The Stalin Epigram

D1353798

Also by Robert Littell

FICTION

Vicious Circle

Legends

The Company

Walking Back the Cat

The Visiting Professor

An Agent in Place

The Once and Future Spy

The Revolutionist

The Amateur

The Sisters

The Debriefing

Mother Russia

The October Circle

Sweet Reason

The Defection of A. J. Lewinter

NON-FICTION

For the Future of Israel (with Shimon Peres)

The Stalin Epigram

a novel

ROBERT LITTELL

Duckworth Overlook

First paperback edition 2011
First published in the UK in 2010 by
Duckworth Overlook
90-93 Cowcross Street, London EC1M 6BF
Tel: 020 7490 7300
Fax: 020 7490 0080
info@duckworth-publishers.co.uk
www.ducknet.co.uk

© 2009 by Robert Littell

The right of Robert Littell to be identified as the Author of the
Work has been asserted by him in accordance with Sections 77 and 78 of
the Copyright, Designs and Patents Act 1988.

Reprinted with the permission of Scribner, a Division of Simon & Schuster, Inc., from
HOPE AGAINST HOPE: A MEMOIR by Nadezha Mandelstam, translated from the
Russian by Max Hayward. Copyright © 1970 by Atheneum Publishers. All rights reserved.

By Anna Akhmatova from *Poems of Akhmatova*, selected, translated, and introduced by
Stanley Kunitz and Max Hayward. Originally published by Houghton Mifflin/Mariner
and used courtesy of Darhansoff, Verrill, Feldman Literary Agents.

Excerpt form "Where are the Swans" from *The Demesne of the Swans* by
Marina A. Tsvetaeva. Copyright © 1980 by Ardis books.

Reprinted with the permission of Scribner, a Division of Simon & Schuster, Inc., from
OSIP MANDELSTAM SELECTED POEMS by Clarence Brown, and W.S. Merwin
(translator). Copyright © 1973 by Clarence brown and W.S. Merwin. All rights reserved.

All rights reserved. No part of this publication may be reproduced, stored in a retrieval
system, or transmitted, in any form or by any means, electronic, mechanical,
photocopying, recording or otherwise, without the
prior permission of the publisher.

ISBN 978 0 7156 4073 9

Printed and bound in the UK by
CPI Bookmarque, Croydon, Surrey

For my muse Stella

for whom the stars

(to borrow an image from Philip Sidney's

Astrophel and Stella, 1591)

"still dance"

... et chacun effectuera avec son âme, telle l'hirondelle avant l'orage, un vol indescriptible.

Mandelstam

I am alone; all round me drowns in falsehood:
Life is not a walk across a field.

From Boris Pasternak's banned poem "Hamlet," which his
friends defiantly read aloud at his funeral in 1960

THE VOICES IN THIS BOOK
BELONG TO

Nadezhda Yakovlevna Mandelstam, Nadenka to her husband, the poet Osip Emilievich Mandelstam. She is thirty-four years old when we first hear her voice in 1934.

Nikolai Sidorovich Vlasik, Stalin's personal bodyguard and occasional family photographer. He is in his mid-thirties when we meet him in the villa of the writer Maksim Gorky.

Fikrit Trofimovich Shotman, a popular Soviet weight-lifting champion. He is thirty-two years old when we come across him for the first time. Originally from Azerbaidzhan, Shotman won the silver medal at the All-European games in Vienna in 1932. He subsequently retired from competition because of a botched operation on damaged knee cartilage. After his weight-lifting career was cut short, he worked as a circus strongman.

Anna Andreyevna Akhmatova, born Anna Gorenko, close friend to both Mandelstam and Pasternak, and a widely admired poet even though the Communist authorities have banned publication of her verse since the mid-twenties. Tall and slender, she was the lover of the then little-known Italian painter Amedeo Modigliani in Paris in 1911 and sat for nude portraits he did of her. Akhmatova, a "decadent poetess" according to her father (who forbid her to use the family name, Gorenko, professionally), "half nun, half harlot" in the eyes of the Bolshevik cultural watchdogs, is forty-five years old when we meet her in these pages.

Zinaida Zaitseva-Antonova, a very young and very beautiful theater actress who is on intimate terms with the Mandelstams.

Osip Emilievich Mandelstam, Osya to his wife, Nadezhda. The publication of his first book of poetry in 1913, entitled *Stone*, established him in the eyes of many as *the* great Russian poet of the twentieth century, a view that Stalin clearly shared.

Boris Leonidovich Pasternak, famous lyric poet, forty-four in 1934, son of the painter Leonid Osipovich Pasternak. His first book of poems, published in 1914, was *The Twin in the Clouds*, which may explain why Stalin, who had a certain admiration for Pasternak, nicknamed him *the cloud dweller*. It took years for Pasternak to accept that Stalin himself, and not the Chekists operating behind his back, was responsible for the deportations and purges and executions.

ONE

Nadezhda Yakovlevna
Saturday, the 13th of January 1934

Since that white night our lifelines first coiled themselves around each other, fifteen years ago come May Day, in Kiev, in a seedy bohemian cabaret called the Junk Shop, I must have heard Mandelstam give public readings scores of times, still the pure pleasure I take from the poetry of his poems is undiminished. There are moments when I am reduced to tears by the unspeakable beauty of the words, which take on another dimension when they enter one's consciousness through the ear, as opposed to the eye. How can I explain the miracle of it without sounding like the doting wife swooning in blind admiration? This high-strung, headstrong, life-glad *homo poeticus* (his description of himself, casually offered up when he mooched that first cigarette from me in the Junk Shop in what now seems like a previous incarnation), this nervous lover (of me and sundry others), is transfigured—becomes someone, something, else. (It goes without saying but humor me if I say it: when he metamorphoses into someone else, so do I.) With one arm sawing the air awkwardly, the arc of his body scores the rhyme and rhythm and layers of multiple meaning buried in the text. His head tossed back, the unmistakably Semitic Adam's apple working against the almost transparently thin skin of his pale throat, he loses himself in the thing we call poetry; becomes the poem. When he materializes at the lectern at the start of an evening, there are usually several barely suppressed groans of mirth from the audience at the sight of this fussy, stage-frightened figure of a man dressed as if for his own funeral. On the particular evening I'm describing, he was wearing his only suit (a dark and itchy woolen twill purchased at the hard currency shop using coupons bought with a small inheritance I once received), along with a silk cravat (a relic of his trip to Paris before the Revolution) knotted around a starch-stiffened detachable collar. He reads as only the creator of the poem can read: with a slight pause for breath, an inaudible sucking in of air, at the places where the lines break or bend or double back on themselves. This pause is critical to understanding the impact of a Mandelstam poem. I have compared notes with several of what Osya calls his first readers (with him doing the reading and them doing the listening) and the savvier among them agree that he appears to be inventing the next line as he goes along. And this in turn gives even the listener who is familiar with the poem the eerie feeling that he is hearing these lines for the first time; that they haven't existed before, haven't been composed, reworked, polished, memorized, copied out on onion-skin paper by yours truly and stashed away in teapots and shoes and female undergarments in the hope against hope that our Chekists, when they come for him, will be unable to arrest his oeuvre.

The line, the pause for breath, then the next line spilling freshly minted from his bloodless lips—that, my darlings, is at the heart of the heart of a Mandelstam recitation. For reasons I have not entirely grasped, the effect is even more remarkable when he is reading a love poem—and still more startling when the love poem in question isn't addressed to me, his best friend and comrade-in-arms and lawful wedded wife, but to the plume of a theater actress perched on the folding chair next to me in the front row of the dingy *Literary Gazette* editorial office, my fleshy arm linked through her slender arm, the back of my wrist grazing as if by inadvertence the curve of her very beautiful breast.

At the lectern Mandelstam turned away for a sip of water before starting to recite the last poem of the reading. The actress, who used her stage name, Zinaida Zaitseva-Antonova, even offstage, leaned toward me, crushing her breast into my wrist. "Which poem is next, Nadezhda Yakovlevna?" she breathed, her voice husky with what I identified as sexual anticipation.

"It is the one he composed for you, my dear. *Shamefaced glances*."

Mandelstam set down the glass of water. "*Mistress of shamefaced glances*," he began, the stubby fingers of one hand splayed above his balding scalp, his pupils burning into the eyes of the woman next to me.

> *Suzerain of little shoulders!*
> *Pacified the dangerous headstrong male . . .*

I leaned toward Zinaida. "Tonight you must conduct yourself decently," I instructed her. "You must stop teasing him."

"But it's you I tease," she whispered back, flaying playfully at my knuckles with the end of one of the long braids that plunged down her chest. "You excite me as much as he does."

> *Why, like a Janissary, do I prize*
> *That swiftly reddening, tiny, piteous*
> *Crescent of your lips?*
>
> *Don't be cross, my Turkish love,*
> *I'll be sewn up with you in a sack . . .*

"In Ottoman Turkey," I told Zinaida, my lips grazing her ear, "adulterous wives were sewn into sacks with their lovers and cast into the sea."

Never lifting her gaze from Mandelstam, her reddening, tiny, piteous lips barely moving, she murmured, "Oh, I shouldn't mind drowning like that."

> *I stand at a hard threshold.*
> *Go. Go, I say!—Yet, stay a while.*

"Hard threshold," Zinaida repeated.

"Hard indeed," I said with a snicker of suggestiveness.

The eleven souls apart from us who had braved a January snowstorm to attend the reading broke into fervent applause. Two or three of the younger members of the audience stomped the wooden floorboards with the soles of their galoshes. The *Literary Gazette*'s chief editor, a brave fellow who had published Mandelstam when Mandelstam was publishable, had been bitterly disappointed by the turnout, which he attributed to the subzero weather. Despite my husband's low profile in recent years, there were still many poetry lovers who considered him to be an iconic figure, so the editor had reassured us. We liked to think this was true, but we were no longer as sure of it as we had been in the late twenties when a Mandelstam reading could fill a small concert hall.

Mandelstam, suddenly breathing with difficulty (he suffered from occasional palpitation of the heart), swayed drunkenly, then stepped to the side and, steadying himself with a hand on the lectern, bowed from the waist.

"Has he been drinking?" Zinaida asked me above the clamor.

"He drank half a bottle of Georgian wine before the reading to calm his nerves," I told her. "But he is not intoxicated, if that's what you mean. I have never seen Mandelstam intoxicated on alcohol, only on words."

Standing at the back of the room, the woman editorial director of a state publishing house, who was known as the Pigeon (it was widely believed she kept our Chekists informed of who said what at gatherings such as this one), called out, "Questions, answers."

I waved a warning finger at my husband, hoping to get him to end the evening then and there; I feared the Pigeon would try to provoke him into saying something that could land him in hot water with our minders. When his instinct for survival (mine as well as his) had dominated his fine sense of right and wrong, he used to beat about the bush. No longer. In the months since we'd returned from the Crimea, where we'd seen hoards of rake-thin and bone-weary peasants, victims of Stalin's collectivization rampage, begging for crusts of bread at train stations along the way, Mandelstam had become dangerously outspoken. In recent weeks he had taken to quoting lines from an old 1931 poem of his whenever one of his acquaintances passed through our kitchen: *How I'd love to speak my mind, To play the fool, to spit out truth.* I lived in dread he would do precisely that—I was terrified he would repeat in public things he'd confided to intimate friends in private: about the individual he called the Kremlin mountaineer, about the utter failure of the Bolshevik Revolution to improve the lot of common people, about the transformation of Russia into a police state far worse than existed under the miserable tsars, about how the Communist apparatchiki who kept an eye on artists had deprived poets of the right to write boring poems.

With a courteous wave of his hand, Mandelstam gave the woman leave to pose a question.

"Tell us, Osip Emilievich, where in your experience does poetry come from?"

"If I could be sure, I'd write more verse than I do." Mandelstam savored the laughter his comment elicited. "To respond to your question," he went on when it had subsided, "Pasternak claims the artist doesn't think up images, rather he gathers them from the street."

"Are you telling us that the poet is something like a garbage collector?" the Pigeon asked.

"Garbage represents the dregs of capitalist societies," Mandelstam observed, smiling blandly at the stool pigeon over the heads of his listeners. "Our Soviet Socialist Republics don't produce garbage, which explains the absence of garbage collectors."

This, too, drew a laugh; a functionary in the Moscow City Cooperative had recently been arrested on charges of sabotaging the capital's sanitation department by failing to hire a sufficient number of garbage collectors.

"No garbage, no garbage collectors," Zinaida agreed under her breath. She uttered it in a way that dispatched a pang of jealousy through my soul; for the instant it takes an eyelid to rinse the eye, she actually *sounded* like Mandelstam.

"What about Akhmatova?" an intense young poet demanded from the row behind me.

"As for Akhmatova," Mandelstam said, "it is inaccurate to say she writes poetry. In point of fact, *she writes it down*—she opens a notebook and copies out lines that, during what she calls prelyrical anxiety, have already formed in her head. I have known her to substitute dots for a line that has not yet come to her, filling in the missing words later." Closing his eyes, angling his head, exposing his throat, Mandelstam recited a verse of Akhmatova's that, like much of her recent poetry, remained unpublished:

> If only you knew from what rubbish
> Poetry grows . . .
> An angry cry, fresh smell of tar,
> Mysterious mold on the wall,
> And suddenly lines ring out . . .

"Enough of Pasternak and Akhmatova," Zinaida cried. "Where does *Mandelstam* poetry come from, Osip Emilievich?"

Mandelstam favored her with a conspiratorial half-smile, as if they had covered this very ground during one of their so-called literary evenings together. "A poem begins with a barely audible voice ringing in the ear well before words are formed," he replied. "This signals that the search for lost words has been initiated. My lips move soundlessly, so I'm told, until eventually they begin to mouth disjointed words or phrases. Gradually this inner voice becomes more distinct, resolving itself into units of meaning, at which point the poem begins to knock like a fist on a window. For me, the writing of poetry has two phases: when the first words make themselves known, and when the last of the foreign words lodged like splinters in the body of the poem are driven out by the right words."

"God, he makes it sound easy," Zinaida was saying as we waited in the lobby downstairs for Mandelstam to finish signing slim volumes of his early poetry or scraps cut from newspapers with more recent poems printed on them (a rarity since our minders decided that Mandelstam wasn't contributing to the construction of socialism). "I could listen for the inner music from now until the Arctic melts," Zinaida continued with what I took to be a practiced theatrical sigh, "and still never come up with a poem."

"What Mandelstam has," I informed the young actress whom we were both lusting after, "is a gift from the Gods. Either you have it or you don't. If you have it, the music and the words are delivered to you on a silver tray."

"Is it true, Nadezhda, what they say about your knowing every poem he has ever written?"

"I am of course extremely familiar with his several volumes of published poetry. But our literary minders pretty much stopped publishing Mandelstam's verse, with the occasional exception, six years ago. In the late twenties, he went through what he calls his *deaf-mute* phase, when he abandoned the writing of poetry entirely. Every poem he has composed since I have had to memorize—I repeat them to myself day in and day out. This way if anything happens to him, the poems could survive."

"And if, God forbid, something were to happen to you?"

The little persifleur had touched a nerve. I wondered if Mandelstam had spoken of the matter with her. Knowing him, probably. Confiding intimate secrets was an unerring way of gaining a woman's confidence; of persuading her you were not violent in order to seduce her into what, in the end, is an essentially violent act. "You have put your finger on a sore point between my husband and me," I admitted. (I was not above sharing intimate secrets to tempt someone of either sex into my bed.) "Mandelstam has few illusions about his own survival, or that of his oeuvre. Since Stalin decreed that nothing contradicting the Party line could be published, Mandelstam considers his fate has been sealed. Let's face it: an unpublished poet makes as much noise as a tree falling in a forest with nobody around to hear it. Stalin's position—which boils down to *Either you are for us or you are against us, my darlings*— leaves no middle ground for the likes of Mandelstam. So you see, my dear Zinaida, my husband had something in addition to his literary legacy in mind when he encouraged me to commit his poems to memory. As we have chosen not to have children, he has convinced himself that my being the last repository of his oeuvre would give me an incentive to survive."

"Would it?"

I must have shrugged, which is how I usually evade answering silly questions. Who can say what, besides the hard-to-kick habit of breathing or the ephemeral gratification of sexual congress or the utter satisfaction of disappointing those in power who wish you dead, would push one to cling to life?

Zinaida studied her reflection in the glass door. "If my husband were to disappear into a camp—they have been arresting agronomists of late to account for the long lines at bread shops—it would solve all my problems." She tossed her pretty head to suggest she was making a joke, but I knew enough about her marriage— her husband was twelve years her senior and had little interest in the theater or in the arts—to understand she was at least half serious. "I would be legally entitled to divorce him and keep the apartment, as well as my Moscow residence permit."

Mandelstam turned up before I could educate her—wives of enemies of the people were more often than not being sent into exile with their arrested husbands these days. Catching sight of him, Zinaida arranged the shabby fox stole around her delicate neck so that the head of the animal, its beady eyes surveying the world with unblinking indifference, was resting on her breast. Never one to let pass something he considered sexually suggestive, Mandelstam noticed this immediately. "For the first time in my forty-three years of existence I am green with jealousy of a dead fox," he confessed, causing Zinaida to avert her eyes in feigned embarrassment. (She was, you will remember, the mistress—and I might add, the master—of shamefaced glances.) I pulled the ratty collar of my late aunt's winter coat, made, if you believed my husband, of skunk fur, up around my neck and dragged open the heavy door of the building. A blast of icy air filled with frozen clots of snow singed our faces. Mandelstam lowered the earflaps on his fur-lined leather cap. "Cigarettes," he announced, and linking his arms through ours he pulled us into the wintry Moscow street.

Like many men—perhaps I should say like *most* men— Mandelstam sailed through life with a cargo of manias. He lived in terror of his muse and his erection one day deserting him. He lived in everlasting fear of fear. He never thought twice about where the next ruble or the next hard currency coupon would come from—he simply assumed that when he needed one or the other, I would somehow magically produce it, which was more often than not the case. But he worried himself sick that he would run out of cigarettes in the middle of the night when the ringing in his ear roused him from a troubled sleep and he spent the restless hours before dawn prowling the miniscule rooms of the flat we were lucky enough to have, sucking on cigarette after cigarette as he waited for the arrival of those disjointed words and phrases. And so, having sponged two cigarettes from members of the audience upstairs and discovering that he himself had only five Herzegovina Flors left in a crumpled packet, he led us, gripping the white knob of the walking stick he had begun using because of occasional shortness of breath, on a mad quest for cheap cigarettes. We wound up, our heads bent into an eye-tearing snowstorm, making the rounds of the coffee shops and the canteens in the neighborhood, hoping to beg or borrow or buy a full packet of cigarettes. It was at the third stop, actually a late-night canteen for trolley car workers hidden in a small alleyway behind the Kremlin terminal, that Mandelstam found what he was looking for (a shady character who claimed to have a vendor's license was selling individual Bulgarian cigarettes from a cigar box), along with something he wasn't looking for: humiliation.

"Osip Emilievich! What brings you out on a night like this? It's New Year's Day according to the old style Julian calendar. So happy new year to you, friend."

The voice came from an unshaven ruffian holding court at two tables dragged together at the back of the canteen. The five young women around him, all wearing padded winter overcoats and sipping what I supposed to be vodka from tea glasses, turned to gape at us as if we were ghouls wandered in from a cemetery. I could tell from the way Mandelstam saluted the speaker with his half-raised walking stick that he wasn't sure of his identity; Mandelstam often had a hard time putting names to faces when people were out of context.

"Hello to you, Ugor-Zhitkin," I called, and I could see my husband nodding in relief as he grasped the identity of his interlocutor.

"Ugor-Zhitkin, at long last," my husband exclaimed, turning from the seller of Bulgarian cigarettes. "I have been leaving messages with your secretary for weeks."

"This time of year is always a madhouse," Ugor-Zhitkin grumbled, as if that would excuse his failure to respond. "A thousand and one things to do, a thousand and one people to see . . ."

Mandelstam had learned from Pasternak, two or three months before, that the editor Ugor-Zhitkin was offering hard cash for original manuscripts for the new Literary Fund Library. The only manuscripts my husband possessed, of unpublished (and according to our literary minders, unpublishable) poems, had been written out by me, and he would not part with these even if someone were reckless enough to want them. We were desperate for money—my translation work had dried up as Mandelstam had become *non grata* in the literary world, and we were ashamed to ask Pasternak or Akhmatova for yet another loan that we had no hope of repaying. Which is how we came up with the scheme of concocting a manuscript that Mandelstam could then pass off as an original and sell. Bent over our small linoleum-covered kitchen table with a crust of bread under one leg to keep it from wobbling, he copied every poem from the original green-covered edition of *Stone*, his first published volume, into a grade school exercise book. The chore took the better part of two full days. Getting it to look authentic became something of an obsession with us. Mandelstam remembered or invented earlier versions of some of the poems and filled the pages with crossed-out words and lines. When he finished we took turns thumbing through the exercise book until the edges of the pages became dog-eared, after which we aged the manuscript by baking it under a low flame in a neighbor's oven until the paper turned brittle and yellow. Throwing himself into the project, Mandelstam even went so far as to copy off cryptic notes to himself and a recipe for Polish borsht (a heavy-handed reference to his having been born in Warsaw) on the blank pages. The finished product was carefully wrapped in a page from a 1913 newspaper that I pinched from the university library, and personally delivered by Mandelstam to Ugor-Zhitkin's secretary, who agreed to bring it to her boss's attention the moment he returned to Moscow.

"Come drink in the new year with us," Ugor-Zhitkin was saying, waving to the free chairs at the end of the two tables. He was clearly hoping to avoid the subject of Mandelstam's *original* manuscript of *Stone*. "The girls and I"—the females at the table, who enjoyed the reputation of being his protégées, were counting on Ugor-Zhitkin to use his considerable influence to get their short stories or poems or plays into print; what they gave him in return for this service was the subject of more than one supper conversation in Moscow—"the girls and I are celebrating something beside the Julian new year. Listen, Osip Emilievich, this is a great occasion in Soviet history. We've just come away from seeing our first talking motion picture. Surely you've read the fabulous review in *Pravda*—there are some who are convinced that Stalin himself wrote it since he is known to admire the film. I'm talking about *Chapayev*, by the Vasilyev brothers. It's based on the Furmanov novel about the Civil War hero Vasily Chapayev."

The expression on the face of the Mandelstam who no longer beat about the bush darkened. I knew what was coming and tried to catch his eye and head him off. No such luck. "The trouble with Soviet films, silent or talking," he allowed, slipping into an exaggerated Georgian drawl that was supposed to remind people of how Stalin spoke Russian, "is that they are marked by a wealth of detail and a poverty of ideas, but then propaganda doesn't need ideas."

Mandelstam might as well have poured ice water from the Moscow River over Ugor-Zhitkin and his entourage.

"What is he saying?" gasped one of the girls.

"He is suggesting that Soviet filmmakers are propagandists," another said.

"It sounds awfully like an anti-Soviet declaration to me," a third girl observed uncomfortably.

Rummaging in his pockets, Mandelstam came up with the receipt the secretary had written out for "One original manuscript of the 1913 edition of *Stone*." He strode across the room, past the streetcar drivers and conductors who were fortifying themselves for the night shift with stale beer, and flattened the receipt on the table in front of Ugor-Zhitkin.

"I've been meaning to get back to you about this," Ugor-Zhitkin said.

"Have you looked at my manuscript?"

"The value of any given manuscript depends on the writer's specific gravity. Frankly, the general opinion is that you are a minor poet. I am afraid it's not worth more than two hundred rubles."

"Two hundred rubles!" His hands trembling with rage, Mandelstam brought his walking stick crashing down on the table. The tea glasses jumped. Two of the girls sprang to their feet in fright. Ugor-Zhitkin turned pale. "*Stone*," Mandelstam plunged on, the metal tip of his stick tapping the table top, "is a classic of twentieth-century Russian poetry, so the reviewers concluded at the time of its publication. You paid five times what you're offering me for a piece of shit by—" Mandelstam named a writer whose three-act drama glorifying Stalin's role in the Civil War was playing to full houses in Moscow.

My great friend the poet Anna Akhmatova claims there are moments in life that are so momentous, it appears as if the earth has stopped dead in its tracks for the beat of a heart. This was such a moment in the life of Osip Mandelstam.

"Who are you?" one of the girls demanded. "Who is he?"

I caught my breath. Mandelstam elevated his chin. "I am the poet Mandelstam."

"There is no poet of that name," another girl declared. "Once, long ago, there was such a poet—"

"I thought Mandelstam was dead," said the first girl.

The earth resumed rotating around its axis, though nothing would ever be the same.

"The two hundred rubles," Ugor-Zhitkin said, determined not to let himself be pushed around in front of his protégées, "is a take-it or leave-it proposition."

My husband started toward the door, then turned back to the editor. "You are living proof that a man's character is written on his face," Mandelstam said so agreeably it didn't dawn on Ugor-Zhitkin he was being insulted. "Do you happen to have cigarettes?"

Ugor-Zhitkin collected the two partially filled packets on the table and handed them to Mandelstam. "Happy nineteen thirty-four to you, all the same," he said.

I saw my husband nod as if he were confirming something he didn't like about himself. "I accept the two hundred rubles," he announced.

"Come around in the morning," Ugor-Zhitkin said, barely swallowing a smile. "My secretary will have an envelope for you."

Kicking at a drift of snow outside the canteen, Mandelstam managed a cranky laugh. "Mandelstam dead!" he said, making no effort to conceal the anguish in his voice. The words that then emerged from his mouth seemed to be transported on small billows of frozen breath. "Dead—but—not—yet—buried."

I can tell you I shivered, not from the gut-numbing cold but from a presentiment of terror. What in the world did he mean by *Dead but not yet buried?*

Zinaida asked the hour. Mandelstam never wore a wristwatch but always knew the time; he was never off by more than a minute or two. "It is twenty past eleven—too late for you to return to your own flat. You must come home with us and spend the night."

I took Zinaida's elbow. "We simply will not accept no for an answer, darling girl."

"You owe it to me as a poet," Mandelstam said a bit frantically. "Nothing so depends on eroticism as poetry."

"That being the case," she said with a pout, "I shall have to say . . ."

I could see my husband was hanging on her reply; the prospect of an erotic encounter with this gorgeous creature had pushed from his mind everything that had happened to him that evening.

"I shall have to say *yes.*"

The three of us fell into lockstep as we headed toward Herzen House and our flat. "I outfoxed that asinine Ugor-Zhitkin, didn't I?" Mandelstam said, his spirits soaring. "Two hundred rubles for a phony manuscript! Come along, Aida. Come along, Nadenka. If I am unable to publish poetry, I can at least produce counterfeit manuscripts until the inkwells run dry in Russia."

Nashchokin Street was caked with ice. Linking arms, we made

as if to skate the last thirty meters to the writers' building. The hallway inside our wing reeked from the rancid insecticide used to kill bedbugs. We were convulsed with laughter as we threw open the door to our ground floor flat and, flinging the overcoats to the floor, sprawled short of breath on the bedraggled sofa in the living room. We could hear the Swiss clock, with the heavy weight hanging on the end of the chain, ticking away in the kitchen. The radiator under the window that I'd painted rose red hissed and belched as if it were human. Somewhere above us a toilet flushed and water rushed through pipes in the walls, but nothing could dampen our spirits. The telephone in the niche at the end of the corridor started ringing and kept at it until one of the tenants answered and then shouted, "Lifshitz, Piotr Semyonovich, your wife would like to have a word with your mistress," which set us to giggling like schoolchildren.

When I'd caught my breath, I said something about how sexual relationships were never uncomplicated in this socialist paradise of ours.

Mandelstam set three thick kitchen tumblers on our makeshift coffee table (actually an old suitcase plastered with stickers from Heidelberg, where he'd spent a semester in 1910) and poured out what was left in the bottle of Georgian Khvanchkara, then raised his glass. "I propose we drink to the health of those who are responsible for this happy life of ours."

"No, no, let's drink to the three of us," I suggested.

"To the three of us," Zinaida exclaimed.

"Well, then, to the three of us," my husband happily agreed and we clanked glasses and drank off the wine.

"Three is a lucky number," Mandelstam said, pulling his cravat free as he licked the last of the red wine from his lips. And he launched into a self-conscious soliloquy (one that I'd heard before) about how the Bolshevik Revolution had had sexual as well as social and political consequences. "In the twenties," he told our guest, "the ménage à trois began to be widely practiced in intellectual circles. Everyone remembers the relationship between Osip and Lily Brik and Mayakovsky. Shostakovich had an open marriage with Nina Varzar. Akhmatova once lived with the very beautiful Olga Sudeikina and the composer Artur Lurye."

I supplied the succulent details. "She used to say they could never decide which of them he was in love with, so they both loved him and each other."

Mandelstam said, "I speak for my wife—don't I, Nadenka?—when I say we consider a three-way marriage to be a fortress no outsider can conquer."

"Is he accurately representing your views?" Zinaida demanded.

"Yes," I said. "It seems to me that in this dead country, where nothing can be reborn, the ménage à trois is the ideal citadel."

"Did you ever see any of his conquests as a threat to you?" Zinaida persisted.

I exchanged looks with my husband. "When our paths first crossed, in a cabaret in Kiev, we appeared to be ships passing in the night until, as he later put it, I blew him out of the water. Soon after we met, Mandelstam and I were separated by the Civil War. I was your age at the time and missed him terribly. He wound up in Petersburg, where he had a three-month fling with Olga Arbenina. What I resented most was not Arbenina—I can understand any female of the species being attracted to Mandelstam. No, what I resented most was Mandelstam. When he took up with that woman, he and I were on intimate terms. He called me sister and addressed me using the familiar *ty*. But when he got around to writing me after meeting Arbenina, he switched into the formal *vy* and I understood we would have to begin from zero in our relationship."

"What did you do?" Zinaida asked, looking eagerly from one to the other.

"The answer is as plain as the beauty mark on your chin," Mandelstam said. "We started again from scratch." And he added, more for my ears than Zinaida's, "Loving a third person is not without risks."

Zinaida wanted to know if we had ever come close to splitting up.

"There was a bearded writer in the mid-twenties," I admitted.

"Oh, do tell me who it was," she demanded.

I could only smile at the memory. "His last name began with the initial *T*. More I will not tell you. It was a time when I was mutinying against my husband's definition of a couple—he expected me to abandon my life to him, renounce my own self, become a part of him. This mutiny took the form of falling head over heels in love with T. But I fortunately came to my senses."

Zinaida turned to Mandelstam. "Do you still expect Nadezhda to abandon her life and become part of you?"

"We have since met on a middle ground," he replied.

"Recount your first experience as a ménage à trois? Were you nervous? Were you . . . inhibited?"

"For me," Mandelstam said, "the baptism of fire was with two sisters who acted in motion pictures—"

That was simply too much for me, even if we were both of us in full seductive flight, so to speak. "He is lying through his teeth," I exploded. "Before we met he knew nothing of such things. He would undress in the dark, for God's sake. I was the one who initiated him."

"But *you* don't respond to the question, Nadezhda Yakovlevna. Were *you* inhibited the first time?"

"The first time one is always timid, darling girl. You are fortunate in that you have us to light the way."

Zinaida crushed a fold of my long skirt in her fingers and pulled me closer. "I confess that I am embarrassed," she said softly, her cheeks burning, her eyes aglow.

"I am able to fix that," Mandelstam said impatiently (the foreplay was taking longer than he had anticipated). "Take off your clothing and the three of us shall repair to the bedroom for a conversation that doesn't require a knowledge of dialectical materialism."

I reached to undo the top buttons of her blouse and, placing the tips of my fingers on the swell of a breast, kissed her lightly on the lips. Mandelstam removed his jacket and his collar and, offering a hand, led her toward the small bedroom. "There were English poets," he told her, "who believed that for each ejaculation, a man loses a day of his life."

"Does that suggest the woman gains a day?" Zinaida inquired with feigned innocence.

"Not," Mandelstam said mischievously, "unless she swallows."

Zinaida's little shoulders shook with soundless laughter. "I should not feel comfortable lengthening my life at the expense of shortening yours."

"Don't worry your pretty head over it," I remarked as I followed them through the doorway. What I left unsaid was this: It was the poems that failed to beat about the bush, not the orgasms with this bewitching sea nymph, which risked to cut short Mandelstam's lifeline. Not to mention mine. When we'd burst through the door of the flat earlier, I'd instantly detected what my husband, too enthralled by Zinaida's petal-of-rose perfume, had missed: the stale aroma of a strong tobacco that only men smoked. And I noticed, as I was meant to, that the glass ashtray on the windowsill was filled with cigarette ends. I didn't have the heart to spoil Mandelstam's Lucullan banquet by telling him we'd had visitors. At least for the space of a few hours, he would put behind him the agony of no longer being published, the indignity of reading his poems to eleven people, the humiliation of *Once, long ago, there was such a poet*.

Dear God in heaven, while he still has a muse and an erection, arrange things so the sun will simply fail to rise tomorrow morning. Amen.

TWO

Nikolai Vlasik
Monday, the 19th of February 1934

The celebrated Maksim Gorky himself, wearing a belted beige greatcoat with an astrakhan collar and strutting like a White Russian doorman at a Pigalle cabaret, was patrolling the portico when I pulled up in the motor pool Packard. "You will be Vlasik," he called out in a shrill voice, looming alongside the automobile to haul open the door on the passenger's side before my chauffeur could circle around and do it himself.

"At your beck and call," I shot back, flashing a tight little smile meant to convey that I was anything but. Nikolai Sidorovich Vlasik was at the beck and call of only one man in the universe, the *caid* in the Kremlin we called the *khozyain*—that's a Georgian expression meaning head of household, though the household in question sprawled from the Baltic to the Black Sea, from the Arctic icecap to the Pacific Ocean. Gorky, his hair slicked back with pomade and a wispy handlebar mustache trickling off his upper lip, led the way into the gaudy foyer of his Art Nouveau villa. An enormous painting of an emaciated naked lady picnicking with two fully clothed gentlemen on the bank of a river filled an entire wall. You could see a smaller version of the same painting reflected in the steel-framed mirror on the opposite wall.

"Playing host to Comrade Stalin is a new experience for me," Gorky declared, pitching his greatcoat into the outstretched arms of a servant. "Where do we begin?"

I can't say I thought much of the villa or the naked lady or Gorky, whom I'd seen from a distance at Kremlin receptions when "Russia's greatest writer" (as *Pravda* called him when it recounted a meeting between Gorky and a young American author named B. Schulberg) was trotted out on cultural occasions. I'd never read anything Gorky'd written, not even his *The Canal Named for Stalin*, nor did I intend to. (Not that I had much time for books; my official duties as the *khozyain*'s personal bodyguard, factotum and occasional family photographer barely left evenings free to service my concubines.) According to the dossier provided by Second Deputy Chairman of the Cheka Genrikh Yagoda, Gorky, a.k.a Aleksei Maksimovich Peshkov, was one of those "vegetarians" (my boss's delicious turn of phrase, derogatory, meant to distinguish between the fainthearted revolutionists and the "red meat eaters") who had abandoned Lenin in the early twenties when the going got a bit sticky. For a time he had been living abroad with a famous beauty of her day, Moura Budberg, who had previously been the mistress of Britain's consul general in Moscow at the time of the Revolution; Yagoda told me he suspected the Budberg woman of spying, but he couldn't figure out for whom. The *khozyain*, for reasons beyond me, had lured Gorky back to the homeland from his lavish Italian exile in the late twenties by offering him this villa in the Lenin Hills that once belonged to the millionaire Ryabushinsky, as well as a couple of *dachas*, one near Stalin's not far from Moscow, the other in the Crimea, each resplendent enough to set the mouths of visitors to watering, so I've been informed. In case this wasn't bait enough the boss, with a stroke of the pen, changed the name of Nizhni Novgorod, the writer's birth city on the Volga, to Gorky. (It was rumored that Yagoda, who also came from Nizhni Novgorod, was furious the city had not been named after him.) No wonder Gorky came back to Russia! As Christ is my witness, I'd seriously consider taking up residence in America if the *khozyain* in Washington, that crass capitalist F. Roosevelt, agreed to change the name of Chicago to Vlasikgrad.

Yusis, the Lithuanian who had been working for the *khozyain* as long as I had, longer even, turned up behind me with my chauffeur, an Ossetian tribesman from the mountains of Georgia; talk about red meat eaters, the Ossete had been a tsarist prison guard in his youth. I gestured for them to search the house and, fingering the small German pistols in the pockets of their leather jackets, they set off in different directions to explore it from attic to cellar. "We'll start with the guest list," I told Gorky as we walked down several steps, our footfalls echoing off tiled walls, into the long mirrored reception hall lined with Chinese vases where my boss would meet the writers.

Gorky, agitated, thumbed his false teeth back into place. "But the list of guests has already been vetted by Comrade Stalin's secretariat."

"I am the head of the *khozyain's* security detail," I informed the fair weather friend of Lenin's who had jumped ship at the sight of spilled blood. "It's me who has the ultimate responsibility for his safety. The list, if you please. The list, even if you don't please."

I am a big-bodied man who keeps fit by doing push-ups every morning and moves with the agility of someone half his weight; it has been said of me that I am able to walk across a room without provoking the creaking of floorboards under my feet. Browbeating vegetarians is what I do to work up an appetite.

Gorky produced a typescript from the breast pocket of a European suit jacket with ridiculously wide lapels. Settling onto one of the steel-and-celluloid chairs, I went over the page, which had thirty-eight names on it selected by Gorky, typed in two neat columns. I uncapped my fountain pen and scratched lines through the names of three film writers and three novelists and two editors whom I knew to be on Yagoda's shit list. When I handed the page back to Gorky, he looked rattled. "These people have already been invited—they will turn up at my door in three quarters of an hour."

"You are not only the host here—you are the head of the Writers' Union. You will station yourself at the entranceway, Comrade Gorky. Tick off the names as the guests arrive. The ones whose names have lines through them are to be turned away."

"What the devil will I tell them?"

"You are an inventor of fictions—tell them whatever comes into your head. Only be sure they do not get in. Now let me see the seating plan."

I studied the page he handed me, which corresponded to the long table that ran the length of the reception room. The *khozyain*, according to Gorky's plan, was to be seated at the head of the table. "Comrade Stalin never presides at receptions," I informed the writer. "You yourself will sit at the head of the table. He will sit immediately to your right with his back to the wall. Instruct your servers that the food he eats and the wine he drinks will be supplied by me. If he desires tea, I will pour it from a thermos flask." Crossing out names and writing in new ones, I rearranged the seating order so that my boss would be surrounded by writers and editors whom I knew to be members of the Party, and returned the page to Gorky, along with one of the Cheka's manila file cards with the names of three of his servants typed on it. "Get rid of them for the afternoon," I instructed the great writer. "We don't want them coming anywhere near the *khozyain*."

Gorky squinted at the index card in disbelief and for a moment I thought he might have more spine than his detractors gave him credit for. "These people," he blurted out, "have been with me since I returned to Russia—"

I glanced impatiently at my wristwatch. "They have Israelite names, Comrade Gorky," I said, assuming that would be explanation enough.

"Israelite names! Some of the comrades closest to Stalin are of

Jewish extraction—Zinoviev, Kamenev, Kaganovich, even your Chekist Genrikh Yagoda. Lenin himself is said to have had Jewish blood—"

I cut him off. "The archtraitor Bronstein-Trotsky is an Israelite. We are concerned that he will attempt to assassinate the *khozyain* with the assistance of the international Zionist conspiracy."

Gorky rolled his eyes in dismay. "Inviting the *khozyain* to meet with writers under my roof has turned out to be more complicated than I imagined when Stalin suggested the idea."

The first of the writers and editors, arriving in private automobiles or taxicabs or on foot, began turning up as the chimes in the Kremlin tower across the river tolled high noon. I could see the hunched figure of Yusis, standing immediately inside the front door, scrutinizing the guests with his unsmiling eyes as they removed their winter coats and piled them on the tables set out for that purpose in the foyer. Gorky was arguing with two men at the door, throwing up his hands helplessly as he turned them away. My Ossetian chauffeur had taken up position in front of the swinging doors leading from the reception hall to the kitchen. I kept an eye on things for a while, then made my way to the servants' entrance off the laundry room next to the kitchen, which gave onto an unpaved alleyway behind the villa. At half past the hour, a 1911 Rolls-Royce with teardrop fenders turned into the alley and pulled to a stop at the back of the villa. At both ends of the alleyway I could make out soldiers armed with rifles fitted with bayonets blocking off access from the street. Two of Yagoda's people in civilian clothing sprang from the car. One of them came up to me and saluted while the other held open the rear door of the Rolls-Royce. The *khozyain* emerged from the automobile, clearly in no hurry to get where he was going; he loathed public functions and held all writers, with the possible exception of Mikhail Sholokhov, the poet Pasternak and another poet with a distinctly Israelite name that escapes me now, in low esteem inasmuch as he considered them to be careerists who served themselves first and the Revolution a distant second. My boss, with a worker's cap on his head and a plain army greatcoat thrown over his shoulders, spotted me at the door and raised a hand to acknowledge my presence. A cigarette bobbed on his lower lip. He treated himself to a last drag before flicking it into an open garbage pail. (Comrade Stalin, who was vigilant about the image he presented to the world, made a point of never being seen in public or photographed smoking a cigarette.) Walking with that distinctive pigeon-toed gate that actors who played him on stage imitated so artfully, he came through the doorway.

"Everything in order, Vlasik?" he muttered.

I nodded once. I'd been the *khozyain*'s bodyguard since the Civil War. He knew me well enough to know I wouldn't let him set foot in a building if it wasn't.

"What kind of humor is the great Gorky in today?"

"I get the impression he thinks he is doing you a favor."

A guttural laugh worked its way up from the back of the *khozyain*'s throat. "Asshole." He shrugged the greatcoat off his shoulders. One of Yagoda's people snatched it before it hit the floor and folded it over the back of a bench. Under the coat Comrade Stalin was dressed in one of the rough peasant tunics he favored when he appeared in public, and baggy woolen trousers tucked *muzhik*-style into soft leather boots with thick heels designed to make him taller. (When he reviewed parades from the top of Lenin's Tomb, he stood on a wooden milk box so his head would be as high as, or higher than, those of the marshals and Politburo members around him. I happen to know this because I supplied the milk box.) I followed my boss through the laundry room and the kitchen and reached past him to push open the swinging doors leading to the reception hall. Word of his arrival spread like wildfire through the room. Conversations died away. The writers and editors who were already sitting at the table jumped to their feet. The others, milling around clutching small glasses of *pertsovka*, a fiery vodka aged with pepper, stood to attention, looking for all the world like gymnasium students in the presence of their schoolmaster. My boss waved his good hand in a vague greeting that took in everyone. A fawning Gorky materialized out of the crowd and made a great show of welcoming him to the villa the *khozyain* had given him. Comrade Stalin pulled a Dunhill pipe from the pocket of his tunic and carefully packed the bowl from a pouch (which I'd filled with tobacco shredded from one of his favorite brands of cigarettes, Kazbek Papirosi). Gorky produced a silver pocket lighter and cupped the flame over the bowl of the pipe as Comrade Stalin sucked it into life. For a moment the two of them were obscured by a cloud of smoke. I ambled between knots of guests to be closer to the *khozyain*. As I drew nearer, a beam of sun streaming through the skylight caught his face like a spotlight and I was struck, once again, by how worn-out the boss appeared. He was in his middle fifties and looked his age, but acted older. His mustache, which his eight-year-old daughter, Svetlana, complained of being prickly, drooped like a weedy plant in need of watering. He had what we laughingly called a *Kremlin* complexion that came from working fifteen-hour days—his skin, pitted with childhood smallpox scars, had turned a sickly sallow. His rotting teeth, clearly visible as he gnawed on the stem of his pipe, seemed to mirror the general decay of his body.

For those of us who were on intimate terms with Comrade Stalin, it was no secret that he was waging a rearguard action against a persuasive despair. Oh, he could put on a show in public, but most mornings found him, after yet another sleepless night, in a black mood ranting about his chronic tonsillitis or the rheumatic throbbing in his deformed arm or an ache in a tooth that the dentist Shapiro (another Israelite for me to worry about!) had failed to alleviate during a visit to the Kremlin clinic the previous afternoon. The women in his entourage—Molotov's wife, the Jewess Polina; Bukharin's new bride, the beautiful twenty-year-old Anna Larina—thought he had never gotten over the sudden death, a year and a half before, of his young wife, Nadezhda. Of course no one spoke of this in front of him lest his legendary Georgian-Ossetian temper, which could burst like a summer squall, put an abrupt end to the conversation, not to mention the Kremlin pass that gave you access to the court. (Everyone agreed that the absence of a serious female companion contributed to the *khozyain*'s depression; I myself had casually offered to introduce him to one or several of my concubines, but he had declined so brusquely it discouraged me from raising the subject a second time.) The men close to Comrade Stalin—his longtime secretary, his chief of staff, assorted members of the Politburo, even Yagoda—had another take on the situation. For them, the boss's obsession with forcing the peasantry onto collectives had come home to haunt him. Tales of deserted Ukrainian villages, of cattle cars filled with starving peasants, of rampaging mobs burning seed grain and killing livestock, circulated in the Kremlin. The forbidden word *famine* was being spread about. Was Comrade Stalin, the man of steel who had held fast during the roll of the dice we referred to as the *Revolution*, as well as the brutal Civil War that followed, losing his nerve? Was he afraid the chaos he had unleashed would spiral out of control; that the Ukrainian breadbasket would be lost forever to the Union of Soviet Socialist Republics; that his Politburo colleagues, faced with the collapse of Bolshevik power, would plot behind his back to strip him of his leadership role—or his life?

The cigarette tobacco in his pipe seemed to settle the boss's nerves. Sinking into the seat to the right of Gorky, he even managed to chat stiffly with the writers and editors nearest him. "That's a good question—our history books skim over this period of Stalin's life because it would be unseemly for a Bolshevik to draw attention to it," he told a writer, speaking a rich Russian with a thick Georgian accent, using the third person form of speech he favored in public appearances like this one. "His mother—Ekaterina, thank God, is still very much alive—is a certified saint. In those days the family lived in a dilapidated shack behind a church in Gori, a dreary sprawl of a town in a mountainous backwater of Georgia next to the Kura River, which was so muddy fish drowned in it. She made ends meet keeping house for a local priest and taking in washing from the bourgeois housewives who lived on the side of town with paved streets and garbage collection. The last time Stalin visited his mother—you're not going to credit this—she asked him what he did for a living. Stalin explained that he worked in the Kremlin and helped govern the country. She shook her head in disgust and said he would have done better to finish the seminary and become a priest. Can you imagine Stalin, a devout atheist, as a priest!"

The *khozyain* tapped the toes and heels of his boots on the floor in a little jig, a sign that he was beginning to enjoy the conversation. One thing my boss relished was talking about himself. It was hard to get him started, but once started, it was harder to stop him. "As for Stalin's late and very lamented father, Vissarion," he went on, "he was a shoemaker by trade, a hardworking breadwinner and a model proletarian, though there is little chance he ever knew the meaning of the word. He struggled selflessly to make life better for his wife and children. Vissarion, to Stalin's everlasting regret, died before he could really get to know him, but his father remains a shining example of what a man should be. You asked about Stalin's names—his mother called him Soso when he was a kid, which is the Georgian equivalent of Joey. Later, when Stalin went underground and began his revolutionary activities, he called himself Koba after a fictional Caucasian outlaw."

"And where did the name Stalin originate?" a fat editor asked.

Around us the waiters were serving chilled white Georgian wine to the guests. Yusis came over with a bottle he'd selected at random from the cartons in the kitchen, uncorked it in front of the boss's eyes and half filled his glass. The *khozyain* wet his lips on the wine. "Koba began using the underground name Stalin in 1913, I think. Yes, yes, it was 1913. He took the name from a bosomy apple-cheeked Bolshevik whose bed he was sharing at the time. Her name was Ludmilla Stal. He transformed the *Stal* into *Stalin*."

"Stalin—man of steel," Gorky said approvingly.

"Wonderful story," an editor diagonally across the table from Comrade Stalin said. "Can I print it in my newspaper?"

My boss bristled. "Out of the question," he snapped. "We Bolsheviks pride ourselves on being modest, on discouraging a cult based on our persons."

While the waiters were distributing silver trays piled high with small salmon wedges, I had Yusis retrieve from the boot of my Packard the straw hamper containing the food that had been prepared at a Cheka laboratory and then sealed and marked *Certified free of poisonous elements.* The *khozyain,* who was something of an expert on poisons—he once informed me that prussic acid smelled like burnt almonds, hemlock like a rat's nest, oleander like chocolate, arsenic like a decomposing supper—categorically refused to eat at public receptions unless he broke the seal and opened the hamper himself. Reaching around him, I set the box down on the table. Comrade Stalin slit the seal with one of his nicotine-stained fingernails and sniffed at the cold *perozhki* filled with ground pork before popping one into his mouth.

At the head of the table, Gorky climbed to his feet and tapped a knife against a bottle of mineral water. "Everyone talks about Lenin and Leninism, but Lenin has been gone a long time. I say, long live Stalin and Stalinism!" he called, raising a wineglass over his head. "Long life, energy, wisdom and stamina to triumph over the many enemies of the first Socialist state on the planet Earth."

In an instant the guests were on their feet. "To Comrade Stalin," they cried in chorus and drank off the white wine.

Stalin wagged a pinky at Gorky. "How can you say that? Lenin was a fist, Stalin a little finger." The guests at Stalin's end of the table who heard the comment broke into applause.

I took a turn around the kitchen to be sure the servants with Israelite surnames had been sent home. When I returned to my post near the *khozyain,* I discovered he was telling a joke; the boss could charm the skin off a snake if he put his mind to it. "If you've heard it before, stop me," he informed the guests within earshot. "So: A Turk asks a Serb why they were always waging war. 'For plunder,' the Serb responds. 'We are a poor people and hope to win some booty. How about you?' the Serb asks. 'We fight for honor and for glory,' the Turk replies. At which point the Serb says"—the *khozyain* started to chuckle at his own story—"he says, 'Everyone fights for what he doesn't have.'"

"Everyone fights for what he doesn't have," Gorky repeated, and he burst into peals of girlish laughter. The guests around Stalin slapped the table appreciatively. After a moment someone asked if the *khozyain* thought Soviet Communism would spread to other industrialized countries.

Comrade Stalin was in his element now. "When we Bolsheviks took power," he said, "several of the more naïve comrades thought our uprising would spark revolutions across capitalist Europe—someone even suggested, half jokingly, that we ought to construct a high tower on the frontier and post a lookout to keep an eye peeled for world revolution. Stalin, who believed in constructing Socialism in one country at a time, Russia first, told them such a scheme would have the advantage of providing permanent employment for at least one worker. Well, you get the point. Which countries are ripe for revolution? Certainly not America, where everyone is too busy accumulating wealth, or holding on to what they've already accumulated, to take to the streets. The French are too preoccupied with eating and drinking and fornicating to make a revolution. As for Great Britain, the English are unable to rebel against the king because revolution would involve ignoring signs that prohibit walking on lawns."

"That leaves the Germans," Gorky offered.

"Every child knows the Germans would be incapable of storming a railroad station without first purchasing tickets to the quay," the boss said with a smirk.

The people around Comrade Stalin, seduced by the *khozyain*'s conviviality, began to relax. Mikhail Sholokhov, sitting across from my boss on Gorky's left, wanted to know if there was any truth to the rumor that the Central Committee was thinking of renaming Moscow *Stalinodar*.

"I can reveal—though it must go no further than this room—that the subject was raised, but Stalin flatly refused."

Sholokhov, a favorite of Comrade Stalin's, asked the boss which in his opinion was the highest art, prose or playwriting or poetry. Stalin gave this some thought. "Clearly poetry is head and shoulders above the other arts. Stalin talked about this very question the other day with the American writer Dos Passos, who is visiting us in connection with the Writers' Congress. Dos Passos agreed with my formulation and quoted the British novelist Maugham, something to the effect that the poet makes the best of the prose writers look like a piece of cheese. That is also Stalin's opinion."

Gorky, his voice pitched higher than usual, said, "I cannot say I agree—"

The boss sucked noisily on his dead pipe. "Nobody asks you to agree," he said in a tone so silkily pleasant Gorky couldn't fail to understand that he had ventured onto a limb. The *khozyain* didn't appreciate being contradicted in public; he once confided to me that it came close to being a criminal offense.

When the waiters got around to setting out bowls of fruit and biscuits, the *khozyain* rapped his Dunhill on the table. "Comrade writers," he called. Whatever conversation there was in the room faded instantly. "So: You will surely be wondering why you were invited to share Gorky's hospitality on this particular February afternoon. We thought there was something to be gained by giving you, who are among the most prominent Soviet writers and editors, a preview of the new cultural policy the Politburo is about to promulgate in connection with the First All-Union Congress of Soviet Writers. We are in the process of redirecting the Party line from modernism to what we call Socialist realism. What is Socialist realism? Henceforth, it is the obligatory aesthetic for the visual arts, for the theater and the cinema, for all forms of creative writing. Socialist realism recognizes that there is no such thing as art or culture in the abstract. All art, all culture either serves the Revolution and the Party or it doesn't. Socialist realism proclaims that art in all its forms must be realistic in form and Socialist in content—it recognizes that writers are engineers of the human soul and as such have a moral obligation to inspire the Soviet proletariat to dream Socialist dreams."

At the far end of the long table a young short story writer raised a finger.

"There is no need to ask permission to speak," Comrade Stalin instructed him. "Here we are all equals."

The young man scratched nervously at the stubble of a beard on his broad peasant's face. "I would like to ask Comrade Stalin how a writer—working in the obligatory aesthetic of Socialist realism—is to deal with the question of collectivization. If we are to be realistic in form, we must portray the chaos, the distress . . ."

The only sound in the room came from outside the windows of the villa—automobiles klaxoning impatiently near a construction site at the foot of the hill. The *khozyain* leaned forward in order to get a better look at the speaker. "What is your name, comrade?"

"Saakadze, Sergo."

"Saakadze, Sergo," the boss repeated amiably. "Stalin thanks you for your intervention. So: Inasmuch as collectivization of the peasants has been a catastrophic success, a certain amount of chaos and distress was inevitable. When a great Socialist homeland moves to eliminate waste and poverty on a grand scale, stuff happens. You—the cultural workers who have the responsibility of justifying collectivization to the masses—must weigh the chaos and distress against what is being accomplished, and this must enter into your *realistic* portrait of the events in question. Collectivization is what makes industrialization possible. To slow down the tempo of collectivization will cripple industrialization, and that in turn will mean that our Socialist Republics will lag behind the West. And those who lag behind wind up in the dustbin of history. One only has to think back to Old Russia—because of her military, cultural, political, industrial and agricultural backwardness, she was constantly being defeated. By the Mongol khans. By the Polish-Lithuanian gentry. By the Anglo-French capitalists. Comrades, let us look reality in the eye. We are behind the leading industrial countries by half a hundred years. We must make up this difference in ten years—either that or perish. This Adolf Hitler has a ravenous appetite—mark my words, when he finishes stuffing himself in the West he will turn eastward. We must be ready to welcome him with cold steel. Stalin and his Politburo colleagues believe we are capable of catching up before the inevitable war with Nazi Germany breaks out. You must never lose sight of the fact that we are armed with irrefutable scientific Marxism, which allows us to foresee the future and to divert the course of history. The capitalists live off religions that promise heaven *after* earth, we are holding out the prospect of heaven *on* earth. Our factory and our farm workers will be rewarded in this world for their labor, not in some afterlife." My boss aimed his index finger in Saakadze's direction. "You ask how you are to deal with collectivization. Take your cue from Mikhail Aleksandrovich here." With an effort Comrade Stalin stiffly raised his crippled arm to indicate Sholokhov across the table. "Take your cue from his masterly novel about collectivization, *Virgin Soil Upturned*. Stalin has read it twice. Comrade Sholokhov manages to dramatize Marx's aphorism about the absolute idiocy of rural life as it was organized under the tsars."

Gorky nodded in vehement agreement. "If the enemy does not surrender," he said, looking around at the writers and editors, "he must be exterminated."

Comrade Stalin said reproachfully, "Comrade Gorky, nobody aside from you has said anything about extermination."

Gorky blanched. "I let myself get carried away by the justice of our cause," he mumbled.

Sergo Saakadze started to raise a hand to speak again, then like a child caught violating a rule hurriedly retracted it. "Comrade Stalin, anyone who keeps an ear to the ground knows that famine is spreading to large areas of the Ukraine, yet according to *Pravda* the Soviet Union continues to export grain. Why aren't we rushing food shipments to the hardest-hit areas instead of exporting to the West?"

The *khozyain* surveyed the faces around the table. "Our comrade is a good storyteller," he declared. "He invented the fiction of famine to frighten us." His heavy-lidded gaze fell on Saakadze. "What do you write—fables for morons? Where do you get your information?"

"I get my information from my mother and my father, who live in"—here he named a district in the Ukraine and a village in that district. "I myself was born and raised in this village. Thanks to Bolshevik policies of egalitarianism, I finished secondary school and was admitted to university in Kiev, where I now teach. I have been a member of the Party since before Lenin's death. According to the law on collectivization, kulaks who have children teaching in state schools are exempt from forced collectivization. Nevertheless my parents were subject to the harshest repression by Chekists. So I ask you, Comrade Stalin, why my parents, who are small plot owners, what Party propagandists call *kulaks*, were not exempt from expropriation and forced collectivization as the law specified?"

I could tell from the boss's body language that he was irritated—his shoulders were listing to starboard, his feet were flat on the floor, he was chomping on the stem of his pipe as if he couldn't wait to suck on a cigarette. "The fact is that collectivization went better and faster than we had anticipated," he finally said. "At which point our people on the ground, dizzy with success, committed occasional excesses—they mistakenly identified a small number of middle peasants as kulaks, they used intimidation to force them into collectives, they confiscated their seed grain and cattle. Still, Stalin can tell you that the overall policy of collectivization is the right policy at the right time. Write down your name and that of your mother and father, as well as the name of their village. Stalin will have his people look into the matter. If it is determined that a wrong was done your parents, we will set it right."

Minutes later I accompanied a riled *khozyain* through the kitchen and the laundry room to the waiting automobile. One of Yagoda's Chekists held open the back door. Comrade Stalin handed me the piece of paper with Saakadze's name on it. "Fuck his mother," he said in an undertone, a soggy Kazbek Papirosi glued to his lower lip. "How did the prick get invited?"

"Gorky."

The *khozyain* was not pleased. "It is the moral equivalent of wrecking to challenge collectivization or raise the specter of famine in public. Have the Organs check him out."

THREE

Fikrit Shotman
Tuesday, the 3rd of April 1934

As wives go, Agrippina was as good as most and better than many, but once she set her mind to a thing, you could lose money betting you would hear the conclusion of it anytime soon.

"I am able to read you like an open book, Fikrit. When you stare out the window like that, fogging your reflection with your breath, you're not hanging on my every word, you're not even in the same room with me. You're back in the mountains of Azerbaidzhan. You're wrestling boulders out of that riverbed behind your father's shed and hefting them onto an oxcart, you're digging in your heels and dragging the ox that's dragging the cart to get both of them up the embankment onto the flat."

She was not wrong. I was homesick not so much for the sweet air of Azerbaidzhan or the song mountain rivers sing when they rush over boulders, I was homesick for simpler times when you could live by the sweat of your brow without worrying that some city folk or other would cast everything you do, everything you say, in a bad light.

"Wishing you were back in Azerbaidzhan won't get you back to Azerbaidzhan," Agrippina said, and though she was only a little more than half my size and not even half my weight, she took a firm grip on my wrist with both her small hands and pulled me over to the bench at the foot of our bed, and pushed me down so that I was sitting on it and she was kneeling at my feet. "Listen up, Fikrit. Pay attention. Brains are not your strong suit so you need to concentrate on each word as it comes out my mouth. Let's go over it again from the beginning. Before we go to sleep, we need to shape out what you will say when they come sucking around with their questions."

"What makes you so sure they're going to come around?"

"You were denounced at the meeting of the circus cooperative, and by no one less than the bearded lady who sleeps with the Chekist representative in the front office. He is bound to file a report, that's what Chekists do for a living. The people he reports to are bound to come nosing around. That's the way it worked when they carted off Dancho the magician for throwing darts at a target he painted on a page of a magazine—how was he to know Stalin's photograph was on the back of it? So begin with the European championship in Vienna."

"I told you that part. I took fifty dollars U.S. from the assistant coach of the American team to let the American Hoffman win the dead lift competition. The only reason I took the money was because he already held the world dead lift record at 295 kilograms. The most I've done was 285 kilograms, so he was going to go and win anyhow. Where's the harm?"

"You used the fifty U.S. to buy the steamer trunk from the porter at the hotel, who found it in the basement storeroom where it was abandoned by a traveling salesman who left without paying his bill."

"I don't see that we need to bring the fifty U.S. into it," I told Agrippina. "We can say the trunk was an added and additional bonus prize for when I won the silver dead lift medal."

"That doesn't explain how an Eiffel Tower sticker wound up on the steamer trunk."

"I could tell the truth—how your half brother Arkhip brought it back from Paris, France last summer when the Red Army Band, of which he is second trumpet, returned from its Europe tour."

"That's the last thing you ought to say! Think what would happen to Arkhip if it became known he was handing out Eiffel Tower stickers left and right. No, no, you say the Eiffel Tower was pasted on the trunk when they gave it to you in Vienna, you say you never noticed it until the matter was raised at the circus cooperative meeting last night."

"That should have the ring of truth to it. The trunk was plastered with stickers from all over Europe. Besides which, even if I had seen it, how was I to know the Eiffel Tower was in Paris, France?"

"You're such an innocent, Fikrit. Sometimes I think you never made it past the safety of childhood. Sometimes I think you got stuck in babyhood. Every idiot knows the Eiffel Tower is in Paris, France."

"I was all for scraping the sticker off when you found it on the trunk last summer."

"That would have been worse. It would have left its outline on the trunk. The Cheka would be sure to spot you'd scraped off a sticker. You can count on them to have all the stickers in the world on file. The triangular sticker with the Eiffel Tower has got to be one of the best known. It would have looked suspicious. Why, they would ask themselves, is he scraping off the Eiffel Tower if it is such an innocent sticker?"

"I never even been to Paris, France," I said. "Vienna, Austria is as far west as I went in my life. I can prove it—anyone can see there are no Paris, France stamps in my external passport."

"Fikrit, Fikrit, look at it from their point of view—the sticker is evidence that you *want to go to Paris, France,* that you think there are things there you cannot find here. How can you be so thick? We have towers all over Russia. They may not be as big as the one in Paris, but every woman knows it's not size that counts.

Dear God in heaven, if only there had been a sticker of a Soviet tower on your steamer trunk instead of that unsightly French thing."

"I never thought anyone would pick out the Eiffel Tower from all those stickers pasted on the trunk."

"Oh, you thought someone would pick it out, all right, Fikrit. I know you better than you know yourself. You wanted the circus people to see it, you wanted word to get around that the Party trusted you so much you'd been permitted to travel to Paris, France. It was your vanity that landed us in this mess."

"You are blowing this out of proportion, Agrippina. It is after all only a sticker. And it isn't as if I scraped it off to hide it. That could count in my favor, that and me being a member of the Party."

"They've been purging members of the Party by the thousands. There's also the matter of the tattoo."

I'd forgotten about the tattoo. I got it when they renamed Tsaritsyn Stalingrad in honor of Comrade Stalin's great victory over the White Guard during the Civil War. "The face of Josef Stalin on my biceps will surely count for more than a sticker on a trunk. It was done by a well-known tattoo artist in Alma Ata. It happens to be a real good likeness."

As usual Agrippina was a jump ahead of me. "Take your head out of the sand, Fikrit. The tattoo is fading. That could be interpreted as a political statement. And the rope burn across it from the time you were putting up the big tent in Tiflis could be seen as intentional disfigurement, which is the same as wrecking."

I got to admit she was making me uneasy. I fumbled for a pinch of *makhorka* in my cloth pouch, rolled it in one of those worthless state loan coupons from the time of the tsars and licked it closed. Agrippina came up with a match and lit it with a flick of her thumbnail. I let the smoke stream out of my nostrils to keep my teeth from turning any yellower. "Some of your tattoos are fading too," was all I could think to say.

"Lenin is fading, that's true enough, but he is hidden under my brassiere between my breasts and they won't think to look there. Trotsky, thanks to God, has almost completely faded—when customers ask me who it is I always say it's Engels, and as nobody remembers what he looked like, nobody is the wiser. The one of Stalin on my stomach is fresh as a daisy. And I don't have a sticker of the Eiffel Tower on my valise."

Agrippina began to sob silently, her head on my thigh, her tears soaking into my canvas breeches. To calm her, I rubbed the map of Africa that started at the nape of her neck and trickled down her spine, but she only whimpered, "What will become of me if they arrest you, Fikrit?"

"You will find another husband from the circus to share your bed," I said. "In Azerbaidzhan, when a man for one reason or another disappears, his woman waits a decent interval and then finds another to take his place. Such a thing is perfectly normal. There is no shame in speaking of it, no shame in doing it."

She shook her head violently. "You were the first man I ever met who loved my body covered in tattoos, and you will surely be the last."

"I remember the first time you showed me all your tattoos, including the ones the public never gets to see."

That brought a shy smile to Agrippina's lips. "Me, also, I remember. Oh, I was a nervous wreck. I took off all my clothing in the water closet and put on one of your shirts, which fell to my knees, and padded barefoot into the room with the oversize bed and stood on it looking down at your beautiful body. And I took a deep breath and threw off the shirt and spread wide my arms and cried out *Ta da!* And I could tell right off from the look in your eyes that you loved what you saw."

"Oh I did. I really did. I loved the serpent snaking up your thigh with its head vanishing into your short hairs. I loved Lenin staring out from between your small breasts. I loved Africa starting with Tunisia at the scruff of your neck and ending at the Cape of

Good Hope right over the crack in your ass. I loved Stalin on your belly. I loved the *Mona Lisa* painting on one of your buttocks, I even loved Trotsky on the other—at the time nobody knew he was a rotten apple who would betray the Revolution. I loved the Soviet slogan about electricity running down your arm. I loved the two peacocks, one perched on each shoulder, their tail feathers tickling your tiny nipples."

"My darling Fikrit, I loved you the more for loving them."

It suddenly came to me—how could I not have seen it sooner?—that we didn't need to lose sleep over a sticker on a trunk. "Listen, Agrippina, if they do come around, we will show them the picture in the newspaper of Comrade Stalin shaking my hand after I won the silver medal in Vienna, Austria. How many people get to shake Comrade Stalin's hand in person? And in the Kremlin no less. He said something about how I showed the world that Socialist weight lifters were as good or better than capitalist weight lifters, even though they did it for money and we do it for the Socialist motherland. He said my second place in Vienna, Austria was evidence, if evidence was needed, of the superiority of scientific Marxism." I was starting to get worked up, starting to hope these Chekists *would* come around with their dumb questions so I could trot out my newspaper articles and my pictures. "I'll show them the article about Comrade Stalin personally intervening when the cartilage on my left knee cracked after I snatched 212 kilograms in Vilnius, how thanks to him I was operated on in the Kremlin clinic, how that fat Ukrainian who's a big wheel in the Moscow Metro project—what's his name?"

"Nikita something or other," Agrippina said.

"Nikita Khrushchev," I said excitedly, "that's it. He was in the room next to me with gallbladder trouble or kidney stones, I don't remember which. Imagine, an important Communist like him next to a weight lifter—when he was up and about, he used to come into my room every afternoon to see how I was getting on. Once he even challenged me to arm-wrestle. Of course I could have beaten him, but I let him pin me. The male nurses had a good laugh watching us."

"They botched the operation," Agrippina reminded me disagreeably.

"It wasn't Comrade Stalin's fault if the Kremlin doctors didn't know about knee cartilage. And that Nikita Khrushchev was the one who came up with the idea of me working as a circus strongman when the doctors broke the news about my weight-lifting days being behind me. Don't you see it, Agrippina, these local Chekists will cringe when they realize they are dealing with someone who has shaken the hand of Comrade Stalin and arm-wrestled Nikita Khrushchev. They will mumble excuses and beg our pardon and back out of the room and close the door behind them so quietly you won't hear the latch click."

The things I said must have comforted her because she drifted off into a deep sleep. Her head was on my thigh and as she had been up most of the night before worrying, I didn't have the heart to wake her when my stiff knee began to throb. I sat there dealing with the pain for I don't know how long. It must have been past midnight when I caught the sound of an automobile pulling to a stop in the street below our apartment house, which was far enough off the ring road to make a car in the dead of night remarkable. At first I thought I must have imagined the thing I feared. Then I made out men talking in the street, I heard the janitor unlocking the front door, I heard the elevator start up from the lobby. In my head I could picture the tenants on every floor, almost all of them workers at the circus like us, staring into the darkness, listening to see where it would stop. You could almost hear the sighs of relief when it passed their floor. Agrippina and I lived on the one-from-last floor and I started hoping and then praying it would stop, please God, before it reached our floor. But it didn't and so I began hoping and then praying it would pass our floor and continue on up to the top floor. But it didn't. And then I heard the heavy elevator door swing open and the footsteps of men walking down the hallway and I started hoping and then praying they would for God's sake knock on someone else's door. But the footsteps kept coming until the men were standing before our door. And then one of them pressed the buzzer.

The bell set high on the wall inside the apartment rang. Agrippina came awake without knowing what woke her. She sat up, rubbing the sleep out of her eyes with the back of her small fists. "Fikrit, I've been thinking about those tsarist loan coupons you use for cigarette paper," she said. "We ought to get rid of them before the Chekists find them."

The bell rang again and didn't stop ringing. Agrippina's eyes opened wide in panic. I leaned over and whispered in her ear, "It's true what you said about me loving your body covered in tattoos. Living with you has been like living with art and history and nature and geography all rolled into one."

FOUR

Anna Andreyevna
Thursday, the 12th of April 1934

I told Nadezhda I would try and I will. She takes the view that it serves some purpose to have it down on paper. So for Nadezhda's sake, for the sake also of our posterity that may one day want to take a closer look at this nightmarish period of Russian history, I'll see how much of it I can recall.

The day in question, Osip, the ultimate gentleman, had risen before dawn and was waiting for me on the platform when the overnight train pulled in from Petersburg. (I'll be damned if I'll call what Dostoevsky referred to as the *invented city* by its Bolshevik alias, Leningrad.) He clutched a small bouquet of white bindweeds in his hand and thrust it under my nose to smell. We were, as usual, elated to see each other but by mutual consent restrained our emotions lest they run amok—Osip once seriously explained to me that most men and some women never cried because they were afraid of not being able to stop. I thought Osip looked reasonably fit, all things considered, and told him so but he waved away the compliment, if that's what it was, saying the episodes of shortness of breath, of dizziness, had been occurring more frequently of late. I asked him if he had been to see a doctor; he answered my question with an embarrassed tight-lipped smile. (Because of his bad teeth, he had taken the habit of smiling with his mouth shut.) I could see he was under a great strain. Nadezhda had spoken to me about the cigarette ends she regularly found in an ashtray when they came back to their flat. She hadn't mentioned the uninvited visitors to Osip, hoping the evidence of their presence had escaped his notice. During a recent telephone conversation he had sounded more depressed than usual. When I asked what was wrong, he had admitted discovering the cigarette ends of strangers in an ashtray; since Nadezhda hadn't raised the matter with him he assumed she took the cigarette ends for his. Such was life in our Soviet swamp these days. Little wonder Osip's eyes were hollow from lost sleep, his forehead dark with worry. He was gnawing on the inside of his cheek more than I remembered. I decided not to raise the subject of the cigarette ends unless he did. He would talk about what was making him anxious if he wanted to; if not, not.

We came back into Moscow by trolley car, careful not to say too much, surrounded as we were by people we didn't know. Borisik, as I called Pasternak, was waiting for us in the small square in front of Herzen House. He had been to see his soon-to-be ex-wife, Yevgenia, who lived with their young son in the ritzier wing of the writers' house, to work out the details of their divorce. We found him, with those cadaverous eyes of his set in a tormented face that broke into a grin when you least expected it, sitting on a bench, his suit jacket and vest unbuttoned, his tie loosened around his neck, his gaunt face turned toward the sun, his lids so tightly shut he had squeezed tears out from under his lashes and onto his cheeks. When I came between him and the light, he instantly felt my shadow. His eyes flicked open in alarm. Seeing who it was, he leaped from the bench to catch me in a bear hug of an embrace.

Pasternak and Mandelstam were two of my closest friends in the world—spending precious time together provided each of us with a breath of fresh air in this stale, stifling country of ours. Every meeting took on an intensity that came from the real possibility it would be our last; that one or all of us might not survive to meet yet again. Their being wonderfully talented poets only cemented the bond between us inasmuch as it gave us a common language, a way of communicating with coded messages tucked out of sight between and under the words. I admired them both enormously. They were unsure enough about themselves to keep them from being boring. (It is this uncertainty, isn't it, that attracts women?) They didn't take their poetic gift for granted, knowing, as we all know, that because you are able to compose a poem one day does not mean you will compose another in your lifetime. What else? They shared an abiding responsibility to be truth tellers in this wasteland of lies.

They brought out the best in each other and in me, no mean feat when you consider the times we lived in, and the place. When the three of us were able to come together, we vanished into a sanctuary of camaraderie and connivance that was not, I'll be the first to admit, without overtones of sensuality. (I had slept with one of them years before and would have slept with the other if he had ever asked me. I won't say which was which; let that be my little secret.)

We started to stroll, and I walked between the two of them, looking happily from one to the other, the three of us not in the least concerned with the getting there, contented only with the going. In the distance we could make out enormous cranes swinging giant wrecking balls—Osip, who excavated metaphors in the most unlikely places, thought it was a sign of the times that they were in the shape of teardrops—against the Cathedral of Christ the Savior, which the Bolsheviks had condemned to demolition. Geysers of chalk and cement particles spewed into the sky with each angry thump of the teardrops. I think I was wearing the rubber mackintosh with the hood for fear it would rain, along with my shiny black ankle-length boots. Yes, yes, I must have been because I distinctly remember Osip teasing me for dressing like a deep-sea diver. (It's amazing the details that come back to you once you start down this road.) Borisik was still under the spell of Shostakovich's new opera, *Lady Macbeth of the Mzensk District*, which he'd seen at the Stanislavsky-Nemirovich the night before. He took a visceral pleasure in reading aloud the inane review he'd torn from a page of *Pravda*. I can still hear his melodious voice in my ear. " 'An ugly flood of confusing sound, a pandemonium of creaking, shrieking and clashes.' Ah, and this," he said, slapping the scrap of newsprint with the back of his hand. " '*Un-Soviet*.' Now what the hell does un-Soviet mean? I can vaguely see what they're driving at with this Socialist realism gibberish, but how can *music*, for God's sake, be realist in form and Socialist in content?" Shaking his head in disgust, he added, "We live under a dictatorship of mediocrities, not a dictatorship of the proletariat."

Osip, for his part, described a visit he'd had from Ehrenburg, the Russian émigré novelist who had been living in Europe since the early twenties. "In tones that left little room for dispute, Ilya Grigorievich let me know how much he admired the progressive politics of the Soviet Union. Needless to say, I could not let that pass without comment."

"Needless to say," Borisik agreed, flashing one of his delicious grins.

"I ripped into him for praising from Paris what writers and artists and poets here had to endure at first hand. I told him how hard it is to compose honest verse in this atmosphere, how I make the rounds of editorial offices looking in vain for someone with the balls to publish a Mandelstam poem."

"The problems of those of us who live in cities pale in comparison to what's happening in the countryside," Borisik interjected.

"Precisely," Osip agreed. He let his walking stick clack against the metal grille surrounding a neighborhood Party building. The racket made Borisik and me uneasy—we weren't keen to attract attention to ourselves. "I described to him the train ride Nadenka and I took returning from the Crimea," Osip continued, "the emaciated bodies stacked like firewood in open wagons queued up before improvised cemeteries, the ribs clearly visible on the horses dragging plows in the fields. I dredged up a line from a poem I wrote a few years ago that pretty much summarizes my attitude toward Soviet power. *The wolf-hound century leaps at my throat.* I could see Ehrenburg's eyes searching feverishly for the way out of our flat," Osip said gloomily. "He didn't believe a word I said."

We spotted an empty bench next to a trolley car stop and sat down on it. A woman pushing a child in a stroller stood in the sun nearby, waiting for the next trolley. As she had her back turned to us, we took no notice of her.

"I feel as if the world is closing in on me," Osip said, his brow knitting. Then he added, "I suppose I mustn't complain. I have the good fortune to live in a country where poetry is respected—people are killed for reading it, for writing it."

Osip was inadvertently opening old wounds with this reference to my first husband, the poet Nikolai Gumilyov, who was shot by the Bolsheviks as a counterrevolutionist one dreadful day in 1921. There was also the brilliant Yesenin, who evoked peasant life like nobody else of his generation and drowned himself in alcohol before he committed suicide in 1925. And there was the insufferably clever Mayakovsky, who killed himself in 1930 after becoming disenchanted with the Revolution he had passionately championed. Osip must have seen me close my eyes. "I beg your pardon, Anna," he said, touching my elbow. "It was not my intention—"

"Spilt milk," I remember saying, "always makes me want to weep. But I shall resist, lest I discover that I am unable to stop."

He favored me with one of his tight-lipped smiles, pleased to see I remembered his observation about crying.

"What are you up to these days, Borisik?" I asked, hoping to move the conversation onto dryer ground.

"My life has become a theatrical performance," Pasternak moaned. "I am beginning to understand why alcoholics get drunk hoping they will never sober up. I am exhausted, not from the difficulties of today's living conditions, but my existence as a whole. I am worn down by the unchangeability of things. I live in faith and grief, faith and fear, faith and work."

"What work?" Osip demanded.

"By all means, tell us what work?" I said.

"I've been reading into Shakespeare's *Hamlet* again. I dream of translating it someday."

Osip said, "You should be writing your own poetry, Boris, not translating the poetry of others. The effect of a Pasternak poem on another poet is liberating—it frees one's voice, one's spirit, one's imagination. In any case, poetry is what gets lost in translation."

"One of the many things I like about you, Osip—one of the many things I *love* about you—is that it doesn't matter who has written a poem, you or another. If it's true poetry, you take pride in it. Unlike me, you are free of envy."

Osip shook his head. "I envy you your being published. I envy you your reviews."

"My reviews! You are rubbing salt in my wounds. Only last week a literary magazine accused me of standing on the wrong side of the barricades of class warfare, of glorifying the past at the expense of the present."

To Osip's delight, I immediately convened a mock court. "Boris Leonidovich Pasternak, how do you plead?"

Borisik announced, "I shall plead madness, in both senses of the word."

Osip said, "What's the difference how he pleads—he is clearly guilty as charged. There's nothing left to do but come up with an appropriately inappropriate sentence."

"As we are under no obligation to have the punishment fit the crime," I said, enjoying the game, "I propose the only rational sentence." And to Osip's immense pleasure, I quoted a line from a gem of a poem he once dedicated to me: *'I'll find an old beheading axe in the woods.'*

"A beheading axe!" Osip exclaimed. "Now we're getting into the Bolshevik spirit of things."

"And where th'offense is, let the great axe fall," Boris proclaimed in English, quoting, as he told us, a line from Shakespeare's *Hamlet*.

We burst into laughter—my heart aches now as I recall the scene, for it was destined to be the last time the three of us would laugh together. In a manner of speaking, laughter vanished from our lives on that sun-drenched Thursday in April, anno Domini 1934.

A trolley came churning along the street, sparks flecking from the electric cable overhead, and with a shriek of metal on metal skidded to a stop in front of us. I waved to the motorman to signal we weren't getting on. Neither, apparently, was the woman pushing the child in the stroller. The motorman called grumpily through the open door, "Thems that aren't waiting for trolleys, comrades, oughtn't be sitting at trolley stops." Jerking closed his doors, he headed off down the street.

Borisik groaned. "What is it about us and the new order that we can't even get trolley etiquette right?"

"It's the story of my life," I said. "Do you really think there is a regulation restricting these benches to trolley passengers?"

"Why not?" Osip said irritably. "There are regulations for everything else, including the writing of poetry."

Borisik said, "According to the article in *Pravda*, Stalin himself spelled out the new regulations during a meeting with writers at Gorky's villa."

"Socialist realism," I said, "makes me want to throw up."

"It will not have escaped you that none of us was invited to this meeting between Stalin and the so-called *engineers of the human soul*," Borisik said. "What do you make of this?"

And then Osip uttered something that astonished us. "Stalin was paying us a great compliment. With his peasant's instinct for what is genuine and what is ersatz, he doesn't put us in the same pigeonhole as his writer-engineers."

I wasn't sure whether Osip was speaking tongue-in-cheek. "Do you really think he is capable of distinguishing between art that is genuine and art that isn't?"

"The Kremlin mountaineer, as I have decided to call him, surely understands the difference between the poet or the dramatist or the composer who is willing to deliver the obligatory monody to the everlasting glory of Stalin and those who, because of moral or esthetic scruples, are unwilling. If I had to make an educated guess, I would bet Josef Vissarionovich Dzhugashvili, to use his Georgian name, is endowed with enough peasant common sense to realize that the artist who coughs up a monody on command delivers something devoid of artistic value; that the monodies he can't get are the ones he must have if his legend is to outlive his body."

We began walking again. I saw that the woman pushing the child in a stroller was a few paces behind us. "We have company," I said under my breath.

Borisik glanced back and grinned at the woman and she smiled back. "You're becoming paranoid," he told me. "She's taking the sun like us."

"Let's return to *Hamlet*," I suggested. "Borisik, explain, please, what you see in the play that brings you back to it, year after year."

Osip didn't understand Borisik's fascination with it either. "Tolstoy hit the nail on the head," he said impatiently. "*Hamlet* is little more than a vulgar tale of pagan vengeance. The plot is relatively straightforward—a Danish prince seeks more and more proof that his uncle murdered his father because he can't bring himself to act, can't bring himself to take revenge even when he has the proof. It's a story about someone who is unable to deal with his own cowardice and so takes refuge from it in madness."

"No, no, I don't read it that way at all," Borisik burst out. "*Hamlet* is not mad; he *feigns* madness to justify his failure to act against his essential nature."

And then something happened that, given how things turned

out, now seems to me to be best conveyed by saying that I thought the earth had stopped dead in its tracks for the beat of a heart.

I will need a moment to collect my thoughts.

What I have recalled up to now is more or less the gist. But when the earth stopped dead, so too did time; things proceeded at the speed of a mountain eroding, so I am able to reconstruct the moment with absolute accuracy. Osip halted so abruptly the woman pushing the stroller had to swerve to avoid him. Borisik and I looked inquisitively at him, then at each other, then at Osip again. He appeared to be shrugging off a great burden. His breathing became as calm as the drafts of air you would expect to find in the eye of a hurricane. "So that's how it is," he said, more to himself than to us. And forgetting his decaying teeth, he smiled a genuine smile.

Both Borisik and I were mystified. "What?" I asked.

"But that puts everything into perspective!" Osip declared. "Hamlet feigns *madness* to justify his failure to act. I feign *sanity* to justify *my* failure to act, since no sane person can be expected to do what I must do."

Osip couldn't have missed the look of confusion in my eyes. "What must you do?" I demanded.

Borisik, who had a sixth sense for matters of the spirit, said very quietly, "He has been putting off confronting his Kremlin mountaineer. What he feels he must do compels him to act against his essential nature, inasmuch as poets don't dirty their hands in politics."

And then, as if a dam had given way, a torrent of words spilled from Osip's lips. "In the beginning, God forgive us, many of us shared Mayakovsky's optimistic view of the Revolution—the Bolsheviks seemed to have a moral dimension, a hunger to improve the lot of the masses. But we didn't reckon on the Kremlin mountaineer climbing over the bodies of his colleagues and reaching the top of the pyramid ahead of them. Stalin makes Caligula, Cesare Borgia, Ivan the Terrible look like humanitarians."

I saw Borisik shaking his head in anxious disagreement. "There is no evidence that Stalin knows what's going on," he said. "It could be Yagoda who is behind the forced collectivization and the famine and the mass arrests. The Cheka has always acted as a state within a state."

"This is not the first time we've had this argument," Osip insisted, clearly exasperated. "What will it take to convince you I'm right, Boris, a photograph of Stalin on the front page of *Pravda* with a smoking revolver in his fist? *Something is rotten in these Soviet Socialist Republics!* He *knows*, for God's sake. He's behind every arrest, every execution, every deportation to Siberia. Nothing happens without his approval in this *unweeded garden*—your phrase, Boris, taken from the lips of the Hamlet who feigns madness. *Absolutely nothing!*"

If I shut my eyes and catch my breath, I can still make out Borisik delivering the lines in English: " *'Tis an unweeded garden that grows to seed; things rank and gross in nature possess it merely.*"

In his eagerness to explain himself, Osip was almost tripping over words now. "Red Terror didn't start yesterday, it began when that poor creature Fanny Kaplan tried to kill Lenin in 1923—that night the order, countersigned by Stalin, went out to execute White prisoners by the thousands. He's been at it ever since, killing hope, pushing us deeper and deeper into a new ice age. He has to be stopped before he runs riot and drowns a hundred and fifty million people in teardrops." Wincing in agitation, Osip came up with some lines I recognized from one of his older poems. "... *Your spine has been shattered, my splendid derelict, my age* ... My dear Anna, my dear Boris, I confide in you because you of all people will comprehend me. *I know how to go about destroying him!* It needs only a spark. We have heard physicists speculate about the explosive power locked inside an atom. I am deeply committed to the proposition that an explosive power resides in the nucleus of a poem, too. I am able to release this power, I can trigger the explosion if I can bring myself to abandon sanity, if I become mad enough, in both senses of the word, to let the scream of outrage stuck in the back of my throat emerge." Osip looked hard at me. "Screaming has a lot in common with crying, Anna—once you start you risk not being able to stop."

I couldn't believe my ears. "You propose to destroy Stalin with a poem!" I said incredulously.

"A poem bursting with truth telling that will reverberate across the land like ripples from a pebble thrown into stagnant water. Something as straightforward as *The king has no clothes*. The peasants will greet his fall with prayers of thanksgiving. The Party will declare a national holiday. The Komsomol will sing it as they march off to fulfill their quotas. At congresses in the Bolshoi, from every balcony and box, workers will shout it out. Young people who have grown old before their time with fear will dance in the streets for joy. It will be the end of Stalin."

"He will kill you," Borisik said flatly.

"Executions fill me with fear," Osip admitted, "especially my own."

Borisik came up with another phrase from *Hamlet*, something along the lines of *Safety lies in fear*. Osip shook his head in irritation. "In an unweeded garden, there is no safety," he said. "No matter— the object is to save Russia, not me."

I was beginning to feel alarmed. Turning on Borisik, I grabbed a lapel of his jacket. "Don't stand there like an idiot, for heaven's sake. Talk sense to him."

I have the image engraved in my brain of these two dear men staring into each other's eyes for an eternity, though it was surely only a fleeting moment. Then Borisik, the consummate ladies' man who wasn't particularly physical with his male friends, did something I'd never seen him do before: moving with exquisite awkwardness, he wrapped his gangling arms around Osip and pulled him into what can only be described as a lover's embrace.

"Believe me, I would talk you out of it if I could," Borisik said in tones usually reserved for funeral orations.

Osip seemed to be in a state of exaltation. His face was flushed, his fingers trembled. "The two of you, along with Nadenka, shall be my first readers," he promised.

Borisik slipped his arms through Osip's and mine and the three of us set off walking again. I became aware of a spring to Osip's step, almost as if the going had given way to the getting there. Nobody said a word for some time. I remember it was Borisik who broke the silence. "If it were possible, I would set the clock back."

"Where would you go back to?" I asked.

"I would return to when Osip feigned sanity to justify his failure to act."

"I would set the clock back still further," Osip declared passionately. "I would go back to Russian literature before the Bolsheviks twisted its arm and tore it from its socket."

I had the sinking feeling he was going to spill more milk. I begged Osip—dear God, when I think of it now my blood runs cold—I begged him to carefully weigh the consequences of his actions. "The last thing Russia needs," I told him, "is the death of another poet."

FIVE

Fikrit Shotman
Tuesday, the 1st of May 1934

Through the planks nailed over the slit of a window high in the wall of my cell, I could hear horns and whistles and kettledrums and trombones in the streets around the Lubyanka. I could picture the mass of workers, some waving banners representing their factory or collective, others carrying small children on their shoulders, flowing in great rivers toward Red Square to file past Lenin's Tomb in celebration of the seventeenth May Day since the glorious Bolshevik Revolution put Russia on the road to Communism. Monitors along the route would keep an eye peeled for those who had drunk too much vodka and could barely walk, and cart them off to dry out in open trucks filled with straw parked in side streets. The workers from my circus collective—as attendance is obligatory, Agrippina would be among them if she wasn't in prison like me—would march in the crowd, the hammer-and-sickle ensign serving as a balancing pole for one of the lady funambulists tightrope-walking on a cable stretched and held taut overhead by the tent men. Oh, how I wished I could join the parade—I would wave wildly at Comrade Stalin looking down from Lenin's Tomb in the hope that he would recognize me, would point me out to his Politburo comrades, would clasp his hands together in a sign of approval and wave his clasped hands for all the world to see he had not forgotten the weight lifter who brought the silver medal home to Moscow from the 1932 All-Europe championship games in Vienna, Austria.

"Turn down the racket," my cell mate said through lips caked stiff with dried blood, as if the noise from the street was coming from a loudspeaker. He had been in the cell, crouching like a wild animal in a corner, his trousers and shirt shredded beyond mending, his bare feet (minus some toenails) planted in a puddle of his own urine, when I arrived something like four weeks before. He was badly beaten and thrown back into the cell in even worse condition after each interrogation. One shoulder was dislocated, all but one of his front teeth was knocked out, his left wrist hung limp, judging from the grimaces when he coughed up blood he must have several cracked ribs, where his nose had been there was a swell of bloody tissue that oozed puss. I didn't for an instant doubt this prisoner was a dangerous criminal who deserved severe punishment. I resented having to share a cell with such a scoundrel and protested to my interrogator the first time I was taken for questioning. He slid a pencil and a sheet of paper across the table and instructed me to write down my complaint. I didn't want to let on I couldn't read or write so I pushed the paper back and mumbled something about not wanting to waste his time on a matter so trivial.

What did it feel like to be arrested? I wasn't frightened, if that's what you're driving at. Why should I have been frightened? I didn't break any laws, I wasn't a wrecker or an assassin or a spy for the Great Britain secret service. I was a member of the Party in good standing. I owed two months' dues earlier in the year (the circus was touring in Central Asia at the time) but I settled the debt as soon as we got back to Moscow, including the ten percent penalty for late payment. Don't take my word for it—I have a receipt to prove it if you don't believe me. I admit I was mortified at being arrested in front of all my neighbors (listening behind their doors, watching from their windows). Everyone in the circus would know the strongman had been taken off by the militia, and as people generally believe there is no smoke without fire, everyone would agree I must be guilty of *something*. I could picture the embarrassment on their faces when I returned to the circus waving a typewriter letter signed and stamped by the procurer testifying to the world that the arrest of Shotman, Fikrit, had been a regrettable bureaucratic error. Out of shame they would avoid my eye when they shook my hand. Certain Chekists would surely be reprimanded. Who could say, there might even be a telegram from Comrade Stalin himself apologizing for any inconvenience the Organs caused me or mine.

I try not to think of the actual arrest because it was Agrippina who suffered the most. She was sobbing so violently she got the hiccups. Between sobs, between hiccups, she kept trying to convince the six militiamen (I have been told the Cheka usually sends four but I am, after all, a champion weight lifter) they were making a terrible mistake as they led me down the hall to the elevator. "We are only going to ask him a few questions, lady," the one with a facial tic growled at her in exasperation. "He'll be back in bed with you and your tattoos before the mattress grows cold."

As you more often than not wind up believing what you hope is true, I took him at his word. "Keep my lunch warm for me," I called cheerily to Agrippina as the elevator door swung closed—but it was a heavy door and it slammed shut as if it was locking me into a prison and whatever cheeriness there was in me vanished like one of those white rabbits in Mr. Dancho's top hat. I could hear Agrippina hollering my name down the shaft as the elevator began its long descent toward what turned out to be a nightmare. Outside the building, I was bundled into a bread delivery wagon that had no odor of bread in it, only the unmistakable stink of human sweat.

They took away the wide belt I brought back from Sofia, Bulgaria, and my shoelaces in a small room off the courtyard inside the back doors of the Lubyanka, along with everything in my pockets, including my Czech wristwatch that was supposed to tell the day of the month but never got it right. I was given an itemized list of my belongings to sign and carefully made my mark on the line that was pointed out to me. I was able to keep track of the passage of time for the first eight or nine days by scratching a mark for each day on one of the thick stones in the wall of my cell with a kopeck they missed when they searched my pockets the night of my arrival. But I came back to my cell from an all-nighter one morning—you knew it was morning when the turnkeys slid hardtack and a fancy chinaware cup filled with lukewarm tea tasting of iodine through the slot in the door—to find that someone had added scratches to the wall to confuse me.

It took me a while to address a word to my cell mate. I had never before been in the presence of an enemy of the people and didn't want to become contaminated by talking to him. When he wasn't being questioned, he spent his waking hours licking his wounds—I mean actually licking them the way a cat licks his paw and then rubs the paw over parts of his body. I understood this to mean he had peasant roots because in Azerbaidzhan it's well known that saliva is a sanative for cuts and bruises and warts and the like. After I don't know how many days in the cell I began to feel sorry they didn't just shoot him to put him out of his misery. And so I worked up my nerve to talk to him.

"So what are you guilty of, comrade?" I asked.

His one eye that wasn't swollen shut stared at me through the dampness of the cell, which was lighted by a dazzling electric bulb dangling out of reach from the ceiling. "What makes you think I'm guilty of something?"

"You wouldn't be here if you weren't. You wouldn't be in this condition if you were innocent."

He tried to laugh but all he managed to do was slobber. "I made the mistake of raising the subject of collectivization in front of Stalin at a public meeting."

"You have personally met Comrade Stalin!" And without waiting for an answer, I told him about how Stalin himself had shaken my hand for winning the silver medal in Vienna, Austria two years before.

"You're that Azerbaidzhan weight lifter who became a circus strongman," he said. "I remember reading about you in *Pravda*. I'm Sergo"—he may have told me his patronymic or surname, but given the sorry condition of his mouth, it was difficult to understand what he said and I never caught them. "How about you—what are you guilty of?"

"I am absolutely not guilty of anything and everything, a fact which will come out when the wheels of Socialist justice have a chance to turn."

"If you're not guilty, what are you doing here?"

"I was denounced for having a sticker of the Eiffel Tower on my steamer trunk. In case you aren't familiar with the tower in question, it happens to be located in Paris, France."

"I will wager a crust of bread the famous Christophorovich is your interrogator."

"How did you know?"

"He is my interrogator, too. I am a writer of short stories. Christophorovich is the resident specialist on cultural cases. As a circus performer, you come under the category of culture."

"He seems an honest Bolshevik—the first words out of his mouth were about me being well treated."

"Honest my ass," Sergo sneered. "Before he's through with you he'll have you convinced you're guilty of something."

I'd been in jail for six days according to the marks I'd scratched onto the wall when three turnkeys turned up at my cell door (only one came around to collect Sergo but I am, let's not forget, a champion weight lifter). This took place late in the day after I fed Sergo his supper soup, a thin gruel of potato peel and cabbage in a china bowl, and settled down on my folded blanket to try to sleep. "Shotman, Fikrit," one of the guards called out, as if he couldn't tell the difference between the wrecker Sergo and a respectable Soviet citizen. Holding my trousers to keep them from falling around my ankles, I shuffled behind the turnkeys along the passageway, past rows of cell doors with numbers painted on them, to an open freight elevator with padded walls and up we went, three floors as I counted them, until we came to a floor that looked more like what you would expect to find in a fancy office building than a prison. There was a long brightly lighted hallway with a worn carpet running the length of it and fine wooden doors with brass numbers on them. The turnkeys, walking on crepe-soled shoes, jingled their keys as we made our way down the hallway and when they heard another turnkey coming toward us jingling his keys, they jerked the back of my blouse over my head and turned me until my nose was pressed against the wall. As soon as the guard jingling his keys passed with his prisoner, we resumed our route. When we reached door number twenty-three, the guards knocked twice, opened it and shoved me inside.

I found myself in an enormous corner room with windows on two sides fitted with thick pleated curtains, which were shut to keep Moscow out. Bright spotlights, the kind used at circus sideshows, was fitted to bars on the ceiling and aimed at my face, causing my eyes to tear. Sitting on a wooden swivel chair behind a long and narrow table was a not heavy, not big man wearing a leather butcher's apron filled with dark stains over some kind of uniform. His hair, which was the color of cement, was cut short in the military style. To protect his eyes from the spotlights, he wore a colored eyeshade like the one the paymaster in our circus used when he tallied up the night's receipts. If I squinted, I could make out on the wall behind him an enormous photograph of Comrade Stalin. He was standing on top of Lenin's tomb in Red Square, towering over the comrades on either side of him, his right hand raised high saluting the person looking at the photograph, which is to say, saluting me.

I must have waited a good quarter hour, shifting my weight

from one laceless shoe to the other, before the man in the butcher's apron looked up. "I am Christophorovich," he said so softly I had to strain to make out his words. "Any complaints about how you're being treated?"

"I am treated fine, Your Honor, except for the tea which tastes of iodine."

"Our medical service has determined that several drops of tincture of iodine diluted in tea can prevent diarrhea, digestive disorders, even psoriasis. I have heard it said that Comrade Stalin himself takes a daily dose of tincture of iodine. If you have no other complaints—"

"I am unhappy about having to share a cell with a wrecker." It was then he pushed pen and paper across the table so I could file a complaint, which I didn't for reasons already explained.

Christophorovich gestured with a finger and the three guards led me across the room and shackled my wrists and ankles to irons embedded in the wall. I could see dried blood, even scab, on one of the wrist irons and supposed Sergo or a criminal like him had been shackled to the same irons. It didn't upset me being chained to the wall—I am, after all, a big man and Christophorovich was not yet convinced of my innocence. How could he be, we'd only just met? Fitting on a pair of those round steel-rimmed eyeglasses favored by important people, he busied himself reading through a stack of dossiers on his table. He didn't look up or address a word to me for what must have been hours. I whiled away the time watching him out of the corner of my eye. He looked the way people who suffer from insomnia look—his lids were half closed, what Agrippina called migraine lines were stitched into his high forehead, his upper teeth chewed away on his lower lip. All things considered, he put me in mind of our trapezists, pacing behind the tent with worried eyes before bursting through the flap to bow to the audience, their nervous smiles hiding their fears of not performing well. I wondered if someone in Christophorovich's situation needed to worry about not performing well. I wondered how his superiors measured whether he was performing well or not. I wondered if he had family—a wife, children, brothers, sisters, uncles, aunts. I wondered if they knew what he did for a living. I wondered if professional interrogators were able to leave their work behind at the office and talk to friends and neighbors like I talked to friends and neighbors, or did they always need to be vigilant, weighing every word, every gesture, looking for evidence of wrecking. Maybe that's what kept him up nights. I wondered if he took vacations at the hotels reserved for the Organs on the Black Sea, sunning himself on pebbled beaches at the foot of cliffs, swimming in the surf, eating in communal canteens where waiters tried to figure out the importance of guests not wearing uniforms so they would know who to serve the best cuts of meat to.

Comrade interrogator's fingers drummed on the blotter of his table. From time to time he uncapped a fountain pen and made a note on one of the dossiers. I could hear the nib of his pen scratching across the paper. The sound reassured me—surely someone who can read and write like Christophorovich was capable of weighing the evidence carefully and figuring out Shotman, Fikrit, didn't belong in prison. Sometime in the early hours of the morning a stocky lady wearing a white chef's smock and a white kerchief over her hair wheeled a cart into the room and set out two plates filled with food on the table, along with white cloth napkins and forks and knives and glasses and a pitcher of beer. I tried to think who the second plate could be for. Christophorovich tucked the end of a napkin under his collar and attacked the food like someone who had worked up an appetite.

The odor of the food—I got a whiff of beefsteak and fried onions—made me light-headed.

When he finished eating, Christophorovich belched into the back of his hand, which I took to mean he came from the intelligentsia and not the working class. Pulling a file folder from a drawer, he drank off more beer as he read through it. At long last he looked over at me and said, "Shotman, Fikrit Trofimovich?"

"One and the same, Your Honor."

"It says here you have been a member of the Party since 1928."

"I actually took the oath of allegiance in December of '27, Your Honor, but the list for that year was closed so I had to wait for an opening, which came in February of '28."

"You consider yourself a good Communist?"

I nodded emphatically.

"What in your opinion is Communism?"

His question threw me off. I don't know all that much about Marx and Lenin and the dictatorship of the proletariat, not to mention dielectrical materialism, but I thought to say, "I am not absolutely certain what Communism is, comrade interrogator, but I am sure I will recognize it when I see it."

"Close your eyes. Go ahead. That's it. Now describe, if you please, what you see when you see Communism."

"I see a country where everyone is sure that tomorrow will be better than today. Don't get me wrong, I'm not saying today is bad, only that as great as today is, tomorrow will be even greater. I see a country where everyone—all the factory workers, all the peasants on collective farms—live the same good life we live at our circus. We are paid by the number of performances even if there is a blizzard and nobody turns up to buy tickets. If you have been employed at the circus for three years and are hitched, which I am, you are eligible for twenty-four square meters in one of those new apartment buildings going up around the Ring Road. The circus has its own shoe repair shop and laundry and a metalworker who makes almost all the spare parts we need for our trucks. We have a trained nurse who says she can even deliver babies, though she has not yet been put to the test. We eat three square meals a day at home or on the road, we drink beer on weekends and vodka on our name days." I had a sudden inspiration. "Communism is when everything works so well we won't need the Cheka to make sure everything works well. Communism is where you, comrade interrogator, will be out of a job."

For a second I was afraid I might have gone too far, but Christophorovich nodded as if he approved my answer. "I have another question for you, Shotman. Would you say you follow orders from the Party?"

"To the letter, Your Honor. You can ask my block captain. You can ask the Cheka representative on the circus collective. When the Party says jump, I jump."

"That being the case, the Party orders you to tell me what you're guilty of. This will save me a lot of time and you a lot of pain. In the West they say that time is money, which is a curious way of looking at it. To me, time is something you allocate, so much to each prisoner, so you can fulfill your quota. You look surprised. Yes, I have a quota to fulfill like a worker in a factory. I am required to produce a certain number of confessions each month. Your voluntary confession will give me more time to extract confessions from the wreckers who want to sabotage Communism but won't come clean without a bit of coaxing from me." Christophorovich pointed to the second plate filled with food. "As soon as you have signed a confession, this beefsteak is yours to eat. Beefsteak and beer, along with an entire night of uninterrupted sleep, will be your reward for cooperating."

I am the first to own up to the fact that my mind turns slowly. But it turns. And this is what I was thinking: If the Party, knowing I was innocent, thought it was useful for me to plead guilty, of course I would do it at the drop of a hat. But if the Party thought I was really guilty and wanted me to confirm it by pleading guilty, I didn't see how I could do that. It would be making the Party, which I worshipped, an accomplice to a falsehood. I wasn't sure I could explain this satisfactorily to Christophorovich, so I said instead, "I would gladly tell you what I'm guilty of if I could figure out what I did wrong."

"Let me help you, Shotman." It was at this point that

Christophorovich asked me the same thing Sergo asked me back in the cell. "If you're not guilty, explain what you are doing here."

"I am here by mistake."

"Let's be clear. You, a Party member since 1928, consider the Party capable of making mistakes?"

"The Party is only human, comrade interrogator. In arresting enemies of the people by the thousands, by the tens of thousands even, the Organs are bound to make an honest error now and then."

Using only one hand, Christophorovich blew his nose into the linen napkin, which made me think he didn't come from the intelligentsia after all. He inspected the results, and apparently satisfied at finding no evidence of illness, turned his attention back to me. "Every prisoner starts off his interrogation claiming the Organs have made a terrible mistake," he explained patiently. "I had a client in to tea earlier today. He was a typesetter for the provincial newspaper that ran the story of Stalin's triumphant reception of Soviet aviators under the headline *Death to Trotskyist Traitors*, and a story of the trial of kulak wreckers under the headline *Hail to the Heroes of the Skies*. He denied the charge of sabotage and attributed the mix-up of the headlines to honest error. The summary tribunal interpreted his stubborn refusal to admit guilt as proof of guilt and I was unable to save him from the highest measure of punishment. He is due to be shot"—comrade interrogator picked up a large alarm clock on the table and started winding the key in the back of it—"long about now. Normally it's me who does the dirty work. I pride myself on finishing what I start—if a prisoner I am assigned to interrogate is sentenced to execution, I don't let a stranger do it, I accompany him down to the cellar vaults and shoot him myself. It's what you might call a work ethic. As I've done two executions already today—one was a magician from your own circus who turned a photograph of Stalin into a target for darts—my assistant offered to stand in for me. So do you still think you're here because of an honest error?"

For years Agrippina has been drumming into my thick skull if I can't think of something halfway intelligent to say, don't say anything. Which is what I did now. Christophorovich shrugged and shook his head as if he was sad about something. He lifted the telephone from its cradle and said very quietly, "Bring it in."

One of the guards who escorted me from my cell wheeled in a mover's dolly with my steamer trunk on it. The guard tipped the dolly and let the trunk slide onto the floor between me chained to the wall and Christophorovich sitting at the table. I could make out the Eiffel Tower sticker with a circle drawn in red paint around it.

Waving the guard out of the room, comrade interrogator came around the table and hiked himself up on it, his short legs stretching so his toes could reach the floor. "Let's talk about this Eiffel Tower sticker," he suggested pleasantly.

"I have nothing to hide," I said. "The first thing to know is that it wasn't me that glued it on the trunk. I got the trunk with it already glued on. I didn't even notice it was there until the bearded lady raised the matter at the circus cooperative meeting. The second thing to know"—I was racking my brain to try and remember what Agrippina had figured out for me to say—"is that I personally think Soviet towers are a hundred times better than this stupid tower in Paris, France that looks like a giant Mechano construction toy. I mean, you only need to look at this Eiffel Tower to see how ugly it is."

"You've been to Paris?"

"Never. You can check my external passport—there are no Paris, France stamps in it."

"Spies have ways of crossing frontiers without getting stamps in their passports."

"Why would I want to go to Paris, France? There's nothing there but unemployed workers and prisons and bread lines in front of bread shops and capitalist police who keep the poor and homeless proletarians out of sight so as not to disturb the filthy rich capitalists who exploit them."

"I also have never been to Paris, but I'm told they have large avenues and great museums filled with art treasures."

"There is nothing in Paris, France you can't find in Soviet cities and Soviet museums, comrade interrogator. Take for instance the *Mona Lisa* painting—"

"Where did you see the Mona Lisa painting?"

"In a book somewhere."

Christophorovich smiled a funny smile. "The *Mona Lisa* painting happens to be in Paris."

I swallowed hard. "I must be confusing it with another painting here in Russia," I said weakly.

"Let's move on. When the bearded lady drew your attention to the Eiffel Tower sticker, why didn't you scrape it off?"

For the first time in the interrogation I felt solid ground under my feet. "The fact I didn't scrape it off surely must count in my favor, comrade interrogator. It shows I have nothing to hide."

Christophorovich chewed on his lower lip until he drew a drop of blood, then licked it off with his tongue. "It doesn't take an experienced interrogator to see that the contrary is true, Shotman. If it was really a meaningless sticker that wound up on your steamer trunk through no fault of yours, you would have immediately scraped it off. The fact that you didn't is incriminating—it can only mean that the Eiffel Tower sticker in question is a secret sign of membership in a Trotskyist plot against Bolshevik rule and the Socialist order. I must make a note to the Organs to this effect—we must begin to look for telltale Eiffel Tower stickers on the valises and trunks of others suspected of treason."

Looking back, it's almost impossible for me to say with any positiveness where that first interrogation left off and the second and the third and the fourth began. Or even how many interrogations there were. In my mind's eye all the interrogations melt into one long bad dream, sprinkled with rides up and down the freight elevator, with tea tasting of iodine, with Sergo screaming in agony when they fling him back into the cell to collapse in his own piss and vomit. There were times when I distinctly remember walking along hallways under my own steam and others where I had to be dragged to and from the corner room with the pleated curtains. I think but I'm not absolutely certain that they began to beat the confession out of me long about the third or fourth interrogation. It happened this way. I remember comrade interrogator pulling open the top drawer of my steamer trunk and taking out a fistful of the worthless tsarist loan coupons. I remember him looking up at me and slapping me playfully across the face with the coupons. I remember him asking, "So tell me, Shotman, do you expect the capitalists to return to power in Soviet Russia anytime soon?"

"I would personally man the barricades if they tried," I said.

"That being the case, how do you explain the presence of these tsarist loan coupons in your trunk?"

"I ask you to believe me, comrade interrogator, when I tell you the loan coupons belonged to my mother's stepbrother, who was a small factory owner in Baku at the time of the Revolution—he employed ten or twelve Israelites that sewed sweatbands into hats. My mother's stepbrother bought the coupons as a joke after the fall of the tsar when they were selling for a tiny fraction of their face value. He was going to wallpaper the outhouse behind his villa with them, but he was accused of being a capitalist exploiter and wound up in front of a Red Guard firing squad before he could get around to it. My mother found the coupons in a shoe box when she cleared out her stepbrother's closet. When she learned they were worthless she started using them to light the cooking fire. I wish to God I'd let her, but I took them to roll cigarettes in."

"How brainless do you think I am, Shotman? You expect me to believe you kept these coupons to use in the place of cigarette paper?"

"It's the God honest truth, Your Honor. They're the right shape and the right size, and they burn slowly. If I had some of my *makhorka* I could show you."

Christophorovich went back to his table and removed a sheet of paper from what I took to be my folder. "Your original application to become a member of the Party makes no mention of your uncle being shot by the Red Guards. So we must add falsification of official records to your list of crimes."

"He wasn't my uncle, comrade interrogator. He was my stepuncle. The application form asked about blood relatives. Besides which, he lived in Baku, we lived in the mountains. I hardly ever saw him. If he passed me in the street today I wouldn't recognize him."

"How could he pass you in the street today if he's dead?"

"I only meant—I don't sleep much, comrade interrogator, so I sometimes mix things up."

"You mix up innocence and guilt," he said with so much conviction it set me to wondering if he knew something I didn't.

It was long about then that the biggest of the guards, an Uzbek with the broken, badly set nose and the long sideburns of an itinerant wrestler, turned up in comrade interrogator's corner office. We sized each other up for a few seconds. I didn't doubt, despite my bad knee, I could take him if it came to a test of strength. The Uzbek, clearly a professional, checked to make sure my wrists and ankles were properly attached to the irons in the wall. Christophorovich came up with a man's sock and the Uzbek, using a wooden soup ladle, began filling it with sand from a red firefighting box. When the sock was half stuffed with sand, he tied the filled part off with a piece of string and tested it against the palm of his hand. Satisfied, he looked over at comrade interrogator, who was back at the table, the napkin tucked under his chin, eating his supper meal. A second plate filled with sausages and cabbage was waiting for me if I signed a confession. Picking gristle out of his teeth with a fingernail, which convinced me he had working-class roots after all, Christophorovich nodded. The wrestler, if that's what he was before he went to work for the Organs, came up to me and gently pinned my head so my right cheek was flat against the wall. There is an unwritten code between really big men like the Uzbek and me—you should not make use of your strength to hurt someone if you can avoid it, you should use it respectfully if you can't avoid it. Which is why the Uzbek said his name.

"Islam Issa."

I said mine. "Fikrit Shotman."

His grip on my chin tightened. "Say when you are ready."

"Do what you must do to earn your bread," I told him.

He locked my head against the wall with one big paw and began to bash the sock filled with sand against the inside of my left ear.

I am not as thick as some who shall remain nameless pretend. I took this as a good, even positive sign—using the sock filled with sand, as opposed to a brick, and concentrating on the inside of my ear meant they didn't want to leave marks on my body. And that meant that without me confessing, they weren't sure they could prove I committed a crime and would have to let me go home to Agrippina. Look, they weren't ticklish about leaving marks on Sergo's body, you see my point? Which can only mean they were confident he was guilty as sin, but didn't rule out I might be innocent like the baby Jesus, though, mind you, I wouldn't say that out loud because, as they drummed into us at Party meetings, Russian Orthodox is the opium of the people, something like that.

The beatings continued over the next interrogations and I began to go deaf in my left ear. It started with a terrible ringing. I tried to get my mind off the pain by picturing, one after the other, all of Agrippina's tattoos—the snake twisting up her thigh, the map of Africa, the faces of Lenin and Stalin and the one she called Engels though I was in on the secret, I knew it was the traitor Trotsky, the *Mona Lisa* painting even though it was in Paris, France and not Russia, the two peacocks, one perched on each of her small shoulders. The painkiller worked for a while, then the throbbing began to blur the tattoos until I couldn't see them clearly. The more they beat me, the farther away the ringing got until it seemed to come from another room, and then from another floor of the prison. After that there was only soreness in the ear, soreness and silence. And through the fog of hurting like hell it came to me that they couldn't beat me on my other ear if they wanted me to hear their questions. I also saw that going deaf in one ear had certain advantages that comrade interrogator probably never thought of— it meant I was able to sleep with my good ear pressed to the blanket on the cell floor and not hear Sergo moaning all day long.

Every now and then the Uzbek went over to the shut-tight pleated curtains to smoke a cigarette while comrade interrogator came at me again with his questions. He wanted to know what political statement I was making with the tattoo of Comrade Stalin on my biceps having a scar across his face. When I explained about the rope burn from when we were putting up the tent in Tiflis, he broke into laughter.

"You have an explanation for everything, which in my experience is a definite sign of guilt."

"I am telling you the way it really happened."

"What about the fifty dollars U.S. you took to let the American weight lifter Hoffman win the gold medal at the European games in 1932? You didn't think we knew about that, did you? Wise up, Shotman, we know everything there is to know about you." Christophorovich didn't even give me a chance to deny the charge. "The Chekists who were watching you in Vienna filed a report. You were lucky that time—the picture of Stalin shaking your hand at the Kremlin reception turned up in the newspapers before we got around to arresting you. But it's a matter of record that you were already in the employ of the Americans in 1932. When did they first contact you? What kind of secret codes did they use to communicate with you when you returned to Moscow?" About then he dramatically pulled open another drawer in my steamer trunk and took out the copy of the American magazine *Strength and Health* Bob Hoffman gave me in Vienna, Austria. His voice dripping with contempt, Christophorovich read in what sounded like American the dedication Bob Hoffman wrote in it. He didn't need to translate the words—I knew them by heart. *To Fikrit Shotman, who took silver when he came in ten kilograms behind me in the dead lift, Vienna, December 27, 1932.* It was signed, *From your friend Bob Hoffman, who took gold.* "Any jackass can see there's a secret message buried here somewhere. Save yourself grief and tell us what it says, Shotman. Our cipher experts will decode it anyway."

The Uzbek stubbed out his cigarette in the box of sand and came back to my side of the room, all the while smacking the sock filled with sand in his palm. Comrade interrogator turned my head so he could talk into my good ear. "I don't need to remind you that Trotsky was in New York at the time of the first Revolution that overthrew the Tsar in 1917. He was without doubt in the pay of the American Organs when he returned to Russia to join the Bolsheviks, and later tried to take over the Party after Lenin's death. You are clearly an accomplice of Trotsky's, like him in the pay of the Americans. If you hope for leniency, confess what we already know, Shotman—you are a key member of the backup Trotskyist Paris-based anti-Bolshevik Center." And he added so triumphantly I could almost make out the *ta da* in his voice, "That is the significance of the Eiffel Tower sticker on your trunk!"

It may have been long about then I began to consider the possibility there might be a grain of truth to comrade interrogator's version of events. I wasn't yet positive of what, but I knew there was a good chance I must be guilty of something. I mean, even a village idiot knows there's no smoke without fire.

SIX

Nadezhda Yakovlevna
Monday, the 7th of May 1934

Spread-eagled on our mattress, Mandelstam listened to the siren song of the sea nymph and, to my immense relief, managed to resist being lured to destruction on the rocks surrounding our citadel.

Since the night of that poetry reading back in January, Zinaida had more or less separated from her agronomist husband. She hadn't actually moved in with us bag and baggage—she was careful to make it appear she was still living with her husband so as not to jeopardize her rights to their flat, and eventually her Moscow residence permit. But she had taken to spending two and sometimes three nights a week with us in Herzen House, more often than not in our bed, the other times on a thin mattress in the tiny kitchen if my husband was exhausted or preoccupied with what I delicately called *his mountaineer mission.*

The timid mistress of shamefaced glances, with her burning cheeks and incendiary orgasms (half stifled in deference to the thinness of the walls of our bedroom), had become adept at the protocol of a *ménage à trois.* She devoted as much attention to me as she did to my husband, partly to compensate for his paying more attention to her than to me, partly (I flatter myself) because she found me, as I found her, physically attractive and sexually stimulating. Mandelstam is on record as saying that loving a third person is not without risks, though the risk in this particular instance was not his falling insanely, or even sanely, in love with Zinaida. I can say that she was the kind of sexual animal who shrinks on you with time. Her constantly on display intelligence, her fastidiousness, her gushing admiration for the poet were already wearing thin. What remained was her body. And *what* a body! She was one of those females who didn't object to being lusted after for their bodies and only their bodies. And even I will concede her adroitness at certain techniques of lovemaking normally associated with harlots. Which is to say, no major orifice was left unexplored. Not one. Mandelstam, enthralled by the newness of the delectable corpus at his disposition and somewhat awed by what I might call the exotic smorgasbord set out on the sideboard, tended to forget that I was present as a participant and not a spectator. I suppose the phenomenon of the male focusing on the third person singular, to the exclusion of the *ty* in his life, is the hidden pitfall of all love triangles. I must remember to compare notes on the matter with Akhmatova one of these days.

Where was I? On the morning of the day I propose to recount, Zinaida stirred in my arms, sleepily fondling my breast with one hand, reaching out for Mandelstam with the other. Finding his side of the bed empty, she sat up abruptly.

"Did you manage to get some sleep?" I asked.

"Afterward I did. After our beautiful white night. My God, that husband of yours is insatiable." She looked around the tiny bedroom. "Where has he gotten to?"

"He's been up for hours," I said. "You can hear him pacing in the next room."

"Is he composing a poem?"

"So it would seem."

"For me?"

I had to keep from smiling. "Not for you, darling girl. Though perhaps he will let you interpret it into existence, as he says, when it's completed."

Talk about insatiable, she melted back into my arms and started caressing my skin with the tips of her fingers. "It's true what you said about women's bodies being far more attractive than men's," she said. Her hand worked its way down over my pelvis. "It's no accident that all the great sculptors and painters preferred the female nude to the male. Our skin is silkier, our curves softer, our sensual penetralia trickier to locate but, once located, effortlessly stimulated. Isn't that so, Nadezhda?"

I cannot exclude that I was unable to articulate a response.

"I especially love our breasts," she went on. "Sometimes I caress my own to remind myself how beautiful women are."

"Did you love your agronomist the way you love us?"

"You *are* mocking me, Nadezhda, aren't you? I married the first man I slept with, and I slept with the first man I came across who had a Moscow residence permit. He was my ticket out of the Urals to civilization. Can you see me spending the best years of my life in a repertory theater in Perm?"

"Surely your agronomist has redeeming features."

"Oh he does, he definitely does. He comes equipped with twenty-two square meters in a communal apartment off the Arbat. He has a job with a regular salary and the use of one room in a communal dacha on the low bank of the Volga for holidays, no matter that brats with runny noses swarm like locusts. Best of all, he is on the road for weeks at a stretch to study which seeds are best suited to which climates, which is his area of expertise."

"When the cat's away, the mouse will play," I teased her.

She confirmed my supposition with one of her shamefaced glances. "Whenever he returns home, it is too soon. Marriage to my agronomist, who is a hundred years older than I am—"

"Twelve," I corrected her.

"Twelve solar years but a hundred psychic years," she insisted. "Marriage to him transformed our Moscow flat into a cage, with fixed hours of the day for eating and defecating, and fixed days of the month for copulating. I often thought I'd be better off on my own, but I didn't want to abandon the flat and, with it, my precious Moscow residence permit, both of which are the price I must pay for a divorce. If it came to it, I think I could actually bring myself to kill for a residence permit. Tell me honestly, do you think I am wicked?"

"We all of us make compromises to keep our heads above water in this workers' swamp. By the way, I saw your agronomist when my husband and I came backstage the night you played one of the sisters in *Three Sisters*. As men go, he isn't all that bad looking."

"Can you explain, dearest Nadezhda, why women like us are attracted to men in the first place? We know next to nothing about what goes on in their silly heads. There are occasions when I look at their bodies and want to gag. Objectively speaking, the penis, dangling limply like the trunk of an elephant between their hairy legs, is the ugliest body part on a male. And yet . . . and yet when I catch sight of the swelling in a man's trousers, my pulse quickens. I long to touch it, to kiss it, to warm my lips with chamomile tea and accept it—ah, Nadezhda, to *welcome* it—into my mouth." She shuddered in my arms. "Only thinking such thoughts could give me an orgasm."

"Good thing for you it's the men, and not the women, who lose a day of their life with each orgasm," I said jokingly.

"Good thing," she agreed seriously. "When all is said, we have it so much better than the male of the species, don't you agree?"

"Speaking of tea, I could do with a cup," I told her.

"What a rich idea," she said.

I threw Mandelstam's old robe over my shoulders and, walking barefoot, headed for the kitchen to boil water on our small paraffin stove. Mandelstam, wearing the secondhand silk robe I'd gotten him with money I earned for a translation, was so absorbed in the intricacies of composition I don't think he was aware of my passing. When I returned to the living room carrying a tray with cups and a pot of tea, I found Zinaida, wrapped in a quilt from the bed, one lovely bare ankle jutting from under it, curled up on the sofa. She was watching in bafflement as Mandelstam paced the room, four long strides in one direction, then four long strides back, all the while puffing frenetically on a cigarette. I settled down next to her and filled two chipped cups with tea, and we warmed our hands around them waiting for the boiling water to cool. From time to time a moth flew near Mandelstam's head—the walls of Herzen House were insulated with felt, which provided a thermal breeding ground for insects. Mandelstam's concentration was so absolute he was able to backhand the moth away without being aware of its presence. It occurred to me he would not take any notice if one of those new air attack sirens being installed around Moscow, now that Hitler was in power in Germany, began yowling. His lips worked, words and then phrases formed. I could almost hear the poem knocking like a fist on the window.

And then Mandelstam stopped in midstride and looked over at us as if he had only just discovered we were in the room. He spied the moth near his nose and, emerging from a trance, went after it as if this particular insect was the culprit responsible for the hole he'd recently discovered in his knitted sweater. Clambering over furniture, clapping his hands wildly, the great moth hunter scrambled around the room until, victorious, he held up his right palm to show us the small spot of blood.

"I think I got it," he cried.

"The moth?" Zinaida said.

"The poem," Mandelstam said. "The epigram to Stalin."

Zinaida, thinking Mandelstam had given in to the many friends who implored him to compose an ode in honor of Stalin, looked relieved. "I know it must have been difficult for you," she told him, "but I for one think you were wise to do it."

I hooked my arm under her elbow. "You don't understand, darling child. Osya has surely composed a very outspoken poem, one that doesn't beat about the bush. You and I will be his first readers."

She looked puzzled. "But there is only one sort of poem you can compose when the subject is Stalin."

Mandelstam's gaze came to rest on the glass ashtray on the windowsill overflowing with cigarette ends, mostly but not all his. (I wondered if he had spotted the ends from a strong cigarette he himself never smoked when we returned to the flat the previous afternoon.) Shutting his eyes, exposing his pale throat, he raised the palm with the spot of blood on it over his head and began to recite.

> We live, deaf to the land beneath us,
> Ten steps away no one hears our speeches,
>
> All we hear is the Kremlin mountaineer,
> The murderer and peasant-slayer.
>
> His fingers are fat as grubs
> And the words, final as lead weights, fall from his lips,
>
> His cockroach whiskers leer
> And his boot tops gleam.
> Around him a rabble of thin-necked leaders—
> Fawning half-men for him to play with.
>
> They whinny, purr or whine
> As he prates and points a finger,
>
> One by one forging his laws, to be flung
> Like horseshoes at the head, the eye or the groin.
>
> And every killing is a treat
> For the broad-chested Ossete.

Mandelstam, transfigured, looked hard at me, an unmistakable gleam of triumph in his eyes and it finally dawned on me what he had meant by *Dead but not yet buried*. Looking back at this defining moment in our lives, I ask myself: How did I really feel? I suppose I was thrilled and proud and devastated all at the same time: thrilled by his audacity, proud to be an accomplice in an act of pure defiance, devastated that his instinct for survival, his *as well as* mine, was effectively moribund. As for Zinaida, she jerked her ankle back under the quilt and wilted against my arm. *"Murderer and peasant slayer!"* she groaned. "But you simply cannot do this to me, Osip. What will happen when they learn I was present when you read this out? Oh my God! There could be a microphone in the wall. They could be recording every word we say right now! Nadezhda, if he isn't willing to act sanely, you must act sanely for the both of you and talk him out of this folly."

The more she protested, the more I supported him. I was, after all, the wife, she was only the occasional mistress. "Get hold of yourself, Zinaida. Osya has paid you the ultimate compliment of making you one of his first readers. Only the chosen few will know of the existence of this epigram. Whatever happens, you can be certain neither he nor I will ever reveal you heard it."

Mandelstam sank to his knees before the two of us. "Zinaida, you must not breathe a word about this to anyone. If they find out, it could cost me my life."

She nodded miserably.

"Nadenka will memorize the epigram, as she memorizes all my poems. But I have decided that you should, too. If something happens to us, the poem absolutely must survive."

Zinaida tugged the quilt more tightly around her naked body, as if it could somehow shield her from an inconvenient request.

"Repeat the lines after me, both of you," Mandelstam said firmly. *"We live, deaf to the land beneath us, Ten steps away no one hears our speeches . . ."*

"We live, deaf to the land beneath us, Ten steps away no one hears our speeches . . ."

"All we hear is the Kremlin mountaineer, The murderer and peasant-slayer . . ."

"All we hear is the Kremlin mountaineer, The murderer and peasant-slayer . . ."

Having memorized Mandelstam's verse for years, I had an instinct for the rhyme and rhythm and layers of multiple meaning buried in a text, for where the slight pause for breath fell. It didn't take me long to commit the sixteen lines to memory. Zinaida was having a harder time of it. It quickly became apparent that she had no ear for the inner music of a Mandelstam poem. She would get four lines right and then mix up the punctuation, or even the order of the words, when she came back to them. Tears of frustration filled her eyes. "I detest being put on the spot—I can't memorize this the way you do. I must see it written down so I can picture the words. That's how I learn my lines for the theater. Even as a child I had to write things down in order to remember them."

My husband and I exchanged looks. "What do you think?" he said.

I shrugged. "As long as we can be sure the paper is destroyed once she has committed it to memory."

Zinaida looked relieved. "I swear I'll burn it," she said. "Next time I come by I shall recite it without an error."

Mandelstam fetched pen and paper. Crouching at the suitcase, using it as a desk, he wrote out the epigram. Zinaida went into the bedroom to get her clothing and emerged dressed a few minutes later. Mandelstam read over what he'd written to make sure it was exactly as he wanted, then handed the paper to Zinaida. She folded it in half and then in half again and tucked it inside her brassiere.

"I am grateful you're willing to do this," Mandelstam said.

"I am grateful to be part of your citadel," Zinaida replied nervously. "I am thrilled to have your trust."

"Perhaps you should be on your way before the conversation becomes too syrupy," I suggested. I remember adding: "Don't forget to burn the poem."

I recall Zinaida's confident "You can count on me."

After she left I dressed and busied myself straightening up the bedroom. Through the open door I could see Mandelstam sitting on the sofa, staring at the ceiling, occasionally clapping his hands together to kill a moth that had wandered within lethal range of him. "Do you think I did the right thing?" he called out to me.

"Are you talking about the epigram or Zinaida?"

"Both."

I joined him in the living room and sank onto the arm of the sofa. He rested a hand on my ankle and we both smiled at the same memory—the first time we'd been intimate, the night we met at the Junk Shop in Kiev, he began his leisurely exploration of my body with my ankle. It was a joke of long standing between us that he was Russia's first and foremost ankle fetishist. "Concerning the epigram," I said, "you have been torturing yourself for months. You needed to get it out of your system. You only must be careful whom you let in on the secret. As for entrusting it to Zinaida, she is a harmless creature who will evolve badly once her body goes. For now, she is enthralled to be the paramour of the poet Mandelstam—"

Mandelstam brightened. "There is a poet of that name."

His grip tightened on my ankle and he looked intently at me, expecting confirmation. "There is," I agreed with conviction. "He is not yet dead."

It was almost midday when I got around to emptying the glass ashtray filled with cigarette ends into the bin immediately outside the alley door of Herzen House. And who should I come across there but Boris Pasternak, throwing out kitchen garbage after having spent the morning in another wing of the building with his future ex-wife and their son. Telling him that Mandelstam needed cheering up, I practically dragged him back to our flat. My husband was tucking his shirt into his trousers when he caught sight of Pasternak at the door behind me. He let out a howl of pleasure. "You will stay for lunch," I ordered. "We have bread and a bit of butter and two eggs—I will scare up a third from someone on our floor."

I found the extra egg at the second door I knocked on. When I returned to our flat I discovered Mandelstam standing in the middle of the living room reciting the last lines of his Stalin epigram to Pasternak, who was sitting on the floor, his back against a wall, his face buried in his enormous hands. When Mandelstam reached the end, Boris sat there without moving a muscle.

"Well?" Mandelstam said impatiently.

"Well?" I repeated from the doorway.

Boris looked up, first at me, then at my husband. "Who knows about this?" he demanded.

"The three of us," Mandelstam said. "And one friend."

"Can you trust the friend?"

I answered from the door. "Yes."

Springing to his feet, Boris went over to the window and pulled the interior shutters closed. Then he turned around to face us. "You're committing suicide," he said, his eyes grown so hollow you could barely make out the pupils in them. "When you said you were going to let the scream emerge from the back of your throat, I didn't dream you would do something this insane."

"What Russia needs," Mandelstam observed, "is more insanity and less sanity."

Boris was so caught up in his own anguish I don't think he heard him. "How could you write such a poem, you, a Jew!" he blurted out.

"You're forgetting I converted to Christianity to get into university," Mandelstam replied angrily.

"Stalin and the people around him have a lot in common with the ecclesiastical tribunals of the Spanish Inquisition," Pasternak said. "For the *calificadores*, a Jew who converted remains a Jew in his heart, in his soul."

It was difficult to get a word in, but I managed. "I'll recite the poem to you again, Boris—you tell me exactly what in it a Jew shouldn't say."

"No, no, I don't have to hear it a second time to know that Osip has not thought this through. He is either stupid or innocent. I don't want any part of it."

Mandelstam sank onto the back of the sofa. "Poetry is nourished by innocence, not stupidity," he said, clearly devastated by Pasternak's reaction. "You yourself took the position that art is risk taking."

"I said that? Where?"

Mandelstam managed a bitter smile as he threw Pasternak's words back in his face. *"One cannot talk of art as if it were a drainpipe or a construction job and so boil the question down to technique. To talk about the technique of writing poetry is to talk about the technique of achieving disaster. One has to remember that one needs to take risks; nothing on earth exists without risk taking."*

Boris muttered something about having said that in another context. He turned on me furiously. "How can you permit him to do this?"

Before I could put a word in, Mandelstam said, very quietly, "We have never had a relationship that involved my asking her permission or her asking mine."

Boris was beginning to exasperate me. "You are angry," I burst out, "because you don't have the guts to do what Osya is doing. You're not the poet he is."

Mandelstam tried to cut me off. "Nadenka, you go too far—"

I remember saying, "I don't go far enough. He must understand that Mandelstam has to be true to Mandelstam, not to Pasternak."

Boris looked bewildered. "My dear Osip, I don't recognize you anymore. You have become someone else."

"When he becomes someone else," I informed Boris, taking, I will own up, a certain satisfaction from his evident bewilderment, "I am never far behind."

Boris raised a hand to his forehead and kneaded the migraine lurking under his brow. "If you are serious about bringing Stalin down," he told Osip, "join in the long-term political struggle."

"My constitution is incapable of political struggle," my husband retorted. "I am too impatient for strategy. I only have the temperament for tactics. I am drawn to the gesture. And I believe in the power of poetry to displace mountains, along with the Kremlin mountaineer."

"At least rework the poem," Boris said with great emotion, "so that it is veiled, ambiguous, written, say, about a historical figure."

"I am through beating about the bush, Boris. A poem needs to be written that spells out the evil of Stalin so that any dense-brained idiot can understand it." Thinking it would put an end to the argument, Mandelstam coughed up one of his favorite mantras. *"If not now, when? If not me, who?"*

Shaking his head in despair, Boris turned to leave. At the door he hesitated. "The very least you can do—if not for your own sake, then for the friends who will hear the epigram—is rewrite the second stanza. The business about murderer and peasant-slayer—it is perilously direct. I ask you, Osip, to do this."

My husband looked at me, thinking I would challenge Pasternak. I took a deep breath and held my tongue. Whether a truth teller was still truth telling if he gutted the truth was something only Osya could decide.

I could see Mandelstam chewing on the inside of his cheek as he considered the matter. Tossing his head in frustration, he said, "The original version had two other lines that I got rid of because they weren't straightforward enough. If it will make you feel easier, I'll eliminate the *murderer and peasant-slayer* and restore the first version." And he closed his eyes and recited the lines he would substitute:

But where there's so much as half a conversation
The Kremlin mountaineer will get his mention.

Boris said, "If you really want to make me feel easier, scrap the entire epigram."

Only thinking about what my beloved husband did then makes my heart beat more rapidly. His fingers trembling, he elevated his chin and repeated the words he'd thrown into the faces of Ugor-Zhitkin and his lady friends at the canteen for trolley car workers. "I am the poet Mandelstam."

I am afraid I couldn't resist driving home the spike. "As for me, I am the wife of the poet Mandelstam, and proud to be."

Boris shrugged angrily as he turned toward the door.

"What about those eggs?" I said.

"At a time like this, how can you think of food!" he growled in annoyance. "With or without those *peasant-slayer* lines, this matter will end badly. They have treated you miserably in the last years, Osip. If you insist on this epigram, at least you will know *why* they are treating you miserably. I esteem you as a poet. I love you as a brother. I wish you long life, Osip Emilievich."

I remember being struck by how devastated Mandelstam looked—he had been counting on Pasternak's unstinting support. In my brain, I can still hear his voice calling after the departing poet, "Long life to you, too, Boris Leonidovich."

SEVEN

Zinaida Zaitseva-Antonova
Monday, the 7th of May 1934

How could the son of a bitch have done this to me! The way I see it, it's one thing if you're fed up with life before death and want to kill yourself. Stop jabbering about it and do it, I say, but you simply don't have the right to take others down with you. This Stalin poem of Mandelstam's is unadulterated madness. He's off his trolley, round the bend, certifiably loony. But it's *his* madness, not mine. I'm not even sure it's a good poem, for Christ's sake. But that's not going to stop him from reading it to all those has-been writers hanging around Herzen House. My God, what in the world can he be thinking, reading such a poem to innocent people? He has no moral right to make others accomplices to what is, after all, *his* crime. We live in an epoch when someone who has knowledge of treason and doesn't denounce the wrecker *becomes* a wrecker, subject to the same punishment as the perpetrator. It doesn't take a genius to see what's going to happen: of the five or ten or twenty who will hear the poem, one or several of them—or *all* of them except for poor Nadezhda, who is blinded by love—are going to reason like me. Mandelstam has a hell of a nerve putting us in the position where we could be treated as traitors for *listening* to his shitty little poem. Which means one or several or all of those who hear the poem will protect themselves the only way possible: they will race to the nearest militia post and denounce the author of the poem before someone else does and the Cheka comes sniffing around asking you to explain, please, how come you heard this treacherous poem and didn't denounce the enemy of the people who composed it. And what would I do? Bat my eyelashes and ask, *What poem are you talking about, comrade militiaman?* By then they'll know the contents of the poem down to the last comma and the name and address and internal passport number of all those who heard it. And the ones who failed to alert the Organs will be up shit's creek, as the saying goes; off to Siberia or, heaven forbid, worse. And for what? I mean, it's not as if this little poem of Mandelstam's is going to change anything.

Except the lives of those unlucky enough to hear it.

Darling Osip really didn't leave me much choice, so I don't feel as if I betrayed a trust or anything like that. Besides which, any idiot can see the poor man is trying to commit suicide. By alerting the Organs, I was only doing what deep down he wanted me to do.

Was I uncomfortable lengthening my life at the expense of shortening Mandelstam's?

Svoloch—bastard! You've been talking to Nadezhda! If anybody's to blame for shortening Mandelstam's life, it's his bitch. They're a *folie à deux*. One eggs the other on. For God's sake, what other lies did she tell you about me?

EIGHT

Anna Andreyevna
Sunday, the 13th of May 1934

I could tell something was terribly wrong the instant I lifted the telephone handset to my ear. Borisik, his speech saturated with static because of the magnetic storm disrupting the line linking Petersburg to the rest of Russia, announced, "You must absolutely drop whatever you're doing and come to Moscow." He said it in a way that left precious little room for argument. Somehow my dear friend Pasternak managed to sound both alarmed and deathly calm at the same time; it was his deathly calm that sent the chill down my vertebral column. I tried to tell him this was not a good moment for me to leave Petersburg. My twenty-two-year-old son, Lev, with whom I had a thorny relationship, was in town and for once we were talking about what had gone wrong between us rather than quarreling about how I could have described motherhood as a *bright torture*; my third husband, the art historian Nikolai Punin, had secured a voucher for a two-week holiday at one of his university's hostels on Lake Ladoga and was dying for a break from the city; and an editor I knew had agreed to publish my critical essay on Pushkin on condition I cut it by half, no easy chore since I had already cut the original version by half. Borisik brushed aside my excuses and

I was beginning to get annoyed when I heard him say: "You don't understand, Anna. Our mutual friend, who shall remain nameless lest the Organs are monitoring this conversation, has decided to kill himself."

"Kill himself?" I heard myself repeating dully.

"You remember the conversation we had, the three of us, when we were watching the teardrops hurl themselves against the Cathedral of Christ the Savior? Well, he has gone ahead with his project. I tried to convince him it was insane but, supported by that mulish wife of his, he claimed what Russia needed was less sanity and more insanity. I take the view that you are the only one who can have an influence on him in this matter. You must immediately come to Moscow and stop him before—" The noise on the line blotted Borisik out for a moment. Then I heard the words "spilt milk."

Which is how I came to disappoint son and husband and editor. My husband tried to persuade me to phone the Mandelstams so Osip could meet my train, but fearing he would only talk me out of coming, I thought it better not to. As it was too late for the night train and far too early for the morning train, I spent hours tossing sleeplessly on the bed (after a terrible row with Nikolai, who argued that Osip was a consenting adult; that if he really was determined to commit suicide, I had a moral obligation to respect his decision). Under the best of circumstances, I am an agitated traveler. Unlike Borisik, who loves to leap onto the last wagon as it starts to pull out of the quay, I prefer to arrive at the station with time to kill. Knowing my disposition, my husband persuaded a neighbor on our embankment who had the use of a city administration vehicle to drive us to the Moskovsky Railway Station well before dawn. In the waiting room, filled with travelers curled up on benches, Nikolai spotted a public telephone and again suggested I call the Mandelstams. Was it because I was exhausted and not thinking clearly that I didn't argue? I dialed the intercity operator and gave her the number of the communal telephone in the first-floor hallway of Herzen House. After a long wait I could hear the handset ringing on the other end. When nobody answered, the operator was ready to hang up, but I explained that it was a communal phone and begged her to keep ringing. When someone finally picked up the receiver, I asked to speak to Mandelstam. *Do you have any idea of the hour?* a man demanded petulantly. Before I could say a word, he informed me that there was no Mandelstam living in Herzen House. I started to insist that he was making a terrible mistake, there was certainly a Mandelstam living in Herzen House, but the line went dead in my ear. "What did he mean, there is no Mandelstam *living* in Herzen House?" I asked my husband, a knob of panic rising to the back of my throat.

"You make a serious error trying to read between the lines," Nikolai said, but I could see from the look in his eyes that he, too, was turning over the words as if they were stones, looking for worms of calamity beneath them.

I had taken my Pushkin article with me on the train, thinking I could distract myself by reworking it, but I wound up catnapping on my hard second-class seat, my scarf bunched into a makeshift pillow so that my ear, pressed against the windowpane, would not become bruised by the jolting of the train. And I dreamed dreams so frightful I had to force myself awake to escape the anguish they imparted to my soul.

No Mandelstam *living* in Herzen House! Had the people who left cigarette ends in Nadezhda's ashtray taken over the telephone? Were they, in the manner of Chekists, announcing the death of the poet Mandelstam?

The sun was sinking below the rooftops of wooden *izbas* as the train crept through the Moscow suburbs, past the first factories and cooperatives with hammer-and-sickle devices over the arched entrances, through neighborhoods with unpaved streets lined with newly fabricated lodgments that had come into this world with a birth defect: ugliness. It was dark out by the time we pulled into the grand Leningradskiya Railway Station on Komsomolskaya

Ploshchad. I lowered the compartment window and leaned out to see if I could spot a familiar face—Borisik would have calculated which train I was on and passed word to Osip, so I told myself, so I hoped. But there were too many passengers milling on the platform, which was dimly lighted in any case. Clutching my carpetbag, I made my way through the crowd to the head of the platform; I am quite tall enough to see over the heads of people, but I climbed onto a block of cement anyhow to get a better view. I instructed my heart not to sink if Osip didn't turn up. He could have had an appointment with an editor who was willing to publish one of his poems that beat about the bush. He could be out scouring neighborhood canteens for cheap cigarettes.

When I failed to spot him, my disobedient heart sank all the same. Borisik might not have been able to get word to him for the same reason I'd been unable to get word to him—*because there was no Mandelstam living in Herzen House!*

How I managed to find my way to the right trolley line with my soul gripped by a presentiment of tragedy, my sight blurred by unshed tears, I will never know. Perhaps it was pure instinct that led me to the trolley, that helped me to purchase a ticket from the woman conductor at the back, that told me where to get off and which way to walk. Something like forty minutes later, with my heart pounding in my rib cage, I found myself standing before the door of the Mandelstam flat in Herzen House. I remember raising my knuckles to knock and then, short of breath, backing away, terrified that no one would answer.

What if there was no Mandelstam living in Herzen House?

And then I stopped breathing altogether and knocked and strained to catch the sound of footsteps. I thought I heard a woman's voice call *Coming* from somewhere inside. A second later Nadezhda was on the other side of the unopened door demanding, "Who's there?"

Somehow I managed to activate my vocal cords. "It's me," I rasped. "It's Anna."

The door was flung open and a stunned smile materialized on Nadezhda's angelic face. As it dawned on me that she wouldn't be smiling if there was no Mandelstam living in Herzen House, I collapsed into her arms.

"Osip, look who has turned up at our doorstep," Nadezhda cried as she led me into their small kitchen. And there was my dear, dear Osip, in shirttails and suspenders, sipping tea at the table.

At the sight of him I sank onto a chair and wept in relief.

When I had calmed down enough to carry my end of a conversation, I explained about Borisik's summoning me to Moscow. Osip chided me for not calling so he could meet the train, at which point I described the voice on the communal telephone claiming there was no Mandelstam living in Herzen House. Osip and Nadezhda exchanged looks. Osip smiled grimly. Nadezhda linked her arm through her husband's and kissed him on the shoulder. "I suppose I should have told you," she said. "For some months now, there have been strangers visiting our flat when we were away. From time to time I find their cigarette ends in our ashtray."

I remember exclaiming, "But he knows about them, Nadezhda—he's been keeping it to himself so as not to upset *you*."

Nadezhda stared at Osip. "You know about the cigarette ends?"

He was incredulous. "Don't tell me you have known about them, too!"

And the two of them, looking for all the world like mischievous children discovering they shared a secret, laughed until the laughter turned to tears.

"This is not a laughing matter," I said.

They both quieted down. "Of course you are right, Anna," Nadezhda said. "If we laugh, it's out of nervousness."

"Nervous laughter," Osip quipped, "is known to be excellent for the bowels."

"Let's talk about the poem," I suggested.

"Will you hear it?" Osip asked.

Nadezhda touched my arm. "Do hear it," she said. "It's glorious."

I agreed with a nod. Rising to his feet, Osip tucked the shirttails into his trousers and buttoned the top button of his collarless shirt. Taking a deep breath, tossing back his head, he began to recite.

> *We live, deaf to the land beneath us,*
> *Ten steps away no one hears our speeches,*
>
> *But where there's so much as half a conversation*
> *The Kremlin mountaineer will get his mention.*

I cannot claim to have taken in the epigram the way I usually absorb a Mandelstam poem, which is to say as a whole that, on first hearing, mesmerizes me with its mood and its music. This one lodged in my consciousness in word splinters—fragments that had no connection with each other or the whole. I admitted as much when Osip pressed me for a comment. "The English poet Eliot, in his *Waste Land*, claimed to have shored fragments against his ruin," I said. "But your fragments will bring about your ruin."

"How can you reduce my epigram to fragments?" Osip retorted, clearly displeased with my reaction.

Nadezhda, as always, rose to his defense. "Exactly what fragments are you talking about?"

I was, truth be told, brokenhearted not to be able to respond more positively. But Osip and I went back a long way—along with my late husband Gumilyov, we'd been poetic comrades years before Nadezhda came into his life. And the hallmark of our poetic camaraderie was absolute, even brutal, honesty. And so I told him which fragments stuck in my mind. "*Kremlin mountaineer . . . fingers fat as grubs . . . cockroach whiskers . . . fawning half-men . . .* ah, and the bit about *every killing* being *a treat for the Ossete*. Good Lord, Osip, people have been known to vanish into prisons for suggesting that Stalin had a drop of Ossetian bandit blood in his veins, as opposed to his being pure Georgian."

Undoing the top button of his shirt, Osip settled down facing me. "You don't think it's a good poem," he said flatly.

I reached for his hand. "Putting to one side its audacity, I don't think it's a good poem, no. To my ear, it doesn't even appear to be a poem. You weren't listening to the music of the words when you composed it. You had something else in mind. It's a polemic, meant to come across as a political argument. This is not something you will include in your collected works if and when they are published."

Osip shook his head. "The insurgent Decembrists had Pushkin's political poems in their pockets when they rose up against the tsar in Petersburg."

I remember Nadezhda bursting out, "Whether it's a good poem or bad poem is beside the point."

Osip said, "It's a truth-telling poem, one that doesn't beat about the bush. It's a cleansing poem that can wipe the slate clean so Russia can start over again."

I felt compelled to point out the obvious. "If it becomes known, it will get you killed."

"That's what Boris said," Nadezhda noted.

"Borisik loves you, Osip, as I love you. It's one thing to risk your life for a genuine poem, quite another to put your life—as well as your future poetic production—in jeopardy for a polemic."

Nadezhda said, "We don't see things that way."

I smiled at the *we*. Nadezhda had always been a bit envious of my relationship with Osip. Looking back on the conversation, I think she was using it to establish that she was, after all, the wife, and I was merely a friend of long standing. The night wore on as we sat at the small four-sided table going around in circles. Nothing I could think to say made the slightest impression on either of them. Borisik would be deeply troubled when he learned that I had had no success coaxing Osip back across the frontier into sanity.

It must have been close to eleven when we heard someone scratching at the door of the flat. "That will be Sergei Petrovich," Nadezhda said, springing to her feet, thankful for an excuse to put an end to the discussion. "He comes around at this hour to use our toilet and to borrow."

"Borrow what?"

Nadezhda said, "Whatever we happen to have in the way of food. He spends everything he earns on alcohol but gets hungry before going to bed. He's not fussy, he'll accept anything—an egg, a cup of kasha, a slice of bread with or without comfiture. A pickle even."

Osip added with a sour laugh, "Even a pickle."

While Nadezhda went to let him in, Osip told me about their friend and neighbor Sergei Petrovich, who was living in the toiletless half of his former wife's apartment on the second floor; as the two weren't on speaking terms, he had to knock on different doors during the day to use the facilities. "He's a decent enough lyric poet, half Georgian on his mother's side—he was dismissed as the literary editor of a regional newspaper some while ago for publishing a Mandelstam poem, so I feel a debt toward him. Since being fired he has been unable to find work. He makes ends meet translating an infinitely long Georgian epic poem. Because it's Georgian, everyone presumes the project is close to Stalin's heart and so Sergei collects a monthly stipend no matter how many or how few pages he manages to turn in."

Nadezhda returned to the kitchen, the lyric poet—with alcohol on his breath—trailing shakily after her. He plucked my hand from the table and kissed it in the French manner, barely grazing the skin with his course lips. "*Ochen rad,*" he said. "To meet the celebrated Akhmatova in person is a consummation of sorts, more gratifying than sex, which, in any case, I have not experienced in years." He pulled over a wooden apple crate and, setting it on end, joined us around the table. Sergei Petrovich was as tall as I but thin as a plank, which made him appear taller. His long dirty white beard was matted with traces of the food he'd been able to sponge. He wore a vest over a soiled white shirt, shapeless trousers and felt slippers with the backs cut out because they were too small for his large feet. Armless spectacles were attached to his head by a shoelace. Nadezhda pushed the page of newspaper folded into a pouch and filled with kasha across the table to him. Sergei Petrovich managed to bow from the waist while still sitting. "Thank you, my dears," he said, "but what I really hunger after tonight is food for thought." He leaned forward and peered at Osip strangely. "Everybody at Herzen House is talking about it, you know."

I smelled a rat. "Talking about what?" I asked.

Swaying on his makeshift stool, Sergei Petrovich eyed Osip. "The poem about Stalin, of course."

"Who's everybody?" I demanded. I turned on Osip in exasperation. "Did you circulate the epigram in writing?"

Nadezhda answered for him. "It has never been written out. We're not fools."

"How many did you read the poem to, Osip?" I asked.

Nadezhda said, "In Herzen House, two or three, not counting me."

Osip tossed one shoulder defiantly. "My dear Anna, it's a matter of creating ripples."

"How many?" I insisted.

"Five or six. Certainly not more than six."

Sergei Petrovich said, "Seven. If the poet does me the honor, I shall be number eight."

And so my poor innocent naïve Osip pushed himself to his feet and recited it for the tosspot shit. All of it. Every word. He omitted nothing, not the *Kremlin mountaineer* nor the *fingers fat as grubs* nor the *cockroach whiskers* nor the *fawning half-men* nor the son of a bitch of an Ossete for whom *every killing* was *a treat*. My God, in light of what happened afterward, only remembering the moment makes me sick to my stomach.

Sergei Petrovich fell silent when Osip had finished. Then, noisily sucking a lungful of air through his flaring nostrils, he announced, ex cathedra, "It is a truly great poem, my dears. There is no doubt about it. I am swollen with pride to have been one of your first readers, Osip Emilievich. On my deathbed I shall boast of it."

Nadezhda glanced at me triumphantly. Osip was so moved he was at a loss for words. Patting the visitor on the shoulder, he kept nodding his thanks.

Sergei Petrovich wanted to know when the poem had been first conceived, whether it had been revised, who outside the eight at Herzen House had heard it, how each of the first readers had reacted. To Osip's credit, he answered evasively. Eventually he got into a discussion with his visitor about the poets who had defied the tsars before the Bolshevik Revolution. He reached for the teapot where Nadezhda hid the poems she copied off, riffled through them until he found the one with lines from the poet Blok written on the back of a draft of a Mandelstam poem and read them out: *Nothing will change. There's no way out.* Carried away by Sergei Petrovich's compliments, Osip went so far as to compare himself to Lermontov, who had openly accused the tsar of complicity in Pushkin's death and railed against the *venomous wretches huddling about the throne in a greedy throng.*

Sergei Petrovich's head bobbed in truckling agreement. "Lermontov's *venomous wretches* is the spiritual father of your *rabble of thin-necked leaders,* your *fawning half-men.*"

"I hadn't thought of it that way," Osip said, "but I will concede there is something to what you say."

When I was able to get a word in, I asked Osip if he happened to recall Pushkin's last words.

He was in an edgy humor. "I'm sure you'll remind me."

I did remind him. "Lying on the daybed, dying from the bullet wound he'd suffered in the duel with that treacherous Frenchman d'Anthès, he said: *Try to be forgotten. Go live in the country.* Which is what you and Nadezhda ought to be doing instead of drawing attention to yourselves with political poems."

I was beginning to wonder how long the conversation would drag on. Having slept hardly at all the previous night, I was bone tired and aching to stretch out on the sofa in the next room. As much as Nadezhda was enjoying Sergei Petrovich's visit, I could see she was suppressing yawns. Over our heads the Swiss clock with the heavy weight hanging on the end of a chain ticked away as slowly and as loudly as ever. I suggested we move into the living room, thinking the visitor would take the hint and depart. I noticed Sergei Petrovich pulling a large watch from the fob pocket in his vest as he followed me down the hallway. "It *is* late," he said as Nadezhda and I collapsed onto the sofa and the two men brought over chairs. But he made no move to leave.

Fumbling in a pocket, Osip came up with a crumpled pack of cheap Bulgarian cigarettes. When he saw there were only two left in it, he leaped to his feet in distress. "I hate to cut short such an agreeable evening," he said, "but I absolutely must find cigarettes."

As if by slight of hand, Sergei Petrovich produced an unopened pack, Herzegovina Flors at that, and tossed it to Osip. "It's yours," he said so grandly you would have thought he was offering caviar and vodka.

"I wasn't aware you smoked," Osip said, examining the pack as he sank back onto his seat.

"I don't," Sergei Petrovich said. "Someone gave it to me for translating a letter—I offer the cigarettes to thank you for the use of your toilet."

"It *is* getting late," Nadezhda said. "Perhaps we should think of calling it a night."

"Am I keeping you up?" the visitor inquired. It was not my place to say he was, but I remember snorting aloud at his shamelessness. Sergei Petrovich nervously checked the time on his pocket watch. "I shall be on my way as soon as I learn how Mandelstam and Akhmatova met," he announced, looking directly at me. "I want to be able to say I heard the story from the horse's mouth."

That was more than I could tolerate—I'd reached the limits of my patience with this inebriated lyric poet who thought my mouth resembled that of a horse. "We met after you were born but before you started drinking," I remarked.

Sergei Petrovich rolled with the punch. "I am not offended," he told Osip who, too much of a gentleman to evict a guest, started to describe our first meeting, in 1911. Nadezhda, who had heard the story a hundred times, went off to the bedroom and came back with the quilt I always used when I slept over. And still Sergei Petrovich made no move to leave.

And then we discovered why.

No matter how much this hurts, I must get it right. The pain is in the details. Someone knocked softly on the door of the flat. Nadezhda glanced anxiously at the tiny watch on her wrist. "Who would come calling at this hour?" she asked in a hollow voice.

Osip buttoned the top button of his shirt again, almost as if he thought it would be held against him if he wasn't presentable. "O Lord," he murmured, quoting from one of his poems I first heard in the early thirties, "help me to live through this night."

Whoever was at the door rapped more sharply. Osip said to Nadezhda, very calmly, "Will you get that or should I?"

She rose to her feet. The blood had drained from her lips. She looked at me to see if I could fashion an answer to the question she feared to ask. I was too terrified to try. Sergei Petrovich came up with a small medicinal bottle filled with a clear liquid and took a quick swig from it. He wiped the lips that had grazed the back of my hand on the sleeve of his shirt. Reeking of alcohol but suddenly stone sober, he said, "I swear on the head of my ex-wife I didn't know they were coming tonight."

"Who's coming tonight?" I asked so weakly nobody heard me. Nadezhda loomed over the guest and hissed, "Utter one word about the epigram, Sergei, and I will circumcise you with a kitchen knife."

She ironed the wrinkles out of her skirt with the palms of her quavering hands and went to open the door.

When she came back, six men crowded into the room behind her. Five of them wore the belted raincoats associated with the secret police. The sixth, dressed in a black suit with a double-breasted jacket, had the features of a raven; I have heard it said that the guttural croak of the raven can resemble human speech but I had never experienced this until then. (It is beyond me how in the world I remember such trivia. I suppose it's because the scene is graven in my memory.) The man in the dark suit, evidently the agent in charge, approached Sergei Petrovich and, looking down at him, said, "I have a warrant for your arrest."

Considering that the arrest of Mandelstam must have been planned down to the last detail, I couldn't help but smile uneasily at this manifestation of mistaken identity. One could almost feel sorry for the drunken shit of a collaborator, who had been dispatched to make sure the individual the Cheka sought would be there when they came around to collect him at the witching hour; who, during the arrest, would play the role of the obligatory civilian witness required by Soviet law. This explained Sergei's endless questions, not to mention the full pack of Herzegovina Flors in his pocket.

Osip stood up and addressed the officer I identified as the Raven. "You are making a mistake, comrade enforcer of the law. He is the witness. I am the poet."

"Osip Mandelstam?"

"I am the poet Mandelstam, yes."

"I am the Colonel Abakumov. I have a warrant for your arrest. You are charged under Article 58, covering anti-Soviet propaganda and counterrevolutionary activities."

"I don't for an instant doubt you are in possession of a warrant. Still, am I permitted to see it?"

The Raven pulled a paper from the breast pocket of his jacket. Osip skimmed the document. "Genrikh Yagoda himself signed it," he informed us. "I suppose I must take it as mark of esteem to be arrested on a warrant signed by the head of the Cheka." He looked at Sergei Petrovich, who was sitting with his chin on his chest, his eyes tightly shut. "Give me your opinion, Sergei. Would it be a stretch of the imagination to consider this signature as evidence that I am not, after all, a minor poet?"

The guest made no move to reply. The Raven addressed Osip. "Are you armed?"

To my astonishment, Osip nodded. "As a matter of fact, yes."

The Raven seemed taken aback. "What are you armed with? And where do you conceal the weapon?"

"I am armed with the explosive power locked inside the nucleus of poems. I conceal the poems in question in my brain."

The Raven didn't think this was humorous. "You are treating this matter more lightly than you should. One of my men will accompany you to the bedroom. You are permitted to dress. You are permitted to collect a few personal items in a bag, including a change of undergarments."

Osip followed an agent into the bedroom. Nadezhda said, "I want to see the arrest warrant."

"That is out of the question. The arrest warrant is stamped state secret. The procedure is to show it to the individual being arrested, not to every person who happens to be present at the arrest."

"Where are you taking him?" Nadezhda demanded.

"That, too, is a state secret."

"Who will question him? How will he be questioned?"

"Methods of interrogation are a closely guarded state secret. It would help our enemies if they were to know how they would be interrogated."

"Surely there are rules that must be followed in any interrogation."

"There are indeed rules," the Raven agreed, "but they are a state secret."

"Mandelstam is a poet, an intellectual," Nadezhda burst out. "He has not broken the law."

"If that is the case, he has nothing to fear and will be sent home in short order."

The agents in raincoats spread out through the apartment and started to rifle through cupboards and drawers and the hall closet, throwing the contents into a heap in the corner of the room.

"Why is Yagoda taking an interest in a poet who is not even published?" I asked.

The Raven shrugged. "The particulars that have resulted in Mandelstam's arrest are a state secret."

Making no effort to keep the irony out of my voice, I asked, "Is there anything that's not a state secret?"

The Raven favored me with a thin smile. "The answer is obviously yes. But what's not a state secret is a state secret."

Osip emerged from the bedroom. He had put on his only suit and a detachable collar and carried a small satchel filled, I supposed, with toilet articles and spare underwear. He lingered in front of the bookshelf to pluck the small copy of Pushkin's collected works edited by Tomashevski from it. The agent snatched it from his hands and shook it by the spine to be sure nothing was hidden inside, then returned it. Osip slipped it into the pocket of his suit jacket.

Nadezhda tried to embrace her husband but one of the agents stepped between them. His lips trembling, Osip delivered a line from his *Tristia* cycle. *"I have studied the science of good-byes . . ."*

Nadezhda, deathly pale, completed the stanza. *". . . The crying of women and the Muses' song become one."*

Only God knows how I remembered lines from the same poem. *"Everything's happened before and will happen again, but still the moment of each meeting is sweet."*

Blinded by the flood of tears in my eyes, I never saw Osip leave. When the front door closed behind him, Nadezhda and I fell into each other's arms.

The collaborator was still sitting there. One of the agents tapped him on the shoulder. "I will take your deposition in the kitchen," he said, and gestured for Sergei Petrovich to follow him from the room.

The officer and the other two agents continued ransacking the flat. Going through the shelves book by book, the Raven was quite puzzled by the absence of Marxist classics. "But where do you keep Marx and Lenin and Stalin?" he asked.

I said, "This is surely the first time you've arrested somebody who doesn't own a copy of Stalin's *Marxism and the National Question*."

"Not owning a copy of *Marxism and the National Question* can count against someone during the interrogation," the Raven retorted. I couldn't tell whether he was saying this in jest or not. Probably not.

The search went on until dawn. Through it all Nadezhda and I sat numbly on the sofa watching them. What they were after were handwritten documents—letters, poems, even (as it turned out) shopping lists—and to this end every book in the library was shaken by its spine. At some point we heard the collaborator Sergei Petrovich let himself out of the flat. Nadezhda called after him, "Don't forget the kasha," but if he heard her, he made no answer. Soon after the agent came in from the kitchen carrying Nadezhda's spare teapot. Smiling triumphantly, he lifted off the lid and turned it upside down and the poems Nadezhda had hidden inside, written on scraps of thin paper, fluttered to the floor. Every bit of paper with writing on it was collected in a satchel marked *State Property*. At one point during the search the youngest of the agents, a pink-cheeked boy with blond hair, came over to offer us rock candy from a small tin in his pocket. Both of us declined. "They're not poisoned," he said with a shrug. By the time the first of the Herzen House residents could be heard rushing through the hallway to catch the morning trolley to work, Nadezhda was dozing fitfully, her head on my shoulder, her body shuddering with muffled sobs.

Near the end of the search an agent emerged from the bedroom carrying a pile of women's shoes that had been stuffed with newspaper to keep their shape. Nadezhda came awake and took hold of my elbow. I knew that she had copied many of Osip's unpublished poems onto the margins of *Pravda* articles and, crumpling the paper, secreted them in her shoes. Seeing that the shoes were filled with newspaper, the agent tossed them onto the pile of clothing near the window. Nadezhda and I dared not look at each other for fear the expression on our faces would give us away.

When it came time for the Chekists to depart, the Raven gathered up the satchel, along with a dozen or so volumes of French or Italian poetry he had decided to confiscate. "If you want to help Mandelstam, mention the arrest to no one," he advised.

"Is the fact of his arrest a state secret?" I asked.

The Raven glared at me. "Step carefully, Akhmatova—you can be pulled in as an accomplice."

And with that they were gone.

I went into the kitchen to make tea. Nadezhda, barely breathing, was sitting motionless on the sofa when I returned with two cups and pressed one into her icy hand. "The bastard took the kasha when he left," I said, but I don't think she heard me.

"If they refuse to say where they took Osip," Nadezhda asked, "how in the world will I find him?"

I sat down next to her. "There is an old trick," I told her. "You will prepare a small parcel filled with soap and socks and the like and address it to Mandelstam, Osip. I will accompany you. Together we'll go from prison to prison and queue at the window where they accept packages for prisoners. They will check the list of inmates at the prison—if he is not there they will turn you away. The prison that accepts the package is where he'll be."

"How do you know such things, Anna?"

Looking back, I can see now that I was taking out my rage at Osip's arrest on her. She was agonizing over the imminent execution of a husband, an unfortunately banal situation in this workers' paradise of ours. I, on the other hand, stood to lose an irreplaceable poet-brother. "Chalk it up to my having led a less sheltered existence than you," I said, my tone more vinegary than it should have been under the circumstances.

"But my life has been anything but sheltered!"

"Your life may have been unconventional sexually, but sheltered from political reality. You don't understand—they are arresting people for nothing now! We are shuffled like a pack of cards. Only someone who has no grasp of political reality could have encouraged Osip in this madness."

"That's simply not the case. We imagined prison and accepted the risks."

I could barely credit my ears. "You *imagined* prison!"

Nadezhda started hyperventilating and I had to massage her solar plexus before she could respire normally. "What do I do after I find out where he is?" she asked in a small voice.

"We must get people to intervene on his behalf," I said. "I will alert Borisik. He will surely get in touch with Nikolai Bukharin. You must seek an interview with Bukharin and explain what happened. He has helped you and Osip before. He will help again if he is able to. Whatever you do, don't mention the Stalin epigram. All you know is that Osip was arrested."

"Bukharin has been out of favor since the late twenties—"

"He's no longer on the Politburo, but Stalin has thrown him a bone, the editorship of *Izvestiya*—he is said to value Bukharin's judgment."

I don't remember how long we sat there in dazed silence, sipping the tea long after it became cold, lost in thought or its absence. The Moscow morning flooded the room with a deathly slate gray light. I do remember that the poet Tsvetaeva came to mind—I'd known the beautiful Marina when she and Osip had been briefly involved before the Bolsheviks came on the scene. At the time of Mandelstam's arrest she was living in exile in Paris, her poetry circulating in her native land in manuscript. One of her poems that had reached me earlier in the year spoke of the Bolshevik Revolution and *the deadly days of October*. Sitting in the empty room that had once been filled with life and love and laughter and poetry, I suddenly heard Tsvetaeva's ominous lines ringing in my ear.

>—*Where are the swans?*
>—*They went away, the swans.*
>—*The ravens too?*
>—*They stayed behind, the ravens.*

NINE

Osip Emilievich
Thursday, the 17th of May 1934

I can see, with the benefit of hindsight, that it is a marvelously liberating experience to be arrested—it liberates you from the terror of being arrested. Being liberated from the terror of arrest has a downside—it obliges you to concentrate on lesser terrors: where your next meal or next cigarette will come from, what would happen if your muse or your erection go absent without leave, how those dear to you will survive if the state in its infinite wisdom decides they are more useful as next of kin, what would be the effect on the poet's literary reputation if it was discovered he was terrified of terror. I was focusing on the lesser terrors when the arresting officer delivered my perspiring body to the inner prison in Lubyanka and got someone to sign a receipt for me. I never set eyes on the receipt, but I supposed it was something (à la L. Carroll) akin to *Received, one mad hatter twitching from mercury poisoning or fear of being dispatched to the undiscovered country from whose bourn no traveler returns.*

For the record, let me say that I'd been jailed before, briefly, in the Crimea during the Civil War, detained by Wrangel's White Guards rounding up citizens without travel permits or enough cash to bribe their way out of prison, then freed when the Reds stormed the city and hanged *their* prisoners from trees on the hill above it. Curiously, I'd even set foot inside the burnt-almond Lubyanka once. It had come about this way. My brother Evgeny had been incarcerated in the Lubyanka Prison in 1922. Desperate to free him, I'd arranged through a mutual friend to see Nikolai Ivanovich Bukharin, a rising star in the Bolshevik firmament whom Lenin had anointed as *the darling of the Party*. His Bolshevik credentials notwithstanding, Bukharin was a cultivated man, inclined to help artists when he could. Meeting Bukharin in his apartment in the Second House of Soviets, in earlier times called the Metropol Hotel, I'd exposed the absolute innocence of my brother and pleaded with him to intercede. Setting aside the broom he'd been using to swat enormous water bugs, Bukharin had immediately put through a call to the notorious chief of the Cheka, the Pole Feliks Dzerzhinsky, and arranged an appointment for me. I have a vivid memory of the *iron commissar*, as Dzerzhinsky was called (behind his back, it goes without saying)—he had a face that looked as if it had been caught in a vise and a stylish goatee that he kept scratching at when he interviewed me in his cavernous office on one of the Lubyanka's upper floors. (When I described the meeting to Bukharin, I elicited a laugh from him by suggesting that Dzerzhinsky's beard may have been infested with lice.) Keen to do Bukharin a favor, the iron commissar had offered to liberate my brother if I would stand surety for him. *Stand surety for him!* Holy God, someone landing from Mars might have mistaken Russia for a civilized country. Within hours Evgeny was taken from his cell and freed, and I was back browsing the bookstalls on Kuznetsky Bridge, a few steps from the Lubyanka, gazing at the heavy granite high-rise that had originally served as the home office of an insurance company, trying to picture what was going on behind the pleats of the large Italian-style curtains that screened the prison windows.

It was small comfort to think that now I would find out.

Moments after entering Lubyanka, I found myself in a morguelike room with white tiles on the floor and the walls. "Name, forename, patronymic?" the warden, a bony man with a shaven head and foul breath, shouted at me.

"Mandelstam, Osip Emilievich," I shouted back, as if I were responding to a drill sergeant.

"Why are you shouting?"

"I'm shouting because you're shouting."

"I am not shouting," the drill sergeant shouted. "I am talking in my normal voice."

He checked my name against the arrest warrant, then moistening the nib of a pen on his charged tongue, carefully copied it out in longhand on what looked like a bank ledger.

"Is Mandelstam your real name?"

I nodded. Without looking up, he shouted, "I did not catch the answer to my question. Is Mandelstam your real name or an alias?"

"Real name."

"Respond in grammatical sentences, not fragments."

"Fragments are what I shore up against my ruin," I shouted.

"Say again."

"Mandelstam is my real name."

"Occupation?"

"I am a poet."

"Poet is not a proletarian occupation recognized by Soviet statutes."

I had an inspiration. "I am an engineer of men's souls."

He didn't seem to recognize the phrase that had been attributed to Stalin in the newspapers. "What services do you render to the state?" he shouted. "Who pays you for services rendered?"

"I compose poetry, but it's been years since I've been remunerated for this service rendered."

"Remunerated?"

"Compensated. Paid."

He scratched the words *Intellectual* and *Parasite* on the register. "Date of birth?"

"I was born in the night of January the second and third in the unreliable year of eighteen-ninety something, and the centuries surround me with fire," I replied, quoting from a poem I intended to write if I survived.

The warden raised his eyes and effortlessly delivered a stinging slap across my face. "You don't take your arrest seriously," he warned.

"I do, I do," I remember insisting through my tears. "I don't expect you to understand, but I am actually relieved to be arrested. It gives me one less thing to worry about."

"Date of birth?" the warden shouted in precisely the same disinterested tone.

"The third of January 1891," I whispered.

"Speak up," he shouted.

"The third of January 1891."

"Place of residence?"

"Herzen House on Nashchokin Street."

The warden looked up again. "Number?"

"I don't remember the number." I winced in anticipation of another stinging slap.

"Name, relationship of nearest relative to be notified in the likely event of death?"

"Nadezhda Yakovlevna Mandelstam, wife."

"Remove your suspenders and shoelaces. Empty your pockets." He snatched my volume of Pushkin and, holding it by the spine, shook it, then dropped it back on the table. "Strip to the skin."

When I was standing naked before him, he added the word *Israelite* to the ledger and rang a small bell. A middle-aged woman wearing thick eyeglasses and a white medical smock entered, stage left. While the warden examined every stitch of my clothing, looking no doubt for items on the list posted inside the door—razor blades, nail scissors, pencils, letters or other written material, photographs, medicine of any kind—the medical orderly, if that's what she was, fitted on surgical gloves and methodically searched through the hair on my head. Then she pushed aside my organ and threaded her fingers through my pubic hair, after which, deftly deploying a tongue depressor, she visited the principal orifices of my body in the wrong order.

If they had offered me a choice, I would have preferred the humiliation of *Once long ago, there was such a poet*.

"Why are you trembling?" the warden shouted.

"I am chilled to the bone," I shouted back.

"You were sweating when you arrived."

"I have a built-in thermostat that takes into account my level of fear. Sometimes I sweat, sometimes I tremble."

With a snap of his fingers, the warden signaled for me to dress. The items in my pockets were placed in a cardboard box and I was instructed to sign the page in the ledger listing what had been confiscated. One internal identity card in the name of Mandelstam, Osip Emilievich. One Moscow residence permit made out to the same name. One cotton handkerchief, frayed at the edges. One half-empty box of Komsomolskaya brand safety matches. One pack of Herzegovina Flors. One Odessa dental floss dispenser. One passkey (to the front door of Herzen House), one latchkey (to our ground-floor flat). One vial of prescription sulfur pills for heart palpitation, another of valerian drops to calm nerves and induce sleep. Forty rubles in banknotes, twenty kopeks in loose change. I was issued an army blanket and a small towel and a bar of laundry soap, along with a chinaware soup bowl so out of place in a prison it could only have been part of the elegant table service used by the insurance company for banquets at the turn of the century. Clutching my trousers and my volume of Pushkin in one hand, shuffling along in laceless shoes, I followed a turnkey through the labyrinthine corridors to the cell block at the heart of the Lubyanka. Every twenty or so meters steel doors clanged open before us, the racket of the gate alerting everyone within earshot that another soul was entering this Soviet *purgatorio*.

Disoriented in the twisting corridors, I penetrated the heart-murmuring terrain of D. Alighieri half expecting, at each turn, to come across Virgil washing the stains of hell off my beloved Dante, to hear his glorious infantlike babbling.

> *E consolando, usava l'idioma*
> *Che prima i padri e le madri trastulla ;*
> *. . . Favoleggiava con la sua famiglia*
> *De' Troiani, di Fiesole, e di Roma.*

I was eventually shoved into a cell illuminated by a blindingly bright electric light suspended from the ceiling. There was a window high in the wall, but it was covered with planks. I shielded my eyes with my volume of Pushkin and made out the two prisoners already in the cell. One was squatting in a corner in what smelled like a puddle of urine and excrement, moaning as he rocked back and forth on his bare feet. The other prisoner, a giant of a man, was sitting on a blanket with his back to the wall. "I think he is dying," the giant said, indicating the moaning figure with his chin. He angled his head so that his right ear was turned toward me and said, "What are you guilty of, comrade?"

I set my belongings on the stone floor and, sitting down on the folded blanket facing him, covered my nose and mouth with my forearm. "I am guilty of being a poet," I said. "I am guilty of not beating about the bush."

"Poetry doesn't strike me as honest work," the giant said, "in the sense that you don't produce something people can eat or wear. Me, I'm Shotman, Fikrit Trofimovich. He's Sergo. His family name and patronymic are known to God, but not to me."

"Mandelstam, Osip Emilievich," I said.

"Pleased. Fact is, I'm glad to have someone to talk to—Sergo is no longer capable of conversation. I work as a strongman in the circus."

"You don't produce something people eat or wear either."

"I entertain the working class. You entertain the intelligentsia. You can't compare the two. I have a common-law wife, she is the tattooed lady in the same circus as me. Her tattoos are art and history and nature and geography all rolled into one, the first time I saw them I fell into love with her. What about you? Are you married?" When I said I was, he wanted to know if my wife had any tattoos. When I said no, he tossed his head. "No matter—she may have other qualities. How did you meet?"

Telling him took my mind off my present predicament. "I first set eyes on Nadezhda—that's her name—in a cabaret in Kiev called the Junk Shop. I'd been watching her for the better part of an hour—she was bantering with her companions, laughing at their jokes, listening intently to their stories, all the while burning with sensuality. I was overwhelmed by the desire to warm myself at her flame. All I could think to do was ask her for a cigarette. She looked up and smiled and gave me one, and we've been together ever since. Tell me, Fikrit, how long have you been in the Lubyanka?"

"Lost track."

"Do they ever turn the light off?"

"Never."

"How can you sleep with it shining in your eyes all the time?"

"Can't," he said. "That's why they leave it on. If you do doze off, the comrade guard who keeps an eye on us through the peephole will hammer on the door until you wake up. My interrogator, an experienced Chekist with the best interests of his prisoners at heart, says being exhausted helps clear the mind of bourgeois delusions of innocence. If you are here, it's because you are guilty of something. The sooner you identify your crime, the sooner your case will be disposed of."

I looked again at the figure squatting in the corner. "If he is really dying, why don't you summon medical help?"

The giant thought my suggestion humorous. "Medical help! That's a good one. They're the ones making him die."

"Why are they making him die?"

"Because he won't admit guilt."

"And what is he guilty of?"

"Article 58—anti-Soviet propaganda and counterrevolutionary activity. He is guilty of wrecking, he told me so himself when he was still able to talk. He raised the subject of collectivization in front of Stalin at a public meeting." Fikrit must have seen I was trembling. "Not to worry yourself sick, Osip Emilievich. They won't beat you if you admit the truth straight off."

"If he admits he is guilty of wrecking, will they stop beating him?"

Fikrit became indignant. "This is the Soviet Union. Socialist justice and the rule of law always triumph. Once Sergo admits guilt they will stop the beatings and shoot him."

"Without a trial?"

"There may be a secret trial, though the law doesn't require that he be present or have access to the evidence against him, so the comrade interrogator told me. As you can see, Sergo is in no shape for a public trial."

"Have you admitted your guilt?"

"At first I didn't, not because I was trying to fool them into thinking I was innocent, nothing like that. I didn't admit it because I didn't know what I was guilty of."

"Did they beat you?"

"They did. The beatings, along with not being able to sleep, helped me to see the light. I have confessed to being a member of a backup Trotskyist Paris-based anti-Bolshevik conspiracy. When the day comes to overthrow the Bolsheviks, the members of this conspiracy will recognize each other because we all have distinctive Eiffel Tower stickers on our valises or trunks. The Eiffel Tower, in case you are not familiar with it, is located in Paris, France. To make my personal situation worse, I kept tsarist loan coupons against the day when, thanks to Trotsky, capitalism is restored and I can cash them in."

"If you've admitted your guilt, how come you're still in prison?"

"Because I was lucky enough to be selected for public trial. They have promised that my common-law wife will be there to see me. I can tell by the suit you're wearing you are a member of the intelligentsia—a poet is the same as an intellectual, right?—so you probably do not recognize me. I am, excuse me for being the one to say it, famous in Russia for winning the silver medal at the All-European games in Vienna, Austria in 1932. A picture of me shaking hands with Comrade Stalin at the Kremlin was printed on the front page of *Pravda*. Comrade interrogator has promised my picture will be on the front page of *Pravda* again when I give details of the Trotskyist conspiracy at my trial. Right now I am memorizing these details."

Poor Sergo—if he was really dying, he was doing it by centimeters. His moaning never let up. Even now when I think back to that cell I hear Sergo whimpering, I gag at the memory of the stench rising from his tortured body. As for Fikrit, you could tell he was a goodhearted soul, but once he'd recounted his childhood in Azerbaidzhan and his exploit in Vienna and his botched knee operation and his life as a circus strongman, we more or less ran out of conversation. When he wasn't summoned for interrogation, he spent endless hours sitting with his back to the stone wall, his large head buried in his large hands, repeating aloud the confession he would deliver at his trial. I caught fragments (that would lead to his ruin!)—how he'd been recruited in Vienna in 1932 and been given a down payment in United States dollars, how he'd communicated with his handler using a secret code buried in the dedication inside the cover of an American fitness magazine, how carried away by his hatred for the new order he had disfigured Stalin's face tattooed on his upper arm. There was more, a great deal more, but it has long since slipped my mind.

I made a stab at keeping track of the passage of time, but this turned out to be a challenge requiring clearheadedness, and thus beyond my capacity. One day blended seamlessly into the next. I believe, though I can't swear to it, that I was taken off for interrogation after I'd spent something like four days and four nights in the cell, never sleeping more than a few minutes at a time before the comrade guard, as Fikrit called him, woke me, along with everyone else in the cell block, by slamming a sledgehammer against the metal door. What I am certain of is that they came for me after the evening meal, which consisted of watery soup splashed into our chinaware bowls. A beefy guard turned up at the door of the cell and pointed what looked like a cattle prod at me. Fikrit must have sensed where I was off to because he offered some last minute words of advice. "I have heard it said that poets are somehow connected with culture. Which means your interrogator will be comrade Christophorovich—he specializes in culture criminals like yourself. Find out what you're guilty of and then confess it, Osip Emilievich, and things will go more smooth for you."

I realize now how difficult it is to reconstruct the fourteen days I spent in the Lubyanka, given the fact that I was frightened out of my skin even when I managed to doze. Which is to say, my brain was functioning sluggishly; it was as if a shadow of a doubt had lodged in my skull with the result that I wasn't certain in what order things happened, or whether they happened at all. My state of mind is probably best conveyed by comparing it to the loss of depth perception, something I actually experienced in the months after my arrest; you perceive things with a hazy lucidity, but you aren't sure if they are in front of your nose or several meters away; you wind up not being sure if they are there at all or fragments of your imagination.

To this day I am haunted by spectral memories that have the graininess of bad dreams: of an open freight elevator rising with excruciating lethargy to a high floor; of brightly illuminated corridors with worn runners that, like the chinaware, looked as if they dated back to the turn of the century when the building served as the headquarters for an insurance company; of a polished brass number twenty-three on a polished wooden door; of an enormous room with bright spotlights that caused your eyes to smart the moment you crossed the threshold; of the clatter of a typewriter coming from behind a slightly open door; of the distant chiming of the hour from the Kremlin's Spassky Tower; of a blurred figure of a man dressed in some manner of uniform and a leather butcher's apron gesturing for the guard to leave.

I heard the man, who was sitting in front of an enormous photograph of Stalin, introduce himself. "Christophorovich."

I see myself shielding my eyes with my palm, then quickly withdrawing it lest he take it for a salute. "Mandelstam."

"Sit."

Squinting to protect my eyes from the light, I dropped onto a wooden stool the front legs of which were shorter than the rear legs, with the result that I had all to do to keep from sliding off.

The interrogator studied me from behind a mountain of folders. "Any complaints about your detention?"

When I didn't respond he asked, "How do you feel?"

"Exhausted." I intended to stop there but, confusing an interrogation with a confessional, I heard myself add, "Exhausted and frightened."

Let me interrupt my narrative to say that when I have been interviewed, in the years before I was *poeticus non grata*, the words, the phrases attributed to me when a given article appeared in print were approximative; a journalist has a natural tendency to filter what you say through the prism of his syntax and style, so that what you hear is his voice, not your own. Which makes me aware that the scenes I am reconstructing for you from memory must suffer from the same defect. The words I attribute to others are surely approximative—with the notable exception of what the interrogator Christophorovich uttered when I admitted to being frightened. Should I live to be fifty, I will never forget his reply. As I summon it now, I can still hear his intonation: soft and threatening like distant thunder that augurs a particularly brutal storm. Here, word for word, is what he told me:

"It is useful for a poet to experience fear—it can inspire verse. Rest assured you will experience fear in full measure."

I was trying to parse this in the hope of finding meanings other than the obvious one when he asked, very quietly, "Have you figured out why you are here?"

I realized, through a film of exhaustion, that I had to tread cautiously. Clinging to the possibility that he didn't know about the Stalin epigram, I started through the minefield. "Is it because of something I wrote?"

"Inspired guess," Christophorovich agreed with a hollow laugh.

"It could only have been my prose piece *Conversation About Dante.*"

My interrogator removed his green visor and tried to flatten down an unruly tuft of hair. "What you wrote on Dante was not subversive," he said.

"You are familiar with my essay on Dante!"

"I'm familiar with your thesis—that for Dante, the inferno is described as if it were a prison." Moistening the ball of his thumb, Christophorovich leafed through a thick dossier, found the page he was looking for and began to read lines I had written. "*All our efforts are directed toward the struggle against the density and darkness of the place. Illuminated shapes cut through it like teeth.* As you will come to understand, I'm familiar with every word you ever wrote. After your wife, after the harlot Akhmatova, I am probably the leading Mandelstam scholar in the Soviet Union."

"If it's not my Dante essay, it must have been a poem that landed me in this inferno."

He waited. I grasped that silence was one of the tools of his trade.

I attempted to distract him with lines from an old poem. "*In the black velvet of the Soviet night—*"

He pulled another page from the dossier. "Vintage 1920, according to my notes. Try again."

"*Whom will you next kill? What lie will you now invent?*"

My interrogator clearly enjoyed sparring with me. "That's from your poem entitled 'January 1, 1924.' We've known about it since January 2, 1924."

By then I was breathing with difficulty. *"The wolf-hound century leaps at my throat . . . my mouth has been twisted by lies."*

Through the raw light, I could make out Christophorovich sadly shaking his head. "You're getting closer in time—that's from 1931."

"How I'd love to speak my mind, to play the fool, to spit out truth."

"You're stuck in 1931, though the spirit of that particular poem is closer to the one that landed you on our doorstep."

My heart was pounding in my chest as I racked my brain for lines to throw him. *"As if wearing silent slippers, the starving peasants watch the garden gate but do not touch the chain."*

"You're getting warmer, Mandelstam. May 1933, if I'm not mistaken. You called it 'Old Crimea' when you recited it to your first readers."

And then Christophorovich, moving in what appeared to be slow motion, removed a single sheet of paper from the dossier and, angling it to catch the light, began to read:

> *We live, deaf to the land beneath us,*
> *Ten steps away no one hears our speeches,*
>
> *All we hear is the Kremlin mountaineer,*
> *The murderer and peasant-slayer.*

The faint hope that I might somehow come out of this alive plummeted like a shot bird. Quicksand sucked at my feet. I could see his eyes fixed on me over the sheet of paper. "Do these lines ring a bell, Mandelstam?"

When I couldn't bring myself to answer, he flung the juiciest morsels of my epigram in my face: *fingers fat as grubs . . . cockroach whiskers . . . a rabble of thin-necked leaders.* He delivered the last two lines from memory.

> *And every killing is a treat*
> *For the broad-chested Ossete.*

Christophorovich came around to the front of the table. "You are said to be skilled at interpreting poems. In your considered opinion, who is this Kremlin mountaineer? Who, the broad-chested Ossete?"

Clutching my trousers at the waistband with fingers that had gone numb, my laceless shoes planted flat on the quicksand and pushing against it to keep myself from sliding off the stool to certain suffocation, I looked up at the interrogator looming over me. I had difficulty bringing him into focus. I heard him say, "Calm yourself, Mandelstam. You must have known what you were getting into when you composed this seditious poem, when you flaunted it to your first readers."

I think I said something along the lines of "I have gone beyond calm, comrade interrogator, never to return. I am experiencing fear in full measure."

"Excellent. This will have the advantage of accelerating the often tedious process of interrogation. The trick is to think of us as collaborators. My job is an exhausting one. If you are questioned all night, bear in mind that I must question you all night. All night, every night until you not only grovel in guilt, but give me the names of those to whom you read the poem."

"How is it possible for a cultural criminal like myself to collaborate with a cultural commissar?"

"We can meet on a middle ground."

"There is no middle ground in an unweeded garden. Stalin himself has decreed that there are only two possibilities—either you are with us or you are against us." Thinking of Nadenka, I added: "I am a great believer in middle grounds. If Stalin had left a sliver of middle ground, I would have jumped at the chance to live out the few years left to me on it."

"What Stalin said was a figure of speech, a slogan designed to rally the troops to class warfare. Here in the sanctuary of the Lubyanka, there is a middle ground on which you and I can meet, Mandelstam. We Bolsheviks are not brutes bent on destruction for the pleasure of destroying. We are builders. We are attempting what no one has ever before attempted—to construct Socialism, and once constructed, use it as a cornerstone to construct Communism. War, poverty, inequality, exploitation will vanish from the face of the earth, or at least that part of the earth we preside over. Are you familiar with the work of the dramatist Nikolai Pogodin? In the early thirties he wrote a brilliant play that sums up who we are and what we're doing. It was called *My Friend*. Stalin himself has commented favorably on it. The play dramatizes the struggle to build a large factory in a backward peasant country—Pogodin's characters are ordinary workers overcoming enormous obstacles, performing heroically to construct Socialism. We are all of us, from Comrade Stalin on down to the humble Chekist interrogating wreckers in the Lubyanka, ordinary workers performing heroically, trying to create a state that functions for the good of all its citizens and not merely the handful of rich capitalist exploiters who own the means of production. Surely you can understand that to succeed at this hallowed project, the first order of business is to protect it from wreckers like you."

Christophorovich hit a small bell with the heel of his hand. The guard who had brought me turned up at the door. "Think about what I have said, Mandelstam. Tomorrow night we will pick up where we left off. Hopefully we will identify the sliver of middle ground on which we can comfortably collaborate."

Here is the second interrogation, or at least in my imperfect memory what I think of as the second interrogation. I remember being led again through the long corridors to the door with the number twenty-three on it. For some reason Christophorovich was not yet at his post behind the table. I stared at the photograph of Stalin on the wall, half convinced that he would personally interrogate me this time, all the while aware of an animal fear growing inside me like a tumor: fear of poison, of suffocation, of strangulation, of decapitation. I must have fallen asleep on the stool because the guard kicked the legs out from under it, sending me sprawling across the parquet floor. With an effort I crawled back onto the stool. When I looked up I saw Christophorovich observing me from behind the table.

"Have you searched out the common ground on which the cultural commissar and the cultural criminal can meet?" he inquired.

In a delirium of terror, I clutched at a straw. "What you have is an early version of the Stalin epigram. The second stanza was revised. There is no mention of *murderer and peasant-slayer* in the final version."

Christophorovich pushed a blank sheet across the table, along with a fountain pen. He motioned for me to move my stool closer. "Write out the final version of the poem in your own hand," he instructed.

My brain was awash with story lines. Had the people who left cigarette ends in our ashtray planted listening devices in the walls of our flat after all? Had they recorded my reading of the first version to Nadenka and Zinaida? Had they heard me offer to copy it off for Zinaida so that she could memorize it? Had they arrested her and seized the incriminating evidence before the poor girl could destroy it? Were Nadenka and Zinaida even now cowering in a cell somewhere in the bowels of the Lubyanka? In the bedlam of thoughts and emotions, one thing seemed crystal clear to me: the fact that Christophorovich possessed the original epigram meant I could no longer save myself. But I still might be able to save Nadenka and Zinaida, along with the others who had heard the epigram. Leaning over the table, I wrote out the lines, including the revised second stanza:

> *But where there's so much as half a conversation*
> *The Kremlin mountaineer will get his mention.*

Christophorovich snatched the new version from my fingers and read it carefully. He had what can be described as a smug smile on his lips when he finished. "But that changes everything, Mandelstam. Without the *murderer and peasant-slayer*, the whole thing is much more tepid. Though we still have to deal with the *cockroach whiskers*, not to mention the *every killing is a treat for the Ossete*. Given this change, there may be a ray of hope for you if—"

He was a delicate interrogator. One couldn't help but admire his skill as he left the *if* hanging in the air between us.

"If?" I repeated.

He shrugged. "You must absolutely name names. If it is any comfort to you, rest assured we know them already—we know to whom you read the poem, we know their various reactions. Still, it will count against you if this evidence comes from us, as opposed to your making a clean breast of things. If you desire to make amends, to cleanse your criminal behavior with collaboration, name names."

"An individual blessed with a poetic talent has a sacred obligation not to betray that talent," I said.

Christophorovich only smiled. "A person blessed with a poetic talent has a sacred obligation to remain amongst the living and exercise that talent."

The interrogation continued on through the night. Christophorovich coaxed and cajoled and wheedled and threatened; at one point he informed me that Nadenka and Zinaida had been arrested as coconspirators in a plot to overthrow Stalin and were being interrogated in another part of the Lubyanka. He accused me of egoistically putting their lives in jeopardy, as well as compromising all those to whom I had read the epigram. Exasperated by my refusal to name names, he summoned an enormous Uzbek with a deformed nose, who attached my wrists to irons embedded in the wall. I fainted straightaway from fear. When I came awake the medical orderly was listening to my heartbeat with a stethoscope and shaking her head. "If you don't want him to die on you, I suggest you suspend the questioning and let him sleep a few hours, comrade interrogator."

I could make out a rose-gristle dawn bleeding through the window where the Italian curtains didn't overlap when the guard came to fetch me back to my cell. Passing through the last of the steel doors, I reached my cell block. The guard left me for the time it took to get fire for his cigarette from the turnkey. Standing with my back against the wall where, improbable as this sounds, someone had taped up pages from a magazine with portraits of the generals who defeated Napoleon, I thought I heard a woman whimpering—the sound seeped from under the door of a cell two cells down from my own. And then, dear God, I distinctly heard Nadenka's voice—she seemed to be trying to comfort another woman. It was a fleeting impression based on intonation more than actual words. But I'd recognize her voice anywhere. Back in my cell, I knelt beside Fikrit and whispered in his good ear, "Have you heard women whimpering?"

"I have," he said. "If I press my good ear to the stone of the wall, I hear my Agrippina crying her heart out, I hear her saying over and over, *Fikrit, Fikrit, what have you gotten us into?* Sergo, when he was still able to talk, warned me about how they play recordings of women's voices to weaken our will to resist. But I no longer resist and still I hear her whimpering. It is not a recording. There is no doubt about it—like me, she is a prisoner in the Lubyanka."

I crept back to my side of the cell and, coiling my body into a fetal position, fell into a sleep so shallow that the guard's failure to pound on the door woke me every few minutes. I dreamed I was sleepwalking through walls, but became so frightened I would be trapped in a wall that I forced myself awake, or thought I did. I wasn't sure whether I was asleep and dreaming I was awake, or actually awake, when I urinated into the slop jar. The sound of urination, the stench coming from Sergo's corner of the cell, seemed real enough, which suggested I was awake after all. Seeing that both Sergo and Fikrit were sound asleep, I checked to make sure the leather flap was over the peephole in the door, then went across to the wall meaning to put my ear to it. On an impulse I shouldered through the wall into the next cell. Two prisoners, one an old man with fine gray hair falling to his collarbones, the other, a young prematurely bald man with a blanket draped across his shoulders, were playing chess on the cement floor with tiny pieces molded from scraps of soap. "Check," the old man declared triumphantly, edging forward a rook with a fingernail. "Ah," his opponent said, "I didn't anticipate that." I cleared my throat to get their attention. They both raised their eyes. "Excuse me for interrupting your game," I said. "If you're looking for the women," the young man said, "they're one cell over," and he gestured with a thumb that was missing its nail toward the far wall. I started to thank him, but he had turned back to the game and was concentrating on how to extricate his king.

I watched them for a moment, uncertain how I'd gotten into this cell, uncertain how I would get out. Then, as if it were the most natural thing in the world, I walked through the wall he had indicated and found myself in a smaller cell illuminated by a bulb so weak you could see the yellow filament in it. As my eyes became accustomed to the density of the darkness, two illuminated shapes cut through it like teeth. Nadenka and Zinaida were slumbering in each other's arms. Nadenka was wearing the dress she'd had on the night of my arrest, Zinaida was in the off-white mousseline costume she'd worn when we saw her perform in *Three Sisters*. I sank to my knees next to Nadenka. Sensing a presence, she stirred. Her eyes opened and she gaped at me in fright. I put a finger to her lips to keep her from crying out. "How in the world did you get here?" she demanded. I heard myself say, "You won't believe me if I tell you, so I'd better not tell you lest you take me for a mad hatter. When were you arrested?" "During the search of our flat, they found the poems concealed in the teapot—the swine Sergei Petrovich must have betrayed the hiding place. When they discovered they were in my handwriting, they arrested me on the spot." "And Anna Andreyevna?" "Anna was still in the living room when they took me off. I don't know her fate." "When was Zinaida arrested?" "They searched her apartment while she was away at the theater and found the epigram—the dear girl feels dreadful about not having destroyed it. They turned up at the theater and arrested her between acts. As there was no understudy present, the performance had to be canceled." Nadenka took my hand and pressed the back of it against her cheek and I could feel the tears streaming from her eyes. "Oh Osya, what shall we do?" With all the commotion, Zinaida was stirring now. She, too, came awake. When she saw it was me, she burst into tears. "I will never, ever forgive myself for not destroying the epigram," she managed to say between the sobs that racked her body.

Once past the initial emotion of seeing me in her cell, Nadenka, true to character, turned practical. "Are you being interrogated?" she asked. Without waiting for a reply, she said, "It must be the one known as Christophorovich—they say he is the commissar charged with cultural crimes. Have they tortured you? Are you hurt?"

I told Nadenka how he had read the original version of the epigram; how I'd written out the revised version without the offending stanza that Pasternak had asked me to remove; how it had all come down to my identifying the people who had heard the epigram, something that I had up to now refused to do.

"But surely they know who heard the epigram," Nadenka said. "They will have planted microphones in your walls," Zinaida whispered. "They will have recorded everything we said." A terrible thought came to her. "They will have recorded everything we *did*."

Nadenka turned on her. "If they had planted microphones in the walls, they would have arrested the three of us months ago. They would have swooped down on Herzen House and arrested Mandelstam the morning he read out the epigram to us to nip the thing in the bud. There are no microphones, which means we only need to concoct a story they can swallow." She reached for my head and, pulling it closer to hers, said fiercely, "Listen to me, Osya. You must give them names. We must be seen to be naïve intellectuals who blundered and are ready to make amends. It is our only chance."

"How can I implicate Akhmatova? How can I implicate Pasternak and the others?"

"You say you recited the epigram without warning them what the subject was. You say they all reacted, like Pasternak, with horror. You embroider—each and every person who heard the epigram was appalled at the idea of maligning the great Stalin. Each and every person tried to talk you into destroying it. That sort of thing." Nadenka touched her forehead to mine. "You can do it, Osya. You must do it, for your own sake, for our sakes. You must give them whatever they want." "Nadezhda is right," Zinaida pleaded. "Please, please, cooperate with the authorities so we can get on with our lives."

And so I named names. I was a nervous wreck—it's not every day you walk through walls—and began talking so rapidly Christophorovich had trouble keeping up with my confession. He summoned a stenographer and made me start over again. He wanted names, I gave him names. "Nadezhda Yakovlevna, best friend, comrade-in-arms, wife, like Mayakovsky an ardent supporter of cracking eggs in order to make omelets, was the first of eleven. How did she react? She came as close as she ever had to throwing me out of the flat. Sheer slander, she cried, insulting to the intelligence of anyone who might hear it because the entire world knows Stalin as the first among equals, someone who leads by collegiality. Zinaida Zaitseva-Antonova, theater actress, poetry lover, friend, was the second. She was sickened to learn I could sink so low as to spread libel about someone as brilliant and at the same time as modest as Stalin. Pasternak threatened to end our long and close friendship if I didn't destroy this scandalous epigram. As for Akhmatova, I thought she would throw up on our living room floor when she heard it. She insisted it wasn't a poem at all but a polemic, a political argument that was wide of the mark inasmuch as Stalin had no connection with Ossetia and was universally respected, even by his political opponents, for his sincerity and idealism. Ditto for Sergei Petrovich, whose family name escapes me. Ditto for the six others who had the misfortune to wander onto the middle ground Nadezhda and I had created, only to find themselves the captive audience of a demented poet. All of them, starting with Nadezhda, argued that I shouldn't be wasting my talents, assuming I had any, doing the villainous bidding of wreckers and counterrevolutionaries, that instead I ought to be composing an ode to the glory of Stalin, to his courage during the Revolution and the Civil War, to his accomplishments as a builder of Socialism in one country, to his inspired leadership that is bringing industrialization and collectivization to backward Russia. I see now that they were right and I was wrong."

When I had run out of breath, Christophorovich asked the stenographer to read back my confession. He copied off parts of it on a sheet of paper, then underlined one sentence before reading it aloud. ". . . *Doing the villainous bidding of wreckers and counterrevolutionaries.* Those were your words."

I wasn't sure where he was going with this and nodded tentatively.

"Which brings us to the core of the crime, Mandelstam. Who put you up to composing the epigram in the first place? Who ordered you to read it to as many people as possible in the hope that its poison would reverberate"—he plucked another page from the dossier and read from it—"*reverberate across the land like ripples from a pebble thrown into stagnant water.*"

My mouth must have fallen open. Christophorovich snickered with pleasure at my surprise. "I presume you recognize your own words. As you will have guessed by now, the young woman pushing the child in a stroller behind you that day in Moscow was equipped with a directional microphone and recording everything you said." Comrade interrogator read the heading on the page. "Transcript of conversation between Mandelstam, Pasternak, Akhmatova,

Thursday, the twelfth of April 1934. Moscow street. *The Party will declare a national holiday. The Komsomol will sing it*—it being your slanderous epigram—*as they march off to fulfill their quotas. At congresses in the Bolshoi, from every balcony and box, workers will shout it out. It will be the end of Stalin.* Clearly, only someone in the Bolshevik superstructure would be in a position to suggest to you how the Party, how the Komsomol, how delegates to a congress in the Bolshoi Theater would react to the demise of Stalin. Was it Kamenev or Zinoviev, both of whom were expelled from the Party as Trotskyists in 1927? Was it that slime Rykov, who has been plotting against Stalin since the death of Lenin? Perhaps it was the *darling of the party*, the great Bukharin, expelled from the Politburo because he sided with Stalin's enemies who criticized revolutionary, as opposed to evolutionary, collectivization. There is, after all, a long history of Bukharin acting as your guardian angel, first to free your brother from prison, then arranging flats and ration cards and a monthly pension for services to Russian literature, even organizing contracts for future volumes that were paid for but never published. The list of Bukharin's favors to you are as long as your arm: he pulled strings to get you travel permits to the Crimea, he used his influence to have several of your prose pieces published, he even offered you and your wife exit visas from Russia in the mid-twenties, which, to your credit, you turned down. Pity. Perhaps you wouldn't be where you are today if you had gone into exile. Was it Bukharin who proposed you return all these favors by circulating a poem slandering Stalin? Or was it the archtraitor Trotsky himself? Actually, the more I think about it, the more I'm convinced *ripples on stagnant water* sounds exactly like a formulation that would appeal to the twisted mind of the Jew Trotsky. We know for a fact that he has set industrial wreckers to throwing cut glass into sacks of farina. He has ordered mechanics to add water to aviation fuel. He has invited kulaks to slaughter their livestock rather than deliver the animals to collective farms. He is not above psychological wrecking—

encouraging a gullible poet to spread poison about Stalin like *ripples on stagnant water*."

"No one put me up to it," I insisted. "The idea for truth telling originated with me."

"Surely you don't expect us to believe that. You're an intellectual. You don't have the profile of a counterrevolutionary." Christophorovich glanced at another report in his dossier. "You do remember what that girl said in the canteen for trolley car workers last January? *Once, long ago, there was such a poet*. Perhaps it was in the wake of this insult that someone whispered in your ear: *As a poet, you have dropped below the literary horizon. If you circulate a slanderous poem about Stalin, your star will rise—you will be recognized as one of Russia's great poets*. Who whispered in your ear? Who organized the conspiracy? The only thing that can save you is a confession."

"I didn't compose the poem to get attention. I am not part of a conspiracy. I am a poet, not a plotter. I wouldn't know how to function in a conspiracy."

"You have been manipulated, Mandelstam, surely you can see that now. You must identify the person or persons who originated this counterrevolutionary scheme. Your confession, your naming names, is not worth the paper it's written on until you identify the instigators." He circled around behind me and began talking to the nape of my neck. "Look at the trouble they caused you. You and your wife and your mistress. Pasternak, Akhmatova, all the others. The traitors who put you up to this don't give a shit about your fate. Why do you protect scum of the earth? You owe them nothing. Save yourself. Save Nadezhda and the others from a fate worse than death: slow strangulation by hanging from short ropes, simulated drowning in laundry basins, suffocation in sealed cells, standing naked for days on end in subzero temperatures, the breaking of bones in the body one a day—your cell mate Sergo's fate. Give me the name of the ringleader."

Gathering what must have been the last shred of outrage in my trembling body, I said, "You claim to be builders, but in the end you are only torturers."

Comrade interrogator was mightily offended. "My poor Mandelstam, we are not torturers. Chekist tradition holds that to be deemed torture, a procedure must shock the conscience."

I thought I'd found the flaw in his logic. "How can a procedure shock the conscience if you have no conscience?"

"You make a grave miscalculation, Mandelstam. We Bolsheviks live by conscience. We are committed to the principle that ends justify means. As the end in question is the construction of Communism, our conscience instructs us that all means, any means, are justified."

I understood what Christophorovich was after—he wanted me to admit, like Fikrit back in my cell, that I was a member of a Trotskyist anti-Bolshevik Center. He wanted to parade the poet Mandelstam at a public trial. Obviously, my confession would have more impact than that of an uneducated silver medalist at the 1932 Vienna games. But it is one thing to name the names of the those who actually heard my sad little epigram, and quite another to invent a conspiracy that could then be used at the show trials rumored to be in the works—of Zinoviev and Kamenev, of Bukharin despite the esteem in which most Bolsheviks held him, of Trotsky himself if Stalin could lure him back, like Gorky, from exile. And so I stuck to my story, which was after all the truth—not that this counted for much in *purgatorio*. Christophorovich was nothing if not tenacious. He brought to mind the doggedness of a lover who refuses to take no for an answer; who is disappointed by a yes because it cuts short the pleasure to be had from breaking your will. He had the endurance of a marathon runner. He kept at me for hours on end, promising me the state would be lenient with me and mine if I testified against the designated instigators, threatening me with execution if I failed to give him what he wanted—what (I'm supposing here) he needed in order for his career to flourish.

I'm aware that Nadenka takes the view that recounting this episode is therapeutic, in the sense that it sheds light on everything that happened afterward. Personally, I am not persuaded it serves any useful purpose. What's to be gained by reliving the execution? To this day, I am amazed they didn't shoot me straight off the night they brought me to the Lubyanka. I half expected to be put to death every time they took me from my cell—I had heard rumors of prisoners being executed in the vaulted cellars that once served as storage rooms for the insurance company, and only managed to breathe again when the freight elevator started up instead of down. Until the night . . . the nightmarish night . . . the heartaching night when it started down.

Now I'll do my execution.

The next evening, at the hour they usually came to get me for interrogation, three brutes I had never set eyes on turned up at the door of my cell. Two of them carried an ordinary wooden chair into the cell and strapped Sergo onto it with canvas belts. The third brought the heel of his boot down on my chinaware bowl, shattering it into pieces. "You won't be needing this anymore," is how he explained the gesture. He reached for my upper arm and, hauling me roughly to my feet, twisted both my arms behind my back and bound them tightly together at the wrists. Fikrit, bless his soul, climbed to his feet as if he intended to intervene. The guard lazily rested a hand on the butt of the pistol in his web holster and stared down the giant until he slowly backed up against the wall. I think I managed to say, "Thank you, Fikrit," though it is entirely possible my lips moved but no words emerged. With the toe of my shoe, I edged my volume of Pushkin across the floor toward my cell mate. "I cannot read," Fikrit said. "Learn," I said. "Start with Pushkin. If you can one day make out his words, you won't need to read anything else in your lifetime." The two guards carried Sergo from the cell on the chair. Prodded along by the third guard, I followed. At the door I turned back to see, through my tears, the giant weight lifter bowing farewell to me from the waist, his knuckles scraping the floor in the style of peasants from the mountains of Azerbaidzhan.

Our little group made its way down the corridor, through several steel doors to the open freight elevator. When the five of us were inside the guard pulled the throttle *back*—no, no, keep recording, I just need to catch my breath—and the elevator and my stomach and my heart and my head began descending deeper into hell.

Christophorovich was waiting in the vaulted cellar when the elevator reached the basement. He was wearing the leather apron over his uniform and holding a large-bored naval revolver. The guards carried Sergo from the elevator and set him down in the middle of a patch of earth covered with sawdust. They forced me to kneel beside the chair. I could see comrade interrogator chewing on his lower lip as he removed the five enormous bullets from the revolver, then thumbed one of them back in and spun the cylinder as if he intended to play Russian roulette. The three guards backed off. Christophorovich said, "Who wants to go first? Age before beauty? Talent before mediocrity? Urban intellectual before rural hick? What will it be?" I heard Sergo spitting words from between his pus-swollen lips. "Fuck . . . Stalin" is what I think he said. Christophorovich called over to the guards, "It would seem we have someone who is impatient to meet his maker, comrades. Never let it be said I don't attend to the last wishes of the condemned." Stepping behind the chair, he held the revolver at arm's length and thrust the bore into the nape of Sergo's neck and he—he pulled—he pulled the trigger. The hammer struck an empty chamber. Sergo produced an anguished groan, almost as if he regretted still being alive. "Your turn, Mandelstam," Christophorovich announced. "You have been condemned and sentenced to the Highest Measure of Punishment." "But there was no trial," I cried out. "The trial was held without you." He pressed the revolver into the back of my neck and pulled the trigger—on another empty chamber. My knees gave way and my forehead pitched forward onto the sawdust.

Christophorovich took a grip on my collar and hauled me upright, then turned back to Sergo and, aiming at his neck, again pulled the trigger. A deafening roar reverberated through the vaulted cellars as the chair and the body strapped to it spilled sideways. The sound came back from so many directions I thought other prisoners were being shot in other parts of the basement. Clots of blood, of brain spattered on my shirt. "Are you a believer, Mandelstam?" the interrogator demanded as he thumbed another bullet into the revolver and gave a spin to the cylinder. I must have said yes because he asked, "In what?" "In poetry." "Poetry won't save you now," he said and he pressed the revolver into the nape of my neck. I could feel warm urine soaking through my trousers as he—oh, Jesus—as he pulled the thing, the trigger. I heard what must have been the dry thud of the hammer hitting the firing pin and vomited on the sawdust under my knees. It took an eternity for me to realize that if I could vomit, I must be alive. Christophorovich and the guards started laughing, piano at first, then louder until they were roaring with laughter and the laughter, like the shot that had put an end to Sergo's suffering, echoed through the vaulted cellars. "You were luckier than Sergo," Christophorovich managed to say. "Take him back to his cell. We'll try again another night."

What was going through my head at the moment of execution? The cliché has it that your life flashes before your eyes. Not with me, it didn't. I made an effort to summon an image of my wife, but I couldn't remember what she looked like. Try as I might I was unable to call up an erotic image. I struggled to remember a line, any line, from one of my poems, and failing that, words. Nothing came to mind. I strained to come up with a single line from the *Divine Comedy* but drew a blank. I couldn't even recall who had wiped the stains of hell off Dante. My brain was devoid of thought; thought had been shoved aside by fear, as if the cells in the lobes of my brain had scattered in their panic to get out of the path of the foreign object about to come crashing into their hive.

I am incapable of telling you what happened after my mock

execution. (Only now do I see that he didn't intend to kill me, only break me.) There are gaps in the story that no amount of concentration can fill. It will have been sometime after my return to the cell—whether an hour or a day I cannot say—that I tried to cut my wrist with a shard of chinaware. Fikrit stopped me as I was sawing at the vein. He tore a strip of cloth from the tail of my shirt and bandaged the wound, which although not deep was very painful. Curiously, the pain became a source of euphoria. I can remember my mother once telling me—when I was stung by nettles while climbing out of a lake near Warsaw—that nothing makes you more aware you are alive than pain. Cowering in a corner of a cell in the Lubyanka, with Sergo's brains staining my shirt, was not what my mother had in mind when she spoke of the advantages of pain; still the terrible truth is that I was elated to be alive.

I must have been in this euphoric state for days on end because if I was again taken for interrogation or execution, I have no recollection of it. It is strange what does surface in a brain under stress. I remember looking a long, long time at my shoes, mystified by the absence of laces. I remember studying the shards of chinaware on the cell floor, trying to figure out what the object had been before it was broken. I remember wondering, when Fikrit shyly handed a small book to me, what an illiterate weight lifter was doing with a copy of Pushkin. When I came to my senses, or what was left of them, I found myself astride the stool with the sawed-off front legs in Christophorovich's office. I had no idea of how much time had gone by since my execution. Comrade interrogator had been questioning me but, complaining of stomach cramps, he had gone off to the toilet and left me alone with Stalin, so extraordinarily lifelike in the photograph on the wall behind the table I half expected to hear his voice. I sat there for I don't know how long, lost in the enormous room with the pleated curtains on the windows and the alarm clock and the remains of a supper on the table, staring at Stalin. I have long subscribed to the notion that, for better or for worse, a man's character is written on his face. Like most Russian intellectuals, I have been mesmerized by Stalin, wondering what he was like behind the mask. I imagined having conversations with him in the course of which his confidences would shed light on what had transformed him into a practicing paranoid (my diagnosis, based on no medical evidence, only instinct) who assumed everyone was guilty of something. Pasternak and I used to circle endlessly around the subject (I have been known to invent biographical details of Soso Dzhugashvili's life that left Boris in stitches). Had Stalin been marked by a violent childhood in Gori, or his bank-robbing exploits to raise money for the Bolsheviks, or his several exiles in the frozen tundra under the Arctic Circle, or some particularly brutal experience during the Civil War, or the death (rumored to be suicide) of his young wife eighteen months earlier? Peering intently into the face of Stalin, I found no ready answers. You couldn't read much into formal portraits or photographs of Stalin because they were always retouched to erase the smallpox scars, to add ruddiness to his cheeks and kindheartedness to the shadow of a smirk playing on his lips. I looked around to be sure the room was empty, then made my way past the table to take a closer look at Stalin's face. I confess, without shame, that I found myself being drawn to him with the kind of mesmeric attraction I up to then had experienced only with members of the weaker sex. His reproving eyes gnawed at me from the wall. And then, weird as this must sound to you, I found myself being sucked into the photograph, sucked *through* it. My ears were ringing with unformed words. Lines from a poem I had not yet written began to knock like a fist on a window:

> *I came to him—to his core—*
> *Entering the Kremlin without a pass,*
> *In pain, and with a guilty head,*
> *Tearing the sackcloth canvas space.*

I hardly dared open my eyes. When I did I found myself adrift in a murkiness that muted all sound and only gradually dissipated, like thick morning fog, at which point I discovered I was halfway along a narrow corridor. Portraits of the generals who defeated Napoleon were hanging on both sides, each illuminated by a small lamp attached to the top of the gilt frame. I touched one wall with the tips of my fingers. It felt cold and damp. I could sense the soft pile of the thick carpet under my feet. I grasped there were two possibilities: either I was not imagining this, or I was imagining that I was not imagining it. At the far end of the corridor two men in tight-fitting European suits were sitting on either side of a low table playing chess with miniscule pieces made out of clay. The older of the two, with fine gray hair falling to his collarbones, struck me as vaguely familiar. "Mandelstam?" he called out, waving me forward. I must have looked mystified because the other man, younger than the first and prematurely bald, repeated the question. "You are Mandelstam?" I nodded. "I don't have a Kremlin pass," I said, hoping to avoid trouble by admitting my blunder straightaway. "What makes you think you're in the Kremlin?" the younger man demanded. "The portraits of the generals behind me," I said, "are known to hang in the Kremlin." Amused by my amateur detective work, he pulled an appointment book from a file cabinet and ran his finger down a list of names. He put a tick next to one of them. "You don't require a pass," he said. "Stalin is expecting you. Through the double doors there. Don't bow or scrape or anything like that. He detests protocol. He's not a tsar, after all, merely secretary general of the Party."

A big man I recognized from newspaper photographs as Stalin's bodyguard Vlasik pulled open the double doors and, never lifting his eyes from me, stepped aside. "Just walk up to him as you would to any ordinary individual and say your name," he instructed me. "If he offers his hand, shake it." I heard the doors close behind me when I had gone through. Josef Stalin was sitting at the far end of the long rectangular room behind an enormous desk piled high with books. One entire wall was lined with ornate Russian stoves. The thick drapes on the window behind him were partially open and I could make out the onion-shaped domes of Saint Basil's Cathedral, illuminated by antiaircraft searchlights, which meant that I was indeed, as I supposed, inside the Kremlin. What light there was in the room came from a low desk lamp and an arched reading lamp hanging over an upholstered chair. The man known in Kremlin circles as the *khozyain*, wearing a military tunic open at the neck and smoking a cigarette, got to his feet and came around the desk. "Stalin," he muttered. "Mandelstam," I replied. "I know who you are," he said. "Your reputation precedes you." I heard myself say, "Yours trails after you like a wake," and immediately regretted my impudence. (Did I actually say these words or is this how I would have liked to conduct myself?) My comment, assuming I made it, irritated the head of the household. "Therein lies the problem," he said. "Wakes fade away after a time."

He glanced down at my shoes. "What happened to your laces?" "I ask myself the same thing," I said. He raised his eyebrows, obviously perplexed, and after an instant's hesitation, awkwardly held out his hand. I just as awkwardly took it. He produced a packet of *Kazbek Papirosi* from a pocket of his tunic and offered me one of the cigarettes with their long cardboard tips. A gunmetal cigarette lighter materialized in his stumpy fingers. I took hold of his wrist and leaned toward him to bring the end of my cigarette to the flame. Stalin couldn't have missed noticing that my hand was trembling but was discreet enough not to comment on it. The drag on a cigarette, the first since my arrest, went a long way toward calming my frayed nerves. "Let's talk," he suggested, gesturing toward the upholstered chair, pulling over the high-backed wicker chair so that we were facing each other, our knees nearly touching. "About what should we talk?" I asked.

"You can start by explaining how is it that every composer and painter and writer and poet in Russia except you is ready to dedicate a work to Stalin."

"With all respect, if you have the dedication of every composer and painter and writer and poet, I don't see why you need mine."

In person, Stalin looked nothing like his photographs. He was a good deal shorter than the figure in his portraits, almost dwarflike even. His left arm, visibly withered, hung stiffly from a hunched shoulder. He had the beginnings of a paunch. His face, filled with smallpox scars and freckles, was ruddy enough, but on closer inspection I got the impression he applied what women refer to as rouge. His teeth were in worse condition than mine, his eyes were yellow, the mustache on his upper lip was thickened and darkened with shoe wax. His scalp was dry and peeling in places. Black hairs protruded from his nostrils.

Like the poet Mandelstam in his most recent incarnation, Stalin didn't beat about the bush. "Let's be clear, Mandelstam—I am not afraid of dying. I looked death in the face dozens of times as a young revolutionist, as the commissar charged with defending Tsaritsyn during the Civil War. No, what I fear, what I *loathe*, is the fading of my wake after the passage of my ship. I send off valises filled with rubles to that Ukrainian rejuvenation quack Bogomolets to finance his experiments—he is said to believe that drinking water from glaciers accounts for Georgians living into ripe old age—but I don't put much stock in the professor's magic potions. With or without water from glaciers, the curtain will one day come down on my life. And then what? All those objects named after Stalin—the tanks, the tractors, the warships, the factories—all of them will sooner or later disappear, to be replaced by new tanks and new tractors and new warships and new factories named after a new secretary general. The limousine I ride in is a ZIS. The initials, as you no doubt know, stand for Zavod Imeni Stalina—the Factory Named After Stalin. When the last ZIS finishes up in a museum for antique automobiles, people will have forgotten what the initials stood for. The streets in the cities named after Stalin, even the cities like Stalingrad, will eventually revert to their original names. So where, I put the question to the poet

Mandelstam, where can I expect to find a flicker of life after death? The answer is: If there is such a thing as immortality, it resides in the poetry of a genius."

Stalin jabbed a nicotine-stained finger into my knee. "You are a stubborn prick, Mandelstam. Your pal Pasternak came up with a poem, albeit quite run-of-the-mill. *So go forward without flinching, as long as you're alive* . . . Shostakovich delivered a whole symphony he described as a creative reply to Stalin's accurate criticism, though it gives me a splitting headache when I am forced to sit through a performance. (Now that I think of it, maybe that's what the asshole intended. I should have Shostakovich arrested for wrecking my sleep!) Thousands of lesser poets and writers celebrate Stalin in a hundred different languages. Nobody in Russia publishes a book, a pamphlet, a thesis on philosophy or philology or astronomy or linguistics without acknowledging his debt to Stalin. Do you know Khachaturian's *Stalin Song*?" He started to hum the first bars in the sweet-pitched voice of the choir boy he once was. "Well, you get the idea." The *khozyain* pulled another cigarette from his pack and lit it on the embers of the one in his mouth, then filled his lungs with smoke. "Don't make the mistake of thinking this conversation is easy for me, Mandelstam. I am not used to *asking* for something. It is more usual that the very few things I require are *offered*. It would seem that Stalin can have anything his heart desires in all of Russia with the exception of your poem. I ask you, man-to-man, face-to-face: Is such a situation normal?"

I was, I can see now as I look back on my encounter with Stalin, so flabbergasted by the turn the conversation had taken that I couldn't find words to reply. Taking my silence for stubbornness, Stalin became exasperated. "It is unusual to come across someone who does not fear the secretary general who runs the Party and, through it, the state. In other circumstances I could admire such a man. Let's be sure you know what's at stake here, Mandelstam." Scraping back his chair, he stood up and came around behind me and began talking to the nape of my neck. "Do you have an idea of how much the state weighs?"

"The weight of the state?"

"Yes, with all its factories and dams and trains and aircraft and trucks and ships and tanks."

"Nobody can calculate the weight of the state. It is in the realm of astronomical figures."

"And do you think one man can resist the pressure of this astronomical weight? I will have your poem, Mandelstam. If for some reason I can't have your poem, you will be crushed under the weight of the state."

His bluntness left me short of breath. "I am not a threat to Soviet power," was all I could think to say.

He circled around the upholstered chair and stood over me, sucking on his cigarette, studying me with his angry yellow eyes. "You are most certainly a threat to Soviet power. Someone who refuses to bend to Stalin's will may bend to the will of his enemies. There is no middle ground between worshipping the ground Stalin walks on and desecrating it."

Stalin hauled his wicker chair back behind his desk and sank into it, lost for a long moment in reflection. "So what's your answer, Mandelstam?" he said. "I haven't got all night. Will you do your part to secure the secretary general's immortality?"

"I would if I could."

His eyes narrowed in suspicion. "What does that mean?"

"Even if I were to compose such an ode, it would be useless to you. I would be going through the motions. I don't really know you well enough to compose something so true it cuts to the bone, which is what a poem must do if it is to have life after the poet's death. For me you are a larger-than-life icon, a legend, a myth, not a flesh-and-blood human being. There is no way I can counterfeit it."

"Stalin is made of flesh and blood like you." He straightened in his chair. "What is your age?"

"Forty-three."

"You look older. I happen to be thirteen years your senior, but the difference in age notwithstanding, we have a lot in common. Both our fathers were in the leather business—yours sold leather in Warsaw, mine was a shoemaker in Georgia. It is not to be excluded that my father made shoes using leather supplied by your father. Stranger things have been known to happen. In addition we share a common interest in poesy. I myself have written romantic verse— several of my poems were published in a Georgian newspaper under the pen name Soselo before I became a full-time revolutionist. That's not all. It is certainly no accident we both married women whose name, Nadezhda, signifies *hope* in Russian—we may hope for different things, but we share an inclination toward hope. And, curiously, you and I have the same forename. During one of my stretches in exile, the locals in Solvychegodsk in the Arkhangelsk Oblast took to calling me Osip, which is a popular Russian form of Josef up north. I even signed *Oddball Osip* on love letters I wrote to a schoolgirl there named Pelageya. Being a revolutionist, robbing banks to finance the sacred proletarian enterprise, was not without advantages—you could get into any girl's pants."

"Being a poet was not without advantages, too," I said, but I could see he was lost in his own life and hadn't heard me.

"By God, those were the days. Exhilarating. Dangerous. Sheer fun. In Gori, in Tiflis, I was a local hero. People in the Caucasus respected me for who I was, not"—he waved the back of his hand at the Kremlin compound—"where I lived." Stalin remembered I was there. "Did you say something?"

"No."

He nodded absently. "Jesus, I haven't thought about Pelageya in years. I even know her name. Pelageya Onufrieva. I must make a note to have my people find out what became of her."

I thought I might stand a better chance of ingratiating myself with Stalin if I could keep him talking about himself. "Siberian exile must have been a bitter experience," I said.

Stalin blew air through his lips. "Bitter doesn't begin to describe it. I was banished seven times, seven times I survived to make my way back to European Russia. I'll tell you what kept me going in exile: aside from shacking up with girl prisoners so the both of us could keep warm at night, there were the books. Reading is what kept me going. Every time a prisoner died we'd fight to see who'd get his books. I usually won. My seventh exile ended when I raced across the country to Petrograd, after the tsar was overthrown, to direct the Bolsheviks until Lenin negotiated a safe passage through Germany and returned from abroad. Siberian winter is best described as hell frozen over. Try to visualize your piss freezing before it hits the ground. Try to visualize sucking on icicles of frozen vodka to get drunk. Summers, which were as short as a blink of the eye, weren't much better with their swarms of mosquitoes. Ha! As soon as the permafrost started to thaw, I joined the other prisoners crawling under the women's shower house—when we spotted water dripping through joints in the floorboards, we would squirm along the ground until we were directly underneath and try to look up through the dripping water to see the naked woman showering above. And if you could keep your eyes open long enough, you could make out the tear—"

"The tear?"

"The slash in the crotch. The slit. The cunt, you idiot. You ought to be familiar with cunts, Mandelstam. I have been told you get laid a lot. The Cheka file on your wife says she is an occasional lesbian, that you and your wife are both having an affair with a theater actress, that you sometimes watch them and she sometimes watches the two of you and you sometimes do it *à trois* in the French manner. I myself have never fucked more than one woman at a time, but it's not for lack of trying. I made several attempts to talk my Nadezhda into experimenting with free sex in the Bolshevik spirit, but for all her revolutionist credentials—did you know she used to type speeches for Lenin before the Revolution?—she was too puritanical to liberate herself from the bourgeois definition of marriage. These days I fuck my housekeeper Valechka. The only thing she knows is the missionary position, which has a certain irony, since what I preach is the gospel according to Marx."

I watched as Stalin poured water into a glass from a pitcher, then measured out drops from a vial. "Tincture of iodine," he said. "I don't trust doctors. I treat my several ailments with ten drops twice a day. Works wonders." And pulling a face in anticipation of the awful taste, he swallowed the contents of the glass. "With luck, all these anecdotes will break down the wall between us. Maybe you'll begin to see me as flesh and blood after all, which will inspire you to write a serious poem to Stalin, as opposed to a treacherous little polemic." I could only nod in agreement. Who could rule out the possibility that, knowing these intimate details of his life, I might be able to fabricate an ode to Stalin and avoid being crushed by the state?

He reached over to angle the desk lamp so that it illuminated a framed photograph on the wall between us. "That's me at Lenin's funeral procession. As you can see, as all of Russia knows, I was one of the pallbearers carrying his coffin on our shoulders toward Red Square. There was so much ice, I was terrified I'd lose my footing and the coffin would fall to the ground and open and Lenin's corpse would spill onto the street. I was devoted to Lenin, it goes without saying, though the old man, as we called him, could be a prick sometimes. To begin with, he wasn't very courageous—while the rest of us were out in the Petrograd streets making a revolution, he hid in that girls' school we used as an H.Q. When he did work up the nerve to leave Smolny, he wrapped his face in bandages so nobody would recognize him. I'll let you in on a state secret, Mandelstam. To speak plainly, Lenin wasn't very Leninist. Oh, he could theorize about proletarian revolution until the cock crowed but when it came to the day-to-day implementation of the theory, he dithered. *Two steps forward, one step back* was his idea of progress. Lenin didn't have the guts to attack the peasant problem head-on—it took a Stalin to do that. History will vindicate me.

Collectivization, despite the occasional inconvenience to a handful of peasants, will be the crowning glory of my legacy."

Stalin had collapsed into the wicker back of his chair by now, smoking his cigarette in short agitated puffs, clearly caught up in recounting his life's story. "Listen, I was the only one in the immediate group around Lenin who had peasant roots, the only one who had been an active revolutionist leading Bolsheviks squads in street fighting, as opposed to a shitty coffeehouse intellectual. Which made me the odd man out, the sore thumb in the superstructure. When it came to the pecking order, no one took me seriously. Well, they all underestimated me, didn't they? That was the real secret of my rise to the top of the heap. They were lulled by my Georgian accent, they laughed behind my back at the grammatical errors I made when I spoke Russian, they took me for a country chawbacon who couldn't survive in the big city. In the end it was child's play to fuck over those Jews—Trotsky and Kamenev and Zinoviev, even Karl Heinrich Marx, the Vandal who had the misfortune to come from a long line of rabbis. He's probably turning over in his London grave at the thought that someone who doesn't really understand all his bullshit is the leader of the world Communist movement. I even outsmarted that asshole Bukharin who understood Marx's bullshit, or pretended to. How did I do it? To begin with I took the job none of them wanted—general secretary of the Party. I did what none of them wanted to dirty his hands doing—the boring routine day-to-day chores. And so they went on theorizing and scheming and preening while I built up an apparat loyal to me and ran the country. And what did I get by way of a thank-you? After Lenin's first stroke, he was surrounded by vultures who did everything they could to turn him against me. I'll let you in on another secret. Days before the old man kicked the bucket, they prevailed on him to write a testament denouncing Stalin for—get this!—his *crude behavior* toward Krupskaya, Lenin's hagfish of a wife who was furious with me for talking about his affairs with girls in the typing pool in front of her.

Needless to say, I suppressed the so-called last testament. I keep the original, written out in Lenin's wobbly hand, in my desk. You don't believe me? Here"—he snatched a sheet of paper from the drawer and, waving his good hand the way I do when I recite, began to read aloud from it. "*Stalin is too coarse . . . I suggest to the comrades that they think of a way of transferring Stalin from the position of general secretary . . . assigning someone more tolerant, more polite, less capricious,* and so on and so forth. Well, you get the gist. Me, capricious! That's a good one. After Lenin cashed in his chips, Krupskaya threatened to circulate a copy until I warned her, to her face, I'd appoint a new widow for Lenin if she opened her trap about the testament. You can bet the bitch shut up." Stalin brought up a laugh from the pit of his stomach. "Just because she shit in the same toilet as Lenin didn't give her the right to walk over me."

One of the several telephones on the desk rang. Stalin plucked the receiver off the hook and held it to his ear. "Agreed," he said. "Of course they were plotting to kill Stalin. That's what I would be doing in their shoes. As for the trial, it will lend credibility to the proceedings if foreign journalists and foreign diplomats are permitted to witness the confessions. On the matter of the opera *Onegin,* which I attended last night, I find it outrageous that Tatiana appears onstage in a sheer gown. Stalin is not giving instructions but merely expressing an opinion. Whatever happened to Bolshevik modesty? Send a memorandum to the director saying Stalin was overheard remarking that Ivan the Terrible, a great and wise tsar, beat his pregnant daughter-in-law for wearing immodest clothing. Let our cultural workers draw the appropriate conclusions." Hanging up the phone, he glanced over at me. "I lost the thread of our conversation."

"You were talking about the people who tried to turn Lenin against you," I reminded him.

"Yes, yes, it's the price one pays for success," Stalin plunged on, lighting yet another cigarette on the embers of the one that had burned close to his lips. "They tried to turn Lenin against me and almost succeeded. Ten years later the same pricks were at it again, trying to turn my own wife against me." I could see that the mere mention of his wife had aroused strong emotions. His brow creased in pain, his eyes narrowed in irritation "Our marriage was never a bed of roses, as they say. To begin with, I was twenty-two years older and more of a father figure than a lover in her eyes. She actually left me once, running off to Petrograd with the children, but I went after her and sweet-talked her into coming home. And then, in the early thirties, with collectivization under way and nobody quite sure how things would turn out, Bukharin filled her head with cock-and-bull stories of starving children with swollen stomachs begging at train stations, of a Soviet-organized famine spreading across the Ukraine, of mass deportations, of summary executions. Looking back, I can see that Bukharin poisoned our marriage. Nadezhda and I argued bitterly. I fended off her accusations, quoting Lenin's line—not that he acted on it himself—about the need for the peasants to do a bit of starving. The trick, he said, was not to lose your nerve. The peasants who resisted collectivization, who destroyed their cattle and horses and grain, calculated we would lose our nerve and feed them. Zinoviev and Kamenev and Bukharin and Nadezhda were losing theirs, but I wasn't losing mine. I was the same Stalin who risked his skin robbing banks in the Caucasus, who forced the defeatist Bolshevik commanders at Tsaritsyn onto a barge and sank it in the Volga, drowning all the traitors and saving the city from the Whites. Things between Nadezhda and me came to a head at the Kremlin banquet celebrating the fifteenth anniversary of the Revolution." Stalin shook his head in dismay. "That was eighteen months ago, but the scene is so fresh in my mind's eye it might have happened yesterday."

"What happened?"

"I knew Nadezhda was in one of her dark moods the moment I put a polka on the American gramophone. Anastas Mikoyan, my Armenian Politburo pal, sashayed across the room and held out his arms to Nadezhda to dance, but she insolently turned her back on him. Anastas, who, with his little Hitler mustache fancied himself something of a dandy, shrugged off the insult and wound up dancing with Voroshilov's wife, Ekaterina. Nadezhda snubbed my old Georgian friend Beria, the Chekist responsible for cleansing Transcaucasia of wreckers, when he tried to chat her up—she once pretended that he was known to have a weakness for raping young female athletes, but I had no reason to believe this was anything more than grist for the Kremlin gossip mill. I worked the room, making small talk with Bukharchik, as I called Bukharin—I like to give everyone in my entourage a nickname—teasing him about the age difference between him and the piece of ass Anna Larina, whom he'd been openly courting. I remember telling him, *You outspit me this time,* an allusion to his fucking someone even younger than my Nadezhda was when I took up with her. As stunning as Anna Larina was, she didn't hold a candle to my wife, who looked particularly beautiful the night of the banquet. She was wearing the black dress, embroidered with rose petals, that her brother Pavel had brought back from Berlin. She'd done up her hair for once, pinning a tea rose in it. When we'd worn ourselves out dancing and singing Georgian songs, we drifted over to the long table piled with soup terrines and platters of salted fish and lamb, along with bottles of vodka with frost on them. I sat down in the middle of the table next to the film actress Galina Yegorova, the wife of a Red Army commander who had been conveniently dispatched to run a military district in Central Asia. The night of the banquet, Galina was wearing one of those low-cut dresses you see in French magazines. Have you ever caught her on the screen? She's not much of an actress, but I am in a position to testify that she's damn good in bed. Nadezhda sat across from me, favoring me with jealous looks every time I let my eyes wander to Galina's tits. For some reason Molotov and Yagoda began boasting about the dizzy success of our collectivization program. Lazar Kaganovich, my railway commissar, had just come back from the North Caucasus where he'd organized cattle cars to ship peasants who refused to join collectives off to Siberia. Kosherovich, as I'd nicknamed Lazar so nobody would forget his Israelite roots, pulled a slip of paper from his pocket and began reeling off numbers. *Ukraine—145,000; North Caucasus—71,000; Lower Volga—50,000; Belorussia—42,000; West Siberia—50,000; East Siberia—30,000.* I tried to shut him up but he was too drunk to spot the dark looks I dispatched in his direction. Nadezhda called across the table, *What are those numbers, Lazar?* His eyes were glazed over from alcohol and he didn't see the storm coming. *Why, deportations, what else?* he replied. I attempted to distract Nadezhda with a toast. *To the destruction of the enemies of Socialism,* I called out, raising my glass. Everyone around the table raised their glasses and repeated the toast. Everyone except my own Tatochka. She sat there in simmering silence, staring at me across the table with what can only be described as hate in her eyes. If, as the peasants say, looks could kill, I would have been struck dead on the spot. *Why don't you drink?* I demanded. *Are you for or against the enemies of Socialism?* When she looked away without answering, my Georgian temper got the best of me and I threw a handful of orange peel at her. *Hey you, drink!* I shouted. And Nadezhda, humiliating me in front of everyone, shouted back, *Don't* hey you *me.* And then she turned insult into injury by storming out of the banquet hall. What could I do? She had offended me in front of the entire Politburo. You could have heard a pin drop as I settled back into my chair. I tried to pass the incident off as a domestic squabble. *I am married to a fool,* I said, flinging cigarette ends at the empty chair across from me. *All women are torn*—I gestured toward the genitals of the actress next to me—*and for some reason unknown even to Marx, we have become prisoners of this tear, we serve life sentences.* Yagoda had the good sense to laugh and the others followed his lead and soon everyone was roaring with laughter. Everyone except me. I'm not boring you, am I, Mandelstam? Do you want to hear the rest or would you prefer to return to your cell?"

"I am certainly not bored."

"When the party broke up, I threw an army greatcoat over my shoulders and took Galina off in one of the Packards to my dacha outside of Moscow at Zubalovo. We spent a few unpleasant hours together—she was worried that Nadezhda, in a fit of jealousy, would have her arrested. I had to reassure her that I was the only one who could authorize the arrest of someone in the superstructure. Still, the damage was done. It's hard to fuck a woman who is not wet with desire, so we wound up playing billiards. In the early hours of the morning, Vlasik drove me home through the deserted streets of Moscow while I dozed in the backseat. I came awake as we passed through the Troitsky Gates into the Kremlin compound. I remember a light snow was falling. It had already erased the footprints of the guests who had quit the banquet hours before. Someone had left a hall light on for me, but no one was stirring in our apartment in the Poteshny Palace. My anger had accumulated, it's true. The daily drumbeat of bad news from the Ukraine made everyone edgy. Yagoda had passed along word that Zinoviev and Kamenev and even Bukharin were spreading it about that Stalin had fucked up—they were accusing me of having launched the drive for collectivization thinking the peasants would greet us with open arms, of not having a plan to deal with the chaos in the event they didn't. Nadezhda's public rudeness that night had been the last straw. I stormed into her bedroom and found her, still wearing the black dress, asleep in the narrow bed she retreated to when she had the female problems that had plagued her since the abortion in the mid-twenties. Leaning over the bed, I shook her awake. *Have you come to apologize for going off with that slut?* she demanded. *It's you who should apologize for walking out on the supper, for embarrassing me in front of my colleagues,* I lashed out at her. *If you do it again,* ubyu—*I'll kill you.* No sooner had the words crossed my lips than I regretted them. Nadezhda was as fragile as chinaware, easily roused to hysteria and bouts of depression. It was then that she produced the small French Label that Pavel had given her along with the black dress. She was strangely calm as she removed all but one of the bullets from the pistol's cylinder and spun it with her long elegant fingers as if she intended to play Russian roulette. *Don't push me too far,* I warned. She made the mistake of taunting me. *Were you hard with Galina tonight? Were you hard with the hairdresser or that girl in the typists' pool last week? I can see from your expression you weren't. Of course they will tell everyone, you'll be the laughingstock of Moscow. For someone who prides himself on Bolshevik hardness, you are often limp. Here,* she said, holding out the pistol, butt first, *prove to the world you are as hard as your alter ego, Ivan the Terrible, who in a fit of rage killed his own son.* And I did prove it. In the heat of the moment I held the pistol to her heart, Mandelstam. I held it to her heart and I pulled the trigger."

"And?" I asked, barely daring to breathe. "Did the firing pin fall on a bullet?"

"*And* is for me to know and you to imagine," Stalin said. "The servants discovered her body, stiff with rigor mortis, in the morning. There were bruises on her face, though I have no recollection of hitting her. The pistol and the five bullets she'd taken from the cylinder were on the pillow next to her head. Vlasik came up with a doctor who was willing to sign a death certificate listing the cause of death as peritonitis, which was the official version published in *Pravda.* But everyone in the Kremlin was convinced she had committed suicide." Stalin's eyes suddenly glistened with what I took to be inconsolability. "She broke my life," he said so softly I had to strain to make out his words. Had I heard him correctly? *She broke my life!*

There was a tap on the door. The bodyguard Vlasik stuck his head into the room. "I have Yagoda's overnight list," he said. Stalin jerked his head, summoning him forward. Vlasik set several sheets of paper down on the desk. "Both Yagoda and Molotov have signed off on it," he said, uncapping a fountain pen and offering it to the *khozyain.* Stalin eyed the fountain pen suspiciously. "Was that made in Soviet Russia?" he asked. "Germany," Vlasik said, mortified.

Stalin's eyes narrowed in displeasure. Ignoring the fountain pen, he selected a red pencil from a jar filled with pencils. Then he ran a forefinger down the list, occasionally crossing out a name, muttering something about how *terror to be effective must be random*, scrawling *Za—Approved*, along with his initial on the top right-hand corner of each page when he'd finished with it. "Who is Akaki Mgeladze?" he asked at one point. "He's the Abkhazian you nicknamed *the Wolf*." "The commissar I sent to straighten things out in Georgia?" "That's the one." Stalin drew a line through his name and moved on. He asked about two other people he couldn't place. When Vlasik reminded him, Stalin left both their names on the list. "What have we here?" the *khozyain* exclaimed. "Mandelstam, Osip Emilievich." He looked over at me. "You will be interested to know that Yagoda has included you for execution. He may be right. I have read your shitty little epigram. When all is said, you should be shot for writing a lousy poem." With my heart racing, he pretended to discuss the problem with his bodyguard. "What shall we do with this Mandelstam? On the one hand, I don't want to go down in history as the one who cut short the life of a Russian poet. On the other hand, it sets a bad precedent if I am seen to *dither*—people will mistake me for Lenin. So what will it be? *Execute* or *isolate and preserve*?" Sucking on his cigarette as he weighed the alternatives, the *khozyain*, to my everlasting relief, scratched a line through my name and, initialing the last of the pages, handed them back to Vlasik. "Tell Yagoda I haven't made up my mind about Mandelstam. He can add his name to tomorrow night's list. I'll decide then." "Will that be all?" the bodyguard asked. "There's one more thing," Stalin said. "Find out what became of a girl I once knew named Pelageya Onufrieva."

TEN

Zinaida Zaitseva-Antonova
Monday, the 20th of May 1934

The last thing I expected was a reward, but the Organs are known to treat collaborators generously, which is understood to be one of their ways of encouraging collaboration. So I can't say it came as a surprise when the Chekist buttonholed me in my dressing room after rehearsal one night and announced, *We are eager to show our gratitude for your loyalty to Stalin and the Revolution. It isn't every day that someone delivers evidence of treason written out in the traitor's own hand.* Several propositions rolled off the Chekist's tongue. An external passport and authorization to travel to Paris or Rome? Better roles in bigger theaters? A monthlong all-expenses-paid vacation at one of those plush Black Sea hotels frequented by the *nomenklatura*? I favored the visitor with one of what Mandelstam called my shamefaced glances. *I was only doing my duty as a Soviet citizen,* I demurred shyly. *I ask for nothing.* The Chekist, an older gentleman whose lips barely moved when he spoke, smiled as if we shared a secret. Several gold teeth in his lower jaw glistened with saliva. *Surely there is some service the state can offer you to make your life easier,* he insisted. His tone managed to convey that my continuing to refuse could be misconstrued; could be taken to mean

I had second thoughts about having collaborated in the first place. I honestly felt I had no choice but to accept. Which is why I averted my eyes in embarrassment and admitted, in the husky tone actors use on stage when they want to convey reluctance, *Perhaps there is one small thing.* And I raised the delicate question of my risking the loss of my twenty-two square meters in the communal apartment off the Arbat and my Moscow residence permit if I divorced my husband. He pulled a small pad from his pocket and made a note to himself. *Proceed with the divorce,* he instructed me. *Leave the matter of the apartment and the residence permit in our hands.* He rose to leave. I saw him to the door and held out my hand. *How can I thank you?* I asked. Curiously, he didn't shake it. *There is no need to thank us,* he replied. *It is a point of pride with the Organs to take good care of the people who work for us.* His words caught me by surprise. A retort spilled from my mouth before I knew what I was saying. *I wasn't aware that I worked for you.* He smiled indulgently, the way one would at a child who has uttered something vulgar, and said, *We don't believe in one-night stands.*

ELEVEN

Nadezhda Yakovlevna
Tuesday, the 21st of May 1934

It was my dear friend Anna Andreyevna who kept her wits until mine trickled back. When we spoke of my husband's arrest years later, Akhmatova claimed I had sobbed until the tear ducts ran dry, at which point I began seething against everything and everybody under the sun: Mandelstam for truth telling in this swamp of lies, the Kremlin mountaineer for equating the rant of a poet with a counterrevolutionary act, the moths who bred in the felt insulation of our walls, the neighbor Sergei Petrovich who had betrayed the teapot to the Cheka, myself for not having had the courage to talk my husband into a joint suicide pact when I realized he was determined to propagate his epigram. Yes, yes, I see now that we should have killed ourselves the instant we heard that late-night knock on the door. It was only after I'd gotten hold of myself that Anna and I began to think constructively. A day after Mandelstam's arrest, we packed socks and underwear and soap and cigarettes and two hundred grams of smoked ham into a small carton and made the rounds of Moscow's prisons to see which one might accept the package for the prisoner Mandelstam. At Anna's suggestion we started with Butyrki, where writers and artists were usually taken for questioning. Ahead of us in line were two little girls, perhaps five and seven, wearing starched dresses and telling everyone within earshot, *Mother has been arrested.* Eventually a soldier turned up from a side door and led the girls away. Behind us one woman told another, *We must send our children to their grandparents before this happens to them.* After two and a half hours of queuing, Akhmatova and I finally reached the window only to be turned away by a baby-faced guard who went down his list and announced there was nobody by the name of Mandelstam there. The Lubyanka came next. We waited for almost two hours in a light rain, the two of us huddled under a broken umbrella, before we reached the window. And lo and behold, the guard on duty checked the name on the damp package against a typewritten list and, without a word, accepted it.

"At least we know where he is," I said, relishing this small triumph.

"We also know he is alive, or was when they typed up this list," Anna said. "I didn't want to frighten you when we were turned away from Butyrki, but if a prisoner is dead, that's another reason they won't accept the package."

Looking back now, I remember that we were both quite astonished that *we* hadn't been arrested as coconspirators, if only because our arrest would have given them more leverage with Mandelstam. I desperately tried to get in touch with Zinaida to make sure she had destroyed the only copy of the Stalin epigram in my husband's handwriting, but whoever answered the telephone in her communal apartment off the Arbat said she was seldom to be found there these days. After I don't remember how many phone calls I managed to get her agronomist husband on the line. Of course I couldn't come right out and ask him if she had destroyed the poem, but I did elicit the information that she was rehearsing a new play and had most certainly not been picked up by the police. *You catch me at a bad moment,* he said. *We are divorcing and I am in the process of moving out. As for Zinaida, she has always steered clear of anything that smacked of politics, so the idea that she might be detained by the Cheka is absurd. In point of fact, they are going to accord her a Moscow residence permit. If I were you, the last thing I would do is lose sleep over her.*

I will concede I was terribly relieved to hear that Zinaida had not been arrested; I would not have been able to look myself in the eye if our friendship had landed her in trouble with the authorities.

While I was trying (without success, as it turned out) to track down Zinaida, Anna got in touch with Boris Pasternak and informed him of my husband's arrest. He was overwhelmed with remorse at not having been able to talk Mandelstam into destroying the offending epigram. *I never find the right words when I need them,* he reproached himself. He promised to immediately contact Nikolai Bukharin to see if he could do anything. He urged me to do the same. *The more of us who talk to him, the more likely it is that he will consent to stick his neck out for Osip.*

"I absolutely must have a word with Nikolai Ivanovich," I told Bukharin's secretary, a thin woman named Korotkova whom my husband had described (in his "Fourth Prose") as a *squirrel who chews a nut with every visitor.*

"You look pale as death," she said. "Has something happened?"

I could only catch my breath and nod. "Mandelstam has been imprisoned in the Lubyanka," I said.

Korotkova had a good heart. She took my hand and squeezed it. "Nikolai Ivanovich has a full schedule this morning but I will somehow work you in."

And she did, between two editors who emerged from his office jotting notes on a pad and a woman waiting to wheel in a trolley with the linotype slugs of *Izvestiya*'s front page locked into a wooden frame. When he caught sight of me, Nikolai Ivanovich drew me over to the couch. "Pasternak has already been to see me," he said in a muffled voice. (Did he fear that microphones had been planted in *his* walls?) "What has that husband of yours done now? Mandelstam hasn't written something outrageous, has he?"

Bukharin was a slight man with a ruddy goatee that in happier times lent him a raffish air. These days he had the preoccupied appearance of someone with a terminal illness. He'd been expelled from the Politburo in the late twenties, but his absence from the inner circle had apparently not poisoned his relationship with Stalin, who anointed him editor of *Izvestiya* and let him keep his Kremlin apartment despite the occasional friction between them. Still, rumors had been circulating in Moscow that Bukharin's days were numbered; that if Zinoviev and Kamenev were brought to trial, which many thought of as a probability, as opposed to a possibility, to save their skins they would implicate Nikolai Ivanovich and that would be the end of him. I felt terrible bringing my troubles to someone who had so many of his own. But what was I to do? He still had the ear of Stalin. If only he would consent to put a word in.

"Nothing more outrageous than the poems you know," I told Bukharin, stretching the truth for fear he wouldn't dare lift a finger for Mandelstam if he knew what was in the epigram. "I come to you, Nikolai Ivanovich, as my last and best hope." And I went on to describe the life Mandelstam had been reduced to living: borrowing money to make ends meet, reading his poems aloud in return for cigarettes; making the rounds of editors who, when he managed to get past the secretaries, invented one excuse or another for not publishing his work. I spoke of the heart palpitation that had rendered Mandelstam's health fragile. I even described how he had fabricated a copy of *Stone* to sell to an editor who was buying up original manuscripts for the new Literary Fund Library. "You helped Osya's brother in the early twenties," I pleaded. "You must absolutely help Osya now."

Bukharin listened so intently the cigarette in his mouth burnt down and singed his lips and he had to spit it out and grind the end under his heel on the floor. "Times have changed," he said. "These days I am not confident I can help myself."

I had steeled myself to come away empty-handed, but tears

welled in my eyes. He produced a handkerchief and awkwardly offered it to me. "Control yourself, I beg you, Nadezhda Yakovlevna," he said and, pacing back and forth in his enormous office, he bombarded me with questions. "Have you attempted to see him?" he demanded.

I explained that, thanks to Akhmatova, we had discovered he was being held in the Lubyanka, but visits to relatives in prison were out of the realm of possibility—they hadn't been allowed for years. I could tell from the expression on Bukharin's face that this came as news to him.

"What article are they holding him under?"

"The usual one for political prisoners, Article 58," I said.

Bukharin paled. "Anti-Soviet propaganda, counterrevolutionary activities—that's a bad omen. If only it had been a lesser charge ..." He let the thought trail off, then came back at me with another question. "What was the rank of the senior Chekist who arrested Osip?"

"What difference does that make?"

"The higher the rank of the arresting officer, the more serious the case, the worse the fate of the prisoner."

"He claimed to be a colonel," I said.

Bukharin shook his head in despair. "The fact that they sent a full colonel is a not good sign. Most Article 58 prisoners are arrested by captains, majors at the most."

The telephone on his desk rang. Striding over, he brought it to his ear. Turning his back on me, lowering his voice, he spoke urgently into the mouthpiece. I thought I heard him pronounce Mandelstam's name. "Don't hold up supper—I will be home late," he said, and he hung down the phone.

"That was my wife," he told me. "Anna Larina is shaken by the news of Mandelstam's arrest but she begged me not to get involved. Someone as well known as Osip Emilievich could only have been arrested with the knowledge of Stalin. It is quite likely that he was arrested on the instructions of Stalin. There is enough contentiousness between us without adding Mandelstam to the list of things Stalin holds against me, so my wife advised."

I rose to me feet and handed the handkerchief back to him. "She's right, of course," I said. "It was thoughtless of me to put you in this situation."

Bukharin threw an arm over my shoulder and accompanied me to the door. "We live in—" He racked his brain for the appropriate word. "We live in *grim* times. Koba," he went on, referring to Stalin by his Bolshevik nom de guerre, "is not the man he was when Lenin was alive. He sees himself surrounded by potential enemies, he suffers from pathological suspiciousness, he trusts no one, he schemes to turn one against the other, to divide and liquidate. He sided with Kamenev and Zinoviev against Trotsky, then with me against Kamenev and Zinoviev. When I was no longer useful to him, he threw me out of the Politburo and the Central Committee. I tell you, it will be a miracle if any of the old Bolsheviks survive."

"Thank you for seeing me, Nikolai Ivanovich."

"You were right to come," he said quickly. "One must do what one can to starve the beast. I will raise the subject of Mandelstam's arrest with Koba."

I had all to do not to burst into tears again. "Words fail me," I murmured.

He managed a pained smile. "Let us both hope they don't fail *me*."

TWELVE

Nikolai Vlasik
Wednesday, the 22nd of May 1934

There was no love lost between me and the so-called *darling of the Party*, Nikolai Bukharin. On my all-time shit list, he was right up there with that Pigalle doorman Maksim Gorky. Bukharin's squeamish take on the usefulness of Red terror, his foot-dragging on collectivization, his patronizing attitude toward the *khozyain*, his intellectual arrogance all rubbed me the wrong way. Even Lenin, in his famous testament, felt obliged to concede that Bukharin was weak on dialectics. I don't have the foggiest idea why my boss put up with this smug son of a bitch. Maybe it was, as Yagoda once suggested, an attraction of opposites—Stalin was everything Bukharin wasn't, which is to say someone who had the balls to follow his instincts where they led, as opposed to the spineless coffeehouse Marxist who didn't want to soil his manicured fingernails constructing Socialism. In the end I suppose the unlikely friendship, if friendship it was, could be chalked up to the *khozyain*'s lingering admiration for book learning, an acquired taste that dates back to his brief stint at a seminary when he was young. To this day, Josef Vissarionovich keeps a stack of books on his desk and another on his night table, and I'm here to tell you they aren't there for decoration. Many's the time the boss, plagued by insomnia, would curl up in a reading chair, his nose glued to a book on the Napoleonic wars or ancient Greece or the Persian shahs or *The Last of the Mohicans*. Which is how I'd find him when I came by with newspapers in the morning. I mention all this to explain why, when Bukharin showed up in the anteroom outside Comrade Stalin's hideaway office—without phoning ahead to ask for an appointment, mind you—I was predisposed to give him a hard time.

"Raise your arms," I instructed him.

"Raise my arms?"

"Which words don't you understand? Raise? Your? Arms?"

"Why would I want to raise my arms?"

"Nobody gets in to see Comrade Stalin unless I pat them down for weapons."

"You're not serious, Vlasik. Since when am I suspected of wanting to assassinate Stalin?"

"I was born serious and become more so as I grow older. Either raise your arms or get out."

Mortified, Bukharin slowly lifted his arms over his head. And I just as slowly frisked him, starting at the armpits and working my way down his trousers to the ankles, then back up the inside of his legs to the crotch. I spared him nothing. When I'd finished, he barged through the door into the *khozyain's* office. I followed him inside and took up a watchful position with my back against the door, my arms folded across my chest.

"Koba, I most strongly protest against this indignity," Bukharin burst out.

Comrade Stalin, sitting behind his desk, pushed aside the pile of state papers wrapped in newspaper. "What indignity are you talking about?"

"Your bodyguard insisted on searching me like a common criminal before he would let me into your office," he sputtered.

I'd been around the *khozyain* long enough to see he had all to do to keep from smiling. "Compose yourself, Bukharchik," he said, the tips of his mustache dancing on his cheeks, his eyes glinting with mirth. "It has nothing to do with you personally. Yagoda has decided that nobody can be permitted into my presence without first being searched for firearms. I was against the measure, but Yagoda insists it is a necessary precaution, given the current situation."

"What situation?" Bukharin demanded.

"Comrades thought to be close to me are known to be openly echoing Trotsky's critique of collectivization, which must be seen as an attack on Stalin's leadership."

"Since when has it become a crime to criticize one policy or another?" Bukharin, uninvited, sank into the upholstered chair under the arched reading lamp. A photograph of Comrade Stalin in the very same chair, a book open on his lap, a pipe in one of his fists, had been published several months earlier in a popular weekly magazine; I know this detail because one of my concubines had cut it out and taped it to her vanity mirror. "In the days after the Revolution," Bukharin was saying, "everyone was free to criticize Lenin in private. The only taboo involved raising the matter in public—of challenging the collective infallibility of the Party— once a policy had been decided."

"I have absolutely nothing against criticism made in private," Comrade Stalin said, "as long as it is made to my face and not behind my back." He lit a Kazbek Papirosi on the end of the one between his lips. "Why is it every time I see you we get into an argument?"

"I wasn't aware that this was the case."

The *khozyain* shrugged. "You surely didn't drop by to compare Lenin's style of leadership with mine. What brings you to my wing of the Kremlin on this rain-soaked day, Bukharchik?"

Bukharin pulled a silk handkerchief from a jacket pocket and mopped his brow. "I want to talk to you about the arrest of the poet Mandelstam."

"In the matter of Mandelstam, I, of course, had nothing to do with his arrest. Yagoda, who signed the warrant, informed me about it after the fact. He has apparently been charged with anti-Soviet propaganda and counterrevolutionary activities under Article 58 of the Penal Code."

Bukharin leaned forward in the chair. "Mandelstam is a first-class poet, Koba, a credit to Soviet culture, but for some time now he has not been quite . . . normal."

"I understand he has confessed to the charges against him," the *khozyain* told his uninvited guest.

"Pasternak got in touch with me about Mandelstam. He is extremely distressed about this. He and Mandelstam are personal friends."

Dropping Pasternak's name into the conversation caught Stalin off guard. He scraped the chair back from the desk and, removing the cigarette from his mouth, brought it up to his eyes and studied the thin plume of smoke drifting toward the ceiling. I was aware my boss had a certain esteem for Pasternak—it dated back to his wife's suicide and the perfunctory letters of condolence that flooded the press at the time. I happened to have brought around the newspapers the morning the news of Nadezhda's death (attributed, if memory serves, to peritonitis) was published. I found the *khozyain* in a foul mood, the rheumatic throbbing in his deformed arm having kept him up most of the night. Flipping open the newspapers, he read aloud the trite letters of condolence, his voice dripping with scorn. *Accept our grief at the death of N. S. Alliluyeva . . . a bright candle tragically extinguished . . . a comrade who will be sorely missed.* That sort of thing. And then he stumbled across a short letter signed by Pasternak, who had apparently refused to add his name to the banal communication from the Union of Writers, preferring to publish a note of his own. The *khozyain* snipped Pasternak's letter out of the newspaper and kept it on his blotter for months. As far as I know it may still be there. I can confirm that Pasternak's letter, which read like a telegram and reeked of sincerity, was the single expression of condolence that brought any comfort to the shattered Stalin. As he took to reading it aloud in my presence every morning for weeks, I pretty much remember what Pasternak said: *The day before her death was announced, I thought deeply and intensively about Stalin; as a poet— for the first time. Next morning I read the news. I was shaken, as though I had been there, living by his side, and had seen it. Boris Pasternak.*

The *khozyain* resumed smoking, sucking on the cigarette in short nervous puffs. "What does Pasternak say exactly?" he asked Bukharin.

"He was stunned to learn of Mandelstam's arrest. He asked me to tell you that in a quarrel between a poet and a political leader, the poet, whether he emerges alive or dead, always comes out on top. History, in Pasternak's scheme of things, is on the side of the poet."

"Fuck the cloud dweller," the *khozyain* sneered, using the nickname he had bestowed on Pasternak. "You can count on these rhymesters to stick together, it doesn't matter where the fault lies." All the same I could tell from his tone that the boss was shaken.

Bukharin realized that Pasternak's intervention had impressed Stalin. He drove the nail home. "He says that Mandelstam isn't in his right mind. Years of humiliation, of not being published, of begging or borrowing money to make ends meet, have pushed him into madness. He is not rational, not responsible for his actions—"

The *khozyain* interrupted Bukharin. "Would you be interested in reading the particular poem, written out in his own hand, that caused him to be charged with anti-Soviet propaganda?"

Bukharin could only nod. Comrade Stalin pulled a folded paper from the inside pocket of his tunic and slid it across the desk. Bukharin reached to retrieve it and, unfolding the paper, started reading as the *khozyain*, smiling in grim satisfaction, spit out phrases from memory. *Kremlin mountaineer . . . murderer and peasant-slayer . . . fingers fat as grubs . . . words final as lead weights . . . cockroach whiskers.*

I had heard from Yagoda that Mandelstam had been arrested

for an outrageous poem, but up to that moment I had no idea what was in it. The contents must have come as a bombshell to Bukharin, too. The color literally drained from his features, leaving him as pale as a peeled pear. When he looked up, he seemed to be in a state of shock. "I had no idea ... nobody told me ... I assumed he would be beating about the bush. They suggested it was no more outrageous than what Mandelstam usually wrote." Bukharin collected himself. "Still, Koba, this poem only proves Pasternak's point. No sane person could have written these lines. They stand as proof of his madness."

"Why?"

"Why?"

"Yes, why are these lines proof of madness?"

From my place at the back of the room, I could almost see the wheels turning in Bukharin's head. He understood it wasn't only Mandelstam's life that was in jeopardy, but Bukharin's. "The lines are proof of madness because they are inaccurate, Koba. He doesn't make a rational argument that one can take issue with. He has resorted to slander of the worst kind. This is evidence of irrationality, and the irrationality must be seen as a symptom of madness."

"You made a big mistake interfering in this affair," the *khozyain* said coldly. "I won't forget it."

Bukharin, it must be conceded, had balls. "There were times when you thanked me for interfering," he snapped. "I still have the revolver you gave me with the inscription *To the Leader of the Proletarian Revolution N. Bukharin from J. Stalin.*"

My boss replied angrily. "If you want to talk about your past merits, no one can take them away from you. But Trotsky had them, too. Speaking between ourselves, few had as many merits before the Revolution as Trotsky." The *khozyain* aimed his index finger at Bukharin. "I will take it amiss if you repeat what I said." He waved the back of his good hand to indicate the interview was over. I reached for the knob and pulled open the door. Bukharin rose to his feet. "You're not the revolutionist I knew when we joined Lenin in the struggle to change the world, Koba," he said. "You used to be grateful for the support of your Bolshevik comrades."

"Gratitude is a dog's disease," Stalin shot back.

Bukharin regarded Stalin for a moment as if he intended to have the last word. Then, shaking his head in disgust, he hurried past me.

When Bukharin was gone, the *khozyain* gestured for the door to be shut. "It's not every day you see someone sign his own death warrant," he noted. "About Mandelstam: The shitty thing is that Pasternak is probably right. History is a bitch, and the bitch is on the side of the fucking poets." He looked up. "Get hold of Yagoda, Vlasik. Tell him not to put Mandelstam on the overnight list again. We'll pin a minus twelve on him—keep him away from the twelve major cities for a few years. That'll give him time to work through his madness. When he comes to his senses, we'll kill him for his sanity."

At which point the *khozyain*—I'll say what happened and leave you to figure out what it means—the *khozyain* dragged the cigarette from his lips and ground it out on the back of his hand. It's something the boss must have picked up during his years in Siberia. Real criminals doing time for murder did this to show the political prisoners how tough they were. Looking at the burn mark, my boss nodded, as if the gesture brought back memories. Then he uttered something that confused me when he said it and makes even less sense to me now. What he said was: "Nobody's innocent, Vlasik. Not Mandelstam, not Pasternak, not that harlot Akhmatova, not Bukharin, not even you. Nobody."

THIRTEEN

Boris Pasternak
Thursday, the 23rd of May 1934

Few things disheartened me more than a row with Akhmatova, probably because she turned out to be right more often than not, which is something I would grasp only after she'd hung down the phone. To add to my general sense of aggravation, I shared my father's old apartment with six other families whose children produced such a racket in the communal hallway you could barely make out what your interlocutor was saying. So picture it: There I was, standing in the telephone niche in the corridor, barefooted after having rushed from the communal toilet to answer a call, my suspenders plunging to my shins, the telephone pressed to my ear, children scampering back and forth kicking a ball made of old rags tied with string, and me shouting into the mouthpiece begging Anna to repeat what she had just said. But of course she had raced on to make another point that may or may not have had anything to do with her previous point. Mandelstam's arrest had put us all on edge and Anna was reproaching herself, and me, and every last member of the Union of Writers, for not fulfilling our duty as poets, in sharp contrast to Osip Emilievich, who was rotting in prison for withstanding pressure that the rest of us bowed to. *Define what you* *mean by the duty of a poet?* I hollered. *Truth telling,* she shouted back. *You can't do an awful lot of truth telling from the grave,* I retorted, but she probably never heard me.

Akhmatova was engaged in truth telling, of course. What I had valued above all in the Revolution, back when I'd valued the Revolution, was its moral side—I'd actually entertained the idea that life would take a turn for the better, that art would be free to cut to the bone, that artists could agree to disagree and still honor one another. (I remember Mayakovsky once flinging a long arm over my shoulder after a bitter argument and saying, *We really are different, Boris— you love lightning in the sky, I love it in an electric iron.*) Nowadays it was no longer possible to harbor the delusion that tomorrow would be better than today, or that today was an improvement over yesterday. And this insight changed my life as an artist. For as far back as I can remember I had devoted myself to poetry, which is to say to the art closest to sign language, code writing and other signaling systems. Now I was drifting toward the view that life had grown too complicated for lyric poetry to express the immensity of our experience; that what we had lived through was best captured in prose. I dreamt of writing a novel that would seal my oeuvre, like a lid on a box. I dreamt of writing a novel that would conquer my incoherence as a poet and show how the Russian Revolution had swept away everything established, everything settled, everything to do with home and order. But I'm wandering from the subject: Akhmatova beside herself with anxiety over the fate of our dear friend Mandelstam, Pasternak trying to defend himself against attacks that were never launched, both of us overwhelmed with guilt because Osip was inside the Lubyanka and we were outside.

Some hours passed. I lay stretched out on the daybed in the half of my father's old painting studio that had been partitioned off and allotted to me, lighting up my fifth cigarette of the day, still hoping to limit myself to six before midnight, when one of my neighbors called out that I had another phone call. I assumed it was Akhmatova ringing back to apologize for things that neither of us could remember her saying. The children, thanks to God, were playing up at the other end of the corridor when I picked up the telephone.

"Pasternak?"

"Speaking."

"Alexander Poskrebyshev on the line. Do you have paper and pencil?"

"One second." I tugged open the drawer and found the message pad and a pencil. For some reason I pulled up my suspenders, snapping them on to my shoulders. "Ready," I said into the telephone.

"I am going to give you a private Kremlin telephone number. Dial it in three minutes." He read out the number and had me read it back to be sure I'd noted it correctly. Without another word, he hung up.

My heart was racing. Why would Stalin's *chef de cabinet* be calling me? And who would I find at the other end of the line when I dialed the Kremlin number? I hauled my pocket watch from my trousers and stared at the second hand, convinced that it had slowed to a snail's crawl; that at its present speed a day would last forty-eight hours, which would make limiting one's self to six cigarettes more difficult. When I thought three minutes had gone by, I dialed the number. I was so tense I got it wrong the first time and had to dial again. Someone answered immediately.

"Do you recognize my voice, Pasternak?"

"No."

The man on the other end of the line laughed quietly. "Stalin here. I want to talk to you about Mandelstam. I want you to know that I didn't authorize his arrest."

The children were kicking the ball back down the corridor and yelling as they ran after it. "I can't hear very well—there are kids playing in the corridor. Can you say that again?"

Stalin raised his voice. "I didn't authorize Mandelstam's arrest. When I learned about it, I found it disgraceful. I am calling to let you know that Mandelstam's case is being reviewed at the highest level. I have a feeling everything will turn out all right for him."

"The fact of your taking a personal interest in the matter will reassure a great many artists and writers," I shouted.

The children had passed. I clearly heard Stalin say, "But he is a genius, isn't he?"

"That's not the point," I said.

"What is the point?" he demanded.

My brain flooded with possibilities. Perhaps Osip was wrong after all, perhaps I was right. Perhaps Stalin *was* living in a bubble, unaware of what the Chekists were doing in the real world outside the Kremlin. If only someone could let him know about the famine, the arrests, the executions, the deportations.

"Josef Vissarionovich, I absolutely must talk to you."

"You are talking to me."

"I mean face-to-face. I mean man-to-man."

He hesitated. "About what do you want to talk?"

I stupidly said the first thing that came into my head. "About life, about death."

I pressed the receiver to my ear as hard as I could so as not to miss his reply. I thought I could hear Stalin breathing. And then the line went dead. I kept listening to be sure there was no mistake, all the time bitterly berating myself for not having found the right words; for having passed up the opportunity of a lifetime with my clumsiness. I cut the connection with a finger, then lifted the phone to my ear and waited for a dial tone. When I heard one I dialed the Kremlin number again. It rang sixteen times before someone answered. "Josef Vissarionovich," I shouted, "I beg you to give me a moment to explain—"

"This is Poskrebyshev."

"Can you put me through to Stalin, please?"

"Impossible. He is no longer in Moscow. Don't dial this number again. It was activated for one call and will no longer exist after I hang up. Do you understand, Pasternak?"

"I do not understand—" I heard the line go dead again.

FOURTEEN

Fikrit Shotman
Saturday, the 25th of May 1934

Ever since Vienna, Austria where, as I may have mentioned, I won the silver weight-lifting medal, I've been accustomed to flashbulbs exploding in my face. To tell the truth, I don't really mind them. It makes me feel important. So while my codefendants at the trial covered their eyes with their arms as we entered the October Hall, upstairs in the House of Unions, I smiled and waved to let everyone know that although I was pleading guilty, I was innocent in the sense I didn't know what I was guilty of until Christophorovich educated me. With its high windows and gold-colored curtains and crystal chandeliers, this was as fancy a room as I ever set foot in, but I decided not to let on that I felt out of my depth. When I spotted the three judges, decked out in black robes and sitting in high-backed thrones on the raised platform, I raised high my right hand and saluted them in the style of Azerbaidzhan peasants. Judging from their grins, they weren't indifferent to my mountain ways. The courtroom was overflowing with spectators—there were more than turned up on any given day to watch the strongman perform at the circus. I tried to count them but I gave up when I reached a hundred (there were easily three times that), which is as high as I count without help from Agrippina who, I was thrilled to see, was sitting in the very first row, protected by men in black suits on either side of her. I waved to her and she smiled back one of the forced smiles she produced when she was really sad. (She had this crazy idea that smiling could suck the sadness out of your heart, the way the juice of an onion could suck a wart out of the flat of your foot.) I recognized eight or ten faces in the courtroom. The woman who had copied down my confession was there, along with several lady clerks I'd run into when they took me to the Lubyanka clothing store to fit me out with a suit for the trial. Christophorovich was there, smiling and nodding encouragement. I even spotted the wrestler Islam Issa against a wall near the recessed gallery with tinted windows in the back where the orchestra used to play for the aristocrats before our Revolution fired the aristocrats. Christophorovich'd confided to me that Comrade Stalin himself sometimes watched trials from behind the tinted windows. Comrade interrogator knew this because the cleaning lady reported emptying ashtrays filled with his favorite cigarette, Kazbek Papirosi. Sitting at the end of Agrippina's row were the foreign journalists. You could tell they were foreign by the lapels on their suits and by the fact that they sat with their legs crossed, which is something no self-respecting Soviet journalist would do in the formal situation of a trial. Procurator General A. Vishinsky, who (as every schoolchild knew) once shared the hampers of food supplied by his rich parents with Comrade Stalin when the two were in jail together, stood leaning on the half-circle bar across from me, studying sheets of paper in a file folder.

As for my codefendants, we were never actually introduced. We were thrown together in the basement holding cell an hour or so before the trial got under way. I never knew their names until Procurator General Vishinsky called them out at the trial.

"Knud Trifimovich Ignatiev." The little man on my right, wearing a baggy suit with a soiled shirt buttoned up to his neck, with a mustache trimmed exactly like Comrade Vishinsky's, stood up. "That's me, Your Honor," he said.

Comrade Vishinsky read out the charges against the accused Ignatiev—wrecking, treason, counterrevolutionary activities in violation of Penal Code Article 58. "How is it you plead?"

"Guilty."

"Kindly tell the court," Comrade Vishinsky said, peering at the accused through his horned-rimmed spectacles, his voice oozing contempt, "how a Russian national like yourself winds up with a name like Knud."

"My mother was Danish, my father Russian. I was called Knud after my maternal grandfather."

Comrade Vishinsky turned to address Their Honors the judges. "As you will see, the accused Ignatiev's connection with Denmark is pertinent to the accusations against him." He turned back to the accused, who was clutching the bar to steady himself. "In your capacity as librarian in chief for the greater Moscow district, how many libraries did you direct?"

"In addition to the great Lenin Library and the four university libraries, I was in overall charge of forty-seven neighborhood libraries."

"In your role as director of all these libraries, am I correct in stating that you were responsible for the destruction of books that were considered to be subversive?"

"That is correct, comrade procurator general."

"And how were you alerted to the fact that the responsible authorities considered certain books to be subversive and thus must be destroyed?"

"At weekly intervals, I received a typewritten list from the office of the commissar for cultural affairs. On two occasions I received a note from Comrade Stalin himself inquiring why such and such a book was still available to the general public."

"Then what happened?"

"Along with a female assistant, I made the rounds of the

libraries in the small van allocated to my department and collected the offending volumes. I drove to one of the waste disposal plants on the outskirts of Moscow and personally supervised the destruction of the offending volumes."

"They were burned in the incinerators, is that correct?"

"That is correct, comrade procurator general."

"On the twelfth of March of this year, you were apprehended while supervising the destruction of volumes at the"—the procurator general bent his head to read from the charge sheet in the folder—"at the Yaroslav District waste station on the Yaroslav Highway. Will you tell the court why?"

"Included in the cartons of books earmarked for destruction were seventeen copies of Lenin's collected works and eight copies of Stalin's collected works."

Comrade Vishinsky came around the procurator general's bar and approached the box of the accused. "Would you be so kind as to tell the court, Knud Trifimovich Ignatiev, how you came to be destroying the widely admired texts of Comrade Lenin and Comrade Stalin."

"I am a charter member of the backup Trotskyist Paris-based anti-Bolshevik Center. I was following specific orders issued to me by Trotsky's son, Sedov, during a meeting in Copenhagen, Denmark, where I had gone, with Party permission, to attend the funeral of my mother's father, the Knud after whom I am named."

Comrade Vishinsky glanced again at the charge sheet. "This meeting took place on the fourteenth of February 1934, at three-thirty in the afternoon, at the Hotel Bristol. Is that correct?"

"No."

People in the courtroom gasped. Comrade Vishinsky's mouth fell open. The three judges on the raised platform conferred in undertones. Comrade procurator general checked the charge sheet. "You have admitted, under interrogation, that you met Trotsky's son, Sedov, in the Bristol Hotel. Are you retracting your confession, accused Ignatiev?"

"Your Honors, I described my meeting with Sedov in a Copenhagen hotel. I never mentioned the Bristol. That must have been added by the stenographer or the interrogator. I couldn't have met Sedov in the Bristol on the fourteenth of February 1934 because the hotel, which I knew well, was demolished in 1917."

Comrade Vishinsky turned toward Their Honors on the raised platform. "Needless to say, it doesn't matter in *which* hotel the meeting was held. The important point, which has been established beyond a shadow of a doubt, is that the accused Ignatiev received his wrecking orders directly from Trotsky's son, Sedov, in a Copenhagen hotel." He turned back toward the accused. "Why did Sedov want you to destroy the texts signed by Lenin and Stalin?"

"I asked him that very question," Ignatiev testified in a dull voice. "He said that cleansing the libraries of Lenin and Stalin was the first phase of the intricately planned counterrevolution that would be launched by Trotsky. I happened to have been apprehended before the library wrecking program could swing into full gear. Stalin, along with you, comrade procurator general, and other members of the Soviet leadership, were to be eliminated, after which we Trotskyists would restore capitalism in Russia."

There were angry cries from the crowd of *Shame* and *Death is too good for the traitor*. Comrade Vishinsky's tone turned mild. "Do you, accused Ignatiev, affirm that your confession is voluntary, that you were not coerced in any manner or form by the interrogators assigned to your case?"

"I do."

"Do you affirm the accuracy of your voluntary confession?"

"With the exception of the Hotel Bristol, I do."

"One more thing," Comrade Vishinsky said. "Be so kind as to tell the court how the members of the backup Trotskyist Paris-based anti-Bolshevik Center were supposed to recognize each other."

"The recognition sign was the Eiffel Tower—it might be an

Eiffel Tower sticker on a valise or a briefcase, it might be an Eiffel Tower pin in the buttonhole of a lapel, it might be an actual miniature of the Eiffel Tower set casually on a table or sideboard in someone's office or apartment."

Comrade Vishinsky returned to his bar and removed another charge sheet from the folder. "Galina Yegorova," he called.

The woman sitting between Ignatiev and me got slowly to her feet. I guessed she must have been wearing the dress she had on at the time of her arrest. I say this because, like Ignatiev's suit, it was very rumpled, the hem of the long skirt soiled as if it had been sweeping the ground for weeks. In addition the dress had a very un-Soviet low-cut bodice that was an insult to Bolshevik modesty. If Agrippina had turned up in an outfit like that, much as I love her she would have felt the back of my hand.

"The accused Yegorova, wife of the Red Army commander until recently in charge of a military district in Central Asia, is charged with anti-Soviet slander, treason and counterrevolutionary activities in violation of Penal Code Article 58. How is it you plead?"

When I heard the procurator general say her name, it hit me that this was the lady who was the talk of the Lubyanka. Prison scuttlebutt talked about a female inmate who was not only a well-known motion picture actress but a personal friend of Comrade Stalin's. (I couldn't help but wonder if he was sitting behind the tinted windows at the back of the courtroom watching her. I couldn't help but think that if he was watching her, he would recognize me from the time he shook my hand in the Kremlin.) Something Agrippina once said when the director of our circus was arrested for skimming off ticket receipts came to mind: *How the mighty have fallen.* Clearly the same was true for the poor lady leaning her weight on the bar next to me to keep from sinking to her knees. She looked to be about forty going on sixty, if you catch my meaning. The skin on her face was white like a clown's, her eyes were scared, her breasts were sagging so badly into her bodice you wanted to turn your head away from embarrassment. She squinted as if she was having trouble focusing on the procurator general and Their Honors the judges. I heard her say, in a hoarse voice, "Guilty."

One of the judges called out, "You will have to speak up."

"I plead guilty to the charges against me," the lady said in a louder voice.

Again Comrade Vishinsky came out from behind the procurator's bar and approached the accused. "Galina Yegorova, on or about sixteen March of this year, at a cocktail party celebrating the completion of your latest motion picture, you were heard to say"— he bent his head to the paper in his hands—"*With all these terrorists loose in Moscow trying to kill Stalin, it is amazing he is still alive.* Were those your words?"

"They were taken out of context," she muttered.

"This is your last warning," the judge said. "Speak up or we will hold you in contempt of this court."

"The words were taken out of context, Your Honor. It was not my intention to cast doubt on the stories in *Pravda* concerning the terrorists known to be operating in Moscow, or the trials of terrorists who have admitted trying to assassinate members of the leadership. I was only suggesting that with all these terrorists active in the city, it was *amazing*, as in *a miracle*, that, thanks to the watchfulness of our Chekists, they had not succeeded in assassinating our beloved Josef Vissarionovich."

On the raised platform, the three judges put their heads together. The lead judge addressed the witness. "Accused Yegorova, it cannot help your case that you refer to our esteemed leader by his name and patronymic. Outside his intimate circle of colleagues and friends, he is known as Comrade Stalin."

Yegorova lowered her eyes. "I will not make the same mistake a second time, Your Honor."

Comrade Vishinsky said, "If it pleases the court, I will offer in evidence the signed confession of Yegorova's husband, who was arrested on the charge of high treason in January and has been cooperating with the interrogator since then." Comrade Vishinsky placed a folder on the table in front of the judges.

"So noted," the lead judge remarked and he began to leaf through the folder, passing pages to the other judges as he finished skimming them.

"Red Army Commander Yegorov has confessed to being an agent of the backup Trotskyist Paris-based anti-Bolshevik Center," Comrade Vishinsky continued. "He has admitted organizing a counterrevolutionary uprising in the Central Asian military district of which he was the commander. He has also implicated his wife, the accused Galina Yegorova, in the plot to overthrow the existing order and restore capitalism under the leadership of the archtraitor Leon Trotsky." Comrade procurator general absently polished the lenses of his eyeglasses with the tip of his tie. "Be so kind as to tell the court what your precise role was in this counterrevolutionary conspiracy."

"Why don't you just read it out from my husband's confession? Better still, why don't you put my husband on the witness stand and let him describe my role himself?"

There was a low growl from the audience in response to this arrogant outburst from the witness. Comrade Vishinsky scowled. "Commander Yegorov was so humiliated when his role in the conspiracy came to light that he attempted to kill himself by hitting his head against the stone wall of his cell. He is currently being treated for a severe concussion in the Lubyanka clinic."

"My husband's confession was extracted under torture—"

Now there was a roar of real outrage from the audience. "Slander," a woman shrieked.

"Defamation of our Chekists, who are the guardians of the Revolution," another woman shouted.

The lead judge slammed his gavel down on the table. "Silence!" he roared. He addressed the accused Yegorova. "Is it your claim that your husband's confession, which we have before our eyes—dated, bearing the interrogator's official seal, signed by him and by two witnesses, signed also by the stenographer—was extracted under duress?"

"I am absolutely certain that Commander Yegorov is a loyal Stalinist and was never involved in any counterrevolutionary schemes," Yegorova declared.

Comrade Vishinsky ran a finger between his starched collar and his neck. "You have admitted, under interrogation, that you served as a messenger for the backup Trotskyist Paris-based anti-Bolshevik Center. You have admitted that you were contacted by Trotsky's son, Sedov, in a Berlin hotel when you attended the Berlin film festival in October of last year. Is the court to understand that you are withdrawing your confession?"

"I maintain my confession. I met Sedov in the Berlin hotel, the name of which slips my mind. He gave me a pack of German filter-tip cigarettes, the brand name of which slips my mind. Several of the cigarettes, so I was told, contained instructions for counterrevolutionary wrecking activities printed on the inside of the cigarette paper. Acting on Sedov's instructions, I crossed the frontier back into the Soviet Union carrying the pack of cigarettes in full view in my leather purse. As I left the hotel room after my meeting with Sedov, he moistened the back of an Eiffel Tower sticker with his tongue and pasted it onto my purse as a recognition sign. He instructed me to deliver the cigarettes to the person in the central librarian's office who had a similar sticker visible on his briefcase. This person, who was to pass on the wrecking instructions to other members of the backup Paris-based Trotskyist anti-Bolshevik Center, turned out to be the accused Ignatiev. At no time did I deliver the cigarettes and the instructions they contained to my husband or any of his officers or friends in the Central Asian military district. This I most emphatically deny."

Comrade Vishinsky tossed his head. "What you are telling the court, accused Yegorova, contradicts your signed confession. You don't deny that that is your signature on the notarized confession, which I have already placed in evidence before this court."

"I was promised my life would be spared if I implicated my husband. In a moment of weakness I signed the confession that was put in front of me. The truth is that my husband is completely innocent. As God is my witness, he was unaware of my counterrevolutionary activities. Isn't it enough that I admit my guilt? Why do you need to destroy the both of us?"

The lead judge said, "Your life depends on your telling the truth in this matter of the backup Trotskyist Paris-based anti-Bolshevik Center."

The accused Yegorova's strength gave out before my eyes and she sank to her knees, her chin resting on the low bar. The soldier posted behind her gripped her under the armpits and started to haul her to her feet. In the process a strap of her dress slipped off one shoulder, exposing a breast for everyone to see. I reached over before the soldier behind me could interfere (he was half my size and would have been hard put to restrain me if I wasn't willing to be restrained) and pulled the strap back up on her shoulder.

Comrade Vishinsky, an experienced procurator, was unfazed by the turn of events. "Let the court note that in the face of two signed confessions, her own and that of her husband, the accused Yegorova has perjured herself to protect her husband; has in fact put loyalty to her traitor husband ahead of loyalty to the Soviet state and the Revolution. The evidence, Your Honors, is overwhelming. The counterrevolutionary activities of the accused Ignatiev and the accused Red Army commander Yegorov, who will be tried in a separate proceeding when he has recovered from his self-inflicted head wounds, bear out the conspiracy initiated by Trotsky's son, Sedov, and transmitted to the Moscow section of the backup Trotskyist Paris-based anti-Bolshevik Center by the accused Yegorova."

Comrade Vishinsky made his way back to the procurator general's bar and opened a new folder, and I knew my turn had come at long last. To my delight, he called out my name.

"Fikrit Trofimovich Shotman."

I saw Agrippina cover her eyes with her hands. I saw the men sitting on either side of her grip her wrists and pull her hands away from her face. I gave her an encouraging smile. "Present," I cried in a loud and firm voice, "and eager to admit my guilt as I have come to understand it." And before comrade procurator general could get his tongue around a question, I commenced my confession. I described in great detail how I had been recruited in Vienna, Austria in 1932 when I was representing the Soviet Union in the weight-lifting competition at the All-European games; how I'd been given a cash payment in United States dollars to finance my wrecking activities; how I'd communicated with my handler, an American secret agent masquerading as a weightlifter, using a secret code buried in the dedication inside the cover of an American fitness magazine; how, carried away by my hatred for the new order, I had even disfigured Stalin's face tattooed on my upper arm. To dramatize the point, I flung off the jacket of my new suit, unbuttoned my shirt and bared my arm, angling my left biceps toward the crowd so they could all see the rope burn across the faded tattoo. In the front row, Agrippina turned her head away and I could make out enormous tears flowing down her beautiful cheeks, but I knew I was doing the right thing. I had Comrade Interrogator Christophorovich's word for it. Comrade Vishinsky tried to interrupt as I was buttoning my shirt but I interrupted his interruption. "There's more," I declared, climbing back into my jacket, and I told about the worthless Tsarist loan coupons I kept in my trunk against the day when Trotsky's counterrevolution, in which I was a foot soldier, drove the Bolsheviks from power and restored capitalism in Soviet Russia, at which point my Tsarist coupons could be redeemed at their face value. Comrade procurator general took advantage of me having to come up for air to inquire about the significance of the Eiffel Tower sticker on my steamer trunk. "I'm glad you asked—I almost forgot about the Eiffel Tower. Let me say, for those of you not familiar with it, that the Eiffel Tower located in Paris, France doesn't hold a candle to the towers you can find in our own Soviet Union. True, they may not be as big as the one in Paris, France but every woman knows it's not size that counts." Some of the ladies in the courtroom started giggling, but shut up when one of the judges tapped his wooden gavel on the table. The judge nodded at me to continue, and I did. "When I was recruited into the backup Trotskyist Paris-based anti-Bolshevik Center during the All-Europe games in Vienna, Austria, I was given the Eiffel Tower sticker and ordered to paste it on my steamer trunk as a recognition signal so that other conspirators in the backup Trotskyist Paris-based anti-Bolshevik Center could identify me as a member of this gang."

The lead judge spoke up from his high-backed throne on the raised platform. "Let me say it is to the credit of the accused Shotman that he has chosen to make a clean breast of his crimes. Anyone with a grain of sense can see that he is not attempting to hide, or mitigate, his guilt, and this will certainly be taken into consideration when it comes time to pass sentence."

I didn't understand what the judge meant by *mitigate*, but I nodded my thanks to him from my place in the box of the accused.

The lady judge sitting to the right of the lead judge raised a finger. "I would like to ask the accused Shotman precisely what his role was in the backup Trotskyist Paris-based anti-Bolshevik Center."

"My role?"

"What were you supposed to do to further the counterrevolution?" the lady judge explained.

I looked over at Christophorovich for a sign of what I might answer—he had never raised this matter with me when I rehearsed my confession—but there was no help to be had from him. I glanced at Agrippina, but she avoided my eye. I turned to the lady judge. "Why, my role was to wreck. I signed on as a wrecker."

"Wreck what?" the lady judge persisted.

I shrugged. "Until my knee went bad, I was a champion weight lifter. Until my arrest, I was a circus strongman. Look at me, Your Honors. Look at my hands. Look at my shoulders. I can wreck whatever I am told needs wrecking."

Comrade Vishinsky came to my rescue. "It is clear from his confession that the accused Shotman was ready to follow wrecking instructions sent to him by the backup Trotskyist Paris-based anti-Bolshevik Center. There may have been specific wrecking instructions from Sedov printed inside one of the cigarettes that the accused Yegorova delivered to the accused Ignatiev, but were never forwarded due to the timely arrest of these two conspirators. The important element to bear in mind is that the accused Shotman was a member of the conspiracy and ready to carry out Sedov's wrecking orders when they reached him."

The lead judge looked over at me. "Does the accused Shotman wish to add anything to his testimony?"

It was here that I came up with the words Christophorovich had drummed into my head. "No matter what my punishment will be, Your Honors, I in advance consider it just." I looked intently at the tinted windows at the back of the courtroom. "Let us all go forward behind Comrade Stalin."

Several in the courtroom—Christophorovich, Islam Issa, the lady who had taken down my confession, some of the lady clerks—began clapping their hands. Others joined them until the entire room was filled with applause. Flashbulbs went off in my face. I felt Agrippina's eyes on me and comprehended that, for once, she would not be ashamed of her Fikrit. I turned to the audience and, my knuckles scraping the floor of the prisoner's box, bowed from the waist.

The rest of the trial passed in a haze of speeches from defense lawyers (until that moment I didn't know we had been assigned defense lawyers) demanding the ultimate penalty for my two codefendants. "These mad dogs of capitalism tried to tear limb from limb the best of our Soviet land. I insist that we do with them what we do with mad dogs, which is to say, we shoot them." The lady lawyer assigned to defend me rose and said, "Fikrit Shotman has demonstrated genuine remorse and cooperated fully with the authorities. For him I ask the judges to impose a lenient sentence of four years hard labor in the Far East."

There were cries from the crowd of "The mad dogs must be shot" and "Leniency for Shotman" as the three judges left the courtroom to deliberate. They filed back twenty minutes later. The lead judge read out the verdicts. The accused Ignatiev and Yegorova was condemned to be shot, sentence to be carried out immediately. Me, I pulled four years. In the courtroom, Agrippina collapsed into the arms of one of the men in dark suits. To my right, the accused Ignatiev blew a kiss to an old lady on crutches at the back of the courtroom before he turned to leave the box. The accused Yegorova sank to the floor in a dead faint. The two soldiers had trouble raising her. I shouldered them aside and lifted her as if she was a child's doll and carried her in my arms back to the holding cell in the basement and, carefully straightening her dress, set her gently out on a bench. The last I saw of her, looking over my shoulder as I headed back to my cell block, the guards were trying to revive her with smelling salts so they could take her to execution.

FIFTEEN

Nadezhda Yakovlevna
Tuesday, the 28th of May 1934

I did a great many things in the days after Mandelstam's arrest that recommended themselves to me as a way to make an hour or two pass without agonizing over Mandelstam's arrest. One day I scrubbed the kitchen pots and the single grill of the paraffin stove with steel wool until my fingers turned raw. Another time I pranced around the small living room crushing moths between my palms and keeping score with chalk marks on a piece of slate. I spent an entire weekend mending garments with wrong-colored threads. Working by candlelight one night, I made copies of the poems we'd hidden in my shoes and gave the duplicates to Mandelstam's brother Alexander for safekeeping. The night of Mandelstam's arrest they had searched through all of our books and then flung them back onto the shelves in disorder. On the day in question, I decided to restore them to something resembling the order they had been in, dusting each book as it came off the shelf, stacking my husband's in one pile and mine in another before returning them to the shelves. It is a law of nature that one never sorts books without pausing now and then to skim through the pages, wondering who underlined certain passages, and why, wondering who scribbled illegible notes in the margins with arrows pointing to other paragraphs. I reread sentences I'd underlined in an excellent Russian translation of Laclos's eighteenth-century French masterpiece *Les Liaisons Dangereuses*. I came across another book that I'd thought I'd loaned and lost, Zinovyeva-Annibal's *Thirty-three Monstrosities*, a novel from the turn of the century that, for the first time in modern Russian literature, openly described lesbian love. I don't recall how the book came into my possession, but I do recall when: I was sixteen at the time, with a terrible crush on a Russian girl I'd met in Paris while traveling with my parents. She had slipped me notes on perfumed paper saying how much she admired my pale eyes and my delicate skin. Curiously, I can't even remember the girl's name now, though this puppy love was as intense as any I'd experienced before Mandelstam mooched that first cigarette from me in the Junk Shop. Perhaps this girl had given me the *Thirty-three Monstrosities*. On the other hand it could well have been my mother, one of the first females in all of Russia to qualify as a physician—she had a bohemian disposition and could conceivably have left the book on my night table to impart to her Kiev-bound daughter a patina of sophistication.

I was leafing through *Thirty-three Monstrosities*, lingering over the pages where the corners had been turned down at one time or another, trying (in vain) to read them with the eyes of the sixteen-year-old daydreamer I once was, when I heard footsteps beating a hasty retreat in the corridor outside the flat. Going into the hallway, I couldn't help but spot the folded paper that had been slipped under the door. My heart started pounding in my rib cage when I picked it up. For a moment I was too frightened of what might be in it to unfold the paper and see. Pasternak had phoned several days before to say that he had learned—he absolutely refused to tell me how—that Stalin himself was taking a personal interest in Mandelstam's case. Pasternak interpreted the information as a positive development, but I saw the dark side of this moon: if Stalin was taking a personal interest in Mandelstam, God have mercy on Mandelstam. Curiosity got the better of me and I unfolded the paper, which turned out to be a printed summons, with my name inked in, to turn up at the Furkassovsky Street door of the Lubyanka at two that same afternoon.

The Lubyanka! Was I, then, being arrested? Or did this have to do with my husband—were they going to hand me a death certificate and his personal effects? I remember that my legs gave way under me and I sank onto the floor, kneeling before the rose red radiator as if it were a religious artifact and I were praying to it. Dear God in heaven, if he still has a muse and an erection, arrange things so the sun will simply fail to rise tomorrow morning. Amen. After a time I managed to collect my strength and my thoughts enough to make it to the communal telephone in the corridor and dial Bukharin's *Izvestiya* number. I reached his secretary, Korotkova. "Oh, dear," she said with a despondent sigh, "he has absolutely forbidden me to put through a call from you, Madam Mandelstam. He won't see you if you come by. He is furious with you—you apparently placed Nikolai Ivanovich in an awkward position vis-à-vis his friend in the Kremlin. I am afraid there is nothing I can do for you."

To say I was shaken would be an understatement. One of the Herzen House neighbors found me sitting on the broken chair next to the telephone, staring numbly at the wall. "Nadezhda, have you had bad news?" she asked.

I handed her the summons. She read it and said, "God help you, I cannot," and crushed it back into my fingers as if the paper were contaminated before beating a hasty retreat.

It occurred to me that I should call Akhmatova, my worldly wise friend who knew if you delivered packages to prisons you could discover where your husband was being held. I fell on Lev, Anna Andreyevna's son by her first husband, Gumilyov, who promised me he would have his mother ring me back the instant she returned from the gastronome. I sat there for I don't know how long before the telephone rang under my fingers. I snatched it from the cradle. It was, thank heaven, Akhmatova. I quickly read the summons to her over the phone. As usual, she considered the matter carefully before delivering her opinion. "I think we can rule out that they have summoned you to tell you he is dead," she said finally. "From what I hear, you only learn of the death of a prisoner when a package or a letter is returned with the word *Deceased* stamped on it. Very occasionally some kind soul writes in the cause of death, though the death of a prisoner, even the ones shot in the basements of the Lubyanka, is almost always attributed to heart failure. On rare occasions the authorities send a formal notice listing the date on which the prisoner is said to have died."

"If he *is* dead, what do they do with the body?"

"I have heard the prisoners who aren't cremated are buried in a common grave on the Butovo Shooting Range outside of Moscow, next to the dachas they built for Chekists. But be reassured, Nadezhda, it is extremely unlikely they would summon you to announce Mandelstam's death. I can't rule out you will be arrested. I understand they are arresting so many people these days they don't have enough Chekists to bring them in. The less important political prisoners are *summoned* to save Chekist manpower for the more important prisoners. On the other hand, it might be something entirely different—one can not abandon hope entirely that Pasternak or Bukharin somehow got word to Stalin and Osip is being given a prison sentence. The thing to watch for, if this is the case, is the notation *without the right of correspondence* after the prison term. *Without the right of correspondence* is the equivalent of a death sentence—it means they are cutting the prisoner off from civilization because they don't expect him to return. There is still another possibility—that Osip will be sent into exile, what they call the famous *minus twelve*. In which case they would need you to bring foodstuff for the journey, and clothing for the winter"—Anna corrected herself—"or winters, plural, ahead."

"I never thought I would pray to God for Mandelstam to be sent into exile," I said.

"It would be the least terrible resolution," she agreed. "I will add my voice to yours on the off chance there is an Almighty and he is listening."

"Will they permit me to accompany him into exile?"

"If it is exile, probably. More and more wives are going into exile with their husbands these days. It frees up flats, it gets nuisances like us out of eyeshot. What time are you supposed to turn up at Lubyanka?"

"Two."

"Dearest Nadezhda, I shall camp by the telephone," Akhmatova informed me. "If you don't call back by five, I shall inform Pasternak and the both of us will start bombarding the Writers' Union with telegrams demanding to know what happened to you."

Which is how I found myself standing before a nondescript door on Furkassovsky Street, looking for a bell to ring or a knocker to strike against the wood. Mandelstam would surely have burst into laughter if he could have seen me trying to figure out how to get *into* the Lubyanka. In the end I wound up rapping the joints of my fingers against the door. A young Chekist in the blue uniform of a frontier guard opened it the width of a fist so that I could see only one of his eyes peering at me.

"Well?"

I slipped my summons through the crack to him. He closed the door in my face. I stood there debating whether to knock again or wait. Women passing on the sidewalk, each carrying an *avoska* filled with oranges, glanced at me. I wondered if they were aware that this was a back door to the dreaded Lubyanka Prison. After a moment the door opened, this time wide enough for me to pass through. I heard it being slammed shut and locked with a bolt behind me. I had all to do to keep from sinking to my knees.

"Follow," the guard ordered.

"Where are you taking me?" I asked, but he had already hurried off and I had to run to catch up with him. We passed through another door into a courtyard, then up steps and through yet another door into an elegant entranceway filled with mirrors set into the walls and a tiled floor so polished one could see the hem of one's skirt in it. A wide staircase with a mahogany banister curled up from the entranceway. The guard led me past the staircase to a large mirrored elevator. He handed my summons to the elevator operator, an elderly gentleman wearing white gloves and a blue tunic with gold braid and brass buttons. I got in and through force of habit glanced at myself in the mirror—my complexion alone was enough to frighten off the devil who, we all assumed, lurked in the shadows inside the Lubyanka. I tucked stray hairs back under the beret that my parents had purchased for me in Paris when I was sixteen. It occurred to me that it would have been more prudent to wear a Russian cap than one with a French label sewn inside. The elevator rose under my feet. I counted the floors as they went by. One. Two. We glided to a stop at the third floor. The operator reached for the brass grill and with an effort dragged it back, then pushed open the heavy hall door and held it for me as if I were a guest at the Ritz. "Room twenty-three," he said, nodding in the direction of a door at the far end of the corridor. I started down the brightly lighted hallway, walking on a worn runner past an open freight elevator with padded walls, past fine wooden doors with brass numbers on them until I came to the one with twenty-three on it. And then, as if I were paying a civilized visit to a publisher who wanted to engage my services as a translator, I reached out and knocked.

What I am recounting does not originate in the lobe of the brain where memory resides. It comes directly from the mind's eye. I relive it as I describe it, or more precisely, I live it as if for the first time. When, on occasion, I recall these awful events, they have the odor of earth at a freshly dug grave.

Here is what my heart saw when the man I came to know as Interrogator Christophorovich pulled open the door and with a nod invited me into the room. I saw Josef Stalin peering at me from a huge photograph on the wall. I saw Christophorovich grinning inanely at me like a maître d'hôtel. I saw a man who resembled—no more than *resembled* —the poet Mandelstam standing next to an absurd stool whose front legs were shorter than its hind legs, clinging with both hands to the waistband of his disheveled trousers to keep them from falling to his ankles.

I stumbled across the room and crushed his body, trembling from head to foot with soundless sobs, into my trembling arms.

I should add here that the stench of urine emanated from his clothing.

"As you can see, Madam Mandelstam, your husband is alive and well," the interrogator said. Settling onto a chair behind a large table, he pushed aside a half-eaten dinner and motioned for Mandelstam to sit. My husband clung to my hand as he sank onto the stool. "Are they letting you go?" he asked in a voice that I didn't recognize as coming from anyone I knew.

"What do you mean, *letting me go?*"

"Have you forgotten? I visited you in your cell, Nadenka. You and Zinaida." He beckoned for me crouch next to him so that his mouth was near my ear. "When they arrested her, they arrested the epigram that I wrote out for her."

"My name," the maître d'hôtel announced from behind the table, "is Christophorovich. I have the honor of being your husband's interrogator. He is slightly disoriented, as you can see, due most certainly to the shock of seeing you." He turned to Mandelstam. "Your wife, along with your wife's friend the actress Zinaida Zaitseva-Antonova, were never taken into protective custody."

"You are lying, of course," Mandelstam said in a voice that sounded more like the one I remembered. "I saw them both in prison."

"He is telling the truth, Osya. You must have dreamed it. I have been in our flat in Herzen House these past two weeks."

Christophorovich cleared his throat. "You have been summoned," he informed me, "to hear Mandelstam's sentence for having violated Article 58, which covers the offenses of anti-Soviet propaganda and counterrevolutionary activities. Your husband's poem is a counterrevolutionary document without precedent." The interrogator extracted a sheet of paper from the bulging folder on the table. "Comrade Stalin has reviewed the case personally and instructed the Organs to isolate and preserve the prisoner. He is sentenced to three years of minus-twelve exile."

"What does that mean, minus-twelve?" Mandelstam asked.

"It means you are not permitted to reside in any of the Soviet Union's twelve major urban centers," Christophorovich said.

My husband's grip on my hand tightened and he began to shake uncontrollably. "I am not to be shot?"

"You won't be shot," I told him. "You will live to compose beautiful poems by the dozen."

"I am not to be shot?" he repeated, as if he hadn't heard my response.

"Rest assured, you will not be subjected to the highest measure of punishment," Christophorovich said. He looked directly at me. "Is it your desire to go into exile with your husband?"

"No," Mandelstam answered for me.

"Absolutely," I said, overruling him.

"Which will it be?" Christophorovich demanded.

"I most certainly will accompany my husband into exile."

"In that case, I will draw up the necessary papers and bring them to you for signature."

He came around the desk and stood over Mandelstam. "Considering the counterrevolutionary nature of your crime, the sentence represents an incredible act of clemency from the very highest level. Count your blessings." With that he left the room, closing the door behind him.

His lips quivering, Mandelstam started to speak. "Be careful what you say," I whispered. "They are surely listening." And I glanced at the walls in the classic gesture indicating microphones could have been functioning in them.

"Did you deny being arrested because he was in the room?"

"No. It's the truth. I have been home all this while."

"And Zinaida?"

"After days and days of phoning, I succeeded in getting her on the line. Her voice was strained. I suppose it was because she and her husband are divorcing. She assured me she had destroyed the copy of the epigram you wrote out for her."

He shook his head in confusion. "If her voice was strained, it's because they arrested her copy of the epigram and she was afraid to admit it. Christophorovich showed it to me. There was no mistaking it—it was the first version before Pasternak got me to change the second stanza. I recognized the handwriting as my own."

"I don't understand—"

"Nor do I understand. Believe me, I am not hallucinating. I visited you and Zinaida in prison, for God's sake."

"And I tell you, you imagined it. Dear God, what else did you imagine?"

Mandelstam mumbled something in Greek: *Ei kai egnokamen kata sarka Christon.* I recognized the phrase instantly, as we had often tried to decipher these mysterious words of Saint Paul's in 2 Corinthians. Paul is said never to have crossed paths with the Christ, yet he claims, *We have known Christ after the flesh.* I didn't understand what Mandelstam was getting at by quoting Paul. "Are you trying to tell me you saw Christ in the flesh in prison?" I asked.

He shook his head in annoyance, then looked over at the photograph of Josef Stalin on the wall behind the interrogator's table. "I saw *him.*"

I still didn't understand. "Stalin came to see you in prison?"

My thickheadedness was beginning to irritate my husband. "Not *in* prison. And he didn't come to *me,* I went to *him.* I saw him in the Kremlin, of course. In the flesh. He offered me a cigarette. We talked. He told me many things about himself, including"—he pressed his lips against my ear again—"including that he shot his wife after an argument. Oh, it wasn't entirely his fault—she produced the pistol, she pushed it into his hand, she dared him to prove that he was as hard as Ivan the Terrible. So he thrust the muzzle to her heart and pulled the trigger. Everyone in the Kremlin is convinced she committed suicide. Only I know the truth."

I couldn't think how to respond. Was it possible that Stalin had brought my husband to the Kremlin and confided in him? If he had confided in him—if he had admitted shooting his wife—why would he now send Mandelstam into exile where he could repeat the story to anybody who would listen? No, no, the only explanation that made a shred of sense was that Mandelstam, on the doorsill of a nervous breakdown, had imagined seeing me and Zinaida in a prison cell, and imagined the conversation with Stalin. "Listen carefully, my darling," I said, breathing my message into his ear. "You must not tell a living soul about having encountered Stalin in the Kremlin. I have no doubt it happened as you said. But if you spread the story about how his wife died, he will have you brought back to the Lubyanka in chains. Do you understand what I'm saying, Osya?"

He kneaded his beautiful forehead with his knuckles. "Yes."

"Are you sure you understand?" I repeated.

He nodded slowly.

"Good. Never mention it again. To yourself. To Akhmatova. To Pasternak. To your brother. Even to me."

"I shall never mention it again," he said in a small voice.

"We must put the past behind us and concentrate on the future."

"Is the future behind us or ahead of us?"

For an instant I thought Mandelstam had come to his senses and was making a typically mordant, not to mention poetic, observation. Then I sank back on my heels and saw his eyes gaping wide, hungering for the answer to the question he had posed.

"The future," I replied, "is ahead of us."

Mandelstam accepted this clarification with another slow nod of his head.

The maître d'hôtel returned to the room, bringing with him

forms in triplicate for me to sign. I scratched my name at the bottom of each page without bothering to read it. What more could I lose that hadn't already been taken from me? Using the side of his table as a straight edge, Christophorovich tore off a scrap of paper and wrote the name of a train station, the track number and the time of departure on it. "Mandelstam will be sent into exile in the town of Cherdyn in the northern Urals," he said. "You have seven hours to collect what belongings you can carry and join your husband in the railway carriage." As I started toward the door—I had no time to lose if I was to prepare for the journey—Mandelstam bounded to his feet. "A swallow," he howled, pointing to the pleated curtains covering the window with the hand that wasn't holding up his trousers.

"What is it you see, Osya?"

"I see the future crashing into a mountainside!"

I turned on the interrogator and began ranting. "A poet has been driven insane," I cried. "This is a major offense against the government you represent. A poet is being sent into exile in a state of madness."

Christophorovich remain unfazed in the face of Mandelstam's madness and my tirade. "You will use the time remaining before the departure of the train to better advantage if you calm yourself and start to prepare for the trip," he told me coldly.

I am afraid the images in my mind's eye blur at this point of the narrative. I seem to remember that Mandelstam was weeping as I tore myself away from the room. I have no memory of how I got back to Herzen House, none at all. I don't recall phoning Akhmatova, but I must have because within minutes several of the younger poets who lived in the small rooms on the second floor turned up to help me pack. I remember feeling as if I were running a high fever. In this delirious condition I crammed my husband's clothing (some of it reeking of camphor) into the suitcase that had served as a coffee table, I packed my own clothes in a cardboard suitcase that someone gave me, I threw saucepans and porcelain bowls and kitchen utensils and linen into a canvas mail sack, I filled a small carton with books from Mandelstam's shelves. Pasternak turned up with a thick wad of rubles attached by a rubber band— he said half was from him, half from Akhmatova. Looking more mournful than usual, he kissed me on the forehead and fled from the flat. Bulgakov's wife, Elena Sergeyevna, couldn't contain her tears when she knocked on the door. She literally emptied her purse on the kitchen table and forced me to accept every last ruble in it. The wives of two editors who had been unable to publish Mandelstam's poems also came by, one with two knitted winter scarves, the other with cash. ("Consider it a loan," she insisted when I tried to push the rubles back into her hand.) Two of the young poets who had spent evenings around our kitchen table listening to Mandelstam read aloud from *Stone*, his first book of poetry, flagged down a government automobile and offered the chauffeur a large gratuity to take me to the train station. They insisted on accompanying me to carry the suitcases and the canvas sack and the carton filled with books. Clutching to my breast a tattered handbag filled with more cash than we'd possessed in years, the two young poets trailing along the quay behind me with our pathetic belongings, I caught sight of my husband in a compartment. He appeared as pale and one-dimensional as the reflection you see in the smudged window of a storefront.

Fleeting images of the trip into exile at Cherdyn—it took three nights and two days for the train and the riverboat to cover the roughly fifteen hundred kilometers— run through my mind's eye like one of those motion pictures where the frames jump on the projector's sprockets. (Akhmatova, quoting an English poet whose name escapes me, often spoke of fragments shored up against one's ruin; what I am about to recount are fragments *of* my ruin.) Except for the three armed soldiers, one of whom was always posted outside the door to keep other passengers away, Mandelstam and I had the compartment and its six berths to ourselves. The senior guard, also named Osip, was a country boy with a broad, open face who hummed roundelays when he wasn't grinning at me. He filled my teapot with boiling water from the carriage samovar whenever I asked him, and so I was able to keep my husband supplied with tea, though I'd forgotten to scrounge for sugar at Herzen House and he pulled a face at every sip. Mandelstam spent hours on end with his forehead pressed against the pane, fogging the window with his breath, staring through his reflection at the taiga and the villages hurtling past, listening intently to the almost human voice of the rails under the wheels of the train. "Can't you hear it?" he demanded, and he deciphered the words for me: *Age before beauty? Talent before mediocrity? Urban intellectual before rural hick?* On another occasion I came awake to find him talking to himself. I remember him saying the same thing again and again, something like, "They want to get me away from Moscow before they shoot me—they want me to vanish without a trace."

Osip the guard must have overheard him because, still grinning, he turned to me and said, "Tell him to calm down, Missus. We don't shoot people for making up rhymes, only for spying and sabotage. We're not like the bourgeois countries. There you could be strung up for writing stuff they don't like."

The frames jump to other images. At some point during that first night the train pulled onto a siding and we had to transfer to an open carriage (the guards slung their rifles across their backs and carried our belongings) on a narrow-gauge line. Mandelstam and I sat on the wooden benches facing each other, the guards sat across the aisle and kept other passengers at a distance with waves of their hands. What people made of the two gloomy city folks, their suitcases and belongings piled on the overhead rack, I cannot say. Seeing that we were escorted by armed soldiers, everyone avoided eye contact—everyone except for one person, a thin, elegantly dressed older woman who looked as if she had stepped off the pages of a Turgenev novel. Oh God, it all comes back to me. I haven't thought of her in years. She boarded the carriage at a remote station, dressed as my mother, rest her soul, used to dress for weddings, in a high-collared cream-colored garment and a small straw hat and crocheted gloves. She held a folded lace parasol under one arm and a covered straw hamper in one hand. She looked at me, then at the soldiers, then back at me and, having grasped that we were prisoners being escorted into exile, she favored me with the saddest smile you are likely to see in a lifetime. She started down the aisle toward us, oblivious to the solders waving her off, oblivious to Osip the guard rising to his feet with one hand fingering the butt of an enormous revolver. Opening the lid of her hamper, she rummaged under a foulard and produced two cucumbers. She offered one to my husband, the other to me. My husband, shaken out of his stupor by this bold act of solidarity, rose and kissed her hand in the French manner, his bloodless lips grazing the back of her glove. And with a courteous inclination of her head, this guardian angel of deported prisoners, this relic from a dying Russia, turned and made her way to a seat beside a family of peasants at the far end of the carriage, from where she never lifted her gaze from me.

I must have dozed when I was no longer physically able to keep my eyes open. As the train was pulling out of another remote station, I shook myself awake to find the woman's seat at the end of the car vacant. To this day I bitterly regret not knowing her name, though given what she had done for us it would have put her in jeopardy to ask. Mandelstam, for his part, never stopped staring at his reflection in the window. He was sure he would be executed at any moment and didn't want to be caught unawares. The season of white nights had begun and one could glimpse copses of birches and aspens on the foothills. I drifted off again but was woken before dawn by the lack of motion of the train. We'd pulled onto another siding in a freight yard to let pass red cattle wagons transporting prisoners to forced-labor camps in Siberia. Women had pushed scraps of nylon undergarments between the planks of the wooden siding so people spotting the wagons would understand the nature of their cargo. In my imagination I see these scraps flying like regimental banners in the chilly penumbra between white night and first light.

Late on second day, with the Ural range rising like a smudge on the horizon, the train crawled through a suburb of brightly painted one-storey frame houses and narrow dirt streets into a rundown terminal with giant likenesses of Lenin and Stalin pasted onto billboards and *Solikamsk* printed over the swinging doors leading to the station's waiting room. A news bulletin echoed from loudspeakers rigged to posts on the platform: *The spies, traitors and turncoats have been swept from the face of the earth.* Our three trusty guards transported us and our possessions to an open truck parked around the side next to the public toilets. Mandelstam and I were ordered onto bales of straw in the back and, with a belch of exhaust, the truck headed due north along the city's single boulevard. Within minutes, the frame houses gave way to dense woods and daylight was replaced by impenetrable shadows. Soon after, we pulled up in a clearing and the truck filled with forestry workers hitching rides to the river. One of them in particular terrified Mandelstam—a big bearded man in a dark red shirt carrying a double-bladed axe on one shoulder. Fearing for his life, my husband . began to tremble. "They're going to behead me, as in Peter's time," he gasped. I hugged him to me and attempted to calm him, but he eyed the bearded giant with dread. "Expect the worst," he told me. "Do everything possible to keep your dignity. When they come for me, I must absolutely run for it—it is important to escape or die in the attempt."

I recall saying, "At least if they kill us we won't have to commit suicide."

This elicited a nervous giggle from Mandelstam. "How can I live with a professional suicide like you next to me?" he demanded.

What I didn't say, what I thought, was: If you decide to die, I won't need to kill myself, my life will simply stop.

I remember his taking several deep breaths, which calmed him, but he never took his eyes off the bearded lumberjack and his double-bladed axe.

The sun had gone down by the time the truck reached the rickety pier on the Kolva River. Even the white night was lost in the shadows of the forest that descended almost to the water's edge. Voices of women singing on the far bank echoed through the woods. The foresters disappeared into a barracklike building on a low bluff over the river. The three guards piled our belongings on the pier and sat down with their backs against the pilings, smoking cigarettes and talking in undertones. I knocked on the window of the small store next to the barrack and managed to purchase several tins of sardines, along with a loaf of bread and, to my husband's delight, two packets of cheap Turkish cigarettes. We settled onto the grassy slope next to the pier, listening to the delicate sounds a river produces at night—the murmur of eddying water, the splash of fish, the croak of frogs. In other circumstances it would have been an agreeable interlude. Mandelstam passed the first Turkish cigarette under his nostrils, savoring the odor, then wedged it between his lips and struck a match. His hand was shaking too much to maneuver the flame to the tip of the cigarette, so I lit a second match and he held my wrist and brought the cigarette to the fire. He exhaled and sank back on the grass. "I held Stalin's wrist when he lit my cigarette," he said absently. God only knows how I forced a smile onto my face. And in the darkness, I could see him staring at me as if I were a stranger.

Shortly after midnight, the river steamer, an ancient vessel with a naked lady for bowsprit and a lopsided pilothouse leaning into the wind high above the main deck, tied up alongside the feeble electric lights at the end of the pier. I found the purser in his office off the midship passageway and, dipping into the wealth of cash in my purse, purchased tickets that entitled us to a cabin all to ourselves, even a toilet with a small tin tub. Mandelstam could not believe our good fortune when the steward unlocked the door with a skeleton key and stepped back to let us pass, almost as if we were vacationers on a cruise to Cherdyn. Our three soldiers installed our belongings under the two beds in the cabin and went in search of the bunk rooms reserved for steerage passengers. The smell of cooked cabbage emanated from the galley at the end of the passageway (Mandelstam pronounced himself dismayed at my familiarity with nautical terminology) and, for the price of several cigarettes, we were able to have our meals brought to the cabin. Before long the shriek of the ship's whistle filled the night. The deck began vibrating under our feet as the steamer drifted away from the pier and started upriver toward our destination.

I can say without exaggeration that we both got our first good sleep in days, so much so that I was quite frightened in the morning to see how still Mandelstam lay in his bunk. I watched him closely to reassure myself that he was still breathing before slipping under his blanket to awaken him with the warmth of my body. He clung to me as a drowning man clings to a life preserver and I thought—I wasn't certain, mind you, it was only an impression—that I felt the dampness of tears on my neck. And then—I record this detail, along with the pain it caused me at the time; despite the pain it causes me now—I heard him say, "With any luck, I may still have a muse."

With or without your leave, I shall skip ahead several hours.

Mandelstam, bathed, shaven (by me while he sat in the tub, his knobby knees jutting from the water; I didn't yet feel comfortable letting him have a straight-edged razor in his hand), attired in clothing that smelled of camphor, one of the new knitted scarves wound around his neck, was taking the air on the narrow main deck, strolling from where I was sitting in a lounger to the forecastle and back again, his copy of Pushkin open in his hand but his attention riveted on the shoreline.

And with good reason. Stalin's transgression against humanity—forcing peasants who survived the man-induced famine and the execution squads onto agricultural collectives—had uprooted masses of people and scattered them across what had become a wasteland. My husband and I had seen traces of the calamity returning to Moscow from the Crimea—the trip that left an indelible mark on Mandelstam and turned him, for better or for worse, into a truth teller. Friends traveling south or east from Moscow reported coming across survivors searching desperately for a village to settle in or a plot of land to work, all the while trying to evade the squads of Chekists who were combing the countryside. Now, from the deck of our riverboat, we could see the detritus of collectivization camping at the edge of both banks of the river, clusters of lost souls huddled under tarpaulins stretched from branches over their heads, cartons and straw trunks piled around them, naked children playing in the shallow water while their parents cooked scraps of horsemeat, hacked from dead carcasses, on charcoal fires. And my befuddled best friend and husband, his brain awash with hallucinations of having visited me in a Lubyanka cell, of having encountered Stalin in the Kremlin, turned to me and, pointing a quivering finger at the shore, cried out, "See, Nadenka— the shortage *is* being divided amongst the peasants!"

To the eternal shame of Russia, he was right. What can one say about this episode after all these years? If, as Mandelstam insisted, Stalin knew what his Chekists were doing, he was surely condemned for eternity to the circle of hell where, as Dante tells us, the fires are so searing one could use molten glass to cool one's body. If, as Pasternak suspected, Stalin didn't know, he was guilty of not knowing what he should have known and will wind up in the same inferno.

At midafternoon Cherdyn loomed around a bend in the Kolva, sprawling over several hills, each surrounded by forest, the whole dominated by the bell tower of an enormous cathedral that had surely been converted by the Bolsheviks into a warehouse. Mandelstam stood on the bow, his palm on the rump of the naked sprit, watching as the steamer turned in the current and drifted down on the cement wharf piled high with bales and crates waiting to be transported back to civilization. Catching the heaving lines thrown by crewmen, stevedores dragged the heavy hawsers through the water and up onto bollards. When the ship was fast to the wharf and the gangway secured at midship, the three guards, carrying our possessions, escorted us to an open carriage drawn by a skeletal mare and followed along on foot behind as we slowly made our way through an enormous gate into the citadel at the center of the city. The commandant, an old cavalryman from the look of his high boots and flamboyant mustache, was hastily fastening the tarnished gold buttons of his tunic as we were led into his office. He sharpened the ends of his mustache with his fingers. "You will be the Mandelstams," he said. "The telegram from Moscow failed to mention a first name or patronymic. Which one of you is the prisoner?"

"It's me, the prisoner," my husband said. "I am the poet Mandelstam."

"And I am Nadezhda Yakovlevna, the wife of the poet Mandelstam," I said, my pride at being connected to Mandelstam overcoming my resentment (which I tended to suppress) at his having gotten us into this predicament.

"Very unusual," the commandant, who never bothered introducing himself, observed.

"What is very unusual?" I inquired.

"The notation *Isolate and preserve* next to the name Mandelstam on the telegram," he replied. "It is the first time I have come across such instructions." He looked directly at Mandelstam. "Whom do you know in the Kremlin?"

My husband's lips fashioned themselves into what on another occasion could reasonably have been described as a smile. "Stalin," he replied.

The commandant exchanged quick looks with his young deputy sitting behind a desk across the room. "This is not something you should joke about," he warned.

"What makes you think I am joking?"

Apparently deciding it would be more prudent to drop the

matter, the commandant announced that we were to be housed in the local district hospital until our final place of exile was decided upon. This was the first inkling we had that Cherdyn was to be a way station for us. The same carriage transported us up a winding road paved with split logs to a brick structure that had been converted, so we learned, from a sausage factory into a hospital. Our three guards bid us farewell at the gate. The one called Osip actually stood to attention and saluted after turning us over to the hospital authorities. A heavyset woman wearing a soiled white smock led us to a large, empty second-floor ward with two metal army cots set at right angles to one wall. As nobody offered to assist us with our baggage, I had to make several trips to the lobby and haul everything upstairs myself. With the departure of our three guards, who Mandelstam thought were under orders to execute him, my husband relaxed ever so slightly. He noticed a portrait of Lenin that had been torn from a magazine thumbtacked to the back of the ward door, and this sparked a memory. "When the Reds took power," he said, "the wife of one of the Bolsheviks came to the flats of writers to pin portraits of Lenin cut from magazines to our walls. She hoped it would save the intelligentsia. How innocent she was." He shook his head. "How innocent we all were."

As night settled over Cherdyn, Mandelstam started to hear voices again. I knew this was the case from the wild look in his eyes. He became convinced he had heard Akhmatova reciting a line from one of her poems—*They take my shadow for questioning*—and concluded from this that she had been arrested and shot. We were summoned to supper in the canteen on the main floor, but Mandelstam flatly refused to eat anything until he had searched the ravines around the hospital for Akhmatova's corpse. I followed him along the dirt paths that ran through the woods around the hospital until the two of us were stumbling from exhaustion. Only then was I able, pushing and tugging, to get him back up to the second-floor ward and onto his cot. By the time I made it down to the canteen, the only food available was leftovers, but, as they correctly say, beggars cannot be choosers, so I scraped some gristly meat and cold potatoes onto a clean plate and brought it up to my husband, who picked at the scraps with a remarkable absence of enthusiasm.

I have reached the part of the story that causes my heart to splinter. It's as if . . . as if reliving this episode has something in common with dying.

Mandelstam was sitting up on his cot, fully dressed, his spinal cord against the wall, listening with his eyes, muttering about how the woodcutters were going to execute him when the moon was high enough for them to find their way through the forest. I was determined not to close my eyes until he fell asleep but, overcome with fatigue, I must have drifted off. I dreamed terrible dreams of alligators plucking children out of the shallow water along the riverbank while their parents fanned the flames of charcoal fires and turned makeshift spits with dead humans on them. The nightmare jolted me awake. The cot next to me was empty. The glass door leading to a narrow balcony was open. I caught sight of the poet Mandelstam in the light of the moon. He was sitting astride the balustrade, one leg dangling over the side two floors above the ground, working up the courage to jump. From the glass door I whispered his name in order not to startle him. He turned his head and gaped at me, his eye sockets dark with terror. I lunged for him and caught hold of the back of his jacket, but he squirmed out of the sleeves and dropped into the darkness. I stood there in the icy night, clutching the jacket in my hands for the time it takes the image on the retina to reach the brain. Then I screamed a scream so piercing it frightened birds into the night sky.

I don't recall how I made it down the wide flight of steps to the ground floor, only of standing in the garden at the foot of the hospital wall as figures carrying kerosene lamps rushed from the entrance. People in white smocks were pulling Mandelstam, moaning in pain, from the hedge into which he had fallen. They set him on a stretcher and had to pry me off his body in order to carry him back into the hospital. I staggered along behind. We wound up in the operating block lighted by candles because the generator was switched off at night to save fuel. A woman doctor, wearing a bathrobe and clearly disgruntled at having been woken up, directed the nurses to strip Mandelstam naked. Her eyeglasses slipping along her nose, she examined his right shoulder and arm, which were twisted out of shape and blue with bruises. "He is fortunate," the doctor said, probing my husband with the tips of her fingers. "He has dislocated his shoulder socket." And with that she took hold of Mandelstam's wrist and gave it a sharp tug, setting the bone back into the socket. My husband's shriek of pain was cut short when he fainted.

By the time he regained consciousness, his shoulder and torso had been bandaged and he was back in his cot, his arm in a sling, a blanket pulled up to his chin. "What happened?" he asked when the effect of the sedative wore off.

"You fell, my darling Osya. Luckily, you landed in hedges, which broke your fall. The ground underneath had been recently turned to make a flower bed. You dislocated your shoulder. The doctor said it will be some weeks before you regain full use of your right arm."

After Mandelstam's attempt at suicide, I have no memory of time, only of light: sunlight, white night, candlelight, moonlight, even starlight. Days folded themselves into one another. The nurses, moved by our plight, turned out to be very caring. They changed my husband's bandages and sponged his limbs and emptied the bedpan and brought up meals from the canteen so I wouldn't be obliged to leave him alone in the ward. Perhaps a week went by. I honestly can't say. What I do remember is that on a sun-drenched morning two male nurses turned up in the ward carrying a sturdy chair on which they proposed to carry Mandelstam downstairs. I never understood why but he broke into a cold sweat and began shaking his head emphatically, and nothing I said could convince him to submit to their ministrations. He ended up descending the staircase leaning his weight on me and wincing in pain with each step. Once downstairs, Mandelstam was lifted, along with our possessions, into the back of a hand-drawn cart, which two strapping peasant boys contrived to drag down the road paved with split logs to the citadel. The commandant, wearing coveralls this time, received us in his office. "I guess you do have a friend in the Kremlin," he said, shaking his head in disbelief. "I have received a telegram with instructions you are to be permitted to select your place of exile. It can be anywhere except one of the twelve biggest cities."

Who was our friend in the Kremlin? Had Pasternak prevailed upon Bukharin to intervene after all? Had the head of the Writers' Union, Maksim Gorky, picked up rumblings of discontent from the poets and passed them on to Yagoda? Had Stalin himself— surely the one behind the order to *isolate and preserve*—decided that Mandelstam would be unlikely to survive a winter immediately under the Arctic Circle?

Offered a choice, Mandelstam didn't hesitate. "Voronezh," he announced as if he had anticipated the question.

"Why Voronezh?" the commandant asked.

The choice surprised me, too. "Why Voronezh, Osya?"

Mandelstam thought about this. "I knew a biologist at Tashkent University who was born in Voronezh, a frontier town in the time of Peter the Great populated with escaped convicts. He told me good things about it. As the city is on the Don and south of Moscow, the weather will be milder than here. I remember the biologist saying his father worked as a prison doctor there." And then, miracle of miracles, the old Mandelstam, that high-strung, headstrong, life-glad *homo poeticus* who was able to find a grain of humor in the darkest situation, reincarnated himself in the commandant's office of the citadel at Cherdyn. He looked at me, a hint of a smile playing in his eyes, and he said, "We cannot rule out the possibility that we may need the services of a prison doctor, can we, Nadenka?"

"Welcome back," I said.

SIXTEEN

Fikrit Shotman
Saturday, the 23rd of June 1934

I love trains. I have as far back as I can remember remembering. To my mind, there's no music more easy on the ear than the whistle of a train in the night. When I was sixteen and already big for my age, I dreamed of working as a coal stoker in a steam locomotive. I admired the uniforms worn by stationmasters and conductors, with their visored caps they looked to me like generals in the glorious Red Army. When I became a professional weight lifter, later when I was a circus strongman, I spent a good part of my life on the road, but the trip that began on the twenty-third day of June in the year 1934 was the first time I ever voyaged in a cattle car. If you're thinking what I think you're thinking, you're dead wrong because traveling in a cattle car turned out to be as close to first class as I ever been when there was a first class in the days before the Revolution. I'll explain. There's no denying we were crowded, ninety-three warm bodies all told, including seven children going to Siberia with their parents and nineteen old people, one of which was paralyzed from the waist downward and needed to be carried in and out of the cattle car when we stopped in the middle of nowhere so we could wash in streams. This kind of situation was ripe for calamity, except we were lucky to have with us one prisoner that everyone called the professor, a short guy with round eyeglasses thick as windowpanes and a pointed goatee that reminded me of Agrippina's tattoo of the traitor Trotsky that she passed off as Engels. Not that it mattered, but the professor must have been an Israelite because he had the same name as that Jew on the Politburo, Kaganovich, for all I know the professor and the locomotive commissar (Kaganovich's nickname when he ran the railroads) may have been near or distant cousins. The professor organized us into what he called the cattle car collective and it was thanks to him that, unlike in the other cattle cars on the same train where they buried dead bodies in shallow graves at every siding, we made the nineteen-day trip from the little-used station in Moscow to the transit camp in Magadanskaya without losing a single life. My size gave me natural authority, so the professor put me in charge of the communal toilet, which was a hole contrived in the floorboards at one corner of the car and surrounded with women's shawls fastened to make a screen. I used a wooden bucket filled with piss and a sheaf of straw to clean the hole after it was fouled by prisoners with the runs, leading the professor himself to compliment me in front of every member of the collective on the sanitary condition of the toilet.

More about the professor. He was an Old Bolshevik, having fought, as he proudly informed us, in the battle for the Winter Palace at the time of the Revolution. Being a diehard Marxist, he gathered prisoners in the cattle car around him at night and delivered lectures on the dictatorship of the proletariat or dielectrical materialism or exploitation by the capitalist class. After the lectures, the professor opened the floor to questions. The night of his first lecture, I raised a finger and he nodded in my direction. "What are you being sent up for?" I asked.

"Violation of Article 58," he replied, looking me straight in the eye. "I was accused of belonging to an anti-Soviet Trotkyist wrecking group that was planning to assassinate Stalin and other members of the Politburo."

Many in the cattle car, me included, greeted this with a buzz of anger. It had not occurred to us that this small man with bushy hair over his ears and bald crown could be a dangerous criminal. "Were you guilty?" a woman called from the back of the car.

"Of course he was guilty," I said, "otherwise he wouldn't be on his way to Siberia."

"I was guilty," the professor said, "but not of what they accused me of. I signed a petition circulated by Communist students at my university supporting Bukharin's criticism of forced collectivization of agriculture. Like Bukharin, we were not against collectivization itself—the idea of peasants being treated as agricultural workers and drawing salaries the same as factory workers seemed to us to be a logical extension of Marxist doctrine. But we favored a more gradual approach—we would have *lured* the peasants onto collectives with good housing and a fifty-four-hour workweek and a guaranteed wage even if the harvest was poor. The other peasants, seeing how much better life turned out to be on the collective, would have drifted in that direction of their own free will instead of destroying their livestock and their crops in protest."

The old man who was paralyzed spoke up. "How is it that despite being falsely convicted, you still call yourself a Marxist?"

"With pride, with hope in the future of Russia and all mankind, I call myself a Marxist and a Leninist," the professor declared. "Progress is not a straight line. It zigs and it zags as it attempts to avoid the Western materialistic mind-set that is indifferent to suffering and find a distinctive Russian path to modernity. Each zig, each zag results in unnecessary distress, even the death of true believers. Let me put it another way. Until the Bolsheviks came on the scene, man was the *object* of history—he was kicked around like a football by tyrannical leaders of religious institutions and capitalist empires. With the coming of Communism, man discredited the religious institutions and the capitalist tyrants and became the *subject* of history. In this cattle car, on this train steaming toward the most remote corner of Siberia, I see myself as a soldier on the front line of the world proletarian revolution.

What's the difference if I lay the foundations for Communism in European Russia or on some Siberian taiga? Comrades, I shall supply the answer to my own question. There is no difference."

Several of the women prisoners started applauding softly. Then the men joined in and the applause grew louder. And me, too, I began clapping my hands together, setting a rhythm to the applause that matched the moan of the wheels on the rails. And soon everybody was applauding and stomping on the floorboards to the rhythm I set, and I knew that I would look back on the trip in the cattle car as one of the high points of my life, right up there with my silver medal in Vienna, Austria and my handshake with Comrade Stalin.

Washing my feet and my one pair of spare socks in an icy stream the next afternoon, I overheard a lady mention what the professor was a professor of. It turned out to be something called linguistics. The lady said he was famous for figuring out the difference between languages and dialects—languages were spoken by people with armies, dialects by people without. The professor was no slouch in geography, neither, because no sooner had our train started out than he marked the route from Moscow to Magadanskaya in chalk on the wood siding of the cattle car, ticking off the cities as he caught glimpses of them through the crack between the boards—Nizhni-Novgorod, Kazan, Yekaterinburg (where, good riddance to bad rubbish, the Bolsheviks executed the last tsar), Omsk, Novosibirsk, Irkutskaya.

That first night out he had all the food and water and water receptacles in the cattle car collected and appointed a committee to distribute rations, to each according to his need, which is to say the children and the old people got to get more water than the able-bodied prisoners like myself. He appointed another committee, made up of peasant women, whose job it was to search for cedar nuts and edible roots whenever the train pulled up on a siding and we were allowed off to fill the receptacles from a rivulet or brook. From time to time, usually after we passed through a city late at night, the guards slid back the heavy door and threw in a paper sack filled with loaves of bread. In the other cars you could hear the prisoners cursing and battling among themselves as they fought over the bread. In our car the ration committee took charge of the sack and doled out the bread so that it pretty much lasted until the next city and the next sack.

Some of the prisoners wrote letters on their own, but for the illiterate there was the professor's letter writing committee, made up of three ex-schoolteachers. To begin with they made the rounds of the cattle car, collecting blank pages from the books the prisoners had brought with them. Writing on the pages in the style of the prison camps, which is to say in a tiny handwriting that filled every square centimeter of the paper, they copied off letters for the prisoners who couldn't write their own. The name and address of the receiver of the letter was printed out on one side, then the paper was folded and refolded so that only the receiver's name and address was visible, at which point it was *mailed* through the toilet hole when we passed a town or village at night. The professor told us there was a tradition that went back to the tsar's penal colonies whereby peasants coming across letters on the railroad tracks would copy the address onto an envelope and, as stamps were dirt cheap, post it. That way relatives and friends back in Moscow would get news of the prisoners being transported to Siberia. I myself didn't take advantage of this letter-writing system because I didn't want people to think I couldn't read or write.

There was another committee, which the professor called the propaganda team. I am not sure I really understood what they were up to, but I'll describe it in case the reader of this account understands it better than me. The committee, made up entirely of city women that were members of the Party, asked all the ladies to contribute scraps of nylon or lace undergarments. (One lady still dressed in the ball gown she was wearing the night of her arrest donated an entire pettiskirt.) And when our train passed through big cities or even middle-sized towns, which was always at night, the committee members stuffed the scraps through the joints between the planking in the side of the car so that they were flying in the current of air caused by the motion of the train. And when we were past the city or town, the scraps of undergarment were pulled back and hidden until we came to the next population center.

The professor's children committee kept the kids distracted with games of buttons and fairy tales. But the adults, notwithstanding what I call the first-class conditions in our cattle car, were all down in the mouth. All except your servitor, Fikrit Shotman. I can honestly say I looked forward to paying my debt to society, wiping clean my slate of deceit and treachery the comrade interrogator had skillfully exposed to the world. The way I saw it, the sooner I reached the transit camp, the sooner I would be packed off to a gulag (a word I picked up from fellow prisoners) to purge my crimes against the Soviet state. Four years was not forever. I was alive and in good health and physically fit and would return to Agrippina and the circus and pick up my life wiser in the ways of the world, but not all that much older. It was important to see the trip east in a positive light. All of my heroes, starting with Vladimir Lenin and including Comrade Stalin, had spent years in exile and returned stronger because of the experience. Don't get me wrong. I am not comparing myself with Lenin or Stalin. I'm just saying that, having conducted myself with dignity at my trial, I was determined to conduct myself with dignity in my present situation. In a word, I was determined to put the past where it belonged, which was behind me.

Our excitement grew as we approached Magadanskaya on the professor's chalk map. The streams we washed in felt colder even though yellow dandelions were pushing up their heads and summer was near enough to smell. The landscape turned rougher, the underbrush near the tracks became tangled with wild berries, the wild goats that came down to drink from a stream we were washing in had long curling claws that hadn't been cut in years, not as many villages were visible from the train and there was more distance between them, you could go for half a day without seeing a plowed field or a break in the forest. The emptiness reminded me of the Kara Kum Desert near Khiva in Turkmenistan, except here there was no sand, only permafrost and mountains with snow still on top of them in June. Pulling through the Magadanskaya marshaling yards, I kept my eye glued to one of the spaces between the planks. I saw wooden houses with small vegetable gardens. I saw cows or goats tethered to brightly painted fences. I saw a lumber cooperative with a hammer over the door and a tractor repair station with a sickle over the hangar. I saw delivery wagons drawn by oxen. In short, I saw what looked like civilization thriving in this Soviet Socialist Republic.

When the train came to a stop at a siding, we were kept waiting in the stifling cattle car for hours. Tempers flared. Two men almost came to blows. Happily the professor found the words to sooth everyone's nerves. We could hear officials dealing with the prisoners in the cars ahead of us. Finally the door to our car was slid open by armed guards wearing gray belted uniform blouses and peaked Budyonny caps. Some of them were holding snarling dogs on short leashes. Two men, one in army fatigues, the other in a rumpled civilian suit, sat at a table on the wooden quay facing our door. The one in civilian clothing called out the professor's name. "Kaganovich, Alter." The professor bid us farewell with a jaunty wave of his hand. Some of the woman turned their heads away to hide their tears. I turned my head away so nobody would see I wasn't crying. (Where I come from, which is the mountains of Azerbaidzhan, men do not cry.) The civilian at the table read from a paper in a voice loud enough for all of us to hear. "Violation of Article 58 of the Penal Code, sentenced to twenty years without the right of correspondence." From the cattle car, we could see the professor hand over his identity card to the man in civilian clothing, then pin what looked like a number on the front of his shirt and join the other convicts already crouching in the back of an open truck parked nearby.

I took heart from the fact he was on his way to construct Communism in Siberia.

One by one the comrade prisoners jumped to the quay when their names were called and presented themselves to the men sitting behind the table. (The two who almost came to blows carried the paralyzed man when his turn came. The army officer seemed puzzled to find himself dealing with someone who was tagged with a tenner for wrecking but couldn't walk. The civilian tossed his head toward something I couldn't see. The army officer agreed and the paralyzed man was carted off in a wheelbarrow in that direction, never to be seen again, at least by me.) And then I heard my name. *Shotman, Fikrit.* "Present and eager to begin serving my sentence," I shouted back, which drew a nervous giggle from the prisoners still in my cattle car. I leaped to the ground and stood to attention before the table.

"*Zek* Sh744239, where are your belongings?"

"Except for a spare pair of socks, I got none, Your Honors."

"What skills do you have?"

"I used to be able to dead lift two hundred and eighty-five kilograms—even with my bad knee I can probably still do two hundred kilograms."

"What does that mean, *dead lift?*"

"There are three kinds of weight lifts, Your Honors—there's the squat lift, there's the bench press and there's the dead lift," I began.

The army officer cut me short impatiently. "Forget I asked." He said something to the civilian next to him, who nodded in agreement. "What do you know about gold, Shotman?" the army officer asked.

"The best I could do was silver, Your Honors."

The two men behind the table exchanged looks. "You mined *silver?*" the civilian demanded.

"I *won* silver, Your Honors. In Vienna, Austria. In 1932. That's what I was trying to tell you. I won silver for the dead lift, coming in ten kilograms behind the American Bob Hoffman, who took gold. Stalin himself shook my hand in the Kremlin when I brought the silver medal back to Moscow."

"I'll repeat my question," the army officer said. "What do you know about gold *mining*?"

I scratched my head. "What I know about gold mining you could fit into a sewing thimble," I said, thinking I would get credit for honesty.

The civilian scribbled something at the bottom of a sheet of paper and handed me a number to pin on my shirt front. "You'll learn what you need to know about gold mining at the Kolma settlement," he said. Motioning me to join the men sitting on a rise behind the quay, he called the next name.

"So you're off to the Kolma River," the soldier guarding the group said as I settled down on the ground with the others.

"Where is the Kolma River?" I asked.

"It's nine days north of here," one of the prisoners, a city man judging from his lace-up shoes, said. He didn't sound enthusiastic.

"Nine days by train? Nine days by boat? Nine days by truck?"

The soldier, who was chewing on a root, grinned. "Nine days by foot," he said. "You'll walk in. If you're still alive at the end of your stretch, which is not something you want to put money on, chances are you'll walk out."

Nine days turned out to be the time it would take if the sun was shining and the trail north was bone dry. Which sorry to say wasn't the situation. No sooner had we hit the road than the heavens opened and it rained more rain than you'd think the sky could hold. The five soldiers who were supposed to be guarding our twenty-four Kolma-bound gold miners kept us trudging through the mud, each step sucking at the soles of our boots as if there was a monster in the ground trying to eat us alive. There were military posts along the way—one convict who was working on his second fiver told me the whole of Siberia was a giant prison camp, but of course I didn't believe him—where we found shelter from the rain for the night, if you can call a cannon cover stretched over tent poles shelter, along with a kind of mutton soup where the soldiers naturally got the chunks of meat and we considered ourselves lucky to wind up with the marrow in the bones. But it was more than we got to eat on the nineteen-day trip to Siberia, and so it seemed like a feast. The rain let up the day we hit the Kolma River, twelve days out of Magadanskaya. We splashed in the fast-flowing water like kids at a Komsomol picnic, then stretched naked on the bank to let our clothes dry in the sun. We had a stroke of luck on the thirteenth day. A shallow-bottomed motor barge went past going upstream to the Kolma settlement to bring victuals to the miners and carry the gold and tin and lumber back down. Our five soldiers, fed up with hiking, got the captain to take us upstream on condition we bailed out his bilge, which we did by making a chain and passing buckets up and back. The barge had a lady cook cooking for the crew. Being an ex-prisoner herself, she snuck portions of rice and vegetables to us after the others had their fill. And on the sixteenth day, with the bilges almost dry, we caught sight of the Kolma settlement upslope from the wooden pilings on the shoreline. The arrival of the barge was greeted with the whine of a hand-cranked siren and we could see from afar people waving at us excitedly from the crest of a hill. A midget of an army officer, holding a leash attached to a silvertip bear standing on its hind legs, came duck-walking downhill. He was wearing exercise pants and the dirtiest uniform tunic I ever seen, open at the neck with discolored silver colonel bars on the collar. Making his way to the dock, he took possession of the vodka that came upriver with the victuals, scratching his initials on each carton as it was loaded onto wooden barrows for transport back uphill. The colonel turned out to be the Kolma commandant. He ordered the five soldiers to line up the new prisoners, then with his bear in tow he strutted past us like a Soviet general inspecting an honor guard. It was then that I caught sight of more ladies than you could shake a stick at, half a hundred maybe, maybe more, spilling downhill toward us as if gravity had lost its influence on their ankles. Pretty soon you could hear them coming as well as see them coming, until the commandant, distracted from inspecting the new consignment of prisoners, screamed, *Silence, ladies!* Their babbling stopped as if the phonograph needle had been lifted off a record. The females fell into a rough line facing us from twenty meters off. The colonel turned back to us prisoners. "Listen up," he shouted. "I'm going to tell you how things function in the Kolma settlement. Here there are no prisons, no barracks, only log cabins hacked out of the taiga by the first convicts to reach the Kolma mountains ten years back. The sixty-two ladies lined up before you are widows, as the expression goes in the Kolma, which means the man they shared their cabin and bed with has either kicked the bucket or served out his prison term and headed back to European Russia. Each of the ladies could do with a man to cut firewood and skin reindeer or hogs and keep her warm in bed, if you get my drift. As there are more ladies looking for husbands than prisoners available, you get to choose. Look them over, pick one of them that fancies you out of the pack and move in with her. Report to work at the entrance to the mine, on the mountain side of the Kolma settlement, half an hour after sunrise tomorrow. Any questions?"

A prisoner at the end of the line raised a hand. "Can we switch after we move in with one of them ladies?"

The colonel laughed. "No. To avoid the women stealing each other's men, your first choice is your only choice. You can always move out, but then you'll have nowhere to live and no female body available to get you through the ten winter months when minus thirty is considered a hot day."

I spotted Magda the second she spotted me. She was a head bigger than all the ladies around her, which made her only a head smaller than me. Our eyes locked. I could see she was smiling at me. The prisoners were starting to drift across the no-man's-land between us and the ladies. One of them wandered near to her but she raised an arm and brushed him away with the back of her wrist. I walked straight across to her.

"Magda," she said.

"Fikrit."

"Kazak," she said.

"Azerbaijani."

"I pulled a tenner," she said. "Counterrevolution, agent of some fellow I never heard of named Litzky or Trotzky or some such. Nine years still to go to the tail end of my sentence."

"I caught four years. Article 58. Wrecking. Key member of the backup Trotskyist Paris-based anti-Bolshevik Center."

"Were you guilty?"

"They said I was so I must be."

"Are you strong as you look?" she asked.

"Stronger."

"Why's your head turned to the side like that?"

"I am deaf in my left ear."

She accepted this with a nod. "Being deaf in one ear don't affect how you screw?"

"Haven't been with a woman since I went deaf, but I don't expect any problem in that department."

Magda laughed. As I had my good ear turned toward her I could hear she had a fine laugh.

"Aside from my height, what made you pick me?" she asked.

I ought to explain that Magda had an enormous head of wild matted hair. She was wearing man's work pants pulled high on her waist with a rope for a belt and a sleeveless shirt that exposed the sides of her large breasts and left her arms bare. "The tattoo," I said. "I saw it right off. I like tattoos on ladies."

She raised her forearm so I could get a better look. "It's lost most of its color. That's what my husband looked like before his arrest."

"What happened to him?"

Magda shrugged. "I caught a glimpse of him in the exercise yard of the Ayagoz prison. He was walking round and round, his hand on the shoulder of the prisoner in front of him. After that I lost track. He could be at another settlement on the Kolma for all I know." She looked at me, her head slanted, her eyes squinting. "You got a wife back in civilization?"

I said as how I did. I said her name was Agrippina. I said she was the tattooed lady in the same circus as me.

"That explains why you like tattoos."

"How come you're a Kolma widow?" I asked.

"Man I was sharing a cabin with went out of his mind. He was on the front end of a twenty-year sentence when I turned up here a year ago. Two, three months back—what month are we now?"

"June."

"It was in February, which makes it four months back. Time goes slow here when you look ahead, it flies by when you look back. In February, like I said, he broke the ice on the river with a pickaxe and took off his clothing and waded into the water. He didn't last half a minute. By the time they was able to find a boat hook and haul him out, he was stiff as a board and blue as the sky."

"So will you take me in his place?" I asked.

"Yes, I'll take you," she said. And tucking an arm through mine, she started to haul me up the hill.

Which is how I came to start a new chapter in my life. I know some will point the finger at me for two-timing Agrippina, but the old saying *Out of sight, out of mind* is as truthful a description as any of what happens to someone in my situation. In my defense, I was on the front end of a four-year stretch, I needed a roof over my head and body heat in my bed at night to survive the winters in this Arctic backwater. I am not trying to let myself off the hook when I say that given how things turned out, I believe Agrippina would have followed my advice. *In Azerbaidzhan, when a man for one reason or another disappears, his woman waits a decent interval and then finds another to take his place.* Agrippina was a good wife to me and would make a good wife to one of the bachelor tent men who live in communal apartments. It would strike me as an example of nature taking its course if she threaded her needle and took in my trousers and shirts and jackets (the tent men are big, but not as big as me) and passed along my clothing to this new husband, which, while I'm on the subject, is what Magda did for me, only in her case she had to let out the waistbands and cuffs of the padded trousers and jackets and shirts of her suicided husband for them to fit me. She was even able to cobble new toes in his cork-soled boots so I could squeeze my feet into them.

And so life flows on. And who is Fitrit Shotman to second-guess what's right and what's wrong at any given bend of the river?

Surviving justifies a lot of what might otherwise pass for wrong.

Magda's cabin was the opposite of Magda. She had a wild beautifulness that some who should have known better took for ugliness. Which is to say, where she herself was untamed, with a fiery temper and uncombable hair shooting off in all directions, her cabin, made of cut logs, round side out with mud and straw in the joints, was clean as a new kopek and ordered. Every tin cup or tin plate or wooden spoon had its place, and heaven help the husband who didn't put it back in its place. Each length of wood I split with the axe was carefully stacked in a corner next to the chimney, the pieces fitted into each other like a jigsaw puzzle so that the pile took up less room in the room. The outhouse behind the cabin had a four-legged stool with a hole cut in the middle, a luxury I had not experienced since I went to the toilet in the Kremlin the time I shook Comrade Stalin's hand. Even the gold-mining work—fourteen hours a day, six days a week—filled me with satisfaction because, like Professor Kaganovich from our cattle car, I knew I was contributing to the construction of Communism. I worked at the bitter end of a kilometer-long shaft that burrowed into the side of the mountain, chipping away at the veins of white quartz rock with a pickaxe, shoveling the lode into the narrow ore carts that we pushed down the tracks to the entrance of the mine when they were full. The air in the shaft was foul, forcing us to wear gas masks from the Great War most of the time. Even without the gas mask, you could barely talk to the miner next to you because of the racket from the pumps pumping water from the shaft. Magda was on the team at the mine's entrance that emptied the ore carts into bins, then worked what they called *stamps,* heavy iron crushers which rose and fell on the quartz rock, smashing it to smithereens, which the older prisoners sifted through. The nuggets of gold were thrown into an acid bath, which reduced the gold to a sludge that was smelted into brick-sized ingots. When the two hundred or so prisoners working in the mine produced ten or more ingots a day, we got to draw double rations for supper that night, which was a cause for jubilation because single rations left your stomach rumbling with hunger. On the one day we didn't work in the mine, the prisoners were expected to turn up after midday meal in the common building next to the commandant's office to listen to pages of Stalin's books read aloud by the flabby officer in charge of political education. The officer lisped. Anyone nodding off risked having to scrub the commandant's latrine with a toothbrush, and then scrubbing his teeth with the same toothbrush.

If there was a downside to life in the Kolma settlement, it had to do with time taking its sweet time. Prisoners with long sentences would tick them off by months. Short-timers would count the weeks or days left. But whether you counted by months or weeks or days, the hours dragged. Here is what I thought—if we owned a clock, like one of the big ones in train stations, the second hand would be turning round the Roman numbers in slow motion. Between Magda and me, we didn't have a wristwatch or a clock. Magda owned a pretty little sand glass that emptied in three minutes, but we only used it to soft-boil eggs when we had eggs, which was on national holidays like the anniversary of the Bolshevik Revolution or Stalin's birthday. Every day at Kolma began with the off-key scream of a bugle when the first spark of sunlight broke through the hills around the settlement. You could hear the men coughing and cursing in the cabins around us. Half an hour later we were all lined up on the flat in front of the shaft entrance and counted off, and the workday began. There was a ten-minute break for lunch, cold goulash ladled out from a wooden bucket into the tin plates we carried in a pouch when we went into the shaft. Since none of the prisoners owned wristwatches (the few that had them traded them off to the guards for cigarettes soon after arriving), and since we were a thousand meters inside the mountainside and the only light came from flickering miner's lamps, you could only guess at how many hours were left in the workday. And as time crawled, everyone, me included, guessed short. But two weeks into living with Magda, I found out she knew how to make time fly. I am not inventing this. There were other prisoners in the settlement who used Magda's trick. If the commandant knew about it, he turned a blind eye. The secret was *tea*. Ordinary kitchen tea with Chinese writing on the cloth satchel. Here's how it worked. Every prisoner had a ration of two grams of tea per day, which meant Magda and me had four grams a day, which added up to twenty-something grams a week not counting what we could buy with the fifteen-ruble-a-month pocket money we each got. Magda would save up our tea until we had a hundred grams. When the officer with the lisp got tired of reading from Stalin's books, we would make our way back to Magda's cabin and I'd get a roaring fire going (wood was there for the taking) under a big pot filled with well water so that the room soon became hot and clammy like one of those Turkish bathhouses in Moscow, and then we'd strip naked and sit on the floor with our backs to the wall rubbing our sweating bodies with straw. While I nibbled on a marinated eel I caught with my bare hands in a shallow reach of the Kolma River, Magda boiled our stash of tea in so little water you'd get no more than two or three small cups. Prisoners had a name for the boiled-down tea, which was loaded with something Magda called tannin. They called it *chaifir*. If you sipped it slow you'd become high, if you drank two cups you'd go into a trance and time would whiz past your ear at the speed of sunlight stabbing between the Kolma mountains in the morning. High on *chaifir*, the second hand on the railway station clock in my head would spin so fast it made me dizzy and a four-year sentence'd seem, for the time the high lasted, like it would be behind you when you came back down to earth.

I guess that more or less covers everything. Except your last question. What was the difference between Agrippina and Magda? First off, it's hard to compare two ladies when they're not in the same room. The presence of the one that's present adds weight to her qualities. The absence of the one that's absent calls to mind her faults. What I can say is that Magda was a lady of few words, but those words said everything that needed to be said. She was, as the peasant's put it, the mistress of the world she lived in. And the center of her world was her bed. She took pleasure in giving pleasure. I won't say more because I don't want to embarrass you by obliging you to listen to things that are none of your business.

SEVENTEEN

Anna Andreyevna
Tuesday, the 4th of February 1936

The trip out was an abomination—forty-nine interminable hours, thirty-six of them in stuffy railway carriages filled with cigarette smoke and Communist bourgeois (apparatchiki going to Voronezh to audit state warehouses or run state farms or, in one case, lecture on Stalin's colossal contribution to what the state calls scientific Marxism), thirteen hours killing time in decrepit stations waiting for a train to pass going in the right direction. The worst part was the small talk: the recitation by one's carriage companions of their bodily tribulations, ranging from boils on their backsides to rotting teeth to gynecological problems that shall remain, by me at least, unidentified. There was one couple in the last rows of wooden benches being escorted by three soldiers who had fitted bayonets to their rifles before stacking them on the overhead rack as if they were ski poles. The man, unshaven but decently dressed in a tie and three-piece suit of foreign manufacture and reading a book, had the look of an intellectual—a professor who had probably been overheard repeating an anti-Soviet joke by the student in his class designated to spy for the Cheka. (I say this because I know of one case where the professor's downfall happened exactly like that.) Passing the couple on the way to the toilet in the vestibule, I established eye contact with the woman, handsome enough but careworn, her hair turned sooty white even though she had obviously not yet reached middle age. My own husband and son had been arrested four months earlier; a glimpse of the misery in the woman's eyes was enough to make me think I was seeing my reflection in a mirror. I stopped to utter a word of encouragement but the soldiers shooed me away, saying prisoners being escorted into exile were excluded from conversing with free citizens of the Soviet Socialist Republics. The woman, refusing to be cowed, informed the soldier that her husband was the convicted prisoner; that she was a free woman voluntarily accompanying him into exile and she could talk to anyone she pleased. The eldest of the three soldiers, with frayed sergeant stripes peeling off the sleeve of his shapeless tunic, raised his eyebrows in a kind of world-weariness and gave her a sharp slap across the mouth with the back of his hand. He wore a ring on one finger and it scored her cheek, drawing a trickle of blood. The husband looked up from his book and I could see tears seeping from his eyes because he was unable to protect his wife.

The young woman with white hair struggled for breath. "Can you describe this?" she asked softly, looking intently at me.

"I can," I murmured and made a silent vow I one day would. I stood there glaring at the sergeant, but I didn't dare protest lest he use his asinine authority to banish me from the train at the next station. Which would leave Osip Emilievich, waiting impatiently for me on the quay of Voronezh, an increment closer to suicide than he would have been if I'd turned up. Nadezhda's letter begging me to come out had been unambiguous. Despite her Herculean efforts, dear Osip was slipping down the treacherous slope into melancholy and madness. And so I swallowed my pride, along with my words of disgust for the regime, and said nothing. And hated myself a bit more than I had before this incident.

The train crawled into the Voronezh station moments before noon. I lugged my two satchels—the smaller one with a change of clothing and toilet articles, the larger of the two filled with books and sundry presents for the Mandelstams—down the quay, peering into faces searching for one that seemed familiar. And then I heard a voice *behind* me call out, *Anna Andreyevna!* I turned back to gape at an utter stranger.

It was, of course, the poet Mandelstam.

My failure to recognize him had clearly frightened him. "Dear Anna, have I changed all that much?" he demanded.

"Osip?"

"In the flesh, though the flesh hangs off the bone."

I was speechless. Osip was wearing a yellow leather jacket that plunged to his knees and a leather cap with the earflaps tied up. He was unshaven, thin as a toothpick, his right shoulder hunched forward, his right arm hanging stiffly from the shoulder. His teeth were in lamentable condition, his lips blue, his cheeks sunken. Standing there breathing in short gasps, he looked a good twenty years older than his forty-five years.

"Don't be embarrassed," he said. "There is no mirror where we live but I have seen my reflection in storefronts. The first few times this happened I saw someone staring back at me whom I also didn't recognize." He thrust a small bouquet of dried forget-me-nots into my hand. "Impossible to find fresh flowers in February. You will have to make do with these."

"Dearest Osip," I cried, and abandoning my satchels on the quay, I flung my arms around his neck. And I remember him saying—dear God in heaven, I can actually hear his voice as I resurrect his words—"Anna, Anna, I am not dead, only dying."

Yes. *Only dying.* I am absolutely certain that's what he said.

Fortunately—I say *fortunately* because it was a struggle for Osip to carry even the lighter of my two satchels—the Mandelstams lived within walking distance of the railway station. We set off at a snail's pace. Osip had improvised a cane out of a wooden curtain rod with a knob at the end, but he didn't appear to have the strength in his right arm to lean on it. (Nadezhda had written me about his fall from the second floor of a hospital, about his dislocated shoulder, but as she hadn't mentioned the matter in more than a year I assumed the injury had healed. How wrong I was.) From time to time Osip stopped to catch his breath. From where we stood I could see the center of Voronezh, flat as a table in a Parisian café. Revolution Avenue ran like an artery through the town. Side streets and alleyways fell sharply off the avenue and trickled downhill into a frozen stream that Osip identified as the Vorona. Needless to say, none of the streets off Revolution Avenue were paved, which was perfectly fine in winter when the ground was rock hard but must have been hellish in summer when rain transformed the pathways into slides of mud. The Mandelstams' abode (if a warped roof of wooden shingles balanced precariously on four decrepit walls can properly be described as an abode), at number 4 Lineinaya Street, stood at the top of a narrow sloping alley filled with tumbledown weatherboard houses that, to my city eye, looked as if they were slowly sinking into their miniscule gardens. Railway signals were across from the door of the house where they rented a room from a kindly seamstress. As I soon discovered, trains whooshed past the windows every now and then. With surprising agility, Osip would bound from his chair and rush to fling open the door and watch the train, as if each passage was a remarkable event in his waking hours. But I'm getting ahead of myself.

Nadezhda, as you can suppose, was elated when I turned up. She bombarded me with questions, barely leaving room between them for answers. What news did I have of my husband and my son, Lev? (None. They'd been summoned by the Chekists and hadn't been heard from since. My telegrams to the Writers' Union and the Central Committee had gone unanswered.) How long could I stay? (One week. I was fearful of being away from my communal telephone longer.) What was Pasternak up to these days? (I had torn pages from *Izvestiya* dated January of this year containing two Pasternak poems in praise of Stalin. I saw Nadezhda and Osip exchange meaningful glances as they passed the poems from one to the other.) Was there any truth to the rumors that Zinoviev and Kamenev were to go on trial in the summer? (How on earth could one know if a rumor was true? On the other hand, newspaper articles reported they had confessed to plotting against Stalin, which would indicate a show trial was likely to be in the works.) Was it possible they had arrested so many people, the trains taking prisoners to detention centers, not to mention the centers themselves, were overloaded and the terror was tapering off? (Certainly not. Compared to the relatively vegetarian year of 1934, when people were more or less arrested for a reason, nowadays anybody could be arrested and for no reason at all. The Cheka didn't require accusations, evidence, even a denunciation. It was almost as if the very randomness of the arrests was the point the state wanted to get across.)

And so, in half sentences and pregnant silences and stifled tears, we brought one another up to date on the ruins of our lives. The Mandelstams had sectioned off the room they rented with a cord strung between two walls and covered with blankets to create a partition screening their narrow bed. They absolutely insisted I sleep in the bed. God only knows where they slept. Perhaps the seamstress let them use the ottoman I spied in the sewing room when I met their landlady. In any case, mornings were a saraband of people passing in the hallway—the three of us, the seamstress and her son, even some neighbors who didn't have running water— to use the only toilet in the house. Soon after my arrival I gave them the books I'd brought (including a new Italian translation of Plutarch's *Parallel Lives*) and the clothing (long underwear and leather gloves for Osip, a no-nonsense German brassiere and thick thigh-length woolen stockings for Nadezhda), along with the sulfur pills for Osip's heart palpitation and the thousand rubles (half from Borisik, half from me) I had pinned inside my underwear for safekeeping. I could sense Osip was annoyed to discover there were no cigarettes in what he called his *Father Christmas* stocking, but

Nadezhda had written me warning that the doctor at the clinic had urged him to give up smoking.

Osip had composed any number of poems in what he called the Voronezh cycle, some of which he'd sent to me in letters, others that he took pleasure in reading aloud now that I was in Voronezh. There were flashes of the old Osip as he thrust himself to his feet and, leaning on the back of a chair, his good hand beating the air, recited bits and pieces from memory.

> *Oh, if only once the stir of the air and the heat*
> *of summer could make me hear*
> *beyond sleep and death*
> *the earth's axis, the earth's axis*

Nadezhda profited from the first occasion when we were alone to tell me that Osip, who frequently fell into black moods of despair, still entertained the thought of a joint suicide, but when he seemed set to leap, she hung back; when she was ready, he would say, *Not yet—let's wait and see.* Apparently the idea of their killing themselves individually was never seriously considered by either of them. They had lived as a couple, Nadezhda said with what can only be described as pride, if it came to it they would die as a couple. On the positive side, Osip exhibited a faint sign that his instinct for survival had not completely withered. He'd been laboring for months, so Nadezhda confided, on a proper Ode to Stalin, one that would expunge the insults he'd flung at the *Kremlin mountaineer* in his epigram to Stalin and, so he hoped, protect them from arrest when his sentence expired. When I accompanied him to Polyclinic No. 1 on Engels Street to see the laryngologist the following day (Osip's sinuses were acting up), I raised the subject of the ode and he grudgingly recited chunks of it. I cannot claim to have committed to memory more than a few fragments of this eminently forgettable poem:

I want to say—not Stalin—I want to name him
Dzhugashvili . . .
Artist, cherish the warrior, he is always with you . . .
He smiles—a smiling reaper . . .
Bending from the podium, as if upon a mountain, he
reaches over mounds of heads . . .

Another appalling line comes to mind:

Stalin's eyes are parting mountains—

My God, to what had Osip been reduced! *Stalin's eyes parting mountains!* Here are two more lines, ending with a play on the nom de guerre Stalin, which as every schoolchild learns, has its origins in *stali,* or steel:

No truth is truer than the warrior's candor:
For honor and for love, for valor and for steel—

I remember Osip stopping in his tracks after he had delivered the last line of the Ode. Lost in self-doubt, he gazed downhill at the half-wrecked Cathedral of Saint Mitrofanius, named after the holy seventeenth-century bishop of Voronezh, rising like an ice palace from the café table center of town. The streets around the cathedral, locked in ice, were filled with peasants who, fed up with getting the dregs after the Bolsheviks carted off the harvest to feed the proletarians in the cities, had fled collective farms. One could make out knots of them standing outside stores, stamping their feet on the ground to keep from freezing while they begged for crusts of bread. Osip had surely seen all of this before, but still he grimaced in empathy. I remember his saying that, contrary to what people claimed, misery *didn't* love company—it preferred to be alone. (I surmised he was speaking from personal experience.) And then, in one of the characteristic ellipsis that left his first readers and his friends struggling to bridge the gap in the conversation, he burst out, "Anna, Anna, when I was younger, poetry came easier and it was often quite good. Now that I am older, it comes much more slowly, but at times it is better. When I read aloud some of the poems in the Voronezh cycle, I don't have to pause for breath so my first readers will know where the lines break or bend or double back. The words speak for themselves. They no longer need the poet. Except for this . . . this Ode to Stalin. These words came up like bile. I feel as if I am babbling. It is beginning to dawn on me that I am in artistic trouble. What have I done?"

I told him that one had to remain among the living as long as one humanly could. I like to think I managed to say it with conviction even if I didn't feel any. "If I could save my son, if I could save my husband," I added, "Jesus, what I wouldn't do. I would fuck Stalin."

"I, too, would fuck Stalin if I could," he said. And then he actually smiled. Yes, yes, Osip produced a cheerless smile. And he said, "Of course I'm using the verb in a different sense than you." And we fell into each other's arms, shuddering in an ecstasy of laughter.

I can't recall if it was that day or the next that Osip, crossing the railway tracks, stooped to retrieve a scrap of paper. I started to tease him—"Have you been reduced to picking up paper, then?"—when I realized that it was folded into a tiny packet. Osip peeled it open and showed it to me. The paper contained a short letter, written in a tiny hand on a page torn from a school exercise book, along with a name and address in Petersburg. "The cattle cars that pass in the night are filled with prisoners being taken off to Central Asia," he said. "Listen to this," and fitting his spectacles over his ears, he began to read:

My dearest and most beloved Axinya,

I kiss your hands, I kiss your feet. My trial ended before I was aware it had begun. The three-man Special

Court read aloud the conclusions of my interrogator.
I tried to get a word in but was gaveled into silence.
The three judges whispered to each other, then the one
in the middle announced the sentence—twenty years
forced labor without the right of correspondence. If this
letter, God willing, reaches you, you will know that you
and the children must get by without me. Don't hesitate
to sell my two violins, along with the bows and my
supply of resin. The Italian violin especially should fetch
a good price. Consult my brother for advice on who
might have the talent to play it and the money to buy it.
Donate my partitions to the music school. Send word to
my friends in the orchestra of my fate. I weep in regret
that I did not commit the crimes I was accused of.

Your loving husband who will go to the grave with an
image of you under the lids of his eyes,
Alexander

Osip carefully folded the paper. I took it from him and moistened the side without writing with the tears accumulating in the corner of an eye. I remember thinking: perhaps I would get word of the fate of my husband or son when some kind soul comes across a letter dropped along the railway ties. I slipped the folded page inside the wrist of my glove to take back with me to Petersburg, where I intended to post it. "Perhaps the musician has stumbled across the formula to put an end to your Kremlin mountaineer," I said. "Perhaps we should all commit the crimes we're *going* to be accused of."

"That would be as good a way as any of killing yourself," Osip said.

Looking back on my week in Voronezh, it strikes me as instructive how, even in Osip's situation, banished as he was to one of the minus-twelve cities for writing a seditious poem, one went through the motions of living a normal life in a civilized society.

The hour each morning after breakfast was devoted to reconstituting Mandelstam's oeuvre. Large portions of it had been confiscated by the Chekists searching the flat after his arrest. With his eyes tightly shut and his head angled back, Osip would help his wife reconstruct the poems from memory (now and then I was able to fill in a missing fragment) as Nadezhda copied them off in a tiny hand onto cigarette paper, one poem to a paper, before secreting them with exiled writers in Voronezh. When his concentration waned, Osip would call a halt for the day. Gleefully stuffing pages of a local newspaper between his shirt and his sweater for insulation against the bitter cold, he insisted on my accompanying him on his daily expeditions into the center of Voronezh. (Nadezhda used the time to meet with local newspaper editors who paid her a pittance for advising them on the merits of literary works submitted for publication.) Osip had picked up work writing radio scripts for the Voronezh station—I remember the one he particularly liked was entitled *Gulliver for Children*. He also had earned three hundred rubles from a theater for writing the program notes for Gluck's *Orpheus and Eurydice*. On our trips into town, he kept an eye peeled for cigarettes. Unlike the old days in Moscow when he would buy or mooch them by the pack, he now considered it a triumph to unearth a single cigarette, which, swearing me to secrecy, he smoked behind Nadezhda's back. He would stop by the radio station and the theater on the off chance they might have something else for him to do; he claimed to be ready to sweep the streets that, in Voronezh, were never swept by anything except the blisteringly icy winds from the steppes. But the main excuse for the walks was it gave us an opportunity to catch up. Oblivious to the wintry temperature, we talked and talked until our lips were stiff from the cold, and the words emerged with muted *b*'s and *m*'s and *p*'s and *v*'s. Osip joked that we were inventing a new language, one that prisoners spoke without moving their lips so that Cheka lip-readers, watching through binoculars, wouldn't know they were talking to each other.

I couldn't help but observe, as we trudged down and up hills, that Osip seemed to recognize very few of the people we passed. Occasionally a man dressed in a winter coat would doff his hat in my friend's direction, and Osip, a distant look in his eyes, would absently nod back. But when I inquired about the identity of the passersby—I was curious whether they were political prisoners or simply souls living in Voronezh of their own free will—he invariably said he didn't know. "I am not familiar with the personal stories of the people I nod to," he said.

"But you must have made some friends here," I ventured.

"Aside from Nadenka, I have only one friend. It's the prostitute who lives immediately next door to us on Lineinaya Street," he explained. "When I became aware that nobody greeted her in the street—none of the men would be caught dead tipping his hat to a prostitute—I began to regularly tip mine and she would smile back gratefully. And then one day she invited us to tea and comfiture, and as we hadn't set eyes on comfiture in two years we immediately accepted."

I should say straightaway that I was intrigued by Osip's friendship with a prostitute. (Was it because I had heard that the Bolsheviks referred to me as *the harlot*?) Over the years I had met almost all of Osip's paramours, including the one he ran off with *after* he met Nadezhda at that bohemian cabaret in Kiev, but I'd never known him, no matter how lustful he felt, to go off with a lady of ill repute, as the gentlemen of ill repute called them. "And did she offer you her services?" I asked with a smirk.

Osip, having stopped to catch his breath, snickered. "No, she never offered. If she had I could not have accepted. I queue on the long line on a side street not far from the railway station where they rent erections, but they always run out of stock by the time I reach the window. Don't look so startled, my dear Anna. I still have my muse."

Osip was reluctant to arrange for me to meet the prostitute, fearing she would take it badly if he brought around a friend to stare at her as if she were a fish in a bowl. He relented only when I persisted. Which is how we wound up taking tea, as the English say, in the parlor of the prostitute, whose name was Varvara Samolova. She turned out to be something of a character. Varvara had arrived in Voronezh as the common-law wife of a political prisoner. When he failed to survive the first winter, she took up prostitution to earn money to raise her son, who was fifteen or sixteen. Her hobby was collecting postage stamps from all over the world depicting works of art—paintings, statues, architectural wonders. Osip claimed that some of her clients paid her in postage stamps instead of rubles, but I found this hard to believe. I thought it quite out of the ordinary that she functioned openly as a prostitute until I discovered, from Osip, that several members of the local Party committee, including one who was a Chekist, regularly made use of her services.

What did Varvara look like? I took her to be in her late twenties or early thirties, fine-boned like a snowbird, with a beautiful complexion and long reddish hair that trailed in fluffy tufts over her breasts. She wore a frock that (as it turned out) she herself had created by sewing together two aprons. The dress was cut low on the bosom and worn over a lace undergarment that left little to the imagination. Planted squarely on her head, even indoors, was a fashionable hat, the kind you might come across in a Parisian magazine. It crossed my mind that she may have received her clients with her clothing removed and her hat on, but I didn't feel it suitable to raise the question with her. She was clearly delighted to discover Osip on her doorstep and immediately fetched the comfiture from its hiding place on a shelf. She took me for a newly arrived minus-twelve and as Osip failed to correct her, she didn't hesitate to talk freely in my presence. Before one knew it she was setting out her son's textbooks on the glass-covered table to show us the pages where thick paper had been glued over the faces of Trotsky or Zinoviev or Kamenev.

"But how did they know to do this?" I inquired.

"The children are instructed at school which leaders have fallen from grace. The schoolmaster regularly receives letters from the editors of the *Great Encyclopedia* with lists of articles or illustrations to be pasted over or cut out. All this is easy enough when you live, as we do, in the countryside because we have our wood stoves. My sister lives in Moscow—she spends half her waking hours cutting articles and illustrations into strips and flushing them down the toilet."

Osip wondered aloud if all references to him had been expunged from books about poetry published in the twenties and early thirties. "Are you famous?" the prostitute asked and when he didn't answer, she turned to me and repeated the question. "You must absolutely tell me: Is he famous?"

"In certain circles, he is famous. In other circles, he is infamous."

Varvara dismissed my comment with a disparaging wave of her hand. "You don't fool me. You are playing with words, which is something I never do. Here you can lose your head if you play with words. And what is he famous for, then?"

"For scrambling across the faults between words," I declared.

Varvara rocked her head from side to side in wonderment. "One could vanish in the faults between words."

Osip held out his hand. "Let me guide you across the faults," he said.

Smiling demurely, Varvara took his hand.

With the prostitute, I saw a side of Osip that I thought had gone the way of his erections. He was teasing, even seductive, with her. (Perhaps rehearsing a role that, by his own account, he could no longer hope to play allowed him to fantasize). With Varvara he let his hair down, as the saying goes, chatting of lighter-hearted things as if he didn't have a care in the world. Nadezhda was another story. In my presence, they talked only of serious matters seriously: the pros and cons of suicide; whether to squander their limited supply of rubles on a bottle of Georgian wine in my honor; whether Nadezhda's *murtsovka* was tastier cooked with *kvass* or rusty tap water; if with *kvass*, where on earth some could be found; who in Voronezh might be prevailed upon to give one or the other of them work.

It was left to me to raise the delicate subject they were studiously avoiding. I remember doing it over bowls of semolina an hour or two before my departure. I cleared my throat to get their attention. "What will you do when your sentence is up next year?" I asked.

My question was greeted with stony silence. "If it grows any quieter in the room," I quipped, "one may be able to hear the earth's axis."

A faint smile appeared on Nadezhda's lips as she quoted the line from Osip's Voronezh cycle. ". . . *Beyond sleep and death, the earth's axis . . .*"

"Well?" I insisted.

Osip rushed to the door to watch a passing train. When he had shuffled back to his chair, he stared out the window and said, very firmly, "When my sentence is up, I shall make my way back to Moscow and resume my life."

Nadezhda turned on her husband. "Resume reading your poems to eleven people who brave the weather to turn up at the *Literary Gazette* office? Resume mooching cigarettes from silly girls who think the poet Mandelstam must be dead? Resume fabricating an original manuscript of the 1913 edition of *Stone* to sell to the Literary Fund Library? Resume the insomnia that comes from listening for the late-night knock on the door?"

Osip controlled his temper. "My new Ode to Stalin will protect the both of us from arrest."

Nadezhda appealed to me. "I had a dream of disappearing so far into the countryside the state would forget we existed, of living in an isolated wooden house with ornamented shutters, of seeing on a distant hill the onion domes of a small village church that was being used to store hay, of growing potatoes and cabbages and cucumbers and beets and turnips on the tiny parcel of land behind the house, of keeping hens and a cow, of exchanging eggs and milk for loaves of bread and tins of roe."

I remember Nadezhda looking away, her shoulders aquiver with anguish. I glanced over at my dear friend Osip. "The night you were arrested, back in 1934, I reminded you of Pushkin's last words," I said. "They haven't slipped your mind, surely. *Try to be forgotten. Go live in the country.*"

"Pushkin breathed his last breath in a city," Osip noted irritably. "It is my intention to follow his example."

"You'd be crazy to return to Moscow," I said. "After three years of exile, there's almost no chance of your getting a residence permit, so you would have to live illegally. The cities are acrawl with minor officials and writers and editors who think they can survive by denouncing someone; anyone. Whether you are there legally or illegally, some ambitious lackey in the Cheka will want to make a name for himself by arresting the poet Mandelstam a second time. If you want to survive into middle age—"

With a sly smile, Osip said, "You don't hold out the hope of old age?"

"Old age," I recall answering, "is beyond the realm of possibility."

"I think the same," he admitted.

I went on as if nothing had been said. "If you want to survive into middle age, if you want Nadezhda to survive, you must keep a low profile, you must take refuge somewhere far from Moscow where nobody knows you, you must cultivate anonymity."

"Anonymity!" Osip exploded. "How can you of all people tell me that, Anna Andreyevna? What do you suggest the poet Mandelstam do—join the ranks of the thousands through the centuries who have published poems signed *Anonymous*?" I could see Osip had lost the thread of the question that had provoked the conversation, but that didn't stop him from ranting. "Yes, yes, you've come up with an idea that recommends itself to me. We shall go to the Bolshevik town committee first thing tomorrow, Nadenka, we shall petition them to formally change our family name to *Anonymous*. Osip Emilievich and Nadezhda Yakovlevna Anonymous. That's the ticket. And we'll move into a hermit's hut in the mountains and keep a cow, and use its shit to pave a path to our door when the Bolsheviks come calling to congratulate me on the publication of my Ode to Stalin in *Pravda* under the name *Anonymous*."

"Calm yourself," Nadezhda said. "If you are dead set on returning to Moscow, then that's what we shall do."

Osip filled his lungs with air. Gradually his breathing became steadier. And he came up with a line I immediately recognized from one of the poems in his Voronezh cycle he had sent me in the post. *"Maybe this is the beginning of madness."*

"If it is the beginning of madness," I said, "you can stop feigning sanity."

Did he identify the remark about feigning sanity as having come from his lips during that memorable conversation with Pasternak a lifetime ago? If so, it didn't show in his eyes. He looked at me queerly, almost as if he could see through me. "A bizarre thing happened to me when I was on my way to meet your train," he said. "I stopped to catch my breath in Petrovsky Square next to that statue of Peter the Great holding aloft an anchor. And for a terrifying moment I forgot who I was and what I was doing there, sitting on the rim of a fountain filled not with water but with garbage, looking up at the statue I call Peter the Anchor. What saved me was a line from one of my Voronezh poems that popped into my head. *What is the name of this street? Mandelstam's Street . . .* And my name came back to me, and with it the memory that I was going to meet my dearest friend in the world after Nadenka."

I repeated the line. *"What is the name of this street? Mandelstam's Street . . ."*

It was Nadezhda who accompanied me to the station that afternoon. Osip's heart palpitation had returned; he had taken several of the sulfur pills but they failed to give him relief and he was feeling too weak to do more than see me to the door. We embraced, neither of us persuaded we would ever meet again. I started down the steps only to hear Osip issuing instructions to me in a voice thick with anxiety. He ordered me to go straight to the Central Committee when my train reached Moscow and tell them he was wasting away in Voronezh from hunger and depression, that he had a letter from Polyclinic No. 1 saying he suffered from cardiologopathy, arterial sclerosis and schizoid psychopathy. "How on earth do you expect me to get in to see the Central Committee?" I cried. "I have no pass. They won't let me in the door."

Osip refused to take no for an answer. "Say you have come from the poet Mandelstam and doors will open," he replied, his eyelid twitching. "They will fall over each other to listen to you."

At the station, Nadezhda and I watched the long train covered with dust creep up to the quay. Children jumped aboard to hold seats for the older travelers bogged down with baggage. Nadezhda pressed pickled beets wrapped in newspaper into my hands and then tossed her shoulders in a fit of despair. "I have taken to praying," she informed me. "I pray to God every night when I climb into the narrow cot alongside my husband." I must have asked her what she prayed for because she said, "I say, *Dear God, who, judging from what I see around me, certainly does not exist, while my beloved Osya still has a muse, please arrange things so that the sun fails to rise tomorrow morning. Amen.*"

"Amen," I said.

No, I don't remember very much of the trip back to Petersburg. It had a beginning and a terminus but no middle. In a trancelike state, I changed trains and scrambled for seats and fell asleep clutching my satchel to my chest so that nothing would be stolen from it. Somewhere along the way I scratched four lines on the back of an envelope, which I have to this day. I don't need to find the envelope to tell you the lines. They are committed to memory, they are etched on my brain.

> ... *in the room of the banished poet*
> *Fear and the Muse stand watch by turn,*
> *And the night is coming on,*
> *Which has no hope of dawn*

EIGHTEEN

Nadezhda Yakovlevna
Monday, the 2nd of May 1938

As far as the state was concerned, our minus-twelve banishment to Voronezh came to an end not quite one year ago—at three-fifteen in the afternoon on the sixteenth of May 1937, to be precise—when a pinched-faced Chekist with a waxed mustache (a client, as it turned out, of the charming prostitute who lived next door to us) signed and stamped an official document declaring that Mandelstam had served his sentence and we were free to live anywhere in Soviet Russia our hearts desired. There was an unstated catch: we needed to have a residence permit, and the only city in Soviet Russia we had a residence permit for was Voronezh.

Which meant for the poet Mandelstam, for his wedded wife, exile was expected to last a lifetime.

Still, we were determined to move on. (Where, how, only God knew.) The first order of business was to get rid of the excess baggage we had accumulated since our arrival in Voronezh: buckets, a chamber pot, a frying pan, a flatiron, a small one-burner kerosene stove, a kerosene lamp, a lumpy mattress and an assortment of very mended blankets and quilts, a carton filled with chipped plates and saucepans. Some of the booty we bequeathed to our seamstress landlady, some we gave to a couple of fresh-off-the-train exiles Mandelstam found wandering in Lineinaya Street desperately looking for a room to rent. (Our landlady had decided we would be her last borders as she wanted to free up the room for her son.) We packed our clothing into a valise and two satchels and a paper sack with a rope handle and, paying the seamstress's son to assist us, made our way to the train station. With or without residence permits, we were drawn to Moscow like the proverbial moth to flame. Mandelstam, who slept fitfully and was despondent most of his waking hours, perked up the moment the train, heading north and west, pulled away from Voronezh. The closer we got to Moscow, the more animated he became. He wasn't composing verse these days, but it was almost as if his muse was breathing down his neck.

I can tell you that Moscow, which we reached after a grueling two-and-a-half-day trek, had changed since we'd lived there three years earlier. The long train crept through suburbs that hadn't existed before—wide dusty boulevards lined with brick apartment houses in various stages of construction. The city itself looked as if it had had a face-lift. Tsarist-era buildings had been steam-scrubbed and you could catch glimpses of massive structures rising inside scaffolding, with imposing stone and steel and glass façades that, to my layman's eye, appeared inspired by what our newspapers called the decadent American ornamental style. The social climate had changed, too, though I would be hard put to say it had changed for the better. For months recent arrivals in Voronezh had been commenting on the existence in Moscow of a class of citizens they described as nouveau rich (to which Mandelstam, in one of his infrequent bursts of wit, had responded: *Better nouveau than never*). Young people acted as if they had money to burn. Cadres were getting promoted rapidly (as those ahead of them in the pecking order were arrested). The latest chic was to actually open a bank account. (When I had money, like Akhmatova I kept it pinned inside my undergarments.) Apartments, dachas, used furniture, secondhand gramophones and records, even luxury items such as electric iceboxes were said to be easier to come by, no doubt because so many people were vanishing into prisons or exile, abandoning their possessions behind them.

The moment Mandelstam set foot back in Moscow I could see that, despite the danger of not having a residence permit, we had done the right thing to return. It may sound as if I am inventing this but I could have sworn the color of his skin changed from asphalt to—well, skin color. An unmistakable gleam materialized in his eyes, almost as if the sights and noises of a metropolis had jogged a memory, had reminded him of life *before* death. He even walked at a pace that would have left a snail behind. Seeing a smile on my husband's lips for the first time in months brought a smile to my lips for the first time in months.

Feeling like Jews who had reached the Promised Land after years of wandering a wilderness, we decided then and there that we absolutely had to find a way to remain in Moscow. The first imperative was to come up with a place to sleep. And so, flagging down one of the ministry pool automobiles whose chauffeurs freelanced as taxi drivers, we headed for Herzen House in the hope of coming across someone willing to put us up for a night or two.

In the event we had to make do with couch cushions on the linoleum floor of the tiny apartment belonging to one of the young poets to whom Mandelstam used to read his poetry. The poet's wife, a plump and pale editor at a monthly literary magazine, made it clear, as she set out the cushions on sheets of newspaper, that we were welcome to stay for two or three days, by which she meant that we were not welcome to stay longer. (I didn't hold this against her. They were already running a risk having people without residence permits under their roof.) Mandelstam, overcome with fatigue from the journey, not to mention melancholy at finding himself back in Moscow, stretched out on the cushions and, pulling down the earflaps of his cap to block the clamor of traffic on Nashchokin Street, drifted into a deep sleep. I covered him with his yellow leather coat and lay down, fully clothed, beside him.

I recall waking at sunrise that first morning in Moscow with a fierce headache. My husband was sleeping so soundly I didn't have the heart to rouse him. Making my way to the toilet, I rinsed my face and the back of my neck with rusty cold water from the tap. That made me feel human again. I decided to go downstairs and knock on the door of our old apartment—when I'd packed in a mad rush to accompany Mandelstam into exile, I'd left books behind and I thought I might be able to recover them now. Which is how I came across the note pinned to the door of our flat: "If anybody asks for Zakonsky, I'm at the dacha until the end of the month." There was also a telephone number. I didn't recognize the name Zakonsky, but if he had a dacha *and* a telephone, it meant he was published, which in itself was an inauspicious sign these days; the only writers published were the ones who toed the Party line. I started to turn away when I remembered the latchkey I'd hidden behind the molding near the communal telephone in case Mandelstam should forget his. To my amazement, it was still there after all these years. Nobody was stirring on the floor as I let myself into our apartment. The sight of the familiar walls, the sound of our old Swiss clock ticking away in the kitchen brought tears to my eyes. The books I had left behind filled the top shelf of our old bookcase—first editions of Derzhavin, Yazykov, Zhukovski, Baratynski, Fet, Polanski, along with Mandelstam's beloved Italians, Vasari, Boccaccio, Vico. I gathered them up and, sinking onto the bedraggled sofa where Zinaida and I had sat listening to Mandelstam read his Kremlin mountaineer epigram, began to leaf through the title pages. And naïve as this may sound, it suddenly dawned on me: *The best way to obtain a residence permit is to possess a residence.* The explanation that came into my head seemed simple enough for even an apparatchik to understand: the poet Mandelstam and I had been allotted this flat in Herzen House, he'd been sent into minus-twelve exile, I had accompanied him; now with exile behind us we had returned to Moscow and wanted our residence back. You won't believe this—I barely believe it as I recount the episode—but my reasoning seemed so commonsensical to my twisted brain that I actually set off to find the district militia office. Imagine the fear I had to suppress simply walking through the front door! To my surprise, the officer on duty, an older man who, from the look of him, was desperately hoping to retire before they got around to arresting him, heard me out and then shrugged. You must understand that a shrug in Soviet Russia didn't mean *no*. It meant *maybe;* it meant *I'm not senior enough to assume the responsibility of giving you a definitive answer.* The officer suggested I try the central militia station on Petrovka. I walked all the way, hoping the exertion would calm my nerves and let my voice pass for tired instead of stressed. A long line had formed and I had to queue for hours to reach the ranking militia official in the main hall of the Petrovka station. He was a baby-faced young man—too young for the post he held, which suggested that he had filled the shoes of an arrested official—wearing perfectly round steel-rimmed eyeglasses. He raised his eyes, but not his head, to peer over the rims at me. I started to explain our situation but he cut me off.

"Impossible to be assigned a residence without a residence permit. Residence permit denied because you are a convicted person. Next."

"I have no conviction," I cried.

The woman behind me said in my ear, "Whatever it is you're after, dear lady, you stand a better chance of getting it if you calm yourself."

I pulled the official document from my purse and flattened it on the desk so the official could read it. Again, he didn't move his head, only his eyes. "It says here you are a convicted person," he said.

"I have no conviction. I voluntarily followed my husband into exile."

I might have been talking to an automaton. "It states here," he said impatiently, *"Osip Mandelstam, convicted person."*

"Osip Mandelstam is a man. I am a woman."

I managed to snatch back my precious document an instant before he slammed his fist on the desk. "Osip Mandelstam is your husband, isn't he? Under Soviet law, arrested persons and their families are deprived of residence rights in Moscow. Haven't you heard of Article 58? What your husband was guilty of, you are guilty of. I can charge you with anti-Soviet activities."

I am sorry to report that I fled the Petrovka station in terror.

After the failure of my pathetic attempt to get back our old flat, we lived like birds on a branch. We eventually settled into one room of a communal apartment in Kalinin, which was near enough to Moscow to come in by train several times a month. Word spread that Mandelstam had returned alive from exile and friends flocked to see him when they learned, through word of mouth, that he was in town. Hoping to save us from a second arrest, my husband gave impassioned readings of his more recent Ode to Stalin to anyone who would listen. We had no shortage of writers and poets offering us loans "to tide us over" ("tide us over *what*?" Mandelstam would ask in agitation when we were alone); among them was the self-described *master of the genre of silence* Isaac Babel, who, during one of our several visits to the rooms he rented on the second floor of a private villa, glumly told us, "Silence won't save me. Mark my words—they will come for me soon."

Quite a few close friends were willing to give us shelter in Moscow, though for their sake we never spent more than a few days in any one flat lest our hosts be denounced to the police. Akhmatova dropped what she was doing and came to Moscow the instant she discovered we were back. Mandelstam and she flung themselves into each other's arms. Did I feel odd man out? No, I'm not offended by the question. They had never been lovers, though in a manner of speaking they were more intimate than lovers, by which I mean they were intimate in ways that lovemaking only scratches the surface of. There were occasions, I won't deny it, when this intimacy fetched up a lump to my throat that I identified as jealousy. They awakened the lost youth in one another.

Employing a private language that by its very nature excluded others from the conversation, they could make each other laugh until one of them got a nosebleed. His hands behind his head, his fingers laced together at the back of his neck, Mandelstam strode the room declaiming poems from the Voronezh cycle. Anna Andreyevna, in turn, recited the poem she had written after her visit to Voronezh the previous year, something about fear and a muse taking turns watching over a disgraced poet. (As far as I know this poem has never been published.) We went to Petersburg once, which turned out, from my point of view, to be a mistake—strolling streets familiar to him from his student days set my husband to trembling with emotion. We stayed overnight at Akhmatova's apartment, drinking toasts to poets and particular poems late into the night.

At one point we could hear the telephone ringing in the corridor. A neighbor stuck his head in the door. "It's for you, Anna Andreyevna."

She went to take the call, only to return a moment later looking quite pale. "Who was it?" I asked.

"There was no one on the other end of the line."

We all exchanged looks. Mandelstam and I left in the morning. Anna Andreyevna accompanied us to the station. I shall never forget my husband's last words to her: "I am ready for death."

On another occasion we spent an afternoon with Pasternak at his dacha in Peredelkino, half an hour out from Moscow; originally the Kolychev estate, the village had became a fashionable retreat for fashionable writers in the late 1920s. (We never did figure out how, in the summer of '36, Boris, who was in and out of favor over the years, managed to get a foot in that door.) It was not lost on any of us that his new (to us, at least) wife remained in the kitchen during our visit to avoid my husband. Boris Leonidovich and Mandelstam pulled up stools next to the ornate tile stove for warmth, I remained on a sofa with a coverlet over my feet. Pasternak, who said he was in the very early stages of sketching the outline of a novel "about us all," produced books he was reading on the subject of the French Revolution. I remember the discussion became animated and I gestured to Boris Leonidovich to calm things down for fear Mandelstam's pulse would start to race.

Pasternak took the view that it was possible to survive a reign of terror, but my husband only shook his head in obstinate disagreement. "If you breathe the air of terror," he said, "you become infected. Everyone becomes a victim—those whose heads are lopped off, the executioners who lop off heads, the masses in the streets who watch, even those who have the decency to look away."

At the train station later, Pasternak—with the dexterity of a cutpurse—slipped money into Mandelstam's pocket when they embraced. We discovered it when I went to hang up my husband's yellow leather coat back in Kalinin.

And so the weeks, the months slipped past with Mandelstam staring out of rain-stained windows in Kalinin or Moscow or Petersburg, repeating the names of people who had vanished into a gulag. If I close my eyes I can reproduce his voice in my ear: "The enigmatic Khardjiev with his oversized head, Hippolyte with his wild scheme to seduce the angel of death, Zhenya with his nails bitten to the quick, Vadik with his poems so convoluted even he couldn't understand them, Pasha with his crazy theory about how Russia would be saved when opiate became the religion of the people."

I should say here the disappearance that gave us the most pain, not to speak of the most anguish, was that of our friend and protector Nikolai Bukharin. We had, it goes without saying, followed his fate closely. His name as editor in chief had been removed from the masthead of *Izvestiya* in the winter of '37 and we'd learned of his arrest soon after over the loudspeakers in the main streets of Voronezh. (Mandelstam was particularly incensed to hear people cheering.) For months on end there was no news of Bukharin. Then came his very public trial for high treason and plotting to assassinate Stalin. (Ironically, Genrikh Yagoda, the onetime head of the Cheka who had personally signed the charges against Mandelstam when he was arrested in 1934, was a codefendant: "We won't waste tears over him" was all my husband said when he heard about this.) The trial began early in March of this year in the October Hall of the House of Trade Unions where, we happened to know, Nikolai Ivanovich had proposed marriage to the young woman who later became his third wife. His confession, published in *Pravda*, was the principal subject of conversation in intellectual circles (Hitler's *Anschluss* of Austria was a close second) where Bukharin, despite his Bolshevik credentials, was considered to be a cultivated individual and a humanist. There were those who repeated the old saw *Where there is smoke, expect to come across fire*, which was another way of saying that, given the circumstances, "the filthy little Bukharin" (as he was described in newspaper articles) would have been stupid not to have plotted against Stalin; there were others, we among them, who supposed that he had confessed to save his wife and young son.

Esteemed Nikolai Ivanovich was taken to the vaulted basement of the Lubyanka and shot in the back of the head, if one believed the execution notice that turned up in the newspaper on the morning of 15 March. Which, curiously, was a few days after we bumped into V. Stavsky, the secretary general of the Soviet Writers' Union. Let me explain. We had all but abandoned hope that we would ever get permission to live in Moscow; abandoned hope of being able to survive the new wave of terror spreading across Russia. The last straw we clutched at was the possibility that in the absence of Bukharin, Stavsky would argue Mandelstam's case to Stalin; would give him the text, which we knew to be circulating, of the Ode to Stalin ("*Stalin's eyes are parting mountains . . .*"). But our desperate and repeated attempts to get an appointment with Stavsky failed miserably. We camped for hours on the hard benches in his waiting room. Secretaries would rush about. Eventually someone would take pity on us. The secretary general was out of town, a woman would inform us. He was attending a conference of writers in the Crimea. He was visiting collective farms in various Soviet Socialist Republics. And so on. And then one day, implausible as this may sound, we stumbled across Stavsky emerging from the office building as we were going in. Or more accurately, he stumbled across us. We hadn't seen him in years and I doubt either of us would have recognized him if he hadn't shouted, "Hey, ho, Mandelstam, I've been hunting everywhere for you."

Stavsky, looking very suntanned, wearing a coffee-colored linen three-piece suit and dark glasses, hurried over to us and shook my husband's hand cordially. "I've been trying to get in touch with you," he exclaimed, "but nobody seems to know where you hang your hat these days."

All Mandelstam, bless his heart, could think to say was: "I hang my hat in its usual place, which is on my head."

Stavsky dropped my husband's hand. "Are you all right?"

"No."

"Ah! Well, I have good news for you, Mandelstam. Your fortunes are about to take a turn for the better. To begin with, we have decided to give you and your wife vouchers for a two-month cure at one of the writers' sanatoriums outside of Moscow. The stay will do you a world of good—wholesome food, country air, plenty of sleep, long walks in the woods. You will be a new man. Then we will look into your rehabilitation. The question of a permit to live in Moscow, the matter of finding appropriate work for you, will be hashed out at the highest level."

Stavsky instructed us to present ourselves at the Literary Fund office to collect the train tickets to Charusti, on the Murom Line, and the vouchers for the rest home in Samatikha, twenty-five kilometers from Charusti. When we reached Charusti, we would find a horse-drawn sleigh waiting to take us the rest of the way.

Elation rose in Mandelstam like sap in a tree. "Pinch me," he said when Stavsky saluted us from the backseat of his limousine as it pulled away from the curb. "I must be dreaming that this is happening."

"The problem," I remember saying, "is to figure out *what* is happening."

"But any idiot can see what is happening! My ode has reached Stalin's ears. Word has filtered back down that the poet Mandelstam must be looked after." He turned on me angrily. "Why aren't you capable of dealing with good news?"

"I am worried."

"About what?"

"That there is no such thing as good news, only bad news disguised as good news. I am worried sick they want to get you away from your friends. I am worried sick you will be arrested again."

"What are our alternatives?"

"We can find an isolated house with ornamented shutters, we can grow potatoes and cabbages and cucumbers and beets and turnips in the garden, we can keep hens and a cow, we can exchange eggs and milk for loaves of bread and tins of roe."

Mandelstam's face flushed in agitation. "You don't fool me—you want me to publish poetry under the name *Anonymous*. Nadenka, don't you see it—they're going to *rehabilitate* me. My muse, perhaps even my erection, will take up residence again. Poems will begin to knock like a fist on the window. I shall make love and write poetry and publish under the name of Osip Mandelstam. Editors will beat down my door to get the rights to my collected works."

I looked into his eyes. He desperately wanted to believe we had turned a corner. I suppose I must have smiled because he said, "I knew you'd come around."

I think I said: "What is there to lose by trying?" I think I thought: "Only what's left of our lives."

Why do you keep pressing me for details? There is only one detail that counts for me now: from the moment we ran into Stavsky, I had the sinking feeling of being on a steep and slippery slope. Yes, the train tickets and the vouchers were waiting for us at the Literary Fund office. Yes, yes, there was a horse-drawn sleigh sitting outside the station at Charusti, which Mandelstam took as a further indication that his fortunes had taken a turn for the better. Luxury of luxuries, an enormous sheepskin rug was folded on the seat. We spread it and tugged it up to our armpits and the driver, an old *mujik* with knee-high lace-up leather boots and a wolf-skin *chapka* on his pointed head, raised a whip to the horse and we set out at a trot to cover the twenty-five kilometers to the rest home in Samatikha.

Winter had persisted into April. As far as the eye could see, the countryside was quilted with blindingly white fresh snow. Fir trees stooped under the weight of the ice on their branches. The sky was pearl blue, with wisps of clouds drifting at high altitudes. Swirls of frozen breath spewed from the horse's flaring nostrils. Mandelstam improvised a pair of peasant sunshades with his gloved fingers and took everything in, sighing from time to time at the splendor of the scenery. After two or so hours, the *mujik* pulled into the yard of a collective farm and we were taken to a room where hot wine and biscuits were waiting on a table, as if we were expected. Mandelstam kept glancing at me with a look of triumph on his face. We reached the writers' sanatorium at dusk. The resident doctor, an old Bolshevik who (he later told us) had taken the job in the rest home in the hope of lowering his profile, met us at the door. He confided that he had received a telegram from Moscow ordering him to treat the Mandelstams as important guests. The doctor looked honest enough—if we were being set up for arrest, I took heart from my gut feeling he didn't know about it. Mandelstam mentioned that he longed for quiet as well as peace. The doctor said there was a cabin at the edge of the woods that served as a reading room for residents. In no time they had set up two cots in the reading room and given us the key. We spread our clothing and books on one of the shabby sofas and lay down on the beds, fully dressed, our fingers laced under our heads.

Lord knows why but it was then that Mandelstam was suddenly overcome with doubts. "You could be right," he said suddenly. "We may have fallen into a trap. If we are arrested here, Pasternak and Akhmatova would not hear about it for months."

When my husband's spirits flagged, I must have felt a compulsion to be positive. How else can one explain that I said, "No, no, didn't the Literary Fund pay for transportation and the two-month stay here? They wouldn't have done this if we were still living under a cloud."

"You really think so?"

"Yes."

Mandelstam cheered up. "You are surely right," he said.

April went by. Hope put down roots in the thawing soil of Samatikha. We went for long walks along the paths in the woods, slept late into the mornings, napped again in the afternoons with books from the shelves of the reading room open on our laps. I would come awake to find Mandelstam listening to music over earphones attached to a shortwave radio post in our cabin. We took our meals in the communal dining room not far from the main building. Occasionally writers or poets whom we knew, or knew of, came by the table to chat with Mandelstam. The wife of a short story writer, herself a translator, asked him what he was working on.

"Staying alive," he shot back.

"Everyone works on staying alive," her husband noted with a dry laugh. "She meant, artistically. Are you writing these days?"

For some reason the two of them brought out the orneriness in my husband. "I never *write*," Mandelstam said innocently. "I compose poetry in my head and dictate it to Nadenka. She is the one who *writes* it down."

The writer's wife was obstinate. "And are you composing in your head here?"

One of those ghostly wry smiles flitted across my husband's lips. "Here I concentrate on clearing the cobwebs from my head.

When we return to Moscow—when we are given back our flat in Herzen House—I shall begin composing poetry again."

And then . . . then one evening . . .

Thank you, yes, I will start over.

And then one evening after dinner, peering from the window of the reading room at the edge of the woods, we watched as two identical black automobiles with whitewall tires pulled up to the main house. The figures in the lead automobile remained inside. Two beefy men emerged from the second vehicle, one in civilian clothing, the other in some sort of uniform that I wasn't able to identify. "Did you see that?" Mandelstam asked in alarm.

I could make out his eyes in the dying light. They were wide with fright. "They have probably come to inspect the rest home," I said.

It was the first of May, nineteen years to the day since our paths had crossed in that seedy bohemian cabaret in Kiev. I say that with certainty because I have a memory of the guests standing around a shortwave radio post in the late afternoon listening to Stalin deliver a rambling speech. When an enormous gingerbread cake with twenty-one candles on it was brought to the head table after supper, people clapped their hands and stamped their feet on the floor; Mandelstam leaned close and told me they were applauding the chef who had baked it, not the twenty-one Bolshevik May Days. After the meal, the guests gathered around a piano to drink brandy and sing Russian folk songs. For hours after we retired to our cabin, we could hear them singing patriotic songs at the top of their lungs. When I managed to fall asleep, I dreamed of icons, which is universally taken to be a bad omen. Death lurks behind icons. I remember sitting up suddenly, gasping for breath. My husband tried to calm me. "We have nothing to be afraid of now," he said. "The worst is behind us."

At dawn I was roused by the birds chirping in the trees around the reading room. I checked, as I always did upon awakening, to be sure Mandelstam was breathing. I heard someone knock. Pulling on a robe, I padded across the room in my bare feet and opened the door, thinking of the reproach I would make to the guest come to borrow a book from the reading room at this ungodly hour. I found myself staring at the doctor, who was hyperventilating as if he had run the length of a soccer field. The two beefy men were behind him. The one in civilian clothing shouldered past the doctor. "We are looking for Osip Mandelstam."

Mandelstam materialized behind me. "I am the poet Mandelstam."

The two men pushed past me into the reading room. "Osip Emilievich Mandelstam," the civilian announced, "you are under arrest for violation of Article 58 of the Penal Code." I seem to remember he showed Mandelstam the arrest warrant, though I'm not absolutely certain of this.

My husband, who was in his underwear, nodded. He collected his thoughts, then went to the sofa and pulled on his gray trousers and a collarless white shirt, tucking it into the waistband and buttoning the top button against his neck. As the two men watched in silence, Mandelstam fitted on his suspenders and suit jacket and socks and shoes. He looked around to see what he'd forgotten, then climbed into his yellow leather coat despite the relative warmness of the season. He retrieved the paper sack with the rope handle from under the cot and began to drop things into it—his one-volume Pushkin edited by Tomashevski, some shirts that I had ironed the previous day, several changes of underwear and socks, the knitted winter scarf that an editor's wife had given him after his first arrest, a bar of soap, a comb, a tin of tooth powder, a toothbrush. I pulled my robe tight around my anesthetized body and sat on the bed as if paralyzed. My husband came over to me.

"Accompany me as far as Charusti."

The man wearing the uniform I couldn't identify said, "That is not permitted."

Mandelstam leaned down and kissed me on the lips. "Good-bye, then."

"Good-bye," I said.

I looked over at the shafts of sunlight stabbing through the panes of the window. When I turned back, my husband was gone. I heard the motors of the cars spurting into life. The door of the reading room yawned open. The doctor stood on the threshold, his palm on his heart. "I have no words," he said, crushed by what had transpired. And he, too, fled, leaving the door open behind him. I could not identify the muscles in my body that would have allowed me to cross the room and close it. I cannot remember how long I remained sitting on the bed. It could have been hours. I do remember talking to myself. I remember trying to come to terms with my new identity by repeating it over and over. "I am the widow of the poet Mandelstam. I am the widow of the poet Mandelstam. I am the widow of the poet Mandelstam. I am the widow of the poet Mandelstam. I am the widow of the poet Mandelstam."

NINETEEN

[A copy of the letter reprinted below was generously given to the
author (in January 1965, on the twenty-fifth anniversary of the
death of Isaac Babel, who was tortured into confessing to espionage
and shot) by Yekaterina Zh., a woman living in Moscow who herself
endured three years in a gulag and preferred to remain unidentified.
She and her late husband, a critic who wrote his (unpublished, later
confiscated) magnum opus on Russian poetry before the Bolshevik
Revolution, were close friends of the Mandelstams and, at some
personal risk, put them up overnight on several occasions when
Osip and Nadezhda were living like Gypsies in Moscow after their
return from Voronezh. The letter arrived in an envelope fabricated
out of course brown wrapping paper and postmarked from Ulaan
Baatar, with the name and address of Yekaterina Zh. printed in
ink in large majuscule letters on it. There was no return address.
Undated, unsigned except for the tantalizingly ambiguous (almost
coded) *Still dancing* at the end, the letter itself was painstakingly
written out in pencil in a spidery handwriting, completely filling
two sides of the title page and two sides of a blank page torn from a
copy of Tomashevski's Pushkin. It begins with the name Yekaterina

Zh. and her address in Moscow printed in a hand-drawn box. That's followed by the word *Hope*, which in the feminine singular, надежда in Cyrillic, is the name of Mandelstam's wife, Nadezhda. This, along with the several references to *Nadenka*, supports the supposition that the letter originated with Osip Mandelstam. If, as it appears, this document really can be attributed to Mandelstam, it was probably written in mid- or late September 1938 while he was en route to a transit camp in Siberia after his second arrest. It is reasonable to assume he *mailed* it in the traditional way prisoners posted letters, slipping it through the floor planks of a cattle car as the train carrying him east sped past a village or town at night.]

Hope: My second arrest, I keep track of them on the fingers of my left hand, I still have three arrests to go before I switch to my right, was extraordinary for being ordinary. I could sense the Chekists going through motions they had repeated, like workers on an assembly line, hundreds, perhaps thousands, of times. They seemed bored to tears as they started back toward Moscow, three of them in the automobile with me, one of them racing ahead in the second vehicle to clear the road with his siren when it became clogged with trucks or cows. The Chekist in charge, the one who showed me the arrest warrant, actually offered me a tin cup with tea from a thermos. I was afraid to accept lest the tea turn out to be poisoned, at which point he shrugged and drank it off himself. He didn't offer me a second cup. At Charusti we stopped at a military canteen for a lunch of [illegible] and black bread. I sat between the two soldiers almost as if I were a guest and, as I helped myself from the general bowl, I was able to eat. None of the soldiers at the other tables paid the slightest attention to me. When we started out again I dozed most of the time in the back of the car, my head against my satchel, which was wedged between the back of the seat and the window. Approaching Moscow, I was awakened by the radio [barely legible; could be *crackling into life*]. A voice announced a change of plans. The Chekists were ordered to bring their prisoner to a militia station on the outskirts of the city. When I heard this I started to shake uncontrollably—I thought they were going to take me down to the cellar and shoot me out of hand, which happened to me once before. We pulled up in front of the station. Trembling so badly I could barely walk, I was led inside, where an officer clearly senior to the others—like you, Nadenka, I was never very skillful at identifying rank from the array of gold or silver on shoulder boards or collars—led me through the main hall and out a door into a courtyard. He directed me into the backseat of a shiny American Packard parked at the foot of the steps, its motor running, an Uzbek soldier at the wheel. The officer took his place next to the driver and the Packard set off, thumping at high speed over the cobblestones of an avenue lined with brick apartment buildings so new they didn't have glass in their windows. (Can windows properly be described as windows if they don't reflect light?) I felt as if I would suffocate and started to turn down the car window, which is when I discovered that the glass was as thick as my thumb, which is to say it was of the bulletproof variety one reads about in newspapers. From this I surmised the vehicle belonged to someone important. For what seemed like minutes, though my sense of the passage of time had abandoned me along with my sense of color and my muse, the Packard sped along Government Highway. We passed a billboard depicting a Chekist wearing steel mittens strangling a snake with the heads of Trotsky and Bukharin. I couldn't tell if it was an advertisement for a motion picture or propaganda. The Packard turned off Government Highway at a railroad-crossing barrier blocking a single-lane paved road that plunged into a wood. The officer in the front seat flashed a small badge through the windshield. The guards saluted and raised the barrier. We continued on for some minutes, then turned left onto an even narrower road. Around a bend we were waved past a checkpoint manned by soldiers armed with submachine pistols. Some of the soldiers held watchdogs on short leashes. A high double chain-link fence trailed off on either side of the checkpoint as far as I could see, which wasn't far because we were in the middle of a thick forest of black pines and white birches. Here comes the curious part, Nadenka. Around another bend, completely blocking the road, was an enormous full-length poster of Stalin. It was the size of one of those motion picture billboards but standing on end, and showed Stalin with his feet slightly apart, his chin raised and staring off over the tops of the trees. He was wearing a plain military tunic buttoned to the neck and soft flannel trousers tucked into ankle-length boots. And to my utter befuddlement, the Packard didn't slow down but drove directly through the giant poster that was hanging across the road. Dear Nadenka, I can almost make out your voice in my ear saying, *Calm yourself, my darling—you're imaging things again.* To say the truth, I wasn't sure if this was really happening or I was fantasizing until I looked back through the narrow slit of a rear window and saw the ripped edges of the poster flapping in the currents created by our passage. (Are you still there, Nadenka? I can't hear you listening.) Familiar words resounded in my head—*Tearing the sackcloth canvas space*—as we drove up an oval-shaped gravel driveway past the dog runs of a kennel, past a one-storey barrack with Uzbeks in fatigues sitting outside cleaning weapons on picnic tables. The Packard pulled up in the courtyard of a villa that was too big to be a dacha and too small to be a sanatorium, surrounded on three sides by closed-in glass porches. Uzbeks with submachine pistols at the ready surrounded the car. One of them pulled open the rear door. When I reached for my satchel, the officer in the front seat wagged a finger. *You will retrieve it afterward,* he said. *After what?* I asked. *After* [illegible]. Clutching my yellow leather coat around me, I climbed out of the Packard. A big man who looked vaguely familiar stepped forward and searched me thoroughly. He removed my yellow coat and flung it over the top of the open rear door. *If you're looking for a weapon, I don't have one,* I said. *If I had one, I wouldn't know how to use it.* To which he replied, *Shut your trap.* When he'd finished patting down my trousers and my ankles, he stood up. *Don't you recognize me?* he asked. When I didn't reply, he said, *Vlasik. I'm the chief Kremlin bodyguard. Our paths crossed when you were brought in to see the boss several years ago.* I asked, *Who is the head of household here?* He appeared surprised by my question. *Why, the* khozyain, *to use the Georgian expression, is the head of household, though the household in question sprawls from the Baltic to the Black Sea, from the Arctic icecap to the Pacific Ocean.* Motioning for me to follow, this Vlasik person turned on his heel and entered the building. Glancing back to be sure I was still behind, he walked slowly enough for me to keep up with him. We crossed rooms filled with heavy furniture. In one a radio was playing classical music and a woman was passing a carpet sweeper at the same time. Ah, dearest Nadenka, here is a detail that will make you smile: there was no art on the walls, no paintings of generals such as I saw in the Kremlin, only pages torn from picture magazines—pastoral winter scenes, the Kremlin seen from various angles, that hideous tower in Kiev, a full page aerial view in a Parisian publication of that marvelous Eiffel Tower. There were also quite a few photographs of film and theater actresses. (One looked amazingly like our friend Zinaida Zaitseva-Antonova. I have sometimes wondered what became of the dear girl. Don't get the wrong idea, Nadenka, I don't miss the sex, I miss the intimacy that came from making love to her with you watching. For me, intimacy was always the ultimate orgasm.) Turning down a long corridor we reached a wooden door with what the French call a *vasistas* over it. I could hear muffled voices behind it. Smiling faintly, Vlasik pulled open the door and stepped aside. I found myself at the entrance to a dining room with eight or ten men in it, some in dark European suits, two in uniforms with rows of medals on their chests and gold on their shoulder boards. I immediately recognized several of those present from photographs I had seen in newspapers. Kaganovich stood at a sideboard, heaping caviar and cream onto a blini in his plate. Molotov, with his distinctive mustache and sallow complexion and watchful eyes, looked up at me, then for some reason shook his head as if to dislodge a fly on the tip of his nose and went back to eating. Nikita Khrushchev, sucking noisily on a drumstick, wiped his chin on a shirtsleeve. Sitting one seat down from the head of the table was the *khozyain*, Josef Stalin. He added a finger of vodka to the wine already in his glass and sipped it. One of the men whom I didn't recognize—a short man with the pale greenish skin of an alcoholic and a pince-nez that flashed when it caught the light from the overhead chandelier—spotted me and said something in Georgian. Stalin looked up. *Here we speak only Russian, Lavrenti Pavlovich,* he said with a scowl. He waved me in with his good arm. *Come on, don't hang back,* he cried out. *Beria is not going to bite you.* He pointed to a vacant seat across the table from him. *Help yourself to food, then we'll talk.* I went to the sideboard and put some herring and pickled onions on a plate, filled a glass with mineral water and made my way to the seat that had been indicated.

Stalin himself had changed a great deal since I'd last seen him in the Kremlin. He had put on ten kilos at least—a paunch swelled under his tunic. He was older and looked it, his hair thinner, the smallpox scars on his face redder. The hand of his crippled arm was tucked into the pocket of his tunic. He rocked back on the chair so that his weight was on its rear legs and inspected me. He noticed the stiffness of my shoulder and arm and asked me what had happened. I explained about having fallen from the second floor of a hospital and broken my shoulder. *Accidents happen,* he observed, hiking his own bad shoulder.

Stalin rocked his chair onto its four legs and, climbing to his feet, walked over to an enormous map of the world filling an entire wall of the dining room. *Why is it towns around Leningrad still bear their original German names from the time of Catherine?* he demanded. He turned toward one of the general officers. *This is an intolerable situation. Change these to good Russian names.* The officer pulled a small notepad from a pocket and jotted something in it. Stalin came across the room until he was standing behind me. Was

I imaging that I could feel his breath on the back of his neck? I heard him say, *You disappoint me, Mandelstam. I have read your so-called Ode. It is far worse than that first piece of shit you wrote about me. What do you think I am, an illiterate peasant? You still despise Stalin—you can't bring yourself to celebrate him. You drag him through the mud a second time.* He circled around the head of the table and sank tiredly into his chair. *You don't eat?* he said. *I have lost my appetite,* I replied. He snickered through his nostrils. *And well you might.* He turned to the others and shouted, *And well he might!* Several of those around the table nodded in vigorous agreement. *There is a lesson here somewhere,* Stalin rambled on. *I wanted a poem from him when he wouldn't write one. Now he has, but it's of no use to me because he is no longer the poet he was when he refused to write a poem for me.* He continued speaking to the others but his angry yellow eyes were fixed on me. *On the surface, this new Ode pretends to venerate Stalin, but in subtle ways it is exactly the opposite.* I think I mumbled, *I don't understand* because he grew more exasperated. *Of course you understand. You're the author of this piece of garbage. How could you not understand?* He turned toward his guests. *Out, out, everyone out. What I have to say is for the poet's ears only.* The kittens, as Stalin was known to refer to his Kremlin associates, headed for the door. Khrushchev left taking his dinner plate with him. Stalin snatched a piece of paper from his breast pocket and, his voice oozing sarcasm, began to rattle off lines from my Ode. *What does it mean: Stalin's eyes are parting mountains. This can only be understood as an echo of that treacherous reference in your first poem to Kremlin mountaineer. What does it mean: I want to say—not Stalin—I want to name him Dzhugashvili. Why are you incapable of letting the name Stalin pass your lips, Mandelstam? Why Dzhugashvili except to draw attention to Stalin's non-Russian origins? Who gives a shit if I have Georgian roots? Napoleon was Corsican, not French. Hitler is Austrian, not German. Even that prick Winston Churchill, who will slip a kopeck out of your pocket if you don't keep an eye on him, is half American.* Believe me, Nadenka, when I say I attempted to defend myself.

You are misreading what I wrote, I began, but he rushed on before I could get a word in. *What does it mean: Artist, cherish the warrior, he is always with you. Are you intimating we live in a police state, with Stalin or his Chekists looking over your shoulder twenty-four hours a day?* He slapped the paper with the back of his hand. *And this, for God's sake. Squirm out of this if you can: He smiles—a smiling reaper. Do you imagine for a split second that someone hearing this wouldn't understand the reference to grim reaper? Ha! And here! I didn't even notice this the first time I read your piece of shit: Bending from the podium, as if upon a mountain—there you go again with your fucking mountain—he reaches over mounds of heads. What does it mean, Mandelstam, this image you project of Stalin reaching over mounds of heads? It comes back again in the last stanza: In the distance where the mounds of human heads diminish. I see now I should have had you shot the first time you pulled off something like this. Out of the kindness of my heart I gave you three years—the notation next to your name, in my own hand, read isolate and preserve—and how do you repay me? With trash! With treason! With references to mounds of human heads in the distance! You might as well have erected a signboard pointing east saying, "This Way to Stalin's Gulag"! My God, what insolence!* His face went slack, his lips barely moved as he said, *You have played with fire, Mandelstam. You must be burned.* Reaching into the big pocket of his tunic, he produced a spent bullet and a folded scrap of paper. He tossed the bullet across the table to me. I picked it up. The bullet was crushed, as if it had been fired into something. In minuscule inked letters it bore a name: Bukharin. *Yes, yes, I can see it's dawning on you,* Stalin ranted on. *This is the bullet that was used to execute the traitor Nikolai Bukharin. I had a surgeon dig it from his skull and clean away the brain matter. Your mentor, Bukharin, wrote pleading with me to give him morphine so he could kill himself rather than die with a bullet in the head, but I didn't dignify his letter with a reply. This note will also interest you. It was written by Bukharin moments before the sentence of the court was carried out.* Fitting on a pair of spectacles, Stalin unfolded the paper and read from it.

"*Koba, why do you need me to die?*" I whispered, *Why* did *you kill him?* Again Stalin mixed vodka with wine and drank off half a glass. *You forget where you are, Mandelstam. I didn't kill Bukharin. The Cheka discovered he was guilty of treason. The judges heard the evidence and sentenced him to the highest measure of punishment. The executioner killed him. Stalin had nothing to do with all that.* The khozyain belched into his sleeve. *Bucharchik was a intellectual hunchback,* he said. *My late father used to say only the grave straightens a hunchback.* I think I half rose from my seat. *But he was innocent,* I exclaimed. Stalin sneered. *Innocent! Nobody is innocent. Let me tell you a story. I turned eleven the day two bandits were hanged on a riverbank in Gori. They were handsome young men with wide trousers and bristling mustaches. Dragging their leg irons in the dirt, they went to the gallows bantering with the constables who escorted them. One of the condemned men winked at me as they tightened the noose around his neck. When the bodies fell through the traps and danced at the end of the cords, two fat deputies hung from their feet to speed up strangulation. In a state of exaltation, I ran all the way back to the shack with straw and mud caulking the walls to tell my saint of a mother I'd found out how to cheat death—you winked at it, you bantered with it, you didn't let on you were scared shitless to quit the only life there was, which contrary to what the Orthodox priests preached, was the one before death. By chance my father, Vissarion, who hired out to a shoe factory in Tiflis, had turned up that morning for his monthly visit, his breath reeking of cheap alcohol, an earthenware jug clutched to his chest. Crazy Beso, as his drinking pals called him, was a thickset man with a scruffy beard. He was coming off an all-night binge, which is what he usually did when he had money in his pocket.* (Are you still there, Nadenka? Pay attention to every word I am about to tell you, repeat it to no one, let it go to the grave with you.) *Vissarion,* Stalin ranted on, adding still more vodka to his wine and drinking until the lids of his eyes turned crimson, *set the jug on a shelf and pulled his wide leather belt out of the loops of his canvas trousers. I knew what was coming and cringed in a corner.*

What has Soso done now? my mother begged. She grabbed her drunken husband by the arm. Grunting, he spun around and punched her in the face. I could see blood spurting from her nose. My father loomed over me. Confess, he blurted out. Confess to what? I cried out. I am not guilty of misconduct. Vissarion cursed me and God the Father and Jesus the Son. Where is it written you have to be caught in the act to confess to misconduct? he told me. My mother pleaded with him. Why do you beat him if he is innocent? And my prick of a father said, I beat him to instruct him there is no such thing as innocence—he knows what he is guilty of even if I don't. And he began lashing me across the arm that I'd thrown up to protect my head. This arm! Stalin raised his withered left arm. *The more I protested my innocence, the harder he whipped me. He beat me until my shirt was in shreds and my arm covered with welts and torn skin and sticky blood.* Breathing hard, Stalin fell silent. I asked him if his father was still alive. *He is burning in hell,* he said. *Biographies of me claim he died a hero's death. My saint of a mother once told me he drank himself into a potter's field. She didn't offer details. I never asked. Fuck him.* After a while I worked up the nerve to ask Stalin why he was telling me about his father. You won't like his response, Nadenka. He said, *I tell you this because I'm talking to a dead man. Bukharin isn't around to save you a second time. Listen, there is going to be a war with Hitler. If I play my cards right, I may be able to delay it until 1942 or '43. I've drawn the appropriate conclusions from the Spanish Civil War, specifically from the battle for Madrid, when the infamous fifth column of Franco sympathizers rose up inside the city to support the four columns of Nationalist troops attacking from outside. Before war with Germany breaks out, I must purify the Party, I must weed out the weaklings and the doubters. The purging of a million members from the ranks of the Bolshevik Party, the several public trials and the thousands of less public tribunals, the punishments that fit crimes which, given half a chance, the wreckers would commit, should be seen as a preemptive strike on the fifth column. I must eliminate the collaborators before they can rise up to support Hitler. My campaign against potential enemies must be guided by the principle that there is no such thing as innocence. It doesn't exist in this world. Every last one of the hundred and fifty million people in Russia, with the exception of my sainted mother, is guilty of something. Lenin tops the list. My own Nadezhda is high on it. All the old Bolsheviks— Kamenev, Zinoviev, Trotsky and the others—are on it. So is the darling of the Party, Bukharin. So, too, the darling of poetry, Mandelstam.*

Oh, Nadenka, my sharer of troubles, I tell you I listened to Stalin as one listens to a madman. And then I remembered Tolstoy's tale of a man who, seen from a distance, seemed to be engaged in something which indicated he was mad. Coming closer, he realized the man was sharpening a knife. The *khozyain*, it can be said, appeared mad but he was sharpening a knife. I pushed my chair away from the table and [illegible]. Stalin was talking to himself as I backed toward the door. His lips moved like those of an old man chewing cud. I heard him say, *The closer we come to success, the more active our enemy becomes. When he is at his most active and destructive, it should be taken as a sign that we are on the brink of victory.*

What transpired after that, dearest Nadenka, was anticlimax. I was taken to Lubyanka and signed in but never seriously interrogated. It was as if my guilt had already been established. I was an enemy of the people, a wrecker, an agent of the discredited and executed Buhkarin. The only thing remaining was to determine the appropriate punishment for my imaginary crimes. Talk about coincidence, for a time I shared a cell with Christophorovich, the Chekist who interrogated me after my first arrest. You surely remember him, Nadenka, though you wouldn't have recognized him if you passed him in the street. He had grown cadaverous, his once fine uniform hung off his body, he'd lost most of his hair and all of his cockiness. He didn't make excuses for himself—he said only that his fall had been inevitable in the sense that Chekists moved up the ladder by unmasking their immediate superior as a foreign agent, so it was only a matter of time before those below

Christophorovich denounced him. I asked him if he had confessed to crimes. He said confessions had been useful in 1934, inasmuch as accusations against an enemy of the people had required a certain plausibility. Nowadays, so he claimed, they concoct charges out of smoke—they don't hesitate accusing Jews of spying for Hitler—and confessions are considered superfluous, inasmuch as the Organs are not required to establish a suspect's guilt, rather he or she must present proof of innocence. Christophorovich was sentenced to twenty years of hard labor without the right of correspondence—he, of all people, knew how to decode this—and taken off on a transport before me. I discovered he was gone when, returning one day from the toilet, I found the cell empty and a note from him saying, *You were my crowning interrogation. I don't understand why we didn't shoot you in 1934.* I was eventually taken before a tribunal and within minutes sentenced to five years at hard labor for counterrevolutionary activities. Given my physical condition, I understood the verdict to be the equivalent of a death sentence. I was transferred to Butyrki Prison, where convicts were assembled for transport to Siberia. On September 9th I and several hundred others were taken in closed trucks to a little-used freight siding outside of Moscow and herded onto cattle cars. I was told by a kindly guard we were being sent to the Second River Transit Camp near Vladivostok in the Soviet Far East to await transport to one of the gulags on the Kamchatka Peninsula. I beg you, Nadenka, to send a package to Second River Transit Camp with sweaters and gloves and soap. I kiss your eyes, I kiss the tears that spill from them should this letter by some miracle reach you. Still dancing.

TWENTY

Fikrit Shotman
Sunday, the 8th of January 1939

The telegram authorizing your servitor, *Zek* Sh744239, to return to Moscow from Second River Transit Camp, where I washed up after my sentence ended, specified first available transport, which happened to be one of those old first-class coaches from before the Revolution. Which is how I came to journey west in a Trans-Siberian passenger carriage filled with Red Army officers going home on furlough. The benches were fitted with cushions, something that would have tickled my camp wife, Magda, if she'd been with me, which, sorry to say, she wasn't. She still had five years to go when she waved good-bye to me as my motor barge pulled away from the Kolma pier. (I didn't take it badly she was sizing up the new batch of prisoners on the hillside, in her shoes I would do the same.) The train back took three hours short of three days to reach Moscow, which was a big improvement on my nineteen days in a cattle car going out. Being as my traveling companions were officers, a field kitchen had been set up in another wagon and mess sergeants distributed warm food—on china plates, no less—twice a day. Me being the only civilian in the coach, the officers took me for an important Chekist and treated me with high regard. I let them think I was as important as they thought I was.

Two Chekists in uniform—one a full colonel!—were waiting for me on the quay when my train pulled into Moscow. "Shotman, Fikrit?" the colonel asked, looking up at me because I towered over him.

"One and the same," I said.

Here's what took place next. The colonel whipped a paw up to his visor and snapped off as smart a salute as you're going to see in Soviet Russia. It actually flashed through my thick skull that he was saluting someone behind me, but there was nobody behind me close enough to get saluted. Not wanting to appear bad-mannered, I saluted back.

"We have a car waiting," the colonel announced, treating me, like the officers in the first-class railway coach, with high regard.

So he wouldn't think I was bowled over by all this attention, I shrugged indifferently and trailed after him through the flood of passengers out the station's enormous entrance hall. Sure enough, an Uzbek corporal was standing to attention next to the open door of a shiny blue American Packard. I squeezed into the back, my knees cramped up to my chin. When I rolled down the window to get some air—Moscow winters are summers compared to Siberian winters—I saw the glass was as thick as my little finger. I supposed this was how Americans made cars, though I couldn't think what advantage thick glass would have over thin. To my surprise, four militiamen on motorcycles leapfrogged ahead of the Packard, blocking cross traffic at intersections so we could run red lights. I got a laugh watching people peering into the car to catch sight of the important apparatchik who could make traffic stop for him. After some minutes I spotted the Kremlin wall ahead at the foot of the street named after the late Maksim Gorky, it sticks in my head he had something to do with books, I remembered Magda reading aloud his death notice in the Kolma weekly newsletter maybe two years back, which is how come I knew he was late. When we reached the wall, with glorious Red Square off on the left, the Packard went to the right, then turned left across a small bridge and drove through a Kremlin gate I happened to know was not open to the public.

All the time I kept asking myself where I was being taken, and why.

Inside the Kremlin compound, the car pulled up in front of a low brick building. The Uzbek sprang from his seat to open the back door of the automobile. Sunlight was shining off the onion dome of a church and I had to shield my eyes with a hand to see. The colonel must have thought I was saluting him because he saluted me again. Darting ahead of me, the Uzbek pulled open the front door of the building. Comrade Stalin's chief bodyguard, the one who frisked me the time I shook Stalin's hand in 1932, I remembered him because he was almost as big as me—his name escapes me, with any luck it'll come back before you finish recording my answers to your questions—was waiting in the vestibule. Only this time he didn't frisk me. He jerked his head for me to follow him down a flight of stairs. We came to a glass door with writing on it and he jerked his head again for me to go inside. Which I did. In a thousand years you'll never guess where I was. I was in a tailor shop, yes, a genuine tailor shop with four men slumped over Singer sewing machines, I know the brand because we had the same ones at the circus to repair costumes, their feet furiously working the pedals. Hanging off hangers along one wall were more suits than you could count, piles of folded shirts and shoes filled cubbyholes along another wall. An Israelite tailor, a stooped man with curly hair, began measuring me with the cloth tape measure draped over his neck. Mumbling to himself, the Israelite pulled a dark blue suit off a hanger. "We will have to let out the sleeves and the trousers," he told the bodyguard.

"How long will it take?"

"Twenty minutes."

"Do it in ten."

The tailor gave the trousers to one of his sewers and the jacket to another and they dropped what they were doing and went to work. While they were lengthening the sleeves and trousers, I was ordered to strip to my underwear. I was given a white shirt with a collar attached and genuine leather lace-up shoes that came to a point in front and pinched my toes. When the sewers finished sewing, they ironed the new cuffs and sleeves with an iron that looked to be attached by a cord to an electricity outlet. What will they invent next? I tried on the suit and buttoned the double-breast jacket and took a look at myself in the full-length mirror. If Magda could see me she would have thought she was high on *chaifir*. The Israelite offered me a choice of neckties but, not knowing how to tie one, I waved him off and buttoned the shirt up to my neck, Azerbaidzhani style. My old clothes—the canvas trousers and the flannel shirt that had belonged to Magda's suicided camp husband, the felt boots with the worn-down cork soles—were thrown into a carton on the floor. When I asked if I could have them back, the bodyguard laughed. The Israelites at the sewing machines began laughing, too. Not wanting to be left out of the joke, I laughed along with them.

With my new shoes squeaking under my weight and the collar of the starched shirt scratching at my neck, I followed the bodyguard down a long underground passage lighted every few meters by overhead bulbs. (I knew electricity didn't grow on trees. I wondered if they turned the bulbs off at night to save money.) At the end of the passageway we climbed a spiral staircase to a locked door three flights up. The bodyguard—ah, his name just now came to me. It's Vlasik. Agrippina used to say brains were not my strong suit, but I'm not doing too bad, am I?—this Vlasik took out a ring of keys and fitted one of them in the lock, and the door, which turned out to be made of iron, clicked open. I followed him up another flight of stairs and down a hallway into a room with polished benches along the walls. Behind a desk with three telephones on it sat a hairless man with acne. On the wall behind him was an inspirational picture of Comrade Lenin, his right hand cutting the air, speaking to a crowd of workers from a wooden platform.

Comrade Stalin's bodyguard said, "He's here."

The hairless man at the desk picked up one of the telephones and said, "He's here." He looked up. "Take him straight in."

I caught my breath as I walked through the door—it was the very same room where Comrade Stalin shook my hand when I won silver in Vienna, Austria. A short man wearing a military tunic was standing at one of the windows, looking out at the Kremlin church with the sun shining off the dome. Vlasik coughed into his fist. The person at the window turned slowly to face me. It was Comrade Stalin in the flesh, smaller and older and tireder than I remembered from when I met him six years before. He hitched up his trousers and, making his way around the desk, stuck out a soft hand. "Stalin," he said.

I shook his hand, being careful not to squeeze it. "Shotman, Fikrit," I managed to say, though I was short of breath from breathing the same air as the person I admired most in the world.

Comrade Stalin took a cigarette with a long cardboard tip from a silver case and offered it to me. "I used to smoke hand-rolled *makhorka*," I said, "but I gave it up, Excellency."

"I wish I didn't smoke," he said, holding the flame from a small lighter to the end of the cigarette. He expelled a lungful of smoke. "I intend to give up cigarettes the day America goes Communist."

He went around the desk and sat down on an ordinary chair and pointed to another chair on my side of the desk. I must have looked at it uncertainly because Vlasik growled at me, "Sit, for God's sake." I did.

Comrade Stalin said, "I remember you very well, Shotman—people your size are not easily forgotten. You were the champion weight lifter with the bad knee. When the Kremlin doctors screwed up the operation, Khrushchev had the bright idea of turning you into a circus strongman. How has life treated you since?"

I was thrilled that Comrade Stalin, with the weight of the Soviet state on his shoulders, not to mention the world Communist movement, remembered someone as not important as Fikrit

Shotman. Naturally I told him the truth. "I was accused of being wrecker for having a sticker of the Eiffel Tower on my steamer trunk, for having tsarist state loan coupons in its drawers. I served four years mining gold on the Kolma River."

"I know about Siberia," Comrade Stalin said. "To speak plainly, that's why you're here." He picked through a pile of what looked like telegrams. "The commandant at Second River reports that you came across the poet Mandelstam while you were waiting for transportation west after finishing your sentence."

"Am I in trouble because of Mandelstam?" I blurted out.

"Only answer Comrade Stalin's questions honestly and all will go well for you," Vlasik said from the wall.

"You are not in trouble," Comrade Stalin assured me. "Take your time. Tell me what you know of this Mandelstam."

"When I reached Second River, around the middle of October, it was crawling with prisoners. There were no free bunks left in the barracks so I camped out under tent canvas rigged between two barracks. I'm not complaining, only giving you information, Excellency. The next morning I noticed naked men sitting on the ground in front of the latrines searching their clothes and each other's scalps for lice, and crushing them between their fingers when they found them. I recognized one of the prisoners. It was Mandelstam."

"How could you recognize him? Had you met him before?"

"I shared a cell with him in 1934 when I was being interrogated in the Lubyanka."

"Ha! So that's the connection." Comrade Stalin sucked on his cigarette, slapping away the smoke with a palm so he could keep an eye on me. "What was Mandelstam like when you met him in the Lubyanka?"

"To tell the truth, Excellency, he was a bit loony at times. He thought he could walk through walls. He boasted about meeting you in the Kremlin, he described going down a hallway filled with paintings of Russian generals. He was very mysterious, he said it would be dangerous for me to know what you talked about. At the end he would have cut his wrist with a piece of broken china bowl if I hadn't stopped him."

I could make out Comrade Stalin scowling. Then he said something I still don't comprehend. "I never met Mandelstam in the Kremlin. I never met him outside the Kremlin for that matter."

"I never bought his story about meeting you," I said quickly. Which wasn't the honest-to-God truth. Osip Emilievich described the meeting with Comrade Stalin in so much detail, it never entered my head he was making it up.

"Tell me about Mandelstam in Second River."

The fact of the matter was that if I closed the lids over my eyes, I could see the poet, which is what everyone in the camp called him, as clearly as if he was standing in front of me. I could almost reach out and touch him. "He was thin like a scarecrow, Excellency. Thin and breakable, like the sheets of ice sliding off the roof of the barrack when the sun came out. He refused to collect the bowls of kasha with fat poured over the buckwheat groats handed out twice a day—he was frightened the guards were going to poison him. I scrounged crusts of bread and potato peelings and bone marrow from garbage bins behind the mess barrack and he ate those, though he didn't have many teeth in his mouth and needed to gum the food. When a convoy of prisoners left for the gulags on Kamchatka, I found an empty top bunk in Hut Number 11, Mandelstam's barrack, and pretty much became his protector, carrying him piggyback to the latrine and back, carrying him to the infirmary when he complained of stomach cramps or pains in his chest or double vision. In November, Siberian winter blew in from the steppes. When we went to shower, which was once every two weeks, our clothing froze in the damp air of the bathhouse—our trousers leaned up against the wall as if somebody was in them. And Mandelstam would clap his hands and do a jig to fight off the numbness in his feet. His yellow leather coat was in shreds and he took to shivering all the time. I wrapped one of his spare shirts around his neck like a scarf but it didn't help. One day a prisoner named Arkhangelski—he was a real criminal, not an Article 58er like us—asked Mandelstam to read to the criminals that lived in the attic space under the barrack roof. The invitation raised Osip Emilievich's spirits. He combed his hair with his fingers and ironed the rags on his body with his palms. I helped him up the ladder to the loft, which was heated by a wood stove and lit by a paraffin lamp. The yellow light turned his yellow skin yellower. I lifted Mandelstam, who was getting thinner and weaker with each passing day, onto a high stool and he began reading from the small book he carried in his pocket wherever he went so it wouldn't get stolen. Every once in a while he would stare out at the criminals and finish the poem without bothering to look down at the page. He recited other poems written by someone with a name like Voronezh, I think. The criminals listened with great attention. Sometimes Arkhangelski or another would ask him to recite the same poem again or say what a certain line or certain word meant. Listening to him along with the criminals, I can't say I understood all that much of what he read, though you could see what Osip Emilievich must have been like when he was young and strong and not sick with fear. Between poems Arkhangelski or one of the others gave him slices from a loaf of bread or pickled mushrooms from a can, even lumps of sugar from a jar filled with lumps of sugar. Mandelstam wasn't afraid of the criminals—he didn't think they were out to poison him—so he accepted. He wound up reading to the criminals two or three times a week until . . ."

Comrade Stalin leaned forward in his chair. "Until?"

"Until spotted typhus struck Second River. The first cases were reported in the middle of December. It spread fast. Anyone with fever was locked in the quarantine barrack. Nobody went in or out. Every morning the infected prisoners emptied slop buckets out the window. Pretty soon word spread that everyone in the barrack was dead. Osip Emilievich begged me not let them take him to the quarantine barrack. He was shivering so hard I hauled him up to my upper bunk because it was warmer, and covered him with his blanket and mine. When the medical orderlies with masks over their mouths came through in the morning to take off prisoners with fever, I managed to hide Osip Emilievich from them by lying on the bunk alongside him. And then one morning, when it was my turn to fetch the ration of kasha, the other prisoners found him shivering and sweating under his blankets. When I got back they told me he had a fever, they threatened to report the both of us if I didn't take him off straightaway to the quarantine barrack. I bundled him up in the blankets and carried him instead to the camp infirmary. The doctor at the infirmary, an Article 58er like us, stripped Osip Emilievich and washed his body, which was by then only skin and bones, with a sponge and warm water. The doctor combed the lice out of his hair and beard and short hairs and put him to sleep in an army cot with a real straw mattress. I spent as much time with him as I could in the next days. His mind drifted a lot. One time he made me promise to send a telegram to the Writers' Union informing them he was under the weather and wouldn't be able to read at their auditorium that night. Another time he ranted about having been injected with rabies. Late one afternoon late in December I must have nodded off next to his bed. When I woke up I saw him staring at me with the wide eyes of a child and I thought to myself, he has made his way back to the safety of childhood before he dies. "Can you hear me, Osip Emilievich?" I whispered. His answer was so soft I had to lean my ear that worked over his mouth to catch it. He said something about how the pinprick of the last star was vanishing without pain. I repeated his words to myself until I had memorized them, though the meaning was a mystery to me. (With or without pain, I don't see how a faraway star can give you a pinprick.) Then he reached under the rough blanket and began to play with his sex and I thought to myself, he has made his way past childhood to the safety of babyhood before he dies. I am not ashamed to say I turned my head away so he wouldn't see the tears in my eyes. After a while I got hold of myself and turned back. Mandelstam was still staring at me with his child's innocent eyes, except they were frozen open and he wasn't breathing. I went into the hallway and gestured to the doctor at the end of it and he understood and came running and pulled out a pocket mirror and held it to Mandelstam's mouth and when there was no cloud of life on it he looked over at me and shook his head. And he said, *Death is not sad when what came before was not life.* He printed out Osip Emilievich's name and the date— twenty-seventh of December 1938—on a valise tag and attached it with wire to the poet's big toe. I wrapped his body in a scrap of canvas set aside for that purpose and carried it to the trench behind the last barrack that was already filled with corpses from the typhus outbreak. A bulldozer was parked nearby, waiting to cover the trench with earth when there was no more room in it. I jumped into the trench and lifted Osip Emilievich down after me and set him on the frozen ground and, opening the folds of the canvas, I put two small flat stones, the kind you skim off water, on his eyes, which is what you do when you bury a notable in Azerbaidzhan. And I thought, Jesus, somebody ought to say a prayer or something, what with him being dead, so I said, *God of the Jewish, don't assign too much weight to the charges against the poet Mandelstam, it's not his fault he wasn't socially useful.* When Arkhangelski saw me that night, he wanted to know if the poet was well enough to come up and read to the criminals. I said no, he wasn't well enough to read, the fact was he would never read again, he was dead."

When I finished describing Mandelstam's death, I could hear Comrade Stalin breathing through his nostrils. He was still holding the cigarette but not smoking it. He pulled another telegram from the pile on his desk and said, "The camp commandant listed the cause of death as typhus."

I must have shrugged because Comrade Stalin burst out, "It was typhus, wasn't it?"

"I am not a medical person, Excellency. Who can say why a person dies? In Osip Emilievich's case, he could have died from hunger, since he was afraid to eat his ration. He could have died from not sleeping, since he spent the nights tossing and shivering in his bunk. At Second River prisoners sometimes upped and died when they lost hope, Mandelstam himself said that a few days before he passed on."

"So Mandelstam is really dead," Comrade Stalin said. "You're positive he was the one you buried?"

I nodded yes.

Comrade Stalin ground out his cigarette in an ashtray even though it wasn't smoked down to the end. (In Kolma, at Second Rivers, prisoners would kill for a half-smoked cigarette.) Climbing to his feet, he turned to stare out the window. I could make out the lights coming on in the GUM office arcades across Red Square. When Comrade Stalin spoke again, I could see he was furious. "If the asshole had given me the poem when I wanted it, none of this would have happened. Well, fuck him. He killed himself with his stubborn-headedness. I had nothing to do with it." And then the tsar of Soviet Russia did something that scared the bejesus out of me—he began to knock his fist against the glass pane of the window, lightly at first, then harder and harder and I was sure the glass would break until I figured out it must be as thick as the glass in the Packard. And he shouted out in a voice I didn't recognize, "The prick! What will I do now?"

Vlasik started across the room but Comrade Stalin, his forehead against the windowpane, waved him off. I felt the bodyguard's grip on my arm, the one with the almost completely faded face of Stalin tattooed on it. I followed Vlasik through the waiting room and down the hallway. Turning on me, he warned, "Don't tell a living soul what you saw in there."

"Comrade Stalin is a great hero to me," I said. "I didn't see nothing out of the ordinary."

Vlasik kicked open the door to a toilet. There was a carton on the floor with the canvas trousers and the flannel shirt that'd belonged to Magda's suicided husband and my felt boots with the worn-down cork soles. "The suit and the shirt and the shoes the tailor gave you were on loan," he said.

I wasn't sorry to have my own clothes back. Something told me that Agrippina, who I was planning to look up, wouldn't think the tailor-made suit with the double-breast jacket suited me.

TWENTY-ONE

Anna Andreyevna
Friday, the 4th of June 1965

No, no, I don't think I can do this again, even as a favor to Nadezhda. Not now, not ever. Nowadays when I summon memories of Osip Mandelstam, a certain amount of sheer pain comes up with them and, frankly, I've had enough pain to last a lifetime—my first husband's execution, my third husband's arrest and death in the gulag, my son's rotting in prison for years a hostage to my "good" behavior. When the American poet Frost, old, red-faced, gray-haired, visited me in 1962 (the authorities insisted we meet in one of the plusher dachas in Komarovo rather than my modest cottage; I suppose they didn't want him to see into what dirt they'd trampled me), I told him I'd had it all—poverty, prison lines, fear, poems remembered only by heart, burned poems. And humiliation and grief; endless humiliation, endless grief. Frost was a kindhearted gentleman, he meant no harm, but when I realized he expected me to talk about Osip, the words spilled through my lips before the lobe of my brain that deals with language could formulate a sentence. What I heard myself say was: "You don't know anything about this. You wouldn't be able to understand if I told you."

Russia, the running riot we know and loathe and love and fear, is reserved for Russians. It's really not very complicated: my body is here in England to accept this honorary doctorate from Oxford, but my head, my heart, my soul, my gut are back in Russia. Even if by some miracle we get our bodies out, we Russians can't leave Russia. And goodhearted people like Frost can't get in simply because their passport bears a Soviet visa stamp. You have to have lived through the thirties to understand, and even then you don't understand.

If you think about it, you'll see I've told you everything I know about dear, dear Osip and what was surely one of the most dreadful chapters in Russia's thousand-year history.

EPILOGUE

Robert Littell
Sunday, the 23rd of December 1979

I phoned Madam Mandelstam as soon as I reached Moscow. Some years before, having led a nomadic existence for decades, she'd been granted a residence permit and installed herself in the capital. She invited my companion and me to come by for tea. With the biggest box of chocolates I could find in the hotel's hard currency store under my arm, I flagged down a taxi. It took us to a bleak apartment house in a distant suburb filled with six-storey brick buildings that looked as if they had come into existence ramshackled and gone downhill from there. When the door to the ground floor flat opened, we found ourselves standing before a short, worn, emaciated woman, ancient when she should have been merely old. Young poets were taking turns caring for the widow of the poet Mandelstam. One was preparing tea and cakes in the tiny kitchen when we arrived. Madam Mandelstam lay propped up on a settee most of the time we were there, occasionally selecting, after some deliberation, a bonbon from the box of chocolates open on her lap. "I was never skilled at predicting how something would taste from its shape," she said absently. The narrow apartment was terribly overheated. She was wearing a white sleeveless shift. Her elbows were bare and jutting, the skin on her arms hanging in soft pleats off her bones. The conversation was in English, which she spoke fluently—she had used it to make ends meet with translation work in the years when the poet Mandelstam was not being published and earning no income. When I began recording the conversation she said, "It's been an eternity since you came around with the infernal taping machine of yours that filled a small suitcase. The time you interviewed Mandelstam, I seem to remember you had to change reels every half hour—after you left he complained that watching the spools go round made him dizzy. Now you turn up with a device not much bigger than a pack of cigarettes."

"In the future they'll get even smaller," I said.

Smiling faintly, Madam Mandelstam looked away. "When I was permitted to see him in the Lubyanka, Mandelstam asked me if the future was behind or ahead of us."

"What did you answer?"

"Damn it, Robert, I can't be expected to remember something I said in 1934. That's why you record these conversations. You tell me what I said."

"A lot of water has flowed under the bridge since then," I remarked. "I'll have to look it up in my notes."

She laughed under her breath. "My great friend Akhmatova pretended that what flows under bridges is spilt milk. She was surely right. When she died, not long after returning from Oxford, I thought it entirely possible she might have drowned in spilt milk." Responding to a question, Madam Mandelstam began to talk about her husband: "He was a silly young man, very gay even when things started to become difficult for him as a poet in the twenties. He was endlessly *zhizneradostny*, which can be translated as *joyous* or, better still, *life-glad*. In the thirties, when we were especially miserable—we experienced hunger, homelessness, fear, filth, abject poverty—Mandelstam would ask me: *Where is it written you should be happy?*" Staring off into space, Madam Mandelstam seemed to pick up the thread of a conversation with her husband that had been interrupted forty-one years before. "I was never disillusioned, my darling, because I never had the luxury of illusions."

We sipped our tea. My tape machine recorded minutes of silence. After a while I asked Madam Mandelstam if she thought her husband had actually come face-to-face with Stalin.

"Mandelstam wasn't the only Russian intellectual of his day to be fascinated by Stalin. He wondered what enigmas lay hidden behind those eyes, he was curious about what had transformed the Caucasian peasant Dzhugashvili into the Kremlin peasant-slayer Stalin, which is to say, into a practicing paranoid."

"But you haven't answered my question."

She thought about this for a moment before coming up with a response that satisfied her. "Mandelstam certainly encountered Stalin," she said carefully. "You must decide for yourself whether the meetings took place in the Kremlin or a dacha, or in the poet's head."

Responding to another question, she said she had no idea why she hadn't been arrested along with her husband. At both of his arrests they could have taken her off as easily as they took him. "After the second arrest I followed Pushkin's advice. *Try to be forgotten.* I worked at so many jobs, and in so many places, I've lost track. I was a teacher, a translator, I once cleaned government buildings. I never lived in any one city for very long. I heard there were arrest warrants issued for me but I kept moving and managed to stay one jump ahead of the Chekists. I had to if Mandelstam's oeuvre—a portion of which existed and still exists only in my head—was to survive."

"In the end, obliging you to memorize his poems saved your life."

"You are mistaken if you think he *obliged* me, Robert. I committed his poems to memory because I wanted them on the tip of my tongue. Only later did it occur to either of us that memorizing his oeuvre would give me an incentive to survive if something were to happen to him." Madam Mandelstam closed her eyes for a moment. "Well, against all the odds I did survive. And here I am back in Moscow, if you can call this Moscow"—she waved tiredly at the window looking out onto another apartment building in her remote suburb. "I'm an old lady now. They have lost interest in me."

I asked her to describe the last months before Mandelstam's second arrest.

"You must understand, he was never the same after his first arrest. He once told me how, at his very first interrogation, Christophorovich promised he would experience fear in full measure, and he did. Something happened to Mandelstam in the Lubyanka that crippled his life-gladness. On several occasions he let slip allusions to his execution, but he never offered particulars and I didn't ask for fear of opening the wound. In exile, even after exile, there were months on end when Mandelstam seemed frightened of his shadow. He was afraid to be left alone. He was afraid to eat unless it was me who prepared the food for him, or he could join others serving themselves from a common bowl. He lay awake nights in Voronezh, later in Kalinin, straining to catch the sound of automobiles braking to a stop or footsteps drawing nearer on the street or doors opening in our building. Like countless millions of Russians, he finally fell asleep at dawn. Looking back, I can see there were long stretches when Mandelstam found refuge from terror in madness. It wasn't what I think of as creative madness, which is what drove him to compose that first Stalin epigram—no, no, it was unadulterated madness filled with auditory hallucinations and demons capable of pushing someone to leap into the darkness from the second storey of a hospital. There were also intervals when he would claw his way back to something resembling sanity. It was during these saner moments that he composed the wonderfully wistful poems in his Voronezh cycle. *In splendid poverty, luxurious beggardom I live alone—both peaceful and resigned.*" Madame Mandelstam shook her head as if to clear it. "It was during a saner moment that he got off a last letter, written on pages torn from his copy of Pushkin, asking me to send warm clothes and soap to him at Vtoraya Rechka, which you call Second River. We learned of Mandelstam's death from his brother Alexander—he received an official government letter informing him that Mandelstam died of heart failure on the twenty-seventh of December 1938. In those days, everyone who died, whether in the Lubyanka cellars, on the cattle cars heading east or in the gulag camps, was said by the authorities to have died of heart failure, so of course we considered the official version worthless, except perhaps for the date. Akhmatova arrived from Leningrad soon after. I didn't know how to tell her the news without breaking down before I could finish the sentence, so I said, *I am the widow of the poet Mandelstam.* And we fell into each other's arms and sobbed until we had used up a lifetime's ration of tears."

I mentioned that I was familiar with the poet's last letter and asked her what she made of the signature.

"You are not the first to be intrigued by Mandelstam's *Still dancing,* Robert. One could tease various meanings out of the *Still* before *dancing.* On one level he was surely signaling, with typical Mandelstam bravura, that despite everything he was *continuing* to dance—a nod to your Roaring Twenties when he used to post lookouts at the door so we wouldn't be denounced for doing the Charleston. But my guess is that Mandelstam, as usual, was being more precise. With the cattle car approaching Siberia, he was, like the stars in Philip Sidney's astonishing poem, dancing in place to keep his feet from freezing, against the day when he could make his way back to his best friend and comrade-in-arms and lawful wedded wife."

"So *still dancing* suggests *hope?*"

"More like *hope against hope.* But *hope* all the same. Absolutely."

I told Madam Mandelstam how much I admired the two books she'd written that had been smuggled out of Russia and published in the West under the titles *Hope Against Hope* and *Hope Abandoned*;

how, like a great many people, I thought they were the best writing to come out of Russia, Solzhenitsyn notwithstanding, about the savage Stalinist period that took the lives of millions, the poet Mandelstam among them. I asked if she thought things had changed for the better. She said she hoped against hope this was the case, but you could never be sure; that, like the Jew sitting on the last bench of the synagogue during the time of the pogroms, you had to keep glancing over your shoulder while you prayed if you wanted to survive.

When I thought we'd worn out our welcome, I thanked Madam Mandelstam for receiving us. With an effort she rose to her feet and accompanied us to the door. Before opening it to the dark corridor, she said something that has haunted me since:

Don't speak English in the hallway.

CREDITS

Pasternak's poem on page ix, "Hamlet," was translated by Lydia Pasternak Slater.

Mandelstam's *Kremlin mountaineer* epigram on page 95 was published in Nadezhda Mandelstam, *Hope Against Hope* (London: Collins & Harvill Press, 1971).

Mandelstam's poem *I have studied the science of good-byes* on page 126 is from *Tristia* 104, from *The Selected Poems of Osip Mandelstam*, translated by Clarence Brown and W. S. Merwin (New York: New York Review Books, 2004).

Tsvetaeva's poem on page 131, *Where are the swans?* is from Marina Tsvetaeva, *The Demesne of the Swans*, a bilingual edition, with introduction, notes, commentaries, and translation by Robin Kemball (Ann Arbor: Ardis, 1980).

The snatches of Mandelstam poems starting on page 147—*In the black velvet . . . Whom will you next kill . . . wolf-hound century . . . speak my mind . . . starving peasants"* are all from *Osip Mandelstam: 50 Poems*, translated by Bernard Meares (New York: Persea Books, 1977).

Akhmatova's *In the room of the banished poet* on page 303 is from the poem entitled "Voronezh" and dedicated "To O.M.," in *Poems of Akhmatova*, selected, translated, and introduced by Stanley Kunitz with Max Hayward (Boston: Atlantic-Little Brown, 1973).

Mandelstam's *In splendid poverty* on page 361 is from the poem dated January 1937, "Voronezh," in *Osip Mandelstam, Selected Poems*, translated by David McDuff (Cambridge, Eng.: Rivers Press Ltd., 1973).

ABOUT THE AUTHOR

Robert Littell, a *Newsweek* journalist in a previous incarnation, has been writing about the Soviet Union and Russians since his first work of fiction, the espionage classic *The Defection of A. J. Lewinter*. Among his numerous critically acclaimed novels are *The October Circle, Mother Russia, The Debriefing, The Sisters, The Revolutionist, An Agent in Place, The Visiting Professor,* the *New York Times* best-selling *The Company* (adapted for a TNT miniseries), and *Legends* (winner of the *Los Angeles Times* Book Award for Best Thriller of 2005). Littell is an American who makes his home in France.